The Shattered Crown

J. W. Webb

Book Three of

The Legends of Ansu

Acknowledgement and thanks to:
Catherine Romano, for editing
Julia Gibbs, @ProofreadJulia, for proofreading
Roger Garland, www.lakeside-gallery.com, for illustration
Debbi Stocco, MyBookDesigner.com, for book design
Ravven, ravven.kitsune@gmail.com, for cover art.

ISBN 13: 978-0-9863507-1-9 (Paperback)
ISBN 13: 978-0-9863507-2-6 (Digital)

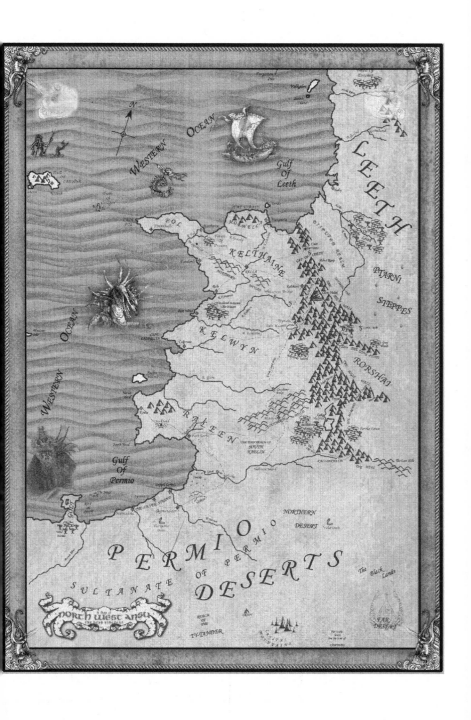

For Rae

Without whom Corin an Fol would still be lost in those woods
May evening starlight guide your path
Nothing is ever forgotten

Table of Contents

Part One

Oracle

Chapter 1

The Smithy

Corin an Fol, recently redundant longswordsman, determined cynic, and downtrodden wretch, was not having one of his better moments. His head hurt, his feet were soaked (leaky boots did nothing for morale), and it hadn't stopped bloody-well raining for three days—and worse—three nights.

He was wet through, his hands frozen and his nose running, and now Thunderhoof, his very expensive foreign warhorse, had chosen to start limping. It was all an act, of course. Thunder did this kind of thing when he'd had enough tromping about the countryside.

Corin wiped the snot from his nose and blinked through the rain. Fog and moor, moor and fog—he remembered why he'd left this place.

"It isn't my fault you were born in the south," Corin told his horse. Thunderhoof had been a generous gift from his former employer, Silon of Raleen, back in the days when they were getting on. It seldom rained down there in Raleen, it being half desert, and Thunder, worthy beast though he was, had scant appreciation for this damp northern climate.

"Besides," continued Corin, "we've only a few miles to go. You can stew in a nice warm, dry stable, and I can get soused." Thunder didn't respond, nor did he pick up his sluggish pace.

A mile marker loomed out of the murk: Finnehalle Seven Miles. The words were barely visible.

"See, look you!" Corin, excited, patted the horse's soggy back. "We're almost there, boy." But if Thunder had been impressed by the milestone, he didn't show it, which wasn't that surprising considering he couldn't read.

A lane entrance yawned off to their right, just passed a stubby clump of hedgerow. Above that a battered sign dripped and creaked on a rusty pole: Polin's Smithy One Mile.

An arrow pointed down the track. Corin reined in as he took in the sign. Down in the wooded dip he could see smoke rising crooked from the smith's cottage and forge. Polin was a stout soul. He'd been a good friend to Corin, back then.

I suppose we could always...

Moments passed. Rider sat thinking whilst horse looked mournful and did something peculiar with his right foreleg.

"Oh, sod it then. Have it your way." Corin dismounted onto the lane with a squishy thud and then hauled hard at Thunder's reins, urging the snorting beast follow him down the side track and on toward the smithy. The horse gave him that superior look—an expression not dissimilar to the one Silon used to visit upon him when he'd just said something obtuse (which happened now and then).

"Horse, I hope for your sake Polin's ale barrel is full," complained Corin. He'd had his heart set on spending a night or two in the Last Ship, the inn he'd frequented a lot —back then. Still, Polin used to keep a decent keg and it would be good to catch up. It had been fourteen years after all, and Finnehalle would still be there in the morning.

Half way down the lane, the rain stopped and a wan sun pierced the grey. Corin smiled as sunlight danced and sparkled in the puddles ahead. This was more like it. But the grin fled from his face when a woman's shriek of rage sent rooks croaking skyward.

What's this?

Corin reached the outer fence to the smithy's lands, tied Thunder's reins to a stump, and then, hand reaching back across his shoulder, slid Clouter, his heavy longsword, free of its scabbard.

"Stay here!" Corin hissed at the horse. Thunder blinked at him but obliged with indifference. Corin left him and approached the gate. He turned the latch and carefully stole inside the stockade, his wet clothes and cold feet forgotten.

Trouble. It was something Corin an Fol understood, its having been his constant companion for over fourteen years.

The woman screamed again—more anger than terror betrayed by her tone. Corin cursed and broke into a run, Clouter gripped between calloused palms and his grey-blue eyes steely hard. It had been two long weeks since he'd last had a scrap. Corin was more than ready.

***

Ulf laughed when the woman threatened him with her rusty knife. His twin, Starki, had already done for her husband, whilst the boy, Cale, had slipped inside the cottage to collect any spoils. That pimply bag of bones had his uses—sometimes.

They hadn't killed the smith yet, just brained him half senseless. The big fellow crouched spewing and moaning in the dirt just outside the stables. Ulf had forgotten him already, having eyes only for the blacksmith's wife.

She was comely, in a spitting, shrieking, red-haired, freckled kind of way. But it wouldn't have mattered if she were ugly. Ulf had never been the fussy kind.

He turned slightly at a noise to his left—Cale returning, his grubby fingers full of silver coin and his bright blue bug-eyes gawping at the scene. Ulf ignored him. Instead he goaded the girl with mock kisses and obscene hints.

Starki, lacking the finer qualities possessed by his twin, grabbed greedily for the girl. She stepped backwards, hissed, and flashed the tiny blade at his blood-shot eyes.

Starki laughed and winked at Ulf. "While you're trying to

prick me with that I'm going to prick you with this." He cupped his groin with a hand and made a lewd thrusting gesture with his hips.

"Get that out and I'll slice it off!" The woman spat in his eye.

"Feisty mare, eh, Starki," observed Ulf. "Mayhap we should draw lots." Behind him the gawky Cale watched in fascinated silence.

"I'm having her first!" Starki grabbed again, but the woman knew what she was doing with her knife. She sliced hard, took a finger.

"Bitch!" Starki's meaty left fist hammered into her face, knocking her prone. He stood over her then, panting, swearing, and flicking the blood from his dripping right hand so that it splattered her linen gown.

She rolled over and tried to get up, but Ulf's studded boot thudded down onto her back, sending her sprawling again. Starki, his eyes lit with murderous rage, freed his dagger and crouched low over the woman.

He froze when the sharp kiss of steel pricked lightly at the nape of his neck.

"Play time's over, ugly," a voice said.

Starki rolled free of the stranger's blade, but only just. He looked up wild-eyed. Where had this bastard come from? A tall nasty-looking bugger clad in dun-leather tunic over a rusty mail shirt. Lean-faced—a white scar crooked up from right brow to hairline—with shaggy brown hair and scary eyes of smoky blue grey. In his hands he clutched a bloody great sword, perhaps five-and-a-half feet long.

But Starki was no craven. In a grunting blur he'd freed his axe and swung out hard and across, aiming to split this lanky impostor in two. To his right his twin watched slack-jawed as Starki's broad swipe cut through air alone.

Clouter did better.

Ulf swore as his brother slunk to his knees, Starki's fingers trying in vain to staunch the great rift opened in his belly. He wept as his guts spilled free, shuddered for a miserable moment, and then lay prone.

Ulf had his sword out, a wickedly curved blade, half sax, half broadsword. He levelled it, roared, and waded in, but the steely-eyed stranger's longsword held him at bay.

Meanwhile, the boy, forgotten by everyone, sidled slowly toward the rear of the stable, believing it prudent to vacate the premises. Trouble was the woman saw Cale out of the corner of her eye. Worse, she was blocking his escape route.

"Stay put, yer little shite," she said. Cale wasn't about to argue with a madwoman armed with rusty knife, however small. She stomped over, grabbed his wrist, and yanked hard. Cale yelped and the stolen coins spilled and sparkled to vanish in the dirt. "I've a rope just perfect for your scrawny neck," she told him. Cale gulped.

Ulf slipped a dagger into his left hand. He circled Corin, the two blades gleaming in the sunshine. Corin smiled at him. Ulf studied the stranger's nasty-looking blade. Barely, he kept a lid on his fury, hearing his twin's dying shudders behind him. Then the stranger's smoky eyes flicked across to where that idiot Cale was succumbing wimperingly to the smith's wife. He seemed half amused at the boy's antics. Ulf seized his moment, tossed his dagger hard and fast. Corin grinned, having expected that. His heavy blade sent the knife spinning away with a blaze of sparks.

But Ulf didn't waste any time. He shouldered into Corin with both hands on his curved blade seeking to hack hard into his enemy's side. Instead Corin's counterstroke clanged into the twin's blade, knocking him off balance.

Still grinning, Corin leapt at Ulf. Reversing Clouter, he rammed the wolf's-head pommel hard into Ulf's chin, breaking the big man's jaw and launching him backward. Ulf groaned once and then lay still.

Corin knelt and wiped Clouter clean on Ulf's woolly coat. He gave its steely length a critical eye before slinging the longsword back in its scabbard, hanging lateral across his back. Corin turned to the woman who had the spitting youth in a headlock.

"You get some rope, girl," he said, "and I'll hoist this fat bastard from that tree out there." He motioned toward Ulf's prone fur-clad lump and then pointed to the large ash shading the far end of the stockade.

"What about this streak of piss?" The woman yanked Cale's left earlobe and he squawked enthusiastically.

"We'll hang him too," replied Corin, grinning evilly. "By the ears," he added. "Over hot coals. Slowly." Corin winked at Cale, who for his part looked wan and sad.

"Aw...you wouldn't," the boy said as the woman left him to source the rope. Corin ignored him. Instead he went to the well across the yard, hoisted a bucket, and spilled the contents over his head.

"I'm hungry," he said to the boy then. Cale didn't reply. He was looking past Corin at someone's looming approach.

"I'm Tommo," said a gruff voice. The smith was big and fresh faced, though blood

matted his sandy hair and rouged his stubbled cheeks. "We are in your debt, stranger," he said.

"Where is Polin?" Corin asked. He didn't like being called stranger. The smithy was only seven miles from where he'd been born. Still, he didn't know these people so why should they know him.

"Father died last winter," the girl answered, returning. She threw a heavy coil of rope on the ground and then stood with feet braced and arms crossed to study Corin.

"I know you." She smiled impishly, which made her look younger, perhaps twenty-five. "You're Corin an Fol," she said, and he nodded. "I used to quite fancy you back then, but you buggered off to foreign parts. I'm Kyssa. Remember me?"

Corin recalled a freckled twelve-year-old girl with wild red hair and a mischievous grin. He nodded, "Aye, I do so, yes." Corin was awkwardly aware of Tommo's lowering brow and somber expression. "I'm sorry to hear of your father's death. He was a good man, Kyssa."

She shrugged. "Everyone dies."

Half hour later, big Tommo helped Corin hoist the kicking, fully conscious Ulf skyward while Kyssa clapped and Cale soiled his pants, this day not going as he'd planned it.

"Well," said Corin, awarding the boy a steely stare. "What have you got to say for yourself, shithead?"

"I've done nothing! I don't deserve...that." Cale's bulging eyes glanced up to where Ulf quivered and kicked.

"We will see." Corin turned and winked at Tommo, but the smith didn't look the forgiving type.

"He's a thief," said Tommo. "Thieves hang, it's the law."

"Bugger the law," said Corin. "How old are you, boy?" Corin asked Cale.

"Almost fourteen winters," Cale replied, and sensing he might have a chance, stuck his chin out. "What's it to you?" Cale was in awe of this stranger and his massive sword but determined not to show it. This bastard had easily bested the two toughest men he had ever known. They might not have been house trained but they had been his only companions.

Cale had wanted to do for them both when they were taunting the woman, but that was different. Cale didn't like that sort of thing, having his own sense of honor. Not that the wench didn't deserve it, the way she'd treated him.

Master Cale had his pride and wasn't about to forgive this weirdo stranger's executions of Ulf and Starki. For three profitable years Cale had accompanied the brutal twins, learning much as they robbed and murdered their way across the wilderness of Kelthaine and Fol.

"Thirteen and three quarters to be exact," he answered eventually.

"Well, be grateful you're not yet fourteen. If you were, I'd slit you open like an overripe melon!" Corin held the boy's defiant gaze for a moment longer, then turned away to spit on Starki's mangled, fly-clustered corpse.

Slowly his anger faded, replaced by fatigue and sorrow. Corin remembered what had occurred on his own fourteenth birthday. The memory of that day would never fade; it was branded into his skull like the sword scar on his forehead. That had been the day of the raid on Finnehalle by Crenise pirates, culminating with the

death of his father and brothers, and later the loss of his mother
and sister too.

"Where are you from?" Corin glared at the boy.

"It don't matter where he's from," Tommo cut in, but Corin
motioned him to silence. Beside her husband, Kyssa fingered her
knife fondly and smiled at Cale. He pretended not to notice.

"Kelthara," Cale muttered then, staring sulkily at the field outside. His quick mind was calculating a way out of this unpleasant
situation. He heard footsteps, and turning back he paled—it was
apparent Tommo's patience had finally dissolved. The ominous
hulk of the blacksmith loomed over him, massive hands bunching
in fury.

"Leave him be." Corin's voice halted the big man's fist. Tommo
turned, glowering at the longswordsman.

"Why?"

Corin shrugged. "There's been enough retribution today," he
said. Kyssa shook her head. She looked disappointed.

Ignored for the minute, Cale seized his chance. With practiced
ease he scooped from the dirt the coins he'd stolen. "I'll be taking
my leave now, masters," the boy announced as he spun on his heels
and fled the yard. "I don't suppose we'll meet again." As Tommo
and Corin gave chase, Cale turned and hurled a dagger he'd kept
stowed up his left sleeve. Tommo dived and Corin ducked as the
blade whooshed over their heads. Corin was angry again. His fast
legs soon carried him ahead of the laboring smith, his longsword
swinging behind him as he vaulted the wall with athletic ease.

To no avail. Cale was a city lad, well used to being pursued by
vengeful adults down the labyrinthine lanes of old Kelthara town.
He'd soon vanished into the thorny knot of woodland enclosing the
western end of Polin's Smithy.

Corin yelled out to him. "If I come across you again it will go
bad for you boy! Remember the name Corin an Fol!"

His only answer was the wind in the trees.

Shaking his head in disgust, Corin returned to the stockade.
Before he reached the gate, the strange sound of laughter made
him stop and glance up at a nearby oak. There, scarce ten feet

away, beautifully balanced on the stout limb of a level branch, sat a girl. Her face was pale perfection dominated by two huge tawny eyes. These

watched him with mocking humor. There was something decidedly odd about this child. Corin felt uneasy under her gaze.

"You did well today," she giggled, her bare legs swinging high above his head. It seemed odd how the chilly breeze didn't bother her, despite her only garment's being a pale blue dress hemmed well above her knees and elbows. Long golden braids cascaded down her back, and she wore shoes of softest red leather. The girl grinned down at Corin with impish delight.

"We are watching you with interest," the strange girl said. Then her lips twisted into a cat's feral grin. Suddenly she looked cruel, spiteful. "Be careful in the woods. *He* is stalking you."

"Who are you, child?" Corin managed before Tommo's heavy footsteps distracted him. He squinted through the afternoon sun to see the blacksmith approach.

"What are you looking at?" Tommo enquired. He awarded the tree a quizzical glance. Corin pointed above, then swore under his breath. The branch was bare.

"I... nothing," Corin struggled, doubting his senses. "The boy's gone," he said, stating the obvious just to change the subject. Corin wondered whether those field mushrooms he'd found yesterday were having an unwholesome effect on him. It wasn't a good sign seeing strange girls in trees.

Tommo shrugged. "I wouldn't have hung him," he said eventually, "just wanted to scare the little shite." Corin nodded. "Why not stay and sup some ale with us," Tommo offered then. "Kyssa's got a three day stew on the stove—turnips, coney, broth and all."

"I thank you, but no," responded Corin. He'd changed his mind after the fight. He desired solitude: time to think on his own. "I wish to watch the sun set on the ocean this very evening, take my leave in the taverns of Finnehalle. It's seven miles away if I read that last marker correctly, though my memory makes the distance shorter." Corin had a sudden notion. "There is a service you can do for me, Tommo, if you will," Corin added.

"Name it."

"My horse, Thunderhoof, is lame, or pretending to be. He's covered many leagues over the last week and isn't happy, doesn't like the wet. Could you stable him and see to his needs? He's a good old boy but gets a bit stiff sometimes."

"Gladly," responded Tommo, insisting once more Corin stay for some respite at least. "Finnehalle *is* only seven miles away, yes, and I've other steeds to lend you. Those rogues left shaggy mounts tied outside the north gate. They'll not be using them again, nor do I expect that young cutpurse will return to reclaim his pony."

Corin could not be persuaded. He made his excuses to the blacksmith and his wife, who joined them, insisting he wanted to walk the last few miles. It would clear his head, Corin told them. Tommo was nonplussed, but Kyssa gazed at him askance.

"You are a strange one, Corin." She yielded a shrug. Corin, feeling awkward, didn't respond. Instead he went to get the horse.

They waited in silence, both worn out by this troublesome day. Eventually Corin returned with Thunderhoof clomping noisily behind him. Then, just a few minutes later the longswordsman bade farewell to the blacksmith, his wife, and Thunder. Heart heavy, Corin took his leave from Polin's Smithy. He vowed to return after a few days' hard drinking. Thunderhoof didn't notice Corin's departure. He was already at his oats. Corin left lane and smithy behind. Time to go home. He wondered if Holly was still in town. He'd liked Holly——back then.

Chapter 2

The Dreaming

She is falling, gliding, sliding down through cold night air. Down and down. She has no fear, knows this to be another dream. Or rather the same dream in yet another guise. Down she falls encased by total blackness.

Things in that void call out to her. Dark things that hint at her ruin and try vainly to reach her. Again she is not afraid. Elanion watches over her—the Goddess of this green world, Ansu, protecting her child as She always has.

The dreamer relaxes as she glides, her pale arms outstretched and her face numbed by icy air. She sees a light, a tiny speck far below. It grows, a small distant globe rising up to meet her.

Ariane smiles. She feels the warmth of the Goddess cocooning her naked body. She is safe—nothing can hurt her now. The light expands, it reaches up, piercing the gloom, and embraces her with blinding clarity. Ariane gasps as her head fills with visions. Wild and giddy, her young mind struggles to make sense of what the Goddess is telling her.

The light takes shape. Its source is in front of her. Ariane no longer falls, instead she stands in an empty hall. Sconces flicker and faint shadows flee from the source of the light, its clarity penetrating every corner. The light, though dazzling, doesn't stop her seeing. Ariane walks effortlessly toward its center, her royal vision enabling her to see through into the very heart.

And there it is, The Crown of Kings. Source of the light. The Tekara. Crystal and radiant, its mystical benevolence banishes darkness from the realm.

Until now.

A shadow has entered the hall. It splits, becomes two shadows. Two men. Intruders. Ariane knows this, having witnessed this outcome twice before. The smaller figure reaches out, grabs the crown, then drops it as the light burns his fingers.

The Tekara falls, impacts with the marble floor.

The dream shifts.

Ariane stands alone in a glade in a deep dark wood. Ahead are tall stones, their shadows long, sloping and narrow. Above her head a diadem of stars studs the night sky. Dark trees creak and stir as she steps forward and enters the glade.

The stones watch her approach. A granite ring, dark and silent. She enters that circle within a circle, turns to her left, following the spiral into the labyrinth's heart. Ariane feels her heart beating with excitement, anticipation, and dread. Voices whisper to her from the beyond the stones.

Knowledge is power, they tell her. Power is corruption. Corruption is the world eater. Ariane ignores them, reaches the core, the very center. Ahead waits a well. Ariane steps silently forward, reaches out with both hands, eager for knowledge and power. But the well is stolen from her eyes by sudden mist. The mist deepens, clings to her face like damp, searching fingers. Ariane cries out at that touch, but her voice is muffled in the murk. Somewhere in the distance she hears the lonely strain of harpsong.

The dream shifts back.

The Tekara explodes as it greets the tiled floor of the hall, shatters into a hundred blazing sparks. Pain fills Ariane's head as she feels those crystal daggers lancing deep into her skin. She falls, bleeding and broken. All around her the shadows dance and whirl like smoky wraiths. She is cold now, icy cold.

Ariane hears laughter and knows the realm is betrayed. Sorcery and corruption. Dream Ariane closes her eyes, lets the darkness consume her again...

***

"My Queen, it is time! The council is gathering in your throne room." Ariane opened her eyes, the rough voice having jolted her back into consciousness. Outside the lofty towers and spires of Wynais, called by some the Silver City, sparkled with morning sunshine.

A cough. She turned her head, saw Roman Parrantios, her champion and trusted friend, leaning over her. Ariane blinked and grimaced as sharp pain lanced behind her eyes. She ignored it.

"I need to speak to Dazaleon. Go find him."

"But the council?"

"Bugger the council, Roman. Go get me the High Priest!" Ariane watched bleary-eyed as Roman left her, his expression grim. He was a good man, but he was a soldier, tough, resilient and practical. Not one to share the Dreaming with.

Ariane checked the hour. It was still early despite Roman's urgency. And it was *her* council, and they could bloody well wait until she was ready for them. Ariane had had Kelwyn's responsibilities thrust upon her just six months past, after her father's untimely death. She was still getting used to the governing process, and patience wasn't her strong point.

She was only twenty two, slight of build and tomboy in shape and nature, with shoulder-length black hair and dark, piercing eyes. But Ariane was clever—she was sharp of tongue and didn't suffer fools. She took after her father in that. Ariane took after her father in most things.

But not the Dreaming. Those dreams had always been her mother's province. But her mother had died whilst birthing a still-born eighteen years past. She'd loved the Queen, but the memory of her childhood was fading fast these days and along with it Queen Cailine's gentle face.

Besides, Ariane was always her father's girl. King Nogel had doted on his daughter, always letting her accompany him on royal visits to Kelthaine, Morwella and Raleen —and even once the island, Crenna, a dangerous place infamous for piracy, dark sacrifices and insurrection.

When Ariane had asked to learn sword craft her father had indulged her. It was Roman who taught her back then: rapier, spear, knife, and bow; elbow, fist, palm, heel, and toe.

Ariane loved learning how to handle weapons. She was deft and moved like a dancer. The Queen was a fine horsewoman, too. Not for her the cozy courtesan life of other high-born ladies, like her cousin, Lady Shallan of Morwella.

But ruling her people was not so easy. She'd not been ready for such responsibility, but her father's falling from his horse and breaking his neck during a hunt had thrust it on her. Ariane was abrupt at council, easily distracted and short tempered as a rule. That said, she was kind hearted and generous. But those were not necessarily the most useful characteristics in a ruler.

She loved her country, though. Kelwyn—the second kingdom. Second in size to only Kelthaine, her northern neighbor, where the High King held court.

Or had done until last week.

A discreet cough at the door jolted her thoughts back to the immediate.

"Your Highness—"

"A moment, Dazaleon, if you please." Ariane fussed her maids get her trousers and tunic as she slid into her small clothes. She liked to dress practical at councils. They went on forever, and Ariane found court uncomfortable enough without being laden down by jewelry and fine lace. It was a point of discussion among her maid servants, though none dared speak their thoughts in her presence.

Ariane grabbed the doeskin trousers from a maid and hoisted them up her legs. She donned the green-suede tunic and girded it with a broad leather belt. Finally she stepped into short black boots of worn expensive leather.

That will suffice.

"You may enter." Another maid opened the door, allowing the tall figure outside to approach her.

Dazaleon, High Priest of Wynais, Kelwyn's royal city and Ariane's birthplace, was an impressive figure. Robed in Goddess green, he stood almost seven feet tall and broad at shoulder, his long hair snow white and thick, and his lined features nut brown around penetrating blue eyes.

Dazaleon looked to be a man of sixty, but he'd already seen his seventy fifth summer. The Goddess gave him power, they said. Strength in body and in mind. He was the young Queen's mentor, spiritual advisor, and closest confidante. But more importantly, Dazaleon was the only one who knew about the Dreaming.

Dazaleon loomed over her, his heavy brows knotted with concern. He was garbed for council, his high-priest robes immaculate emerald and the long rod of office clutched in his left fist. He shifted, fingered the rod, and waited for his Queen to speak.

"I dreamt of the crown again, Dazaleon." Ariane seated herself by the bed and bid her High Priest do the same. Stiffly he joined her, folding his long body into a chair. At her curt wave the maids scurried from the room.

"I guessed it were so, Highness. The third time, is it not?"

"The third time this week, yes."

"The same dream—the Tekara shattering."

"The same, yet subtly different."

"Tell me."

And she did.

***

An hour later Ariane sat at her throne at council whilst her court buzzed and fidgeted across the throne room. Gossip spread flame-fast throughout that airy hall, fed by hinting whispers. Rumors were afoot, the whisperers said, dire portents warning of war and darkest sorcery. Something bad had happened in the north. The Queen knew about it, Dazaleon too—and Roman. Perhaps a few others also.

The Queen raised her left hand and the court fell silent. All eyes were on Ariane and the High Priest standing tall behind her. They shuffled and waited: her nobles, notaries, priests, surgeons, steel-clad officers, silk-wrapped merchants, and other men and women of account. They numbered over fifty, each one known for their discretion and loyalty, thus trusted by the Queen. Most gathered were garbed in expensive cloth. The colors were bright, saving the priests, who wore green and the soldiers dun brown. As one they waited, their expressions tense and their manner unsure.

Eventually the Queen spoke. Despite her awkwardness, Ariane braved a confident voice, easily reaching the double door-ways where the two helmeted guards stood silent with halberds crossed. Like the nobles gathered inside, these guards loved their Queen, though they were concerned she'd taken too much upon herself. King Nogel had ruled with compassion and strength. Everyone loved him, and the realm feared little whilst he was alive. Ariane had his metal in her veins, but she was so young, had not expected to have this responsibility for many years. How would she cope?

"You have heard rumors, this I know," Ariane said. "Events are unravelling fast up in Kelthaine. There is no way to say this easily, my people. High King Kelsalion is dead." There followed shocked gasps and startled looks. Everyone wanted to speak, but none dared utter a sound.

"Yes, it's true, our overlord is dead. Murdered, apparently, by Permian assassins. It happened late last week. We received word via pigeon only three days hence."

"Permian assassins my arse!" Roman Parrantios stood facing his Queen. The champion's bearded jaw was set resolute. "This is that bastard Caswallon's handiwork."

"I concur with our respected champion's opinion," Ariane told the court. Then turning to Roman, she added, "I don't, how-ever, appreciate the interruption." Roman muttered an apology.

"There is worse news," she continued. They waited. Even the guards looked apprehensive at the doors. "The Tekara—Kell's crystal crown, which has protected his descendants and our four realms for millennia—is shattered. Broken beyond repair. I know this because for three nights the Royal Dreaming has visited upon me."

"Treachery!" This from a young officer standing to Roman's left. Fierce looking, tall, and hawkish, with long black braids spilling down the length of his back.

"It's fucking Caswallon," Roman again under his breath—he just couldn't help himself.

"Sirs!" Ariane's withering gaze silenced them both. "Hold your tongues else I'll have them removed!" Roman raised his brows while the courtiers shifted nervously. *She could do that.* "You will have your piece. In the meanwhile, I will not be interrupted." She gazed to her left, where the High Priest loomed imperious.

"As I said, the Dreaming came upon me—the Goddess Herself speaking nuances inside my head. Not once—three times. Star Bright Elanion would protect her children from the approaching storm."

Ariane shifted on the throne. "High Priest Dazaleon understands these things far better than I do. As some of you may know his interpretations of the Queen's—my dear mother's—dream-fuelled visions gave her some solace before she died. Dazaleon is the wisest among us. His counsel is without flaw, and he alone can interpret the Dreaming. So I suggest you listen. (This last was aimed at Roman and the young officer beside him.)

Ariane motioned her mentor step forward. "Come, my lord, impart the wisdom of your knowledge."

Dazaleon leaned heavy on his rod: a long, inch-thick length of ash capped by a globe of solid emerald almost four inches in diameter. The Staff of Elanion—it was this rod enabled Dazaleon speak directly with the Goddess, either in his temple or down by the lake. His heavy gaze swept the courtroom, commanding attention.

"All royal dreams are important," he told them. "Dreams direct from the Goddess are rare indeed. In my entire life I have received only two. Our Highness has had three in three days.

"These dreams bring visions we call the Dreaming. During these visions the Goddess speaks to the dreamer. Not as I speak to you today but in subtler ways. Queen Ariane, though grasping a good deal herself, has given me the task of translating those dreams so all present may comprehend what the Goddess wishes." He turned to the Queen, seated pale on her throne.

"Your Highness, tell us what you saw."

Ariane, feeling uncomfortable, kept it brief. "I fell through darkness. Then there was warmth and a light. The warmth I knew to be the Goddess cocooning me from harm. I knew I journeyed through the void—nothing else could be that dark. The light I recognized as coming from the Tekara, our holy Crown of Kings. I walked toward it. There were creeping shadows, but the light kept them at bay." She turned to Dazaleon, who nodded and stepped forward again.

"Those shadows are our enemies, Your Highness, within and without. Skulkers and deceivers. Always they have tried to undermine the Tekara's power."

Ariane nodded. "Two of those shadows became people—I couldn't see their faces, though one was taller than the other. The smaller one took the crown from its resting place..."

There was hushed silence in the courtroom, even Roman looked pale.

"That was Prince Tarin doing the bidding of Caswallon," Dazaleon told them. "Long has Kelsalion's mentor worked on that boy. Caswallon first got his claws on Tarin after the Queen's death. Torn by grief, the High King was fast losing grip over the realm, and Caswallon saw his chance. Young and impressionable, the boy Prince was easily swayed by the high counsellor's cunning."

"Little prick," muttered Roman under his breath again. "Needs something sharp shoving up his—"Ariane shot him the warning glance of a weary mother, part love, part exasperation.

"Prince Tarin dropped the crown. I..." Ariane exchanged looks with her High Priest. "The dream changed then: I stood in a wood—a sacred grove. Ahead were tall stones—a circle within a circle. I entered...saw a well...felt the Goddess calling me from inside it, so I reached out. But the well faded from view."

"Our Queen speaks of Valen Durrannin—the Oracle of

Elanion. It lies deep within the Forest of Dreams in a wild corner of northern Kelthaine." Dazaleon's long fingers drummed the huge emerald capping his staff. He looked uneasy. "Are there any present familiar with this forest?"

"Well?" Queen Ariane glanced around at the faces watching her. "Someone help us. What about you merchants? You're always on the roads." She hinted to a small group of wealthy looking individuals clustered to the right of the main party.

I've been close, Your Highness." Ariane recognized the speaker as Porric of Port Wind, a city on the coast.

"And saw what?"

Porric muttered a reply.

"We cannot hear you sir!" Ariane snapped.

"I said, it's a dangerous place, Your Highness. Unsettling—even when you see the line of trees only in the distance as we did. Beautiful but sinister. Creepy—that's how I felt about it and my men were edgy too. We stopped at a nearby village. The inn's keeper hinted the forest was once the province of the Faen. The Oracle is rumored to lie deep in its midst. That's all I know."

"You have our thanks, Porric. So there it is—the Forest of Dreams." Ariane twisted in her throne's velvet-padded seat. "Back to my dreams. My visions changed again, I saw the Tekara shatter. At that point I woke because someone interrupted me." Roman had gone a bit red, the Queen's cold glare having fallen on him again. Kelwyn's champion shifted his feet and scratched an ear. She was feisty, this Queen—just like her father had been. Despite that, she needed looking after and he determined to do so.

"Three warning dreams—each one more or less the same," Ariane said. "Our realm is in peril, is it not, Dazaleon."

"It is, Your Highness. Direst peril. Your champion's suspicions are correct, I fear. Caswallon is to blame. I believe he has total power in Kelthaine. A usurper—clever and conniving. With the Tekara shattered, evil will take hold in the Four Kingdoms again. And Caswallon carries darkness with him. I have long mistrusted Kelsalion's favorite councilor. Caswallon is a twisted man. Worse by far, he is a sorcerer.

"The meaning of the Dreaming is clear enough," Dazaleon's voice rose as he addressed all those present. "Queen Ariane must needs ride north, attend the Goddess's Oracle, and gain council on what to do next." "Forgive me, my lord—but that's total crap." Roman strode forward.

"Roman, the court will hear your thoughts," said Ariane, attempting to exert at least a semblance of control over her champion. "Please keep your tone respectful."

Roman wasn't having any of this witchy nonsense, however. "If Caswallon is our enemy, then what we need are swords and strong arms, not dream quests and portents." And the last thing Kelwyn's citizens needed was their beloved young Queen faring out on some wild caper deep within what was now enemy country. That part he kept to himself.

Dazaleon summoned patience. Roman Parrantios was beloved by all. He was steadfast and formidable, Kelwyn's greatest warrior. But sometimes he was hard work, even for a priest.

"The Goddess has spoken, Roman—her words are clear. Besides, Caswallon *is* a sorcerer, and you cannot defeat sorcery with swords. We need knowledge on how to defeat him. We also need to discover what happened to Prince Tarin."

"Hopefully Caswallon slit his throat," muttered Roman.

Dazaleon ignored that last comment. "Our contacts in Kella City sent word that the Prince fled after his treasonous act. No doubt Caswallon will hunt him down."

"So...?" Roman wasn't backing down. "Why should we care?"

"Because he shares my blood, Roman!" Ariane snapped. "The Prince may be a damned fool, but he is not wicked. I would help him if I can."

"And we need to know what happened to the shards," added Dazaleon.

"But why seek out yonder wood, spooks or not?" This came from a fair-haired noble with a lazy smile. He was easy on the eye and had a soft arrogance often shared by those blessed by good fortune and leisure. He'd just emerged from tasting wine at the far tables, where he'd been listening half-heartedly to all that was said.

The newcomer was dressed in cool lapis lazuli and looked politely bored. He stood beside Roman, who glanced briefly in the newcomer's direction and grunted a welcome.

"I wondered when you would show up." The braided officer glared across at the other man. "Surprised you're not at the taverns already, Tamersane."

The blonde noble shrugged. "We cannot all be as assiduous in our duties as you, brother. But pray, what of my question, dearest cuz? Sorry I mean, Your Highness."

Ariane took a deep breath. Roman, Tolranna, and now Tamersane, his younger brother. Trouble piled on trouble. She ought to have them flogged. Trouble was she liked them too much.

Yail Tolranna and his brother, Tamersane, were both highly accomplished swordsmen. Whilst Tolranna was moody, tough, and blunt, Tamersane owned to a fondness of poetry and song. And attractive women. His idle charm and easy tongue were feared by husbands at court far more than his sword. The other thing about Tamersane—he was beyond disrespectful. Despite that, his sword play was second only to Roman's and his loyalty to his royal cousin, assured. "Isn't the answer to it obvious?" responded Dazaleon when Ariane refused to answer Tamersane.

Tamersane raised a lazy brow whilst Dazaleon explained further. "If our Queen dreams of the Oracle, it means she is needed there. Elanion's power is strongest in that forest. There we can reach her directly—nowhere else in the Four Kingdoms. And whatever knowledge she imparts will be crucial in the forthcoming war."

"War?" Ariane asked of her High Priest as the rest of the court drew a collective breath. "Is our outlook so bleak, Dazaleon?"

"I believe so, Highness. Caswallon may be clever, but his objective is transparent. That one wants to rule over all Four Kingdoms. He'll break any rebellion in Kelthaine, smash little Morwella, and then turn on us, and finally Raleen. Aided by his sorcery and with the lands no longer protected by the Tekara, what chance do we have?"

"Then I'll lead a host forward comprising two hundred cavalry," urged Yail Tolranna. "We'll escort Your Highness up there."

"Don't be ridiculous, brother." Tamersane's gaze was on the nearest arched window spilling sunlight in from the courtyard outside. Fine autumn day. Shame he was missing it. "The smaller the number, the safer she'll be."

"Your brother's right in this, Yail." Dazaleon stared hard at the two brothers fidgeting either side of Roman. One dark, one fair. Both shifted uncomfortably under his gaze, but Tamersane couldn't help looking just a little smug.

"A host would only draw Caswallon's attention," Dazaleon said. "We need stealth not armored horse, not yet anyway. Disguised as Elanion's priests, a small party, including Your Highness, could perchance reach northern Kelthaine without detection. It's risky, however."

"But necessary." Ariane had made her mind up. Stewing in court would achieve nothing. "I'll brook no argument," she said. And then, raising her voice so that none could mistake her words, the Queen announced: "Elanion has spoken to me, and my duty is clear. I will ride north to this forest." Ariane's dark gaze then fell on her High Priest. "Do you agree, my lord?" Dazaleon nodded. "I believe it to be our best option, Highness, however dire. But there is some heartening news. We have allies."

"I don't see them. Are they invisible?" Roman ferociously opposed this proposition. His beard bristled and his face grew redder.

"Let me explain," said Ariane. "Under Dazaleon's wise council, we reached out to sympathizers. For months we've been watching Caswallon sharpen his claws up north. Others have, too."

"We formed a secret league," explained Dazaleon. "We communicate only by coded messages sent via birds. Among our confederates are General Belmarius of the Bears regiment; Halfdan of Point Keep, former general of the Wolves regiment and brother of Kelthaine's late King; and down in Port Sarfe, a certain merchant called Silon. This last contact has proved invaluable. Silon has promised us a guide to lead our Queen to the Oracle. The man is rumored to be coarse and ill-bred but apparently trustworthy and useful with a blade."

Ariane studied her court. If only her father were here. King

Nogel would have known what to do. She remembered as a child how he had single-handedly killed two armed would-be murderers with his bare fists whilst she, her mother, and the King walked the leafy streets of Wynais. Not for King Nogel a cavalcade or palanquin. Kelwyn's rulers loved their people and mixed with them whenever they could. The assassins were traced back to Kelthaine. Ariane suspected they'd been in Caswallon's pay. Even back then, Caswallon was on the rise, and he had no love for her father, Nogel having seen clean through the knave, unlike the High King, who doted on Caswallon's every word.

Father, what would you have done?

Ariane saw how Roman's face was still red with emotion. Her champion was clearly not happy, and she didn't blame him. Yail Tolranna looked hungry—eager to be part of the quest. Tamersane looked thoughtful whilst others watching looked worried and confused.

"Enough for now." Ariane stood and her court bowed obeisance. "We need a little time to cogitate and plan. I will hold a second council this evening when my mind is clearer. Only my closest advisers need attend. You few I would have return in three hours, the rest of you enjoy the evening." Ariane bid her court depart with a dismissive wave.

At her word those in the courtroom departed briskly amid chatter—all save Dazaleon and Roman, whilst Tolranna hovered with the guards at the doorway, Tamersane having already departed for the taverns at speed. Ariane turned toward her High Priest.

"Can this Silon really be trusted, do you think?"

"I don't know, Highness, but we don't have a choice but to trust him. Certainly he's no friend to Caswallon, who will most likely impose trade-strangling tariffs. Silon's artful and has many contacts. He's been around a long time, and like us, he fears the usurper's ambitions. We need cunning allies like him, not just armies with steel."

"Armies would be better," growled Roman.

Ariane stared at them both and then turned away. After a moment she spoke, her gaze still on the courtyard outside.

"Summon them back, Roman."

"You said three hours, Highness."

"I know what I said."

"But—"

"My mind is set, Roman. We ride north today. Three shall accompany me, yourself included. We leave before dusk, so I suggest you tell the others and get ready."

"First I need to know who they are." Roman was looking worried.

When the Queen told him, Roman's concerns worsened. He kept his tongue, however, just stomped moody out of the throne room. Dazaleon, watching the champion depart, raised a quizzical brow.

"Strange choice, Your Highness."

"Strange times, Dazaleon." Ariane smiled briefly up at him and then reclaimed her seat on the throne. *Father, what would you have done?*

***

It was actually quite dark by the time they left Wynais, a quiet party of riders garbed in priestly green. Few heeded their passing.

They rode north, deep into the night, finally taking shelter in a small wood beside the rocky stream marking the boundary between the Queen's land and Kelthaine. Roman insisted they take stag despite small risk of danger this close to home. Ariane complied, and the champion took first watch. Soon the other two men were snoring hard beneath their blankets.

But Ariane couldn't sleep. She was restless and edgy, her mind racing about her decision and this trip. She opened her eyes. It was hopeless—she was wide awake.

On a whim, she rolled free of her blanket and sat hunched and bleary over the fire. Roman turned, raised a brow.

"Get some sleep, old friend, I'm wide awake."

"But my Queen, the watch is a soldier's task."

"A soldier is what you trained me to be, Roman," the young Queen smiled at her champion, and he shrugged. "We are a team now, each of us must contribute. I am no exception. Besides, I really cannot sleep so you might as well turn in. I've no doubt we'll need your strength and council the next few days."

Roman smiled. "You have your father's mettle, my Queen."

"I hope so."

"Do not doubt it. I see him in you all the time. But thank you. Yes, I am weary, so I shall happily retire. Don't forget to wake that lout Tamersane. You know what he's like, and I don't want you on watch all night."

"I'll wake him." Ariane waved Roman lie down. "Go get some shut eye."

Time passed, the fire guttered. Ariane sat hunched and dreamy. Close by, Roman's snores eclipsed the other two's. Ariane was not sure how late it was. Perhaps she should wake Tamersane, but what was the point? She knew she wouldn't sleep tonight.

She felt rather than heard a noise in the bush behind her. Close by, the horses shuffled and clustered as though disturbed. By whom? Ariane turned, glimpsed *his* shadow standing there beneath the waxing moon.

King Nogel, her father.

He stood thin as smoke and pale as mist, his sad dead eyes watching her from beneath the trees.

Father!

The King turned his back on her and faded into the night.

"Father!" Ariane found her feet and noisily approached the place where he had been. She saw him again watching her from the edge of the forest.

"What would you have me do?" Ariane called after him.

"Hold to courage, little one," King Nogel's voice was dry leaves on a windswept path. "You ride into danger, a peril far greater than I ever faced."

"Caswallon?"

"He is part of it but only part. From where I stand now, I can see the bigger picture. But it is bleak, my love, so bleak."

"What can I do?"

"Follow your heart. You have your mother's intuition and

my...strength. But you're smarter than I. Trust only those your heart allows. Seek out the Goddess, but be prepared. This is only the start. And be careful who you love."

"Love?"

The pale shape of her father turned away. She could see clear through him. *Love?* He was fading fast, barely a wisp of drifting fret as light paled the fields beyond the wood. Night was nearly over.

Ariane called out one last time. "Why did you leave me, father? You were so strong. I-"

"I was murdered, child."

"Caswallon." Ariane bit her lip, tasting the blood in her mouth.

"He and his accomplices, among them one we trusted."

Ariane's pale face whitened. "A Kelwynian? A traitor? Who?"

But King Nogel no longer stood there. Instead the morning's breeze put paid to the fire's last breath, and behind her she heard her men mutter and groan as they woke beneath their blankets.

Tamersane approached her with a sheepish grin.

"I must have slept through, cuz. Have you been up all night? You look awful, like you've seen a ghost or something."

Ariane glared at Tamersane. "You, my dear cousin, can take the first two watches tonight." She turned to where the others were stirring. "Galed, get breakfast underway. While you've been sleeping I've been thinking. Ten minutes gentlemen. Then we're on our way." Throughout that morning, Ariane stayed quiet. The Queen was clearly troubled. But the men all knew her well, so they let her be. Besides, they were in enemy country, and the fewer words said the better.

✳✳✳

That night, whilst Queen Ariane of Kelwyn and her aids rode north, Caswallon's spy sent urgent word up to Kella City. He had the perfect guise to travel freely in Wynais, being robed in green as one of Elanion's sacred priests. He smiled. Both his masters would be pleased, and he stood to gain much.

When he returned to his quarters, a letter awaited him.

Caswallon's spy recognized the hand and paled slightly. A summoning—his other master.

Ten minutes later, shaky and worried, he tapped the door on the officer's chamber.

"Enter."

He complied and stood silent as the dark-eyed officer watched him from behind his desk—a nobleman, handsome and intelligent, and very dangerous.

"You sent word?" The noble asked him.

"I did, my lord—three birds."

The officer sighed. "It's regrettable. There are few who love our Queen like I do, but we must think of the realm. Ariane is reckless and naïve. Caswallon is invincible. He will rule all Four Kingdoms sooner or later, war or no war. So it's in our interest to court his affections. What we do is for the best, hard though it surely is. The letter I sent you bears my seal. Caswallon will reward you well."

"I'm to go to Kella?"

"Yes. One cannot rely on pigeons alone."

"But, my lord—"

"Report back on your return." The officer looked up sharply. "Well? Away with you, man! No time to waste!"

The man in the priest's garb nodded and left the highborn officer to his thoughts. As he gained the stairs, he had the nasty feeling he had been played. The sorcerer in Kella was not known for his equanimity.

Meanwhile the young noble returned to his papers. It was a difficult business. He loved his Queen and had respected her father. But he knew how the world worked. Sink or swim—the only choice. Ariane's devout passion would destroy Kelwyn, whereas were he to rule (as he could so easily with Caswallon's blessings) the country would surely prosper.

Caswallon would probably kill the spy, but that didn't matter—he would send other birds tomorrow.

Chapter 3

The Last Ship

Corin loosened Clouter's harness and sloped the long blade across his left shoulder, allowing him to walk faster and avoid trapping the hilt on branches and twigs. His second blade, a sax—broad and nasty, one-edged and slightly curved toward the tip— hung at his left hip, adjacent to a heavy knife.

This one he called Biter—good for up-close work. Gut slicing and tripe spilling. The knife he hadn't named: he hurled it at people who pissed him off. Corin knew he'd lose it one day, hence no name. He had smaller knives secreted in various compartments. You can never have too many sharp things in this world.

All Corin's blades weighed him down today. A long stiff walk and him a rider too. Still, it felt good to stretch the legs.

And he was coming home. Actually Corin had mixed feelings about that. Fourteen years and he hadn't left with the best grace.

Ahead a high ridge showed dark through a gap in the woods. Eagerly Corin crested it and gazed down past the trees at the distant smoky dwellings of his childhood home. Finnehalle.

There it lay as it always had, framed by tall bluffs; its harbor washed by the fathomless waters of the Western Ocean. Corin drew a deep breath and soaked in the sight. Finnehalle, his village, scarce more than a chaotic scattering of stone dwellings. Rain-washed houses and wooden fishing huts clustered around the old granite harbor.

Finnehalle, a place of crowded taverns and wind-swept markets, where local tradesmen plied their wares and days followed nights without event. Beyond the confines of the Four Kingdoms, few of its folk paid heed to what happened elsewhere.

Corin's eyes followed the course of a familiar stream spilling out beneath the trees and disappearing in the tangle of smoke-veiled roofs below. Beyond these the stone arm of the harbor jutted forth. Past that, the ocean's green-grey expanse sparkled and danced ever westward until it embraced the autumn sky.

Corin felt a sudden pang of loneliness seeing the storm lanterns swaying in the breeze at the harbor's end. *Come back* ...they called to him. *Come home*!

Corin shrugged away his melancholy thoughts. This was proving a peculiar day—he was a fighter not a bloody philosopher. He liked things simple and straightforward. Didn't go with moping much.

Besides, he needed to press on. The taverns would be filling by now. They'd all want to hear his story—not that Corin was much of a talker. But if they provided the ale he would happily comply.

Corin increased his pace as his thirst demanded, soon losing sight of the town in the autumnal canopy of trees. No bird song nor squirrel chatter? Odd that.

Corin stopped by an old oak. He didn't know how he knew, but someone was watching him. He turned, looked back up toward the ridge.

Silhouetted between the trees was the stooped figure of an old man, bearded features buried beneath a wide-brimmed hat. His cloak hung limp despite the keen breeze. Weird. He was a way off, but Corin could see the old fellow clearly.

The greybeard leant heavily on a long spear, its tip blazing suddenly when a shaft of sunlight pierced the clouds.

Corin slowly inched the fingers of his left hand toward Biter's bone hilt. No room to swing Clouter here. His mind was working fast, trying to recall where he'd seen this stranger before. Friend or enemy? He dare not take the chance. That hat was familiar and so was the spear.

A soft sound to his left. Corin turned sharply, sliding the sax free of its scabbard. He let out a slow breath, watched the rabbit scurry beneath a clutch of briar. Reluctantly Corin returned his gaze to the high ridge.

The old man had vanished. Gone. Disappeared in murky autumn air. There was no sound save the wind and restless sighing of trees. Corin slammed Biter back in its leather, cursed profusely, and then resumed his pace, swifter than before. He needed a drink and fast.

Something fluttered to his left. Corin saw a raven settle silent on a branch. An evil-looking bird, it glared at him in accusation.

"Sod off," Corin told it and swiftly resumed his pace. The raven croaked at him and took wing again. Corin cleared the woods. Open fields led down to the town. These he took at a trot. He reached a gate. Finnehalle—he was home.

Pushing open the gate, Corin entered the town. Slate-dressed houses loomed over him as he hastened by in long eager strides. Gulls weaved high above, their white shapes ghostlike in the fading light. Corin hadn't known what to expect really, but the town seemed quieter than it should be, despite the lateness of the hour.

Where was everybody? Corin nodded whilst passing a burley figure shouldering a sack of grain. The man glanced in his direction before disappearing behind a house. Corin frowned at the open hostility of the gaze.

Miserable bugger.

Corin shrugged off his misgivings and hastened down the main track, cursing as a dog snarled, making him jump. He needed that drink badly and sincerely hoped the taverns were still the same, the patrons happier than that grump had been.

Corin shivered, unrolled his woolen cloak, until now stowed on his back alongside Clouter. He threw the cloak over his shoulders, stopping in a doorway to clasp it with his golden wolfs-head broach. Nearly there—hearth and brew.

It was almost dark when Corin reached the harbor. At least the wind had eased. He took to strolling along the quay, not quite ready to enter the busy taverns (he hoped they were busy) despite his urgent need for ale.

Corin passed fishing huts and stinking piles of nets and ropes. There didn't seem to be anyone about. They must all be in the taverns. Maybe something bad had happened.

Despite not wanting to, Corin pictured that old man in the woods leaning on his spear. He recalled the strange girl's warning and frowned. Behind him the sun sank crimson over western water, and the sea murmured its timeless incantation, luring him to gaze into its fathomless depths.

Corin tugged his cloak close to keep out the chill. He leaned idle on the harbor wall, letting his eyes follow the moonlit waves toward the darkening horizon.

He spied movement at the far end of the harbor's arm. Someone stood there watching the water as he did. Corin wondered who it was.

He stared closer. The stranger seemed unaware of Corin's scrutiny in his silent vigil of the waves. There was something familiar about the way the man was standing. *Silon?* Corin grinned, imagining the wealthy merchant leaving his beloved vineyards and moving north to rain-washed Finnehalle. No chance.

Enough nonsense. Corin drank in the briny air one last time. He felt ready to confront his past. With a final curious glance at the distant stranger, Corin turned and briskly strode toward the nearest inn, his favorite.

A faded sign swung creaking above the well-used door, announcing the establishment: *The Last Ship*. Corin grunted as he pushed the door inwards and entered inside. This had better be the same.

***

Inside the inn a sudden welcome rush of heat greeted Corin, together with the rich smell of roasting flesh. A roaring fire cast dancing shadows across the busy room, sending bellows of smoke backwards to hang in foggy clusters beneath darkened oak beams. Shabbily dressed men glanced up warily from their mugs of ale, muttering as the rangy newcomer shouldered his way moodily to the taproom. A bald, sweating man greeted him in friendly fashion.

Corin grinned, recognizing Burmon, whose family had always managed matters behind these stout walls. The innkeeper was a merry soul and had been a friend to the young Corin. Back then he'd spent most of his time in Burmon's fine hostelry.

The Landlord looked at him askance, clearly not recognizing this hard-faced, scarred longswordsman, currently looming over the ale counter and grinning evilly at him.

"Can I be of assistance, sir?" Burmon asked, glancing nervously to the corner by the fire, where three shaggy men were seated around a table, playing dice. "Have you come far?" Burmon was evidently worried about the huge sword slung low across Corin's shoulders (Corin had loosened Clouter's harness to move through the inn.) Corin felt uneasy. Something was clearly amiss in Finnehalle if a jovial fellow like Burmon looked so strained.

"Far enough to need a large ale," Corin responded, softening his smile. "Don't you recognize me, old friend? I know it's been a while, but well I hoped that—"

"Corin!" blurted the innkeeper and then covered his mouth as the three strangers turned to glower in their direction. "Elanion bless us," he whispered, "but it is good to see you again, lad. It must be ten years!"

"Fourteen."

"Fourteen, you don't say. Where does the time go?"

Corin waited with eager anticipation as Burmon poured him a large mug of ale. "Where have you been lad? By the Goddess you've changed. I must tell Holly. She'll be delighted!"

Corin smiled. He hadn't forgotten the innkeeper's comely daughter. Ale wasn't the only reason he'd chosen *The Last Ship*. Corin had shared many a happy hour with Holly in gentler times. Warmed by ale and hearth, Corin's mood brightened anticipating an enjoyable evening ahead. Draining his tankard, he requested another before the busy landlord slipped away to serve other customers. Corin's eyes smarted as he glanced about the smoke-filled room.

The atmosphere of the inn was reserved, considering the number of folk seated at tables and propping the walls. Corin frowned. A few faces were familiar, farmers mostly and fishermen he remembered from his boyhood. None appeared overly cheerful.

Corin studied them from his half-drained ale mug. They kept their voices low as if worried to speak out loud. Corin's eyes drifted toward the tough-looking men by the fire. Mercenaries by the look of them, or else brigands like those shiteheads at the smithy.

Strangers to Finnehalle, of that much he was certain. Corin suspected these outlanders were the sole cause of the taught atmosphere. He resented their presence at his favorite inn. Corin had come home to get away from bastards like this. The nearest man caught his eye, glanced at the longsword and dropped his gaze. He turned to whisper to his friends. Corin smiled and sipped his ale, anticipating confrontation.

The innkeeper returned, accompanied by a young woman who laughed eagerly when she saw who it was visited their taproom.

"I don't believe you've come back!" Holly grinned, pushing blonde tresses behind her left ear with a well-scrubbed hand. She stretched up on tip-toes, placing a wet kiss on Corin's grinning lips.

Corin recalled how fond he'd been of Holly back then; almost she had quelled his wildness. She still looked good. A bit worn round the edges, maybe, and a nonce thicker in waist. She still had that smile, though, and big cornflower eyes. Corin grinned visualizing good times in the days ahead. But then a swift glance at Burmon sobered him.

"What is it, my friend?" Corin asked, seeing the worry on the landlord's face. "What troubles you?"

"Those strangers," muttered the innkeeper. "They're Morwellan cutthroats and seasoned fighters, too. They worry me, Corin. I don't know why they came here. Some trouble back east, I expect. There is always trouble back east."

"What about them?" Corin casually turned to stare at the

three. They were watching him carefully, their faces far from friendly. Corin remembered a man called Hagan, a Morwellan killer, a man from Corin's bloodstained past. His mood darkened, and a shadow fell across him, recalling bleak days he intended to bury forever. Hagan Delmorier: lethal killer with sword and knife. Cunning fox, wily card cheat, Corin's former comrade at arms.

If ever I see you again, Hagan, one of us will die.

These three Morwellans had a similar look to them. They reminded Corin of all the things he despised in himself. Unlike those clowns who had molested poor Kyssa, these three were professionals.

Burmon handed Corin a plate of steaming fish and refilled his glass. "They frighten my customers," he continued. "There was trouble the other night with some farmers from across the valley. You remember the Breen brothers?" Corin nodded. "Well those three set about them and almost beat them to pulp in this very room. Since then, folk have been afraid to speak out. Now things are worse, for one has taken a fancy to Holly."

"If he comes near me, he'll get a kitchen knife in his ribs." The woman's blue eyes flashed angrily. Corin raised a brow at the lass, admiring her spirit. Her father was looking more worried by the minute. Burmon noted Corin's hostile stare and placed a sweaty hand on the longswordsman's shoulder.

"Have a care with your expression, my friend. Those rogues are watching, and they're always spoiling for a fight."

Corin shrugged nonchalantly, then waded into his fish with hearty relish. The girl and her father left him to his meal as they saw to their guests. Corin wolfed his supper down and drained his tankard a third time. He felt much better. Burmon's strong brew soon banished the chill. From his bench in the corner, Corin could see the Morwellans still watching him with dark expressions. He locked eyes with the nearest and scowled. They didn't belong here. Well then, that settled it. Time for a bit of gentle persuasion.

Yes, ugly, I'm looking at you.

Corin unfastened his cloak, allowing it to drop to the rush-strewn floor. He unslung his harness and rested Clouter against an adjacent bench. Then he stood up flush-faced, savagely kicking his own bench out from under his feet. The room was suddenly silent. Eyes gaped and nerves tautened like bowstrings. Corin confronted the three, glancing warily at the broad blades hanging at their waists.

"Have you got a problem with my face?" Corin growled at the nearest and biggest. The inn was deathly quiet. From over at the bar, the landlord and his daughter looked on, worry creasing their brows. "I said do you have a problem, shite for brains?" Corin rested a lean hand on Biter's hilt. There was no room to swing Clouter in here.

The big one turned toward his companions and laughed. "I think he wants to die," he said. This Morwellan was even uglier than Ulf had been, a scarred, round-faced brute with shaggy beard and missing front teeth. His friends chuckled at his words, lowering their hands and reaching slyly for their blades.

"So, you are a longswordsman," spat the leader. "Can you use that bloody great thing over there, or is it just for show." He leered across to where Clouter leaned redundant. "Maybe I'll try it out on your skinny arse before I keep it as a trophy."

"Sirs, please I beg no trouble!" Burmon's plea drew more laughter from the three Morwellans.

"Be silent, porky, and pour us more ale." The leader wiped his mouth on his dirty sleeve and spat green phlegm on the straw-covered floor. "Our lanky friend here demands our full attention." He turned to the others. "I can always use another sword, however unwieldy, and those leathers would look good on me, though that mail shirt looks a bit knackered. What say you, Balian?"

"Aye," muttered the one-eyed, grizzled fellow to his left. "That sword belt would fit my waist," he grinned. "Are those studs real silver?" The third man said nothing, eying their confronter with eager loathing.

Corin stifled a yawn. "Typical bloody Morwellans," he said, "always yabbing instead of stabbing." Panther quick Corin leaped onto their table, kicked the quiet one hard in the face with his left boot, splitting the Morwellan's nose with a sickening crack.

Bearded moon-face grabbed his leg, but Corin brought his right steel-girded boot down hard on the man's hand, snapping his fingers and making him howl in pain.

The Morwellan with the eye patch had his sword out. He lunged at Corin's thighs. Corin grinned, deftly leaping back off the table. He seized a vacant stool and hurled it into One-eye's face, sending him crashing into the crowd watching open jawed from behind.

"Come on!" Corin snarled, grabbing the bearded leader's sword arm, preventing him from freeing his blade. Corin, after winking at Big-Ugly, rammed his head hard into the leader's chin. Crack! The Morwellan's eyes glazed over and he sank groaning to the floor.

The quiet one with the broken nose stabbed out at Corin with an evil-looking sax. Corin blocked the thrust with his forearm, knocking the flat of the blade aside. He leaped forward, jammed his fingers into his antagonist's neck, and squeezed. Number three crumpled unconscious to the ground. Corin grinned. The Morwellans were a mess of groans and broken bones. The day was getting better.

Corin gulped deep breaths, then laughed. A great movement of feet announced the town folk had unanimously decided to be rid of the troublemakers once and for all.

"Found your courage at last," Corin jeered as they clustered like hornets around the Morwellans, kicking and cursing, stomping and spitting. They dragged the battered three out into the street, and then kicked and punched them some more amid hoots of gleeful laughter. Finally tiring of their sport, the vengeful posse returned to the taproom to replenish mugs and congratulate themselves on their victory. The Morwellans slunk away like mangy curs to lick their wounds.

And plot revenge.

Corin wiped the sweat from his brow. He winked at the shiny-eyed Holly and held his mug out for her to replenish. She obliged with a grin and a moist kiss in his left ear, Corin having just turned his head. Corin stooped, fastidiously removed the fresh bloodstain from his faded leather jerkin. It was nice being center of attention for a change. Or would have been if he'd had the chance to reflect on it. But someone had nudged him from behind, interrupting his reverie.

"Greeting, Corin an Fol," said someone with a foreign accent. "I see that you retain your subtle ways."

I know that voice. Corin turned, found himself staring gormlessly into the canny black eyes of Silon, his former employer.

"So it *was* you on the quay. What do you want?"

"Your assistance."

"Bugger off."

"Does the word *gold* interest you?" Silon rolled a coin between his fingers.

"It might." Corin eyed the coin as if it were a snake.

"Well then, I suggest you listen," the merchant said. And Corin did.

Chapter 4

Outcast

Jen recognized Prince Tarin instantly. She had seen him just last spring whilst she and Cullan were making their annual trip to Kella City. But the Prince looked very different now. His apparel was torn and disheveled, and his young face a mask of dried tears and cuts.

Jen turned and yelled back at the cottage. "Cullan, quick! A rider in need!" Moments later her husband loomed blearily above his wife. Big Cullan rubbed his sleep-filled eyes in disbelief at what looked to be young Prince Tarin swaying in exhaustion on his lathered, filthy horse.

Calmly Jen helped the boy slide exhausted from his saddle, then guided him inside, saying nothing. Her son, Dail, had emerged from his bed amid grumbles and, at her word, was seeing to the Prince's exhausted mare.

"You need rest," she told the Prince as she guided him to a bench and a rough-hewn table. "Here, drink this. There are herbs inside that will restore your strength. I am not without knowledge in such matters. Drink it all, then you must rest. Sleep as long as you need to."

Tarin thanked the woman and her husband. Did these people know who he was? Her soft grey eyes hinted they did, and in any case, anyway his raiment surely gave him away. He gulped the concoction down, relishing the fresh taste, and gratefully accepting another.

"I am Prince Tarin," he informed them as regally as he could manage. The woman had wise eyes and was attractive despite being well into her middle years. Her face was careworn but there was strength there, Tarin thought.

The big man beside her looked like a soldier—hard and tough, not one to cross. Both were clad in plain linen shirts with tunics and trousers, faded and homespun. The husband wore a sword belt.

"I know who you are." Jen smiled slightly and waited for the Prince to continue.

"I am in need of haste," Tarin informed Jen and her husband. "Something most regrettable has occurred of which I cannot yet speak, though you will hear of it soon enough. I dare not remain here but must leave at once. And I believe I am being followed."

"You're not going anywhere, young Prince," the husband this time. "With respect, you are in no fit state. I'm Cullan. I served your father under General Belmarius. If there is one that seeks you ill, he will have to get past my sword-arm first. This is my wife, Jen. We are poor, but what we have is yours, Highness."

Tarin thanked them once again. For the first time in days he let himself relax. These were good people, and he felt safe in their cozy home. It was small but clean despite the beasts stalled in the second room.

Tarin's mind was racing. Perhaps he had been wrong about that rider he'd seen late last night? It was hard not to give in to paranoia. At least he was safe here. For the moment.

"Very well, and thank you," Tarin smiled thinly. "I will spend this day and night in your company, though I've no coin to pay for my lodging and fare."

"You honor us, my liege." Cullan's smile softened his careworn face, but his wife's shrewd eyes were troubled.

"Sleep for a good long time," she urged him. "I will call you for late supper."

They gave him their bed. Cullan attended his duties outside whilst his wife set to tasks on the range. Now and then she called in and checked on him lying there.

***

The brew Jen had given him allowed Tarin some respite, but sleep still evaded him despite his fatigue. Calmed by the drug, Prince Tarin let his mind wander down dark corridors as he lay prone and sweating. Was he ill, he wondered? No,—just scared. Terrified and ashamed. And so he should be. His mind drifted back to that long terrible ride. Once again, Tarin felt the darkness closing in as he fled Kella City, fading deep into the night. He must have dozed off at that point....

Traitor... the wind called out his name. *Coward, fool*...the long grasses sighed up at him. *Murderer*...

Tarin jolted upright in the bed. He was hearing voices. It was gloomy in the room, the dark drapes keeping out the light. A candle guttered to his left. How long had he slept? Tarin felt giddy. Perhaps the kind-faced woman had poisoned him. Trust no one, his instinct told him.

I'm no murderer!

A voice laughed from the shadow in the corner.

Tarin, Prince of Fools, you have cost them the realm...

Caswallon, you duped me—it wasn't my fault.

Fool. The laughter continued. It stopped when Jen entered, lit another tallow candle, and drove the darkness from the corner.

"Sleep," she said and faded from view. Tarin nodded, dozed and almost at once the nightmare tore into him.

Pain and terror. A cold dark room comprising weird shapes, tables and cages. It reeked of decay and putrefaction. And fear. On the nearest table were tools laid out in fastidious order. A man watched him with cat-green eyes and a silent smile.

The smiling watcher chose a tool from the table and turned toward Tarin. Only then did the Prince realize he was lashed and naked, spread akimbo on a frame. Green-eyes flicked the tool at his face. When Tarin saw what it was, he tried to scream, but no sound issued from his mouth. Blackness claimed him at that point.

Tarin woke sweaty and chilled. It was quite dark now and the candle burned low. He couldn't stay here, he decided. What if the rider came back? And perhaps Caswallon had sent others. Tarin gazed at the wall as he tried to make sense of the harrowing events of last week. Once again he recalled his wild flight from the city.

At first he'd ridden blindly, driven by speed and panic, stopping only for water and to rest his exhausted steed. His freezing fingers clung to the crystal shards still wrapped in the blood-stained cloth, safely secreted in the hidden pocket inside his velvet tunic. At least he'd had the sense to salvage the crown's remnants before Caswallon got to them.

I still have the shards. They won't get them.

The day he fled Kella City had passed like judgment, each hour an accusation. Tarin had dug his heels into the horse's flank, spurring her on without compassion. His destination, Port Fardoris and the sea, were many leagues distant. Tarin, half crazed with fear, had felt the ghost of his murdered father riding on his back.

That first night the young Prince had hardly slept. He was up before dawn lightened the sky.

By the third morning, as the pitted road threaded the northern wolds of Kelthaine, Tarin's thoughts had levelled out. He was famished, penniless, and armed only with a knife. But he was alive. Desperately he'd began sketching a plan in his head.

Once he reached the port, Fardoris, Tarin would reveal his identity, invent some dire story explaining his shocking state. He'd board ship, take swift passage south to Kelwyn, arrive at Port Wind or Calprissa. There were always vessels sailing south these days. Once there, he could seek aid from Queen Ariane. Tarin had only to hold his nerve and he would escape.

And so the week had passed, each day a blur of hunger, weariness, and guilt. The nights were worse; shadows stalked his dreams. Tarin had slept little, snatching what meager fare he could along the way and tightening his belt. He'd pushed the mare as hard as he dared.

Then he'd seen the rider clad in black a half mile behind him at a turn in the road. Tarin had felt real terror then. But the horseman didn't notice him and appeared to be waiting for someone else.

Tarin had left the lane at that point, urging his horse into a steep coppice of woodland to lie low for a time. He'd waited but neither heard nor spotted the other rider. Finally satisfied, he'd rejoined the road and urged his steed west toward evening and another troubled rest.

But that night was the worst. There had been eeriness in the chilly air. There were no trees nearby and Tarin had felt exposed. He'd taken shelter under a hedge but had woken abruptly, hearing hoof beats approaching from down the lane. He'd glanced up from his hide just in time to allow the wandering moon to spill silver on rider and horse. The rider had stopped for a moment, glancing his way.

"Who are you?" Tarin had called out—stupidly, he realized now. The horseman hadn't replied. Moments later he'd spurred his beast forward and faded off into the murk, leaving Tarin cold and scared.

That following afternoon, the welcome smell of brine had announced the fugitive Prince's destination grew near. But as the light faded, a peel of thunder summoned dark rainclouds and hail. Glancing up, Tarin had witnessed a host passing high above at speed. The Wild Hunt was abroad. Horns blew and hounds bayed. Tarin had covered his ears as he tried to calm the panicked mare. Both horse and rider had nearly reached breaking point.

But the sky had soon cleared, as the ghostly host fled east. In minutes the doleful notes of the Huntsman's horns were swallowed by distance. Tarin had reined in at that moment, on the point of collapse. Then he'd seen the cottage and the woman waiting with folded arms at the door. Jen. She was leaning over him.

"How do you feel, Highness?"

"Call me Tarin. I don't deserve a title anymore. I have done something terrible, Jen."

She took a stool beside the bed and fingered a pale lock back behind her ear. "Will it help to tell me?"

"I cannot—there are no words."

Jen's mouth tightened. "Never mind, you need to eat to get your strength back. Did you sleep?"

"A little."

"Well...that's something. Supper is ready when you are."

That night Prince Tarin feasted on pheasant and cabbage and decided he'd never eaten better, nor drank finer ale. He'd kept his council all evening; neither hostess nor her man probed him with questions, though their son, Dail was less subtle, despite his parents, swatting his ears. Tarin held evasive, was about to retire, when a loud rap announced a visitor at the door.

The rider has come for me. Tarin's face blanched. He looked about for a place to hide. Jen placed a placating hand on his arm.

"It's alright—Cullan will deal with this."

"Two guests in one day," grunted Cullan, reaching for where his polished sword hung close and ready beside the hearth. "Wait here, Prince. I'll go see."

After a minute or two, Cullan returned with someone else close behind him. Tarin gaped at the newcomer. This stranger was very tall, his features half concealed beneath a hooded blue cloak. He appeared grizzled and grey and was forced to stoop beneath the oak beams as he entered the smoky cottage.

"And who might you be?" asked the Prince ungraciously, on his guard again.

"Just an old wayfarer seeking lodging for the night," answered the stranger in a melodic voice that hinted irony. "However, at least *I* can pay for my stay." His piercing blue eyes were uncommonly large. They surveyed Tarin with sardonic amusement, unsettling him further.

"I smelt roast pheasant—my favorite." the man winked at Jen. "This is a nice little cottage, my dear. Very clean." Wife and husband exchanged glances whilst Dail looked excited and Tarin glared.

The stranger, once seated in a corner, reached deep into the folds of his cloak and brought forth a golden harp. "I am a fable-weaver and bard by profession," he announced amid whoops of delight from Jen and Dail, their eyes dazzled by the golden harp, a thing of rare, uncanny beauty.

Cullan grinned. "Well, you are most welcome. We've little excitement here. Please be seated, sir singer. There is still hot food aplenty left in the kitchen."

Cullan knelt, placed a frothing mug of ale on the table in front of his new guest. This was consumed with zeal, then followed by another and after that a brace of piping hot pheasants fresh from the spit. Once he'd crunched through those, the stranger winked at them.

"I've a yarn or two if you care to listen."

And of course they did.

And what a songsmith he was! That night Tarin heard of wonders: tales of mythical beasts, vengeful gods, and far-flung steaming oceans where golden-haired warriors sailed metal ships beneath broiling, copper skies. The Prince almost forgot his plight for a time, so entranced was he (and his hosts also—especially Dail) by the melodic voice and the skillfully plucked harp of this uncanny visitor.

Sleep finally beckoned. Prince Tarin retired together with his hosts. The stranger sat for a while longer, warming his hands at the fireside, his gaze distant and remote. He had much to peruse of late, but events were generally going as planned.

The songsmith waited for the fire to fade and splutter before making silent for the cot he had been allotted in the eaves above. Once there, he stared up at the ceiling letting his swift mind filter and focus. The Dog Lord was back and war soon would follow.

A sacrifice was needed to make things go as they should. The Dog Lord was wary, crafty as he himself was—these two were old adversaries after all, opposite sides of the same coin. Light and darkness, good and evil—the worm consumes its own tail. He'd have to play things very close to the wire, lest Dog Face see his gambit.

But then sorcerers were renowned for doing just that.

***

When Prince Tarin woke, it was pitch-black night. Someone snored in a room close by. The Prince felt edgy again. He leaned forward, carefully peeled back the drapes just enough to see outside.

His heart stopped in horror.

The rider was there, scarce twenty yards from the window! A silent figure masked and clad in black, cloaked and booted, gazing up at his room. Tarin, shaking, made for the door, but a cold voice stopped him dead in his tracks.

"Stay still, fool!" It was the songsmith who had spoken—the stranger. His manner was sharp and his oddly bright eyes gleamed like sapphires in the dark. "You cannot evade him; this was always part of their plan."

"Whose plan...what?" Tarin managed in a taut whisper. "Who is that rider?" When he looked out again, the masked horseman had vanished and the lane was empty.

"That, young Prince, is none other than Rael Hakkenon, Lord of Crenna, Master Assassin, and usurper's spy," answered the stranger. "He has been paid to apprehend you, boy, and has followed you from Kella City most assiduously. Surely you didn't expect to escape, Prince Tarin? Caswallon is an accomplished schemer."

Tarin felt an icy tingle in his stomach; the Assassin of Crenna was the most feared of all brigands currently troubling the outer fringes of the Four Kingdoms. His father Kelsalion had had a particular loathing for him. He'd placed a price of three hundred gold crowns on the villain's head, together with his pirate followers, the scourge of the Western Ocean.

"What can I do?" Tarin pleaded. "Who are you, songsmith, and how do you know all this? Can you help me escape?"

"Questions, questions, and questions. You speak too much, boy. Time to shut up and listen." Tarin gulped a complaint but was ignored.

"I am called Zallerak in these parts, and you, boy, have much to learn." The stranger pinned Tarin with that sapphire gaze, measuring the boy's courage as a fox gauges chickens. "You must hold your nerve, young Prince," Zallerak told him. "You cannot undo your folly, and... there is a high wergild to be paid."

"But the Assassin!" hissed Tarin. "He will surely kill me!"

"That's no more than you deserve," snapped Zallerak with sudden brutal bluntness. "However, there is just a slight possibility you may yet find redemption, if you follow my guidance, Prince, and do just as I tell you." Zallerak smiled his songsmith smile.

"It concerns the remnants of the Tekara that I know you still possess. Yes, that suspicious bulge beneath your shirt, and no, I don't need to see it—seen it before a while back. Now, listen in..."

Zallerak leaned closer as he imparted his strategy. Tarin's eyes widened in horror when he heard the strange bard's plan. Under his tunic, he clutched hard at the crystal shards of his dead father's crown, so hard that his fingers bled openly again.

***

When Jen woke next morning she discovered her guests gone. On her kitchen table were two gold coins. Throughout that day she felt baffled and confused. Something bad had happened, something that would affect them all. A growing feeling of wrongness tightened like a noose around her neck.

That evening a rider stopped by, pausing only briefly to tell them the news. He was bound for Fardoris and the ocean. He returned later that night, his horse lathered and his news worse than before.

It wasn't long before everyone knew the High King had fallen and that the Tekara, the sacred crown, was no more. That same night the messenger informed them of Prince Tarin's abduction by the cunning snares of the Assassin of Crenna.

Even now, he told them, Rael Hakkenon flees west to his island lair, the royal captive bound and broken on the deck of his black ship. Rael had made no secret of his prize. He was doing what he did best—goading Kelthaine, the land he hated so much (no one knew why). Hakkenon and his pirates would be celebrating in Crenna for days after landing their catch.

Jen's gaze followed the setting sun as it sank like an open wound behind the brooding hills of Fol. She felt sad, deflated, and wept silently as strong Cullan hugged her close. Jen wept for Prince Tarin and for Kelthaine, her fallen, lovely land.

"Whatever will become of us now?" she asked her husband, but he didn't respond, just hugged her tighter. The following day there was more bad news.

And the noose tightened again.

Chapter 5

Silon

The richly garbed merchant bid Corin pull up a chair and sit opposite him at table.

"Please spare your champion a moment," the merchant said to Holly and her father. "We two are old acquaintances, and I've a matter of some import to discuss."

Holly curled her lip whilst Burmon glanced at the merchant, then at Corin, and then back to the foreigner again. He shrugged.

"Be my guest."

Burmon bid his daughter lend a hand clearing the mess the brawlers had made. Holly, wanting to stay close and eavesdrop, rolled her eyes and went dutifully off to assist her father. During all this, Corin stood gawping. He was torn. He'd wanted to explore the inside of Holly's shift before he got too drunk. Gold, though. That spoke volumes.

"Well, are you going to take a seat or just stand there looking vacant?" Silon's crisp words severed the smoky atmosphere. The Raleenian, though small, had a commanding tongue few men ignored.

Corin shrugged, feigning indifference. He was baffled by the merchant's bizarre arrival in Finnehalle. Must be a big job. He shrugged again (Corin always did that when he was confused), reclaimed his cloak, folded it neatly, and pulled up a chair, glancing sideways at Silon. Eventually he found his tongue.

"Don't tell me, merchant," Corin said. "You owe me money and have journeyed all this way north to settle the debt. Gold is always welcome in my pocket." Corin recalled the last time he had seen Silon and the argument that had followed.

"No, indeed," responded the merchant with his customary half smile, "although I've interesting work for you if you'll take it. And gold aplenty will follow on contract's completion, I assure you."

"Forget it, Silon, the Permian Wars are over." Corin had met the wealthy merchant whilst fighting as a mercenary in the Permio Desert a thousand leagues south. Silon had spotted Corin's skill with that big ugly blade during a bloody skirmish near Syrannos. He'd offered the dour northerner a contract that had served them both well for over five years.

But that was finished. Corin had parted company with his employer scarcely three weeks ago over a misunderstanding relating to the merchant's dangerously suggestive daughter.

It wasn't Corin's fault Nalissa had been attracted to him, had thrown herself into his arms. Corin had tried to explain things to the merchant, but Silon hadn't seen the funny side. The merchant showed scant humor that morning, and Corin, found standing bollock naked in the girl's closet, had felt a tad defensive. Nalissa had giggled then fled at her father's withered stare.

Harsh words had been exchanged. The following morning Corin had stormed from the merchant's villa in a cloud of wrath, vowing never to return. He couldn't begin to comprehend why Silon would have travelled all this way north to enlist his services again. It made no sense no matter how big the job.

Corin saw Holly watching him with interest from across the room whilst pretending to assist in the cleanup. He had a bone on below and cursed the merchant's untimely intervention.

This had better be bloody good.

"Still thinking with your groin, I see?" Silon had seen how the girl watched Corin too. "Perhaps you will have the manners to hear me out for a few minutes, then you can go see to your needs with yonder wench. You're the hero of the hour, after all."

Corin no longer felt like the hero of the hour. Rather, he felt crestfallen, like he'd peaked too early. He mouthed "three minutes" to Holly and then turned and glared at the merchant.

"Out with it, then. Night's passing."

Silon winced at the bitter taste of his ale. The merchant preferred wine, but there was a desperate shortage of good grape this far north, so he had to make do with Burmon's heavy brew. He leaned forward, jet orbs pinning Corin's steely stare. "When were you last in Kell's City?"

"Kella? Ten days ago, just passing through," replied Corin, puzzled by the question. "What of it?" Corin scratched his arse and yawned. Silon persisted.

"How did you find the mood in the city?" Silon thoughtfully rubbed the small diamond stud sparkling his left lobe.

"Tense, unfriendly, but I've never liked Kella City," Corin answered. "It's a shitehole like Kelthara in the east. Like all Kelthaine's cities. Where is this leading to, Silon? I've scant leisure for idle chit chat, so get to the bloody point."

"Charming as ever." Silon shook his head in resignation. He had not looked forward to this meeting but knew it necessary. "You would find Kelthaine's greatest city even less endearing now, my hasty friend. Perani of the Swords has placed it under curfew."

"Why would he want to do that?" Corin was almost interested. Perani, the former Champion of Kelthaine, was not a man to flap in a crisis.

"Because the High King has been murdered, Corin an Fol," responded the merchant, smiling slightly at the stunned faces of the occupants of the room (having until now feigned deafness.) The last stragglers had recently returned from finishing punishing the Morwellans. These now joined their friends in eavesdropping unashamedly.

"Yes, my friends," the merchant raised his voice so all could here without straining.

"Kelsalion the Third is slain. Murdered, it is said, by Permian assassins. Although I suspect that to be untrue.

"All Kelthaine is in turmoil. The white cities of Kelwyn are quaking with the news, as are the lush markets of Raleen, my own realm. In Morwella, rumors speak of invasion. They say the Duke of Vangaris is surrounded by foes.

"All Four Kingdoms stand at the brink of war." Silon paused, gauging the reaction in the room. He sipped his ale and grimaced before continuing.

"A dark time has come to this region of Ansu. The benign rule of the Tekara is over, its protection gone. Enemies muster at our borders, and the Wild Huntsman rides the night skies again. Seeing that old crow gatherer up there in the clouds never bodes well."

"What has become of the crown?" Corin *was* interested now. The Tekara, Crown of Kings, was beyond legendary. It had held the Four Kingdoms together for a thousand years. Surely no harm could have come to it. "Who has the Tekara?" Corin demanded.

"It is broken," the merchant's face was bleak. "Shattered into a dozen crystal shards."

"But who has done this?" gasped Burmon, standing pale faced at the bar. "Permian cutthroats or savages of Leeth—or else those wicked bastards over in Crenna?"

"None of the above, master innkeep," responded Silon, dabbing his forehead fastidiously with an immaculate kerchief, "although I've no doubt all our enemies are overjoyed by the news."

"Who, then?" Corin's eyes were hard and probing. He'd forgotten about Holly and his groin.

"Caswallon, the High King's most trusted councilor, together with the aid of Kelsalion's surviving son, Prince Tarin."

"Tarin? What part has that spoilt twat played in this?" Corin had seen the young Prince on two occasions whilst passing through Kella City. Corin was no staunch monarchist, and like most commoners, considered the boy Prince a pompous weakling and a drain on society.

"Is he a traitor?" Corin spat the words out.

"Just a fool, I suspect," answered Silon. "Prince Tarin allowed crafty Caswallon to persuade him don his father's crown, after news of the old King's death, or so I heard. I got word via pigeon the following morning. I informed the others and set sail at once—fortunately Captain Barin obliged by having his trader ready in Port Sarfe harbor." Silon took a furtive sip at his ale.

"Tarin was distraught, having lost his father, and easily swayed by the councilor's smooth words. Of course he obeyed Caswallon and took the crown, thus breaking the sacred law of Kell and imperiling us all."

"What's become of crown and Prince?" Holly asked. She'd taken seat at table near Corin, though he hadn't noticed.

Silon shook his head slowly. "I'm not certain," he replied, fiddling his diamond again. "Rumor is Tarin fled for the coast with the shards gathered in a cloth. They say he never reached Fardoris and was abducted by no other than Rael Hakkenon of Crenna himself."

Corin spat after hearing that name. "Crenna!" he leapt to his feet, feeling the old hatred return. "It's always fucking Crenna! What part have those bastards played in this?"

"Rael the Cruel has long served Caswallon in secret, Corin, as have some others you know, Hagan of Morwella among them. He is in the pay of Rael just as the Assassin is funded by Caswallon. The whole thing stinks." Silon took a pull at his ale. He was getting used to it, the strong content having lulled his prior misgivings.

Corin was at a loss for words. He'd never been good with words apart from expletives. Now even these evaded him. Behind Corin, the patrons leaned forward with elbows on tables, eagerly awaiting more news. The only sounds were the crackling of the fire in the corner of the room and the creaking of the sign outside as the night wind cuffed it to and fro. Silon continued in a quieter voice as hushed faces watched from the shadows.

"There is more," he added. "Caswallon rules Kelthaine and Perani murders all who speak against him. The old champion has sold out. He too is in the usurper's pay. Kella City is in meltdown. Together usurper and general are ruthlessly quashing any opposition. Caswallon has studied sorcery for years awaiting this chance." Silon stared morosely into his tankard.

"And that still is not all," he added wearily. "There is cause to believe a darker menace aids Caswallon from beyond the grave. An ancient evil long banished from these hallowed shores. That evil fuses him with lethal power. Caswallon has become its mortal conduit and foremost servant."

"What evil is this?" Burmon cut in, his face paler than usual.

"I speak of the Urgolais," replied Silon in a whisper. Corin, Holly, and several others looked blank, but Burmon and two of the oldest men listening paled visibly hearing that word. "The Dog People."

"And who might they be?" Corin, despite being intrigued, was getting restless again. He caught Holly's eye and grinned. Silon ignored the question.

"I fear also that Caswallon harbors lustful designs toward the young Queen of Kelwyn." The merchant was almost at a whisper. "Queen Ariane knows and loathes Caswallon. She's brave but vulnerable, having recently lost her father, King Nogel. He was a statesman; she's just learning the craft. Caswallon wants to break her." Silon let his words soak in to his audience. He took a slow sip then turned toward Corin again.

"I need your longsword to help defeat this usurper," he said.

"I wondered when you would come to the crux of all this, Silon." Corin barked a laugh. "Well, you're out of luck. My fighting days are over." Holly sniggered, and Corin cast a pained look in her direction. "Well, almost," he owned.

"What care I, or anyone here for that matter, about Kelthaine or her allies? I hail from Fol, master merchant, bleak, windy little Fol, which is, and always has been, happily independent from Kelthaine's haughty rulers. Good job, too. Let the Four Kingdoms deal with their problems. It's of little interest to us... rustics." Corin turned to face the other occupants of the inn. One or two nodded in agreement, but Burmon's face showed concern.

"Fol would be nothing without Kelthaine's protective influence, Corin," said the landlord. "Those three Morwellans are probably renegades from Vangaris, doubtless now we'll see more of such folk."

"Doubtless," concurred Silon, taking to his feet. "And be wary of spies. Caswallon's arm is long. Trust no stranger, and keep your lips together. These days the wind itself has ears." Silon drained his flagon and drew his kerchief across his mouth.

"My friends, many thanks for your attention," he turned for the door. "I must be leaving you, the hour is late and I am weary." Silon waved a "thank you" to Burmon, who nodded. The merchant then placed a tanned hand on Corin's arm. "I would see you tomorrow. There is still much to discuss."

"I'm not interested," replied Corin. "Go back to Raleen, and take your troubles with you. I want no part in them. And you can keep your bloody gold, too. Ain't no price high enough to mess with sorcerers and politicians. That's a greasy pole. I'd rather keep my head, so to speak."

"We will see," responded the merchant, draping his heavy fur cloak over his shoulders. "I shall expect your company for supper tomorrow on board *The Starlight Wanderer*."

"The Starlight what?"

"Captain Barin's ship from Valkador, an island in the distant north. You, Corin, will not have heard of it. Barin's worthy vessel bore me to your misty shores this very afternoon," Silon explained. "You will find her moored beyond the western side of the harbor—out in the deep water. A fine sight she is, too. Until then, I bid you goodnight, my friend."

"A moment, Silon." Corin stopped the merchant in his tracks. "What is it?"

"I've cause to wonder what you're getting out of this. Merchants aren't known for their altruism, especially rich ones from Raleen. I mean, why get involved with foreign politics? Isn't there enough shite happening down there in Raleen?"

"Suffice it to say, Corin an Fol, there are powers at play here greater than anyone present can guess at!" snapped Silon. "A time is coming soon when all men must choose sides, you included, my reluctant friend. Good night to you!" The inn door creaked open, and the merchant's brisk footsteps faded out into the murk.

Corin watched him leave, then shrugged. He waded across to the nearest barrel and helped himself to more ale. His earlier lust had departed but not his thirst. He needed more beer to think. Ale helped everything.

Actually, it didn't. Corin was becoming morose, and even looking at Holly's ankles couldn't raise his yard. The whole thing stank. Corin's heroic homecoming was obliterated by the kerfuffle following the merchant's brisk departure. Silon stealing the lime- light again. Loved being the center of attention, that one.

And everyone had an opinion on the dreadful business, and Corin's altercation with the Morwellans was presently forgotten. Corin felt deflated both above and below waist. True, Silon's news was all a bit of a worry. That said—it wasn't his worry.

Bugger Silon and bugger the Four Kingdoms.

Corin moodily reclaimed his seat in the corner and immersed himself in ale, becoming more befuddled by the minute. Holly joined him. Her bright company cheered him for a while, but Corin found it hard to relax, even when she deftly fumbled inside his trousers to see if he had anything going on in there, which he didn't. Holly sighed at that point and wandered off to help her fa- ther again.

Corin brooded. An odd homecoming. Polin dead, the freak child up that tree, a strangely familiar greybeard lurking in the woods, and now bloody Silon of Raleen, his former boss, turning up in Finnehalle like a bad penny.

It was enough to give honest men indigestion. Corin felt pro- foundly sad, like someone else had control of his organ. Perhaps they did? The ale wasn't helping. The more he slurped the more addled he became.

Must be a shite barrel.

Try as he might, Corin could find no cheer as the hours wore on. The rest of that night faded into fog and shadows. Corin was dimly aware of a draft's announcing people leaving for the cold street outside.

A thoughtful cough returned him to his senses, almost. He

glanced up, bleary-eyed, saw Burmon leaning over him. "I take it you've found a place for the night," the innkeep grinned knowingly.

"Er... not exactly. I was hoping that—" Corin fumbled inside his jerkin for some coins. He thrust two silver pieces into the landlord's corpulent palm. "That should be enough for several nights lodging and slupper." Corin's tongue wasn't working properly. Burmon grinned, nodded thanks, and yelled up to his daughter.

"Holly, get a room made up for our paying guest." He winked at Corin. "A nice bedroom overlooking the courtyard should suffice. Care for a nightcap before you retire? I've just the thing—Wynais brandy. Stiffens the yard, so to speak."

"Er, no ... think I've had enough." The room was spinning. Corin tried hard to look sober, much to his friend's amusement. Holly laughed too as she carried fresh sheets upstairs. Corin had no notion what they found so funny.

"You always were trouble, boy," Burmon laughed. "Come, follow me, I'll show you to your room."

Corin reclaimed Clouter, still leaning where he'd left it against the table. He stooped beneath the low entrance leading to a narrow hallway beyond. Once he'd navigated that passage, Corin staggered up some stairs and wearily followed the innkeeper to his rented room.

The moment Corin's spinning head hit the pillow, deep slumber claimed him. Outside, the night wore on. Somewhere an owl hooted twice, and shadows lengthened in the courtyard. The roving moon was chased by cloud dragons. Its silver sheen revealed a hooded figure crouched low under the eaves at the far end of the courtyard.

The Dog Lord had come to pay Corin visit in bed.

Chapter 6

Allies

From the shadows, he'd witnessed Prince Tarin's terrified departure. He had smiled back then, relishing the horror on Tarin's face as the boy clattered passed. He had waited for a moment before following. There had been no need to rush things. This was *his* game—his price and prize, and he had so relished the following chase. Hunting. It was what he did best bar one thing only: killing. He'd mounted up only after the Prince cleared the gates, this black-clad rider, and urged his beast quietly follow the dull echo of hoof beats out into the night. That had been days passed. Now the hunt was over and the best part still to come.

Rael Hakkenon, Master Assassin and Lord of Crenna, smiled, revealing perfect teeth. Everything had gone to plan—well almost. The Tekara's shards were missing, so Caswallon wouldn't be pleased. No matter. That was the sorcerer's problem, not his. Rael had been paid. He had his gold stowed under the hold. Gold, the only thing that mattered, bar pride. Gold, the only deity he revered.

Rael laughed at the crumpled, bloody body shivering miserably on the heaving, tossing deck. Poor Prince Tarin—his to hurt and his to punish. Crimes of the father revisited on the son.

Rael had killed the High King too quickly, as needs must. With the boy, Rael would take his time. He'd let Tarin rot and stew in the dungeons over winter, so he could dwell on his fate. Of course, Rael would venture down upon occasion, whisper sweet nuances in the boys terrified ears, relating to certain excruciations pending. Such a fool! Rael had laughed when the Prince chose the coast road for his escape route. That had made things so ridiculously easy for him, and Rael didn't like to work too hard. He'd sent word via bird to Cruel Cavan, his second:

Ready my serpent outside Fardoris. I have the prize.

And so he had watched on as early that morning the boy Prince had ridden out white faced from the cottage, like a lamb attending slaughter. Rael had followed with indolent ease, letting the boy slip out of sight for a time. Early that afternoon he'd reached the rise revealing Fardoris harbor and spied *The Black Serpent,* his shark, lean and clean, waiting close by in the shallows.

Rael had watched from the hill as Tarin rode weary into town, urging his horse through tangled streets down toward the waiting docks. He'd followed on then, urging his mount canter down from the hill.

The game was over. Time to close the gap. Rael's noose had pulled Tarin from his saddle yards from the quay as seamen and dockers gaped stupid. Let them watch! Let all know who had the Prince of fools!

Rael laughed again at the sackcloth of misery behind him. The boy groaned, and Cavan kicked him to silence. Rael turned his gaze west again, to angry sky and distant thunder. Storm coming soon. No matter, they'd raise Crenna before it arrived. This very evening, Rael Hakkenon would feast his chiefs and parade his prize for all to see.

***

That same afternoon back in Kella City found Caswallon, former High Councilor and recently self-imposed Regent of Kelthaine, reflecting on the last few days. No word from the Assassin, but Rael was ever perverse in his communications. No need to fret,

Hakkenon was the finest killer in the realm. Kelsalion had loathed him, hence the irony that it was Rael's poisoned blade that skewered the High King. But Rael Hakkenon was a random weapon. Caswallon dare not trust him. He had other servants, though he didn't trust them either. But then, Caswallon wasn't big on trust. When you sleaze and murder your way to the top, it pays dividends to treat everyone close as a potential knife in the dark.

Still, the Assassin was efficient. Tarin would be in Kranek Castle soon, the poor fool. Caswallon almost pitied the boy—almost.

And he had won! Kella was his, with Perani flushing out the few stubborn royalists. Perani was no fool. He'd sided with Caswallon after seeing how things stood. Sensible fellow—he'd much to gain. Caswallon's hands controlled the city coffers. But it had taken its toll, this long and urgent scheming, plotting, and waiting. Caswallon was just over sixty years old but looked nearly seventy. That was sorcery for you—it played havoc on the body. He had everything he wanted, though—his new masters had been obliging in that area. So though he looked frail, Caswallon's battery was charged to full by an alien power. He had never been stronger, thanks to them.

The Urgolais.

A knock on the door interrupted his peruse.

"Enter."

A nightmare shuffled in, its two hairless heads scraping the lintel supporting the heavy door. It was rangy, its lean body more dog-like than human. It wore a heavy tunic of tanned leather studded with iron, and at its waist hung a heavy mace. The skin that showed was black and hoary, and the thing's paws were tipped with steely nails two inches in length.

Caswallon frowned. Even one-headed Groil took some getting used to. They resembled their masters, with canine eyes and doggy snout. They were tall, long in limb, and fleshless. Creatures of sorcery created by the Dog Lord, Caswallon's new powerful accomplice. This was their leader, Drol. Caswallon's new lieutenant, the Groil chief had arrived last night with two hundred followers, all gifts to Caswallon from their Urgolais master. Gifts that would make sure he kept his side of the bargain.

"What do you require, Drol? I know little of your needs. Your master was unforthcoming."

"We need feed." Most Groil didn't speak. Drol could at least make himself understood.

"On what would you feed?"

"Warm flesh, hot blood—army needs sustaining."

"Oh, I see. Best go clear the dungeons, then. It's too crowded down there anyway. No loss for a few score prisoners to go missing, they've few secrets left to tell me."

"Thank you, C'swollen." Drol practiced what might have been a smile. It was lost on Caswallon.

"Do you know how to find the dungeons below?"

"I can smell them."

"Then go hence swiftly and help yourself."

Scrape, bump, and drag. Two-heads left the chamber.

Caswallon knew he had delved too deep into the realms of ancient thaumaturgy when, of course, *they* had found him. The Dog People. Ancient beings rumored long dead. Like their Aralais foe, both races had ruled this country before the coming of Kell, Kelsalion's legendary ancestor.

Most were gone, but a few lingered still, and these had pounced on Caswallon. Only his guile had saved him. Caswallon was a survivor and had glibly won them over—he was ever a master with words. Their leader had sensed a champion for their ancient cause, to root out the surviving Aralais and annihilate them, and so sorcerers old and new had formed a tenuous alliance.

But there was a price...

Another knock on his heavy door, this one urgent yet tentative. A servant no doubt.

"What is it?" Caswallon's dark brows joined in irritation. He cared not to be interrupted once, let alone twice. "I said, what is it?"

"Messenger, my lord. Fresh from Wynais."

"Ah, then you had better let him in." Caswallon's mood lightened just a jot. This could prove constructive, diverting even.

There followed a shuffle and crunch of steel-shod feet. The

door creaked open, and three men entered: two guards, both Perani's men, both nervous having just met Drol on the stairs. Between them, a shabby sweating mess with shaven head and recently soiled green gown. The messenger (and presumably this was he) had found the chief Groil a sight more unsettling than had the guards.

Caswallon glared at the wretch in utter contempt. "And what is that?" he demanded from the biggest guard."

"He's the messenger, my lord. He sent pigeon to you apparently but thought he'd better ride north himself lest the bird go awry."

Caswallon turned his coaly gaze on the messenger. "You sent only the one bird."

"Three, your worship."

"And yet I remain uninformed."

"I...your—"

"Speak your news, else lose your tongue! Already I weary of you."

And so the messenger told him.

"Just the three men, you say, and only two of them warriors."

"The third man is Galed the—"

"I couldn't give a toss who the third man is," snapped Caswallon. And he couldn't. What mattered was that that arrogant child-bitchling Ariane was calmly riding north into his domain, with only three men to protect her. She might as well go naked.

How diverting. Even stupider than her father, Nogel the Dense, he who had pitched from his horse thanks to Caswallon's men's carefully placed caltrops. Once he was down, they'd helped him break his neck on a stone. Dreadful accident. Shame. There were a lot of accidents back then. It paid to remove the main obstacles long before the endgame.

"When did they leave?"

"Four days ago, my worship—I've not tarried but have ridden hence at speed."

"Not tarried?" Caswallon's black eyes narrowed dangerously. "You, maggot, have cost me time. I could have *her* in chains by now had you the wit to send more birds."

"Worship—"

"Silence, knave!" Caswallon's leaden gaze fell on the big guard. The man looked very pale (though not so pale as the messenger gripped in his and his comrades' steel-coated arms).

"Sergeant, I trust you are acquainted with our new allies, the Groil."

The sergeant nodded and shuffled his feet. The whole bloody city knew about the Groil. They'd been seen by the watch last night marching silently toward the Sorcerer's Roost (the lone tower above the palace had a new name now). Who or what they were no one had a clue. But then no one was about to enquire further, especially since the rumor went they had just materialized from thick night air onto the soiled city streets.

"I am, my lord." The sergeant kept his gaze on the flags at his feet.

"Well, it appears they are hungry fellows. I've bid their leader enter the dungeons and help himself. There are hundreds of prisoners down there, more than enough to keep the Groil legion well nourished and content for a time. Take this idiot below, gut him open, stuff his belly full of pigeons, and introduce him to master Droll, with my kindest compliments."

The guards nodded and hurried to drag the unconscious messenger out of sight. The stench of the wretch's piss smarted Caswallon's eyes and darkened his mood again. He mouthed a spell and both puddle and stink vanished.

Caswallon frowned at the door as the guards' heavy footfalls faded down the stairs. Life was strange and full of change. There were but two choices: Adapt and thrive, else grow stale and die. He'd chosen the former, but of course there were risks. Caswallon enjoyed the new powers awarded him by the Dog Lord. He grew stronger daily as the alien magic filtered inside his veins. But the feeling someone else controlled his actions gnawed at him rapaciously. Keep your enemies close, particularly warlocks. Caswallon would do just that.

He hadn't always been as he was now. When a young man,

Caswallon an Kella had been a staunch advocate of Kelsalion's father, Kelperion the Third. But when that wise King passed in his bed, the heir showed little promise. Kelsalion was weak and his Queen controlling. Anyetta was shrewd. She distrusted Caswallon from the start. But conveniently she had drowned off Fol those many years ago.

After that blessed day, Caswallon changed tactics. He became bolder. In his defense the High Councilor got things done in the realm. He despised weakness and saw it daily in the High King. Kelsalion's first born had been lost with his mother, as had his sister Leanna (Lord Halfdan's wife) and her own baby son, the rightful heir to the throne.

Thirteen years later the despairing King proclaimed his heir to be Prince Tarin, a by-blow of a courtesan, thus not fully royal. And Tarin was weak, too, which again proved useful.

Thus aided by his Urgolais mentors, Caswallon had steered the realm in the direction he desired. He'd fed Kelsalion lies and had subtlety bullied the boy Prince. Soon both father and son became his puppets. Then the joyous day arrived and Rael Assassin struck the deathblow, leaving Caswallon to see to Tarin.

But Caswallon had made one mistake back then. He, who for so long had been meticulous in planning, had neglected something important. He'd been overcome with joy when Tarin had given in, taken the crown for his own. And after witnessing its noisy destruction, Caswallon, laughing out loud, had foolishly allowed the boy to scoop up the shards and flee the palace.

An error that, Caswallon admitted now. Still, the Assassin would have reclaimed the shards by now, so in a short while Caswallon could destroy them utterly with the correct word spell. His new masters had warned him if any of the shards remained there was a chance (a very slight chance, admittedly, but still a chance) that things might go awry. But Caswallon owned to confidence. It was one small oversight and soon would be forgotten. Or so he hoped. And now Ariane...

Caswallon leant back in his high-arched chair, his manner almost content. Once the Groil had feasted, he would summon Drol back, bid the leader send a squad of his creatures out into the wild lands surrounding that haunted forest. They needed to apprehend Ariane before she got tangled in the woody maze. Once beneath those trees Ariane would be hard to trace. Only Elanion knew what lurked in that awful wood. Caswallon had no love for Elanion or any of the gods. He saw them as self-seeking and hostile. Not that he had a problem with that, but why court such fickle beings? But Ariane and her people were devout followers of Elanion. If the goddess were to help her.... He couldn't afford to take that chance.

Caswallon allowed himself a smile. Things in the main were going rather well. Soon he'd have Ariane naked and chained for his pleasure. Then the real recreation would start.

Chapter 7

The Northman

Drip, drip, drip and what's that bloody snuffling below? Corin opened an eye, barely. He felt like shite, what with the room spinning and his head thudding and his belly growling rebellion. Never mind all that. Something lurked outside. Something *nasty*. Corin shoved the pillow over his head.

Bugger off...

It was useless. He'd have to get up and check the courtyard for spooks. What was up with him lately? Corin wondered if he'd pissed off one of the gods, or else a spiteful bog faerie like that wee blonde girlie in the tree. They were a capricious bunch, these otherworld beings. Once you upset one they'd ride on your back for years. Well, if some evil imp had cursed him, Corin had the perfect antidote. He would shove Clouter up its arse.

A scraping noise. Corin groaned, grumbled, rolled out of bed, and stubbed his toe, grumbled again and reached over to where Clouter leaned against the table. He slid steel from leather and pulled open the drapes.

It was foggy and damp out there, but not foggy and damp enough to hide the apparition lurking at the far side of the courtyard. Corin couldn't really see much more than a vague dog shape, half hidden beneath cloak and hood. Now and then he caught a glimpse of snout and yellow eyes. Dogs in cloaks. Of course. Why was he surprised?

This isn't good.

Corin got a very nasty feeling then. A kind of bowel-loosening, cock-shrinking, head-shrieking, knee-knocking crazy fear. That thing out there (whatever it was) was evil incarnate. Corin watched with numb lips as the dog-thing half shuffled, half hopped across the courtyard. It reached the door below. Corin glimpsed a blackened claw.

Corin felt a sudden urgent need to visit the privy. He held on to his bowels, just, but Clouter slid from his sweating fingers. The dog-thing below was working a spell on him. Fortunately it didn't seem that familiar with door handles, its claws scraping and slipping but gaining no purchase. Corin reached down and retrieved Clouter. But just as he did, the dog-thing glared up at the window with those ghoulish yellow eyes and Corin dropped the longsword again. Then the latch turned click and the door creaked open.

Before Corin could react a rush of wings swept down on the dog-creature. There followed a cacophony of croak, snarl and snap. From somewhere a horn sounded. The raven took wing into the gloom. Corin, too startled to blaspheme, gaped at the open door below. The creature had vanished into thick air.

Again Corin retrieved Clouter. He waited a few minutes, minding the door just in case the dog-thing had got inside the building and was about to come visit. But somehow Corin knew it had gone.

The horn sounded again, closer this time and making him jump. Outside, a sudden shaft of lightning lit the courtyard, and rolls of thunder echoed off the cliffs beyond.

A voice boomed, silencing the thunder. Maybe it was the thunder.

The storm trawled high overhead. Corin heard distant voices and something else, hoof beats followed by more ghostly horns. Hounds bayed in the distance. Corin shivered and gaped skyward and saw that the fog had cleared to reveal storm dragons and something else. Corin leant on Clouter as his head thudded and stomach squelched. This had not proved an enjoyable week.

A shadowy host filled the heavens, their moonlit shrouds piercing fog and gloom. The leader rode a corpse-horse, lightning lanced down from the moonlit spear he brandished on high. At his lips was a huge horn on which he blew. Beneath this dreadful rider's feet were shadowy hounds, and behind these baying hell-dogs marched the damned.

It was the Wild Hunt free to ride again.

Corin recalled the old man in the woods and shivered. The Huntsman had many guises, but this was how he was most often seen. Corin saw him up there, riding the night sky. He caught an urgent glint of blue fire beneath that wide-brimmed hat, and then the old Sky Wanderer was gone.

The horns grew fainter, fading from earshot. Inside moments, all was quiet and still, once again, the only sound the constant dripping of water from the lantern on the wall. Corin's knees buckled and he slunk, sat gaping gormless on the bed. He wiped the sweat from his face, farted, and groped for the covers. Corin clambered beneath the cloth and again shoved the pillow on his head. At some point he must have nodded off.

**

Corin woke groaning as bright light stabbed beneath his eyelids. Outside, some infernal blackbird warbled cheerfully close by.

Shut up, bird.

Corin moaned and scratched his ear. He stretched and yawned and then lurched out of bed and, after filling the basin with the shite-awful water, immersed his throbbing head.

Corin felt horrendous this morning, which wasn't surprising considering the amount of ale he'd put away last night. He would give up drinking, he decided, wincing as the morning sun lanced into his now half-open, bloodshot eyes.

Not a good night, really. Ghouls and warlocks stomping about in the wee hours. It wasn't something that happened to everyday folk. Had he dreamt up that dog-horribleness? Corin was unsure. Bit of a worry. He had no idea what was going on inside his head. The girl child up that tree was to blame, he suspected. Some spiteful wood-sprite that had decided to plague him out of sheer caprice. It didn't make for a happy state of mind, what with throbbing head and log-thick tongue.

I need to eat.

Tired of the conundrum, Corin focused on breakfast instead, willfully banishing the harrowing events of the last twenty-four hours to a later time (probably much later), when his addled mind could cope with it.

He squinted at the mirror. What he saw there wasn't reassuring either. Dark rings shadowed his eyes, and he badly needed a shave. The old scar on his forehead itched, adding to his general wretchedness. That scar had been a gift from the sword master in Kelthaine. A hard lesson from a man Corin had never got on with, it had taught him keep his guard up ever since. He had caught up with said sword master years later and settled the score.

Corin an Fol wasn't big on forgiving. He'd seen much in the last fourteen years: wars, betrayal, hunger, and cold (and sweaty, stinking fly-horrible heat) would cover some of it, and then add on the treacherous whoresons, backstabbing weasels, and slippery merchants, not to mention those dark-eyed vixens who had cost him so much coin. Upshot: Corin trusted little and liked less. He had a certain attitude, and this morning was no exception.

That said, Corin considered himself more than just a mercenary. He had panache (so he believed anyway) and a flair for killing quickly, which he thought placed him above the common soldier. Despite this, he was kinder than most of his type, never hurting those smaller and weaker. Well... not without just cause.

Corin hopped and fell clumsily into his leather jerkin and trousers. He'd left the mail shirt with Thunderhoof, half hoping Master Tommo would repair the few broken rings and give it a polish (you never know your luck).

Corin's garments were functional, basic and shoddy, but they served well enough. The boots were newer, recently purloined from a dead traveler in a wayside inn. Corin, never one to miss an opportunity, had helped himself to those nice expensive boots lying vacant by the bedside.

Corin shrugged indifference, commenced fastening the broad belt to his waist. This came from Permio, almost six inches thick with silver studs. Quite pretentious, but he liked it. It not only protected his stomach but also sported a bracket for his shoulder harness that kept Clouter erect. Aside the bracket hung the scabbard of Corin's sax, Biter, and his horn-handled hunting knife.

The latter he'd won in a game of dice in Morwella some years back. There was also a small dagger hidden in the lining of his left boot. This too had come in useful on numerous occasions. As had the two he kept up his right sleeve, and the other one he hid inside his shirt. You can't own enough sharp things in this world.

Corin glanced lovingly at his longsword. Clouter was well balanced, razor sharp, and over five and a half feet in length. Most opponents shat themselves and legged it when they saw it, which saved Corin considerable effort.

The longsword had been gift from Lord Halfdan of Point Keep to replace his worn-out blade. The High King's brother had been fond of the wild-eyed Corin. He'd rewarded him well in the years of his service. Clouter had seen a great deal of use during the Second Permian War, and later whilst serving Silon of Raleen. Corin cherished its fine workmanship. Apart from Thunderhoof and his golden wolf-brooch, the longsword was his only possession of worth.

Corin left his woolen cloak on the unmade bed, as it looked warm outside, and made his way down to the kitchens seeking sustenance. No one was about, so Corin grabbed a large ham from the pantry and painfully squinted his way out into the sunlit courtyard.

Finnehalle was a hive of activity. Carts clattered their way up and down the cobbled streets, and traders shouted their wares at Corin as he trudged by, doggedly munching his breakfast. The market square was full of stalls and banter. Everywhere the noise of people's chatter and barking dogs filled his senses. It did little to ease his throbbing head. The smell of stale fish drifted up from the quayside accompanied by the salty breeze.

Corin felt better. The warm sunshine brightened his mood, banishing morose thoughts. Today was another day, after all. But when he overheard a couple of traders discussing thunderstorms, he hurried by not wanting to listen.

Several of the village folk glanced warily at Clouter, remembering the tall fighter from the evening before. Corin ignored them. He casually tossed the remnants of the ham bone to a grateful hound in a corner. Evidently, word of last night's brawl in *The Last Ship* was already spreading through Finnehalle. No great surprise.

Corin recognized a few of the villagers, but most faces were strange to him. There was no sign of the three Morwellan troublemakers. Lucky for them.

Corin spied his patron struggling back from the market, laden with cheeses and bread. He greeted the innkeeper cheerfully enough, thanking him for his kind hospitality and patience the night before. He even offered to replace the damaged furniture. Burman wiped a sweating brow and told him not to worry.

"You look haggard this morning," he beamed annoyingly. "Enjoy the day, master Corin, it certainly is a beauty. But have a care," he continued in a whisper. "Those Morwellan thugs are probably still lurking in the neighborhood. They will want revenge. You made fools of them last night, and they won't have liked that."

"Let them lurk," replied Corin with a shrug. He reached out to grab the innkeeper's shoulder. "Did you hear those horns last night Burmon?"

"Horns? No, I slept like a troll," answered the innkeeper. "Good day to you—horns indeed."

"Aye, good day, landlord."

As Corin entered the busy marketplace, memories of his childhood flooded back. He recalled his mother chiding both him and his brothers as they ran amok among the wagons and stalls. They were dead now, all dead. Taken from him on that brutal bloody morning. He trudged on.

Reaching the last market stall Corin turned, stared dreamy at the sparkling water of Finnehalle harbor. It was a fine autumn day and the Western Ocean shimmered, reaching out and merging with cloudless sky beyond. To the south, sheer cliffs spilled wailing seabirds into the brine. Corin's eyes followed their whirling dance, taking pleasure in the sight.

It was then that he noticed the foreign ship. It lay anchored in deep water a short distance from the shore. A two-masted vessel with yards and rigging, it towered over the small fishing craft of Finnehalle like a lion amongst cats. The yards were neatly furled and the proud figurehead was embossed with the emblem of a golden sea eagle. Although somewhat out of place in Finnehalle, the brigantine looked splendid in the morning sunshine. That must be the *Starlight Wanderer,* thought Corin, remembering the name from his conversation with Silon yesterday. He turned briskly away. Corin had no desire to speak with the merchant today.

Silon was his past, as had been Lord Halfdan and the commission in the Wolves he'd held out to Corin. Those days were gone forever. It was time for a new start, a fresh chance to make a go of life. Finnehalle would take him back. He was fit and strong, able to turn his hands to most things. Work wouldn't be a problem.

Then there was Holly—still single and lusty (both excellent qualities, in his opinion); Corin reckoned he was in with a good chance there. A decent honest Fol girl wouldn't fleece him like those Raleenian hellcats had. Elanion take Silon, his daughter, and their schemes...

An angry shout shattered Corin's thoughts, and he looked over at the stalls. A heated exchange had broken out between a stroppy leather trader and a colossal foreigner dressed in furs and gold. Corin studied the outlandish stranger, wondering if he had come down from the wild land of Leeth in the remote northeast. But the barbarians of that land had an unkempt look about them. This fellow carried himself like a nobleman.

Curious, Corin strolled over to the stall and feigned a shallow interest in the goods whilst listening with both ears. The giant's booming voice was clearly terrifying the diminutive trader. A formidable figure, he sported long fair braids in hair and beard. At his side hung the largest battle-axe Corin had ever seen. It was double headed, at least two feet across, the wooden shaft the thickness of a small tree and at least a foot longer than Clouter.

And as for its owner...Corin squinted up at him. What was he, eight, nine feet tall? More like seven and a half. Scary, though. Corin wondered what would bring such a one to this far-flung region; the giant surely didn't expect much profitable trade here. Most sailors tended to steer clear of the rocky, dangerous coast of Fol. Instead they fared south to trade in Fardoris, or else Port Wind and Calprissa. Finnehalle was usually overlooked.

"What's occurring here, then?" Corin interrupted the quarrel with a sharp glance at the trader, whilst eyeing the giant's formidable axe in admiration, his fingers resting lightly on the hilt of his sax.

"This worm has cheated me in coin," growled the giant. His voice was foreign sounding but not unpleasant, quite cultured for such a beast of a man. "I'm at a loss whether to chop him into little pieces or merely stamp on him like a beetle!"

The giant winked at Corin. The trader, missing the joke, winced at this, and his bug eyes pleaded with Corin.

"What do you think, warrior?" The stranger's pale eyes gauged Corin shrewdly and the longswordsman knew this man was no fool.

Corin thought for a minute, then smiled. "Perhaps you should cut off a finger or two? Maybe crack the odd rib. Can I assist? I've a sharp knife or two readily available."

"Masters, please!" the horrified trader wailed, pitifully flapping his arms about like a courting crow in springtime.

"Well, then," continued Corin, his eyes never leaving the outlander's massive axe. "May I suggest you reunite our large friend here with his coin, and we'll hear no more about it? The traders of Finnehalle are renowned for their honesty, are they not?"

The leather trader grumbled, complaining to several of the old gods about the manners of his customers these days. Nevertheless, he hastily cast a few silver coins down on the table. The huge stranger snatched them up quickly, very quickly for someone his size. Corin noted that, too.

"There's a good fellow. That wasn't too hard was it?" The blonde giant guffawed, slapping the scowling trader on his bald head with a palm the size of a dinner plate. The trader was propelled backwards over the table to fall face first onto the dung-covered street.

"Whoops, sorry old lad." The outlander turned to Corin with an evil grin. "My thanks, longswordsman," he growled, rubbing his golden beard. "I have no wish for trouble on this sunny autumn day." Corin smiled back. The giant possessed a genial manner despite his fearsome appearance. He was in his middle years, weatherbeaten, with cheerful blue eyes and a blunt freckled nose.

"My name is Barin of Valkador." The big man grinned. "Well met."

"So you are the master of the *Starlight Wanderer*!" exclaimed Corin.

"Aye, you know of her?" asked Barin.

"Very little," replied the longswordsman with a shrug. "I believe you have a certain merchant from Raleen onboard. A former employer of mine that has requested I dine with him, this very evening."

"Oh, has he, indeed? What a presumptuous fellow!" snorted Barin with mock indignation. "So you must be Corin the adventurer. Silon has spoken of you. Well met, I say! This calls for some sustenance. Fancy a bite to eat and some ale, Master Corin?"

Corin shook his head, then shrugged. "Oh, why not," he replied, questioning his wisdom, and the unlikely pair made their way back toward the nearest tavern.

***

Valkador (Barin's home) was a remote island far to the north, near the realms of everlasting ice. It was a short distance from the coast of Leeth, but the relationship between the two lands wasn't good. Some years ago, Barin had clashed bitterly with Daan Redhand, eldest son of the King of that wild country. This heaped fuel on a bloody feud that had waged ruthlessly between the islanders and the brutal Kings of Leeth for over a hundred years.

Barin's prized possession (aside his brig) was the massive double-headed war axe called Wyrmfang. (Corin considered that a rather ponsy name for such an impressive weapon but kept his lips together on the matter.) Barin told him he'd named the axe after some notorious dragon that used to lurk nasty up in the ice woods. Corin didn't believe in dragons, but he let that one go too.

Despite his bellicose appearance, the Northman claimed he preferred trade to warfare. Judging by his apparel, he had no shortage of funds. The giant informed his new friend that he was on his way back from Sedinadola on the northern coast of Permio. He often traded there, selling furs and amber and purchasing silk, jewels, and spice. Neither man mentioned Silon again. Instead they wiled away several hours consuming hearty fare and speaking of their travels. Corin asked the axe man what he knew of the rumors Leeth had allied itself to Caswallon. Barin's answer did little to reassure him.

"Haal of Leeth is hungry for glory and gold. He has long coveted the wealth of the Four Kingdoms," Barin growled into his mug. "That King and his filthy sons prowl Kelthaine's eastern borders like ravenous wolves, Corin. I fear it's only a matter of time before they attack in force."

Corin nodded. "Silon suspected it were so."

Barin grunted, slurped, and wiped his mouth on his sleeve. "This is a pleasant little village," he said, gazing out the window and squinting in the glare. "You're from these parts?"

"Aye, I lived in Finnehalle once," replied Corin thoughtfully, and then added under his breath. "There are problems here also, Barin. Morwellan renegades are stirring up trouble. I had a slight altercation with three of them last night."

"Morwellans, heh, well I'm not altogether surprised," replied Barin with a nod. "Morwella is in a state of flux. Outlaws and rogues have become only too common in that land, and their boldness grows daily. Word is Daan Redhand sailed his ships into Vangaris last month, seizing booty and women. Though the city guard fought the raiders off, they still managed to set fire to the port.

"They say Duke Tomais is in failing health and still mourns

the loss of his wife, and now his daughter Shallan is grown wayward and headstrong. There's faerie in that one, they say." Barin shook his head in resignation. "Morwella's days of freedom are numbered, Corin. Nor do I see Kelthaine rushing to her aid now that master Caswallon sits at the helm." Barin brooded into his tankard, clearly not wishing to speak more on the subject. Corin didn't press the matter. Instead, he yawned and looked out the window.

It was quiet. They were the only customers in the tavern, and outside the noise of the marketplace had dwindled to a distant murmur. Time was wearing on. Barin's scowl deepened until he could contain his thoughts no longer. He glanced at Corin, straightened his tunic, and farted vehemently.

"Those sons of the King of Leeth are the vilest of men, and of the three, Redhand is the worst."

"I have heard of Daan Redhand," replied Corin softly. "I once fought alongside a Morwellan called Hagan who knew him. He is a dangerous foe, Barin." Corin drained his ale before glancing around at the empty room, almost expecting trouble.

"Redhand slew my sister's son," muttered Barin. " There is bad blood between us." Corin was sympathetic, thinking of Crenna, but chose not to respond. He turned away, gazed out the window.

Barin's shrewd glance caught the shadow of past pain in Corin's distant gaze. He sipped his ale thoughtfully for a moment, then coughed.

"So, longswordsman, tell me why you chose leave this quiet peaceful corner of the world."

"Corin shrugged, his gaze still on the marketplace outside. "It's boring, uneventful, or so I thought back then. Needed adventure, see the world, and all that stuff. Always been restless by nature."

"So you enlisted in the Wolves in Kella."

"Eventually."

"A tough bunch."

"We had a certain reputation, and I had a desire to kill people." Barin's eyes narrowed slightly, but he kept his lips together. Corin continued.

"The Wolves were frowned on by the other regiments. Even the High King despised us. The rankers (and most officers) were lowborn, you see, unlike the Tigers and Bears, who recruited only from nobility. Spawn of the gutter, we Wolves were, even felons and thieves were welcome in the Wolves if they could handle a blade."

"I heard they were the loyalist and toughest soldiers in Kelthaine," said Barin before taking another sip. Corin shrugged. "You don't strike me as the cruel type, Corin an Fol. Hard, bitter, not cruel."

Corin turned and pinned Barin with his blue-grey gaze. "Witnessing my family's murder tainted my angle on things."

"That would do it. I'm sorry, Corin."

Corin shrugged. "It was sixteen years ago."

"Who were the culprits?"

Corin drained his tankard, then flung it hard through the window, spraying glass on the yard outside and startling two women talking close by. The innkeep (who until now had been ignoring them) came over red-faced and alarmed, but after seeing Corin's expression decided to let the matter be. He too had heard about the wild man in the 'Ship last night.

Corin stared at the broken window as one surprised by his actions. After a moment, he spoke again. Barin said nothing, just watched his new friend.

"They cut my father down and butchered my two brothers that sunny morning, then they raped my mother and sister and the other women present before dragging them off to their ships to become slaves.

"They didn't get far. A rogue wave drowned the bastards but took the women too. At least they were spared from more suffering. I'm grateful for that much."

Barin nodded, let his blue gaze sweep the room. "Raiders— from where?"

"Crenna."

"Ah...then you were lucky to survive. Usually they butcher every living thing within a mile of habitation."

"They tried to butcher me." Corin's smile was venomous.

"I killed three with my father's blade, then someone clouted me from behind and I lost consciousness."

Barin ordered more ale. When the innkeep arrived, he looked hesitant and wary. Corin placed a silver coin on the table. "Sorry about the mess," he told him. The landlord said nothing but deftly retrieved the silver and departed.

"So you left Finnehalle and fared east." Barin took a long pull at his ale and belched.

"Not at first," Corin replied. "Finnehalle was lucky, though my kin were not. Most folk survived, for the raiders were few in number. I expect they were a rogue crew that split from the other ships.

"I was only fourteen, Barin. Wild, angry. But I had a friend. Two, really—Burmon across the quay in *The Last Ship* was good to me. His daughter and I were..." Corin took a sip of ale. "Then there was Polin the smith. He was an old soldier that kept forge just outside town. A good friend. Dead now.

"I raised havoc for two years, Barin, eventually even patient old Burmon had to have words. I left Finnehalle, took in with the smith.

"Polin told me about the Wolves, and at sixteen I was eligible to enlist. He gave me sword and council, and off I went."

Barin scratched his beard and picked snot from his nose. "We've much in common," he said. "One day I'll tell you my story."

"I'd like to hear it."

"It's dark, Corin, very dark. A green-eyed witch cursed my kin to share a certain doom. She was comely back then, married to my grandfather but lusted over my father. When he spurned her, she—" Barin's eyes were on the table. Suddenly he grinned. "What a cheerful pair we are."

Corin smiled. "I better go. Time presses." He made to depart, but his large friend produced a curious set of dice.

"Care for a game first?" Barin asked.

"Why not?" responded Corin. He was fond of dice. Besides, what else did he have to do?

They discussed lighter matters as they played, drank, and farted their way through that sunny afternoon. Barin spoke of his pretty daughters and blue-eyed wife, who he described as plum ugly and ill-tempered.

But Corin soon got the measure of his new friend and could tell that Barin loved her deeply. As for himself, he invented pillow conquests and vengeful husbands until Barin guffawed and slapped his back.

Outside, the sounds of the marketplace ebbed and flowed, accompanied by the distant thud of breakers on the harbor wall. After being soundly beaten at dice three times, Corin took his leave of Barin.

He felt better and had almost forgotten the events of yesterday. On a whim, he took to strolling through the village again. Avoiding the market crowds, Corin sauntered back up to the gatehouse to get a better view of Finnehalle. It was a glorious afternoon. Above him, mewling gulls swooped and dived in elaborate circles through clear salty air.

Corin needed time to think. He turned, gazed down whimsically at the ocean, watched it heave and sparkle into the distant west. He had not known what to expect coming home after so long away. Home to where no family would greet him. He was lonely and lost but daren't admit it.

Corin thought about Holly. They shared memories good and bad, although she had been away at the time of the raid and, thankfully, been spared that horror. He could do worse—

What's that?

Corin froze, hearing a soft noise from behind. He turned just in time to see the knife hurtling toward him. Corin dived low, Clouter's crosspiece and pommel clanking as they struck the stone lane's surface. Corin rolled, reached for Biter.

"Slippery bastards! Show yourself, yellow-belly scum!"

Nothing. Then a shadow flitted behind a nearby wall, and footsteps scurried away back down to the harbor. Furious, Corin slammed his sax back into its scabbard, straightened Clouter's harness, and scanned the breezy streets. There was no sign of his attacker. Corin cursed and vowed he'd pay the Morwellans a visit before too long.

Corin was still angry when he passed a bakery, but the smells that greeted made him feel hungry, so he forgot the Morwellans, returned to the 'Ship and, with Burmon's kind permission, raided the kitchens again. Once his stomach was full, Corin felt sleepy after his ale and excitement. So he slipped into his room, unslung his clutter, and sprawled akimbo on the bed. Once comfortable, Corin an Fol slept soundly for a couple of hours.

Chapter 8

The Merchant's Story

When Corin woke he felt well rested and better than he had in days. Outside, it was quiet, evening settling peacefully on Finnehalle harbor. The market stalls were dismantled, and one by one the grumbling traders of Fol packed up their remaining wares and retired from their busy day. Even the seabirds had withdrawn from the harbor, returning to their lofty crags. Beyond those cliffs the setting sun spilled crimson into western water.

Corin, feeling brisk and sharp for once, slung the faded cloak of blue wool over his shoulders. He'd shaved and looked almost respectable, if a man like him could ever look respectable. The cloak was warm and the gold brooch pinning it depicted a snarling wolf standing alone at the edge of a forest. Another gift from the Lord of Point Keep for his service in the Permian Wars; it marked Corin as a veteran campaigner. He wore it with pride.

Corin had liked and admired Halfdan of Point Keep and had enjoyed fighting under the canny general's wolf banner. Corin had served in the Wolves for seven years before his rebellious nature spurred him to pursue his fortune as a mercenary. It was a decision Lord Halfdan had frowned upon.

"You are worth more than a common hireling, lad," the High King's brother had told him. "You sell yourself short; there is a good future for you here with the Wolves—even a commission, if you keep your head screwed on and control that nasty temper of yours."

His temper was the problem. After Corin gutted the sword master in a brawl, Halfdan had no choice but to let him go. Disgraced and downtrodden, Corin had left the Wolves that very week.

He hadn't seen Halfdan since that sorry day. Corin wondered what the general would do now. He guessed he was still holed up in Point Keep—the Wolves had taken the brunt of the coup two years past. Those remaining had accompanied their general to that remote fortress. Word was Halfdan had fallen out with the High King. He despised Caswallon and that old crow had got him banished from court.

But as the slain High King's brother, Halfdan was needed more than ever. Someone had to stand up to this bastard, Caswallon. Halfdan and Belmarius, leader of the Bear regiment, were the only two strong enough to do so now that Perani had sold out.

Lord Halfdan's heir had been the true successor to the throne of Kelthaine. But as Silon had reminded him, that child had perished at sea long ago, together with his mother and the Queen during a perilous crossing south of Fol.

Corin was still chewing over these thoughts as he made his way along the quayside. All was quiet, save for a couple of scruffy dogs gnawing possessively on the scraps left by the traders. They growled at him as he passed by, tails bravely tucked between their legs.

Corin stopped at the southern side of the harbor, admiring the great vessel moored just beyond the harbor's arm. The *Starlight Wanderer* was a splendid sight to behold; she appeared over a hundred feet in length, her clinker hull painted bright blue and silver, with the golden sea eagle's head carved at her prow. Above deck, tough-looking flaxen-haired sailors sauntered to and fro, adjusting ropes and mending sails.

Corin paid a fisherman to row him across to the waiting ship. Curiosity had got the better of him after his talk with Barin. He didn't have to commit to anything but might as well go see what slippery Silon wanted.

Corin was acknowledged and welcomed aboard by the boson, a wiry freckle-faced redhead announcing himself Fassof.

"Lord Barin awaits you in the main cabin, me old cock." Skinny Fassof motioned below with a toothless grin. "With him is the merchant of Raleen."

Thanking the boson despite being addressed as 'old cock' (which in Corin's opinion was beyond impertinent), Corin descended the narrow hatch to Barin's cabin.

Below decks the *Starlight Wanderer* was even more impressive. The master's spacious cabin was built of dark wood carved to depict hunting scenes in the northern forests of Enromer, of which Corin had heard many stories.

Golden-threaded tapestries hung on the walls, and priceless rugs from Permio were strewn across the polished wooden floor. Hanging lanterns tilted gently as waves passed. At the rear of the cabin a large round window let in the last of the evening light.

Silon was seated at the far end of a heavy wooden table studying a worn-out chart. In one hand he held a crystal goblet of wine, and from this he sipped thoughtfully.

"We will not be disturbed," the master of *The Starlight Wanderer* assured them after welcoming Corin on board his ship and offering the longswordsman a seat. Barin looked immaculate in a knee-length blue tunic trimmed at collar and sleeves with silver lace. The giant's beard was neatly combed, and his golden hair braids were tied back with a silk ribbon. He stooped low, filling glasses for Corin and himself and then placing the heavy crystal decanter on the table.

Silon looked up from his chart. He too was dressed like a nobleman. His scarlet jerkin looked very expensive and made Corin feel something of a vagabond in his well-worn garb. He'd left his faded but respectable cloak in Fassof's care, as he knew it would be warm below deck. Silon's close-cropped hair was whiter than Corin remembered. The merchant appeared troubled as he thoughtfully rubbed the diamond stud in his left earlobe.

"So, Corin, you have met my friend Barin of Valkador," he said eventually. "The master of this fine vessel has worked with us for some time."

Corin had no idea who "us" referred to. He chose to ignore the remark. Instead, he raised his glass to toast their host.

"I have indeed, master merchant." Corin's eyes narrowed. "You've something of interest to tell me, I believe."

"All in good time," replied Silon, with an impatient wave of his hand. "Supper will be arriving shortly, and what I have to tell you will sit better on a full stomach."

Just after Silon spoke came a knock on the door, and Ruagon, the ship's red-faced cook, emerged carrying three large steaming plates. The food was excellent and wolfed down eagerly without a word. After another helping for Corin and Barin each, and some more wine, Barin ordered the table cleared. Ruagon, sweating profusely, hurried to comply. The galley master left them alone, closing the door quietly behind him.

"And now to business," announced Silon, leaning back into his heavily carved chair. "You, Corin, must bear with me. In order for Barin to understand what we are up against, I need to delve way back into our history."

"Aye, get on with it," belched Corin as he replenished his glass.

Silon gave the longswordsman a sideways glance, the irritation evident in his dark eyes. He sighed, sipped his wine, then began...

"A thousand years ago, Kell the Valiant and his sons fled the ruin of Gol and discovered this fog-bound coast, so say the Legends of Ansu." Corin rolled his eyes. He hadn't expected a history lesson. "The exiles claimed this country for their own but soon discovered they were not alone.

"Back then this continent was dominated by two ancient peoples locked in a hideous war. These were the Aralais and the Urgolais. Both races are now almost forgotten save by a few scholars and some country folk who usually refer to them as 'elves and goblins' in the tales they tell their children.

"The Aralais, the elves, were a beautiful people, noble and wise and apparently ageless. They dwelt around these western lands between the mountains and the sea. Proud and serene, they built crystal towers and rode across the lands in chariots of multi-colored glass.

"The Urgolais, or goblins, were very differentshort of stature and hideous to behold, dwelling mainly in the wild lands far to the east of our Four Kingdoms. They became known as the Dog People due to their canine-shaped skulls. Although related to the Aralais, they loved them not.

"A clandestine, clever people, the Urgolais studied alchemy and became wise in the deepest secrets of Ansu." Silon paused to take a sip of wine. Corin yawned.

"For many years both races prospered," continued the merchant. "But hungry for lore, the Urgolais delved too deep and were snared by the evil one we call Old Night, who claimed their souls in return for dark power. They vowed to serve Him forever.

"The Aralais were skilled also, and they fashioned great treasures deep beneath the Crystal Mountains, far to the south of what is now known as Permio." Corin mouthed the word *shithole,* but again Silon ignored him, continuing, "The Tekara, the sacred crown of Kelthaine, was one such artefact. Callanak, the lost crystal sword of legend, another. They made many more, and in each placed a special power.

"The Urgolais had their own mines far from these lands. The stunted folk were envious of the Aralais artefacts and sought to emulate their beauty.

Spurred on by their leader, Morak (called the Dog Lord by his enemies), the Urgolais captured the crippled god, Croagon the Smith, he who had made the Tekara and Callanak. They blinded Him, demanding Croagon show them his craft."

"If they blinded the Smith how could he show them anything?" challenged Corin. Silon paused, sipped his wine, and awarded Corin a pained look. Barin was looking at both of them, a half grin on his face.

"I'll cont—" Silon stopped midsentence when Corin stood up, shaking his head, and wandered over to the porthole to watch the waves dance westward into the gloaming.

"This wine is excellent," Corin murmured as he gazed out.

Barin nodded, watching his restless friend closely. Silon struggled to quell his annoyance. "Corin an Fol, please let me continue."

"My apologies," replied Corin, winking at Barin. "Cramp in left buttock." Barin nodded sympathetically.

Silon rubbed his eyes, shook his head, and counted to ten.

"The Urgolais..." (Silon paused to look at Corin, who beamed back at him) "...learned much from their prisoner, Croagon. He taught them to forge weapons of power and how to wield them in battle. Once ready, the 'goblins' turned on their kin." Silon paused to reach for his glass, taking another sip whilst Barin lit the swaying tallow lanterns against the fading light.

"The Urgolais were now powerful sorcerers, and this Morak wielded a terrible spear. Golganak was its name, a lance crafted wholly of black crystal. They say Golganak was dipped in the poisonous blood of Old Night's severed head and His malice corrupted it.

"True or not, panic and dismay exuded from its midnight shaft, scolding the flesh of those it touched, including the Dog Lord himself." Corin scratched his ear and yawned again. He was feeling sleepy, bored. Stories were all right, but he'd rather be looking up Holly's shift.

"But the Aralais were undismayed," continued Silon. "They were a mighty race, and among their leaders were wielders of magic. So began the war that raged throughout Ansu for eons until the time when Kell, our ancestor, arrived out of the west and unfurled his silver banners on the shore."

Corin's eyes were glazing over; the wine was starting to mess with his head. He didn't usually drink this stuff, preferring the hearty taste of ale. Wine smelt of flowers, and flowers made him sneeze.

Besides, he'd heard the story of Bold King Kell and his heroic sons too many times. Such patriotic yarns held little interest for Corin, coming as he did from Fol and not the Four Kingdoms (which, in Corin's opinion, took themselves far too seriouslyparticularly Kelthaine).

His country, although tiny, was an independent land claiming ancestry from the mythical god who'd given it his name. The folk of the Four Kingdoms laughed about Fol. They said its people were backwards and had horse's ears. It was a small matter Corin had had to put right on several occasions.

"By this time"Silon's neatly manicured fingers tattooed the crystal glass"the war had taken a terrible toll on both races. The opaque towers of the Aralais were cast down and destroyed, that ancient beauty lost forever. The Urgolais were now few in number. Only a scattering of their most powerful wizards remained. Foremost among them was Morak." Silon shook his head and smiled wryly.

"It was by a strange twist of fate that our ancestors came upon these two warring races in what was to be their final deciding battle. The Aralais were surrounded and it seemed all would be lost, but then Kell led his warriors into the bloody fray. Legend says he received a sign from Elanion bidding him lead his force against the Dog People. Whatever the truth, the newcomers' arrival surprised the Urgolais, defeating them utterly. Few of that ancient evil race survived, and of their necromancers only three remain. But I fear one of them at least has returned from the catacombs of Old Night's cavern."

"The Dog Lord?" inquired Barin, his clear, blue eyes glinting fiercely in the lamplight.

Silon nodded his head. "I pray not, for all our sakes. But we shall see."

"This Morak? Is he an ugly fucker with a long doggy snout?" Corin felt a chill penetrate his skin. He was interested now.

"I know not, but it's likely, since he's called the Dog Lord, isn't it?" replied the merchantrather tartly, Corin thought. "His skin, they say, was burned black by the terrible spear he wielded, and his face rumored hideously scarred."

Silon's dark eyes locked on Corin's blue-grey. No give there.

"Why do you ask? Showing some interest at last, Corin an Fol?"

Corin felt a strange unquiet enter the room. "I just wondered," he replied lamely.

Silon looked at Corin curiously for a minute then continued his story. "Though the Aralais were nearly wiped out and their ancient power gone, they looked on this new race with wonder. In gratitude their leader, Arollas the Golden, gave Kell their last remaining artefact. This was the Tekara; the crystal crown fashioned long before, in times of peace. Arollas, with an immortal's wisdom, knew that his people's time was gone and that these mortal warriors from across the sea heralded the dawning of a new age—"

"So he stinks of wet dog and wears a hood?" asked Corin, interrupting.

"Who wears a hood?" Silon was getting annoyed again.

"The Dogshite Lord," replied Corin, waving an arm energetically, knocking his glass over, and spilling crimson contents on his lap. Barin reached across, righted the glass and refilled it. Corin thanked him and took a slurp.

"He might, Corin an Fol. I don't know. And you shouldn't mock things you don't understand. Now, kindly stop fucking interrupting." Silon gulped a swallow.

"Continue," replied Corin, taking another pull. He had a suspicion who'd tried pay him visit last night. That discovery was far from comforting. And why would this Morak creature single him out?

Silon shook his head in resignation and drained his wine glass. He remembered why he hadn't felt that sorry to see the back of Corin an Fol. Despite his lethal efficiency with that mile-long blade of his, the man had the subtlety of a mountain troll. Just what had Nalissa seen in the idiot? But then his daughter was as perverse as she was wayward.

"So it was," Silon continued under duress, "that Kell the Mighty wore the Tekara upon his head. And his rule was long and righteous. You see, the power within the crown gave wisdom and strength to the rightful monarch.

"Arollas informed Kell to protect the bloodline for future generations. The crystal crown could pass only to the firstborn of his eldest sibling. Kell's only heir was Wynna, his lone surviving son and founder of Kelwyn. But Wynna was able to honor the Aralais wisdom. From his time on, the Tekara passed from uncle to nephew.

"This custom has held true for a thousand years—indeed, until relatively recently." Silon paused to study his companion's faces in the lamplight. He carefully poured himself out another glass of wine. Outside, the only sound was the gentle lapping of the ocean against the ship's wooden hull.

"What happened to the surviving Aralais'?" asked Barin.

"Little is known," replied Silon, shaking his head slowly before continuing. "It was believed that in the end only seven of them endured, and like the Urgolais they departed far from these lands to regions unknown.

"They are a strange, alien people. Before he left, Arollas informed Kell of the prophecy warning of a time of great peril, a dark time when the Crystal Crown would be broken and the Urgolais would return to avenge their defeat.

"'Guard your crown well and it will protect your people,'" Arollas told the King. "'Remember, if the Tekara is lost, the kingdom will founder. Only the rightful heir to the throne must be allowed to place the Tekara upon his head!'

"And so tradition remained for many generationsuntil idiot Prince Tarin tried shoving the crown on his own unworthy head, plunging our realm into ruin. Now everything has changed. Kelsalion the Third is murdered and we have no successor. As everyone knows, Halfdan's baby son was lost at sea years ago."

Silon scowled and looked into the depths of his wine glass. The succession was always going to be a problem with the true heir long dead, but Tarin's inane actions had brought things to a bitter head. "It's all a bit of a mess, quite frankly," Silon added.

"So both the remains of the Tekara and the fate of the King's son lie in the hands of our enemies," growled Barin. "What a disaster. I think"

"What's Caswallon hoping to achieve?" cut in Corin before his big friend could continue. "Surely the old tosser wielded enough power as King's high councilor. It's well known Caswallon was the real strength behind the throne. Why change the status quo and open the doors for our enemies?"

"Caswallon is clever," answered Silon. "His influence stretches to every corner of the Four Kingdoms, and his spies are everywhere. Ambitious and hungry for domination, he's not content ruling Kelthaine alone, Corin. Caswallon means to rule throughout the civilized world. Who can stop him now that the crown is shattered and the High King dead?

"But that's not all, gentlemen. Caswallon is steeped in sorcery. He wields a dark power, learned from an ancient source." Silon rolled his glass deftly between his brown fingers; he stared hard at its liquid contents before continuing.

"I have watched the cunning games of the High King's councilor for some time, and I fear he is under the sway of an Urgolais warlock—perhaps the Dog Lord himself. It explains why there's a malevolence loose again in our land.

"Captain Barin tells us that the Barbarians of Leeth have united under King Haal and are planning to invade Morwella and eastern Kelthaine. Why now? These things take months of preparation.

"In the south the Permians continue to plot against us, and over the mountains our allies speak of sightings of mysterious warriors on the Ptarni steppes. Finally, closer to home, the Assassin of Crenna will surely aid Caswallon to bring an end to the Four Kingdoms and in its place set up a single brutal oligarchy with the usurper at helm and Rael his trusted lieutenant. Freedom, honor, and truth have never been in greater peril."

"Where do I fit in all of this?" asked Corin, folding his arms and leaning back in his chair.

"I was coming to that, Corin an Fol. Thank you for your patience and discretion," said the merchant with a sardonic curl of his lip. "There is a place across the border," he added. "A deserted inn that lies at an old crossroads in a wild part of Kelthaine. I believe it known to you, my young friend."

"The Inn at Waysmeet." Corin nodded with a frown. "I know it well enough to avoid it. An unpleasant place."

"Therefore unlikely to be watched by Caswallon's spies." Silon helped himself to the last of the wine whilst Barin shouted for another. "I need you to ride out there, Corin, wait for some important friends of mine to arrive." Silon pursed his lips, gauging Corin's reaction.

"Friends? I didn't think you had any," Corin answered, making Barin laugh beside him. Silon smiled, but Corin's steel gaze pinned the merchant to his seat. "What friends?" he demanded.

"Queen Ariane of Kelwyn, together with two of her warriors and a trusted aid. One of the warriors is none other than the renowned Roman Parrantios, champion of Kelwyn." Silon stared hard at Corin before continuing in a softer voice. "Queen Ariane seeks the Oracle of Elanion."

"But that lies deep within The Forest of Dreams!" Corin hollered. "Is she mad?" The thought of meeting a royal certainly appealed to Corin, but the Forest of Dreams was a very peculiar place. Some said it was haunted, and although he had been there once before, he had no desire to repeat the experience.

"Queen Ariane has dreamt of the Oracle," continued Silon, ignoring Corin's protestations. "She believes Elanion's help will guide us in the oncoming struggle against Caswallon and his allies. Her Highness has formed a secret council of which I am honored to be a member. With us are Halfdan of Point Keep, General Belmarius, and Captain Barin, here. And some others that you do not know.

"The Queen chose to journey to the forest with three companions only. More would have drawn the attention of unwelcome eyes. The remaining two are Tamersane, a young nobleman and Ariane's cousin, and Galed of Wynais, her trusted chief scribe and notary." Silon placed his hands on the table.

"Her trusted scribe?" Barin and Corin exchanged glances.

"I know. But Ariane, though young, is no fool, I assure you. You must await Queen Ariane's arrival at Waysmeet, Corin," Silon said.

"Must I?"

"Yes, if you care at all about the future of these lands of ours.

They will arrive the day after tomorrow, and you will know them dressed in green robes like priests of Elanion."

"Why have you chosen me for this quest, Silon?" Corin was still unsure of the merchant's motives. "I'm hardly suited to mix with such refined company."

"Because despite your obstinate ways, I trust you, Corin an Fol," replied Silon. "You underestimate your abilities, my friend."

The merchant let his gaze drift across the cabin toward the round window. It was quite dark outside, and the harbor lanterns could be seen flickering in the distance, casting shadows over the fishing boats that bobbed up and down in the night breeze.

"Go to Waysmeet, Corin," Silon urged. "Lead Queen Ariane to the Oracle in the forest, then make your way to Kashorn on the coast. Barin will await you in the harbor with his ship. I will not be there for I've other matters to attend. Go carefully; Caswallon's spies will be watching all roads."

Corin reached for another glass of wine from the new bottle. He felt tired and overwhelmed and was still unsure of his part in this business.

After a moment's reflection he answered. "My head warns me against this venture. I sense more perils lie ahead than you speak of. But my heart is with you." Corin was feeling awkward. "In some strange way I know I'm already involved, despite having no wish to be." Their looks were quizzical.

"Things happened yesterday," Corin continued awkwardly. "Things I don't understand. Things I'm not sure I want to understand." Silon shook his head and tapped the table whilst Barin refilled Corin's glass.

Reluctantly, Corin told them of his journey to Finnehalle the day before. He recalled the fight with the brigands and his encounter with the old Wanderer on the ridge, finally adding the weird creature in the gloom of the courtyard last night and the Wild Hunt riding above.

Corin chose not to mention the strange girl at Polin's Smithy. Part of him denied seeing her at all. There was only so much weirdness one could take, and Corin didn't want his associates to consider him bewitchedor worse, an idiot. When he had finished, both his companions were aghast.

"So the Hunt rides forth again, and Oroonin the Old is abroad," gasped Barin. The Huntsman had many names throughout the wide realms, and this is what they called him up in Valkador. "This is grim news you give!"

Silon placed his hand on Corin's arm. "The enemy clearly sees you as a danger, my friend. I must confess I find that deeply puzzling. Best be on your guard, Corin an Fol!"

Silon stretched, yawned, and rubbed his tanned hands together. "Time is of the essence, my friends. There are forces at work here I cannot comprehend. It could be that we are only pawns in some greater game."

"What do you know of this Huntsman?" asked Corin.

Silon shook his head. "Only that he is the Lord of the Wild Hunt and a master of riddles. He's sometimes called the Sky Wanderer. The wise say he is one of the great old gods. Oroonin is his true name.

"He was once guardian of Ansu but fell afoul of the Weaver, for he gave heed to Old Night, causing war in the heavens. They say Oroonin was banished from Ansu, that Aralais magic held him at bay.

"His reappearance is grave news. The Tekara's influence held him and others in check, but of course that's all changed now. But why he intervened to save you last night, I cannot hazard a guess. Doubtless Oroonin has reasons he will reveal to none. Be wary of him, longswordsman. He is a fickle spirit!"

Corin nodded and turned to Barin. "Have we finished the wine again?"

"I'll shout cook for another bottle."

They settled down to more talk, and Corin asked who Silon suspected it was that had stalked him last night.

"One of the Urgolais for certain," replied the merchant. "Perhaps Morak himself. We can speculate. What worries and puzzles me is why such a one would come here, of all places."

Silon spoke no more on the subject, and the others didn't

press the matter. For the remainder of the night, their talk was more casual. Corin enquired whether Ariane of Kelwyn was as stunning as rumor told.

"You will have to wait and see," responded Silon with a wry laugh. "Two days from now, the Queen and her party will have arrived at Waysmeet. They will be expecting you, and there will be a full moon on that night, so you should have no problem locating them."

"Neither will anyone else," said Barin. Silon ignored that.

"I wish you well with your venture, Corin. Keep your wits about you."

"I can usually find them if I look hard enough."

The others laughed at that, and Silon (more relaxed) reached across the table and lifted the half-drained bottle. "Come now, my friends, let us finish the rest of this excellent wine!"

Talk switched to politics and plots. Corin learned a lot more about the scheming Caswallon and his plans for conquest. It was very late when he finally bade them both goodnight. Barin yelled Fassof row him ashore.

Slowly, thoughtfully, Corin wound his way back to the inn. Finnehalle lay shrouded in silence. Even the waves gently lapping seemed like a dream. He heard a whisper behind a wall and a shadow crossed his path.

Ahead, two figures emerged from the gloom. Corin turned quickly to see the third man approaching fast from behind. They were not sodden with drink this time; instead, they looked very sober and dangerous in the half-light.

Turning slowly with infinite care, Corin reached down. He freed the hidden dagger from its sheath inside his right boot. With a shout he hurled it at the closest Morwellan, speeding at him from behind. One-eye gave a surprised grunt and slunk to the ground, the knife protruding from his throat.

The other two cursed and rushed in for the kill.

Clouter was quicker.

Cobra swift, Corin swung the longsword low, slicing through both legs of the quiet one. That left one man.

Big Ugly swiped two-handed at Corin's midriff.

Corin leapt aside and swung again—this time higher. Big Ugly's head travelled a full ten feet before landing hard against the wall, bouncing down and then rolling two more feet before finally coming to rest in a gutter.

It's where you belong.

Corin dispatched the legless man and strolled across to where One-eye lay twitching. He knelt, retrieved the dagger, wiped it clean on One Eye's cloak, then shoved it back in his boot and stood up.

After cleaning Clouter in like fashion, Corin shrugged, shouldered his heavy blade, and trudged back weary to his room at the inn. Some idiots just couldn't take a hint. Doubtless there would be more talk in Finnehalle tomorrow.

Chapter 9

Alone Again

Corin an Fol rose at dawn and washed briefly before consuming two helpings of Burmon's fried breakfast. His head felt worse than it had the morning before, and he swore he would never touch wine again. Silon's fault entirely.

Corin muttered incoherent thanks to the baffled landlord and shambled out into the heavy drizzle, which did little to lift his spirits. Iron-grey clouds squatted on him dismally as he mooched up the lane, muttering and questioning his sanity.

And now for the long tromp back to Polin's Smithy.

It was soon raining steadily, and the distant fields and woods above Finnehalle were veiled in mist. Corin wrapped his woolen cloak about his shoulders allowing room for Clouter's hilt to poke free at the top to keep out the damp, and he grumbled to any god that might be listening. He trudged through the sleeping village, back up the hill toward the gatehouse. All was still this morning and very damp.

Corin's mind was everywhere. He wondered if anyone had discovered the dead Morwellans yet. Corin suspected they had. He'd thought about mentioning it to Burmon, but Corin was in no mood for conversation. Those tossers would not be missed by anyone in Finnehalle. They had got what they deserved.

The landlord's face had been full of questions at his sudden departure, but he'd been too polite to ask.

I'll get this job done, then go back to see Holly.

It wasn't just about gold. He was curious about this Ariane. He'd heard she was feisty and a looker. But then she'd most likes turn her royal nose up at him. After all, if he were a Queen, the last person he'd want to be seen with was him.

So actually, it was just the gold—a good enough reason for tromping off in the rain.

Or was it?

Just keep walking.

The dreary weather hung over Corin like a blanket of gloom as he hastened up toward the shelter of the woods. Yet again, Corin brooded on the events of the last two days. He wondered what further pleasant surprises waited for him on the journey ahead. Was he bewitched or something?

One thing was sure; he couldn't stay in Finnehalle. It seemed his lot to leave a trail of corpses wherever he went. Corin was too restless to settle down anyway. Even Holly would tire of him when she realized that. He'd return later and suggest she accompany him someplace where he could ply his trade, though he knew she probably wouldn't.

Things were for the best, really. He might as well go meet this Queen. If she favored Corin (though highly unlikely) he wouldn't need the likes of Silon of Raleen anymore. Corin pictured himself as an earl or something and chuckled. They would never accept his rough manners in court. Wolves were never allowed in court, especially disgraced ex-Wolves.

But you never know...

The rain grew heavier, and Corin shivered. He yanked his woolen cloak down over his shoulders and stared bleakly at the forest looming out at him through the murk. His stolen boots were already caked with mud and had once again begun to leak. Expensive but useless, those boots.

Corin cursed his decision to leave Thunderhoof at the smithy, limp or no limp. The horse had probably had a better time of it than he had.

He strode despondent beneath the dripping trees, stoically attempting to avoid thoughts of the two nights past. Instead, Corin recalled the old stories he'd heard about the deserted inn at Waysmeet.

It was situated at an ancient crossroads, perilously close to that peculiar forest where he was to take the Queen, bless her royal arse. Waysmeet was rumored a place of unquiet spirits. The faerie people, by some called Faen, were believed to frequent it, and honest folk avoided going anywhere near. Stories told of an old curse, and travelers spoke in whispers of weird sightings but when questioned further would go quiet and talk no more on the matter. So the stories grew as the centuries passed. The inn at Waysmeet became a place of fear.

Can't wait to get there.

Corin turned, peered back through the trees at the rainwashed village far below. The stone harbor was shrouded in mist, and there was no sign of Barin's ship.

Corin shrugged, commenced following the muddy track up to the high ridge from which he had seen the old Wanderer. He turned a final time to stare back down past the swaying trees toward the distant village. The harbor lanterns glinted faintly as the morning mist began to lift, revealing patches of the stark coastline until land faded from view into the west. Corin held the sea in his gaze for a time then turned away. Enough brooding. Time to press on.

Corin left the woods behind. Ahead, bleak moors stretched eastward as far as his eyes could see into the gloom. Some miles away stood a line of stunted trees marking the edge of the old road that ran from Cape Fol to the border of Kelthaine and beyond.

Corin was thoroughly sodden by the time he reached Polin's Smithy to reclaim Thunderhoof. Tommo greeted him nonplussed at the door, but then Kyssa emerged from the kitchens and shoved a honey cake in his fist. Corin winked at her and munched happily.

After a few more excellent cakes and a bit of a natter about the awful weather, Corin followed Tommo into the hastily repaired stables, where Thunderhoof waited with the other beasts, stomping and snorting.

"He's been restless since you left, but he's well rested and that leg is better. Oh, you left this behind. Surprised you didn't miss it." Tommo awarded him a knowing smile and thrust the now-very-shiny coat of mended mail into Corin's chest, and the longswordsman grinned.

"My old mail coat. I hardly recognize it. You're a magician, Master Tommo!" Corin slung the weighty coat across his shoulders with a grunt. "I'm indebted to you, mate."

"It is we who are indebted," replied Tommo without returning the smile. Outside in the yard, Ulf's bulk still swayed and creaked from the leaf-bare ash. The ex-brigand looked the worse for wear, what with eyes crow-eaten and face black and bloated. Corin looking out, smiled cheerfully at the hanging corpse.

"Hello big lad! Still hanging about, then?" He turned, feeling Tommo's heavy palm on his shoulder.

"I've a gift for you if you'll take it, Corin. Wait here a moment." Tommo left Corin with Thunderhoof and faded off into the drizzle.

"Well, have you missed me?" Corin asked as he slung his worn saddle over Thunderhoof's back and lashed the steel coat behind it. The horse just looked at him mournfully. "I thought not. Anyway, we're off on our travels again." Thunderhoof snorted. "Don't ask," continued Corin, shaking his head. "And don't look at me like that. You know you will only get fat if you stay here."

The blacksmith returned laden with a sack of supplies and a stout bow together with a quiver of twenty goose-fletched arrows. "Polin's old hunting bow," Tommo said. "I'm a crap archer, and besides, wherever you're off to I'm sure you will need it, if only to bring down a deer for supper in the wild. It's a good weapon made from yew. The shafts are ash and fly true." Tommo thrust a meaty palm forward just as Kyssa reappeared and smiled across at him.

"Farewell, Corin, stay in one piece. And thank you once again." Corin grasped the offered hand, thanked Tommo for the gifts. Kyssa he hugged and cuddled warmly for a minute longer than he should have, ceasing only when he noticed Tommo's lowering expression. At that point, Corin hastily untangled himself from the grinning lass and heartily wished the pair well.

Thoughtful, he led Thunderhoof out into the lane. Corin was secretly delighted with the bow. He wasn't an expert at archery, but it was a fine gift. He stowed the weapon in a holster fashioned for the purpose on the side of his saddle and slung the quiver across his back to hang alongside Clouter's scabbard. Sure, he had a lot of clutter, but you needed such stuff to stay alive these days. At some point the bow would prove useful, he felt sure.

"Come on, big fellow." Corin grinned, launching himself into the saddle and no longer caring about the rain. He felt raffish, adventurous. It wouldn't last. "Let's get some miles behind us before nightfall." Thunderhoof snorted but obliged.

As Corin cantered east, the countryside changed little. The bleak moorland of central Fol offered small cheer for wayfarers, especially today. Now and then a stone dolmen loomed out the fog, but the spirits that dwelt therein were sleeping and Corin, relieved, passed them without event.

Dismal morning dwindled into sodden, dreary afternoon. Rain continued to drench both horse and rider. But as evening approached, the deluge finally ceased, and far behind in the west, the clouds broke to reveal a pale autumn sun.

Corin urged Thunderhoof on, heartened that the rain had ceased. He wanted to cross the river Fol before nightfall. That would allow him plenty of time to reach Waysmeet at the appointed time.

Some while later, Corin recognized an old standing stone and knew he was close to the river. Soon after that, the road became steep, winding sharply upward toward a rocky ridge. Cresting that, Corin stopped to observe the terrain. Some miles ahead, half occluded in a steep, wooded valley, glistened the twisted ribbon of the River Fol. Beyond the river, the dark hills of Kelthaine waited to greet him like a host of ill-tempered giants.

Corin abruptly reined in Thunderhoof as a sudden wash of uneasiness swept over him. He loosened Biter at his side and turned in his saddle to stare back down the road behind him.

Once again, that unpleasant feeling of being watched had crept upon him, but the road was empty, the only sound the constant sigh of wind through heather.

Corin shook himself into movement, goading Thunderhoof on until they reached the edge of the steep bank leading down to the river below. Gripping the stallion's reins tight and leaning back on the saddle, Corin began descending the narrow track.

Once beneath the ridge Corin plunged into a dark mass of stunted oaks. Here it was much more sheltered and very quiet. He concentrated hard on negotiating Thunderhoof down the steep descent. Some way ahead there was a bend in the river, and at that point a ford had been constructed so a rider could cross without difficulty.

As horse and rider approached the ford, Corin tensed. He spotted movement below. Something stirred amongst the tumbled rocks strewn along the riverbank.

He peered closer.

There was someone moving at the water's edge. A huddled figure garbed in featureless rags. Corin guessed it must be some old peasant woman scratching about, though why she was alone in this remote place gave him cause to wonder. There were no hamlets nearby. He stared closer. Beneath him he could feel Thunderhoof's unease.

"Steady boy, easy now..."

Corin steered clear of the figure as he approached the nearest bank. Closer inspection revealed an old woman, emaciated and wretched. But that wasn't all. There was something not quite right about her, and Corin felt the small hairs stiffen on the back of his neck.

"Come on, Thunder, let's not linger here!" Corin dug his heels in, and the big horse commenced wading through the strong current. Corin gasped, feeling the icy water splash around his knees. He kept a constant watch on the ragged figure on the far bank. She was closer and appeared to be searching for something in the water. Her black rags were soaked as they trailed behind her in the rushing current. She seemed oblivious to horse and rider, so intent was she in her search.

After an icy time, Corin reached the far bank and shook the excess water from his garments. A wary glance in her direction revealed the old woman had seen him. She watched him in silence. Her face and features were buried beneath what had once been a shawl, though now it resembled nothing so much as a featureless sack.

Corin ignored her, willing Thunderhoof up the far bank in haste. He heard movement behind him and could feel the woman's raven eyes boring into his back. He turned warily and, seeing nothing, faced forward again.

Shite!

The woman was standing right in front of him. How she had caught up so quickly Corin had no idea. Thunderhoof's eyes rolled in fear and his nostrils flared.

"Steady, boy...." Corin clung to the saddle desperately as the big horse reared in alarm.

"Let me pass, old woman!" Corin yelled at her. His knuckles were white as he gripped Biter's bone hilt. "I mean you no harm!"

She didn't reply, just stared up at him, oblivious of her rags dripping and pooling at her feet. Corin made to free Biter, but the woman raised a withered hand and pointed at him. Corin froze: her bony fingers were covered in blood.

"Heed my words, Corin an Fol, lest you ride to your death!" the old woman croaked, startling a host of distant starlings into sudden flight.

"What words, witch? I've no fear of you," Corin lied.

"Seek out your father beyond the High Wall! He will need your help before the end!" Corin gagged at the stench radiating from her breath.

"My father is dead!" Corin yelled at her, watching in fascinated horror as the blood seeped down her spidery arm and came to rest in steaming puddles at her feet. Whose blood? Surely not hers.

"Dead, do you hear me, hag? Now, be gone, or I will put an end to you! I care nothing for your words, old woman!"

"Then you are a fool, Corin an Fol. Oroonin the Corpse Gatherer will claim you as his prize. He watches you with hungry eye!"

She reached out toward him like a lover and Corin backed Thunderhoof away in disgust. The horse's eyes were wide with panic and he frothed at his bit.

"Oh, my sister will try to save you," she cackled. "In her folly, she deems you worthier than you are. She is such a trusting soul. If I were younger…" She shrieked in delight at the horror in Corin's eyes.

"Have a care, Corin an Fol. Enemies stalk you at every turn. Only with your father's help can you avert the will of Caswallon and the evil one he serves."

"Did you not hear, witch? I said my father is dead!" Corin's face was bleak. "I have no other kin. I'm an orphan, cursed to travel these lands alone. You are mistaken, witch. Now, let me be!" He made a show of reaching for his sax again, but she laughed until Corin dug his heels into Thunderhoof's flank, urging the big horse up the steep bank into the woods beyond. The beast needed little encouragement.

Behind them the old women's weasel laughter was dry as winter leaves.

"You disappoint me, son of Fol. I don't know what Vervandi sees in you! Be careful lest Old Night come claim your soul!"

Corin covered his ears with his hands to dispel her dreadful cackle. He urged Thunderhoof gallop furiously toward the dark slopes ahead, but still the old crone's horrible voice followed him.

"Have a care in the Forest of Dreams. Your way is already watched!" Corin wasn't listening. He brought the sweating horse to a halt when he cleared the woods and crested another rise.

Summoning what courage he could muster, Corin stared down at river and ford, now far below. The witch had vanished from sight, but the dwindling echo of her laughter could still be heard rising above the distant gurgle of rushing water.

Corin an Fol, Corin an Fol… came the words. Corin urged Thunderhoof on as if the witch were strapped to his back, his head still reeling with her chilling words.

My father is dead, murdered years ago. He was my true father, there is no other!

Corin bid Thunderhoof maintain pace throughout that afternoon, but when evening beckoned he eased him back to a walk, allowing the horse to crop at tussocks along the way. Corin shivered as last light faded from the valley behind. He was back in Kelthaine and drew little comfort from the fact. From what Silon had told him, this was now enemy country, and no one he encountered could be trusted. Corin reached down and gave Thunderhoof a hearty pat.

"One last trot before bed, heh."

As the horse's hooves beat out the miles, the crone's words danced around Corin's head. He felt dizzy and tired. He wished he were back in *The Last Ship* with a hand up Holly's thigh and the roaring fire to warm his soul. Gold and a Queen. Both factors had lost their appeal. Corin rode east into the deepening dark, and the shadows followed close behind.

Chapter 10

Fugitives

Beyond Fol, the hills of Kelthaine rise ever eastward until they meet the mountain range known as the High Wall. These towering heights march south for over three hundred leagues, from the Gap of Leeth to the river Liaho that borders the desert realm of Permio.

Beneath Kelthaine's stark terrain lies Kelwyn, a country of round wooded hills and gentle mists, stretching from the ocean to the foothills of the High Wall. Thrust deep into a wooded vale at the mountains feet lies the silver city of Wynais, home of the royal house of Kelwyn. Wrought entirely of white granite, the city commands a fine view westward across fertile fields, toward the great glittering lake that shares its name.

It was the morning of the seventh day after Queen Ariane's departure from the city. A lone figure looked out from a high balcony, his long ashen hair ruffled by the autumn breeze. Behind him the many rooms of the palace lay silent and still, for the hour was early.

Dazaleon leant heavily on his oak staff, weariness and worry wearing hard upon him. Another sleepless night. Even constant prayers to her Holiness had brought him little solace.

I shan't find rest until I know she's safe.

The High Priest let his gaze drift down from the lofty walls of the city to the distant water beyond. Autumn sunlight danced off the polished surface of Lake Wynais. Ripples drifted outwards, whilst the mountain's reflections stared up from the water. Dazaleon cast his trained mind toward the reed-covered shoreline and down into the blue waters beyond, but the old spirit that dwelt beneath was asleep. Dazaleon found no answer in those beguiling depths. Perhaps there was no answer.

He looked up suddenly when the morning quiet was broken by the sound of brisk footsteps approaching rapidly from behind. Dazaleon recognized the crisp tread of Yail Tolranna, the newly appointed Captain of Guard. He sighed, being in no mood for confrontation today.

"A quiet morning, Captain Yail," Dazaleon offered eventually. "Is all well in the city?"

The young captain coughed and shuffled awkwardly, averting his gaze from the High Priest, who watched him with those unsettling eyes.

"The people are uneasy, my lord," Tolranna reported. "What with the bleak news from Kelthaine last week and our Queen's sudden decision to vacate the city. They feel abandoned and alone."

"Understandably so," replied the High Priest. He placed a hand on the young captain's shoulder. "Queen Ariane does what she must, Tolranna. The council approved of her actionsnot that their disapproval would have stopped her."

"But to journey north alone." Yail tugged at his braided mane with characteristic zeal. "Was there no other way, Lord Dazaleon?"

"She is not alone."

"But my brother, your eminence. You know what a wastrel he is." Yail spat down at the gardens below. "And Galed the squire, of what use is he?"

"Queen Ariane chose Galed herself, she knows him well," replied Dazaleon. "Do not underestimate his courage, captain."

"I should have gone." Yail wasn't listening. He could never fully convince himself that his burning love for his Queen was purely driven by duty, despite his efforts in that direction.

"You are needed in the city whilst our champion's away. You have been promoted, Tolranna. You should be honored."

Dazaleon offered no more. Instead, he turned to resume his study of the lands beyond, ignoring the tension radiating from the young captain. Tolranna was like a cat on coals today.

Dazaleon would have preferred Tamersane as captain of guard. He knew both boys well and didn't share Yail's view of his younger brother. Tamersane was bright and resourceful, despite appearing indolent. It was all a charadeTamersane laughed at life, but Dazaleon knew he had depth behind that sunny façade. Tolranna was too wooden, he meant well but lacked diplomacy. Still...

Below, a brisk shout announced it time to change watch and a score of blue-cloaked soldiers hastened out onto the battlements, their long spears shining in the sun. Yail leaned forward and rested his calloused hands on the rail. He thought of Tamersane, his younger brother, away questing with the Queen. It had always been thus; Tamersane had the adventures whilst he, Yail, carried the responsibility. Such was his lot in life.

Tolranna's dark gaze narrowed, scanning the soldiers below and taking note of their actions as they talked casually amongst themselves. There would be a drill tomorrow, he decided, and by Elanion, there would be some sharpening up among the troops in Wynais. Roman had been too soft with them, and Yail was intent on making a name for himself.

Kelwynians weren't natural warriors like their dour northern cousins; they shunned conflict, preferring to philosophize away the hours with soft music and wine, his brother a classic example. They were a light-hearted people, fun loving and intelligent, but Yail knew they would have been conquered long ago were it not for the vigilance of Kelthaine and the steadfast influence of the Tekara.

But his Queen was different. Her heart was solid steel. Her father's daughterstrong, resilient, just like he'd been. Yet also beautiful and passionate, and Yail Tolranna would follow her into the pits of the Dark One himself.

But she was up there with Tamersane and Galed. Thank Elanion, Roman was with them.

It should have been me.

The new captain glanced down irritably at his gold embroidered tunic. He flicked invisible dust from his shoulder. It would not do to mope, for there was much to be done. He turned to leave, then hesitated. Two things still troubled him.

"What do you know of this Forest of Dreams, your eminence?" he enquired. "And what of this guide Silon spoke of, a common mercenary he met in the Permian wars. How do we know the man can be trusted?"

"We don't," responded Dazaleon, wishing the captain would depart and leave him to his thoughts. "But we have known Silon long enough to follow his guidance on this matter.

"As for the forest, what can I tell you? I have never been there and know only this: that somewhere deep within its shadowy glades lies the answer to Queen Ariane's Dreaming. But then, you know this also."

"I"

"I will speak no more on this, captain. Good day to you." Dazaleon showed his back, resumed his study of the lake.

"And to you, my lord." Yail Tolranna fidgeted for a moment then spun on his heels and briskly vacated the balcony. Dazaleon sighed and leant harder on the rail.

Within minutes, the young captain emerged below to vent his frustration on the idle guards. The High Priest managed a slight smile; there would be more than one fellow with a thick lip and sore head by nightfall. Yail Tolranna was determined to make an impression.

Alone with his thoughts once more, Dazaleon let his mind wander, reach out to She who encompassed this green world...

Elanion, Goddess of Dreams, guide my Queen through her journey. My heart is heavy with foreboding that she rides into a trap!

Dazaleon closed his eyes, ignoring the keen breeze and instead focused on his inner vision. He trembled slightly, feeling the familiar rush of power surge through his veins. He summoned the fargaze...

Dazaleon's dreamsight swept north to the border, where the river Kelthara wound its dancing course toward the sea. Beyond it lay troubled Kelthaine, mightiest of the Four Kingdoms, now ruled by a tyrant. His mind's eye passed through the barren hills of that country, staying well away from the brooding towers of Kella. He shuddered at the dark sentience choking that distant city. Menace stalked those silent walls; an alien evil festered there, weaving its web with sable gossamer.

Dazaleon's fargaze wandered north. Anxious, he sought the witch wood but found only the coast, where dark ships battled their way through restless seas. Beyond that loomed the cliffs of Fol. Dazaleon reached out further but found nothing...

***

Miles north, Ariane was feeling increasingly frustrated as she watched the two men battle with the horses. Their mounts had become more and more restless throughout the day and were now scarcely controllable.

"What's wrong, Roman?" she demanded of her champion as he cuffed the nearest beast with his gloved fist. "What's the matter with the bloody things?"

"I don't know, Your Highness," he answered in a gruff voice. "Something's clearly troubling them. Ho! Tamersane! Hold that mare still, damn you!"

"I'm trying, or hadn't you noticed," grumbled the younger warrior, cursing as the agitated horse snapped its head back and caught him under the jaw, sweeping him from his feet.

"This is hopeless," muttered Galed, watching miserably as their steeds continued to buck and kick. Galed didn't want to be here, and the horse's bizarre behavior was only helping convince him that they should never have left Wynais.

And he wasn't a bloody squire, he was a scribe—actually chief scribe. The squire title had been placed on him by the (oh, so witty) Tamersane the other night amid much jovialityat Galed's expense.

And why was he here? Arianelove her though he didwas so evasive sometimes. "You can advise us," she'd told him. And so he had with:

"We should go back," "We never should have come here," and "I knew this was a bad idea, but nobody listens to me." No one was listening to him now.

It had been a week since they'd slipped out of the city unannounced. Every day the "squire" had felt a growing apprehension that something was very wrong. Only his loyal devotion to the Queen kept him where he was. That and stupidity, of course.

But Galed would follow Queen Ariane anywhere, so much did he love her. It would be nice if she informed him why he was here, however. Galed was no warrior, just a weary wordsmith and confidante/counselor to the Queen, as he had been to her father (though fat good that had done him). If only King Nogel had listened to Galed and not gone storming off...

For her part, Ariane was fond of the little man, although most at her court saw Galed as a bit of a fool. But he had a sharp mind, and Ariane knew it. She turned toward him and Galed reddened. Her beauty never failed to move him. He tried not to notice as a lock of jet hair slipped free of her priest's hood when a sudden gust rushed down from the tall ridge above them.

"Highness, I—"

"Galed, stop your fucking dreaming and lend a hand! What the—" Roman gaped as a chilling howl drifted down from the tall pines above. "That was no sodding wolf," spat the Champion of Kelwyn. He cursed again as the Queen's mount reared up and kicked him in the head, pitching him to the floor. Tamersane struggled in vain to control the other animals. They were clearly panicked as more weird howls were carried down by the wind.

"It's no good, cuz!" the fair-haired warrior shouted up to where Ariane scowled. "I cannot hold them!"

"Then let them bloody well go!" growled Roman, who had regained his feet and stood scowling up at the distant ridge. "They are no good to us now anyway." Roman turned, blinked up at Ariane as her squire stood watching beside her.

"Wake up, Galed, you little shite! Grab the blankets and other stuff, and let's get moving! Come on! We'll cut across country. Hopefully, whatever creatures they are, they will content themselves with pursuing our steeds."

The others needed no encouragement, and even Ariane lent a hand with their supplies as Tamersane freed the panicking mounts. Within moments, the four beasts had bolted back down the track and disappeared beyond sight. Almost immediately, the strange howls rose up in fury to give chase, drowning out the terrified neighing of the horses.

"Poor things," muttered Galed. "Will they escape, do you think?"

"Forget them," growled Roman, launching a heavy pack over his back. "We had best worry about ourselves. Come, Queen, let us leave this track and cut northwards. Hopefully, that way we might be able to outfox whatever it is that haunts this shite-awful countryside."

Roman led the way, and Ariane pulled her green priest's cloak down to protect her arms from the twisted tangle of brier and sharp thorns barring their way. Their destination was still two days away, and without their horses they would be hard pressed. It didn't matter. They would get there at the appointed time. That's what mattered, Ariane assured herself as the bitter wind whipped around her cloak.

"Roman," she called out to the big man, "how long before we spot the village? You said we were not that far from the forest."

"Indeed no, Your Highness," her champion replied with a backwards glance in her direction. "By keeping to this course, we will half the distance and should still arrive in Waysmeet before tomorrow night—if our luck holds."

"What luck?" moaned Galed as he struggled to keep up with the lanky Tamersane. "We've had no luck since we left Kelwyn." Tamersane ignored him. They struggled on stubbornly through the rest of that day, making reasonable progress despite there being no regular path. The land about was wild and remote, and there were few homesteads in this region.

It was the realm of eagle and bear, and snowfall was not uncommon this time of year. It was growing colder by the hour, and Ariane watched her breath steam as she listened for any sounds of pursuit.

All seemed quiet. Whatever those creatures were, they had gone for the time being, but Ariane would not drop her guard. Her sharp instincts hinted something was amiss. This land had an unhealthy feel to it, and as evening drew on her restlessness grew. They spoke little—even Tamersane was edgy. Galed looked more worried by the mile. He kept his wittering to himself and fingered a small wood axe, his only weapon.

Darkness closed around them as they ventured on, unwilling to rest until they had to. Behind them the silent stalkers closed the gap. The hunt was on again.

Chapter 11

The Road To Waysmeet

Corin glanced up moodily as he rode. The waxing moon had ridden out from behind dark cloud, spilling its dreamy light on the land. Faerie light, they called it—not a term to inspire confidence in a place like this. This northwestern corner of Kelthaine was known for its chill winds and damp climate. Bleak country—no wonder it had sparse occupants.

Ahead, the wild country rose up in craggy tors. Once or twice Corin caught a glint of torchlight in the distance, showing that someone dwelt near. Mostly the land seemed deserted. No great surprise, considering terrain and climate. Those that did dwell in this region were usually outcasts and oddballs, or else fugitives from the cities scratching a meek living from the land.

Corin continued riding for several hours into the night, knowing the area well and being in no mood for stopping until he had put as many miles between him and the River Fol as was possible. And Thunderhoof had no problem with that.

It was getting cold. A chill wind had risen in the east, and Corin was reminded of the lateness of the year. He finally dismounted when exhaustion overcame him, stopping for the night in a small wooded hollow set well back from the road.

Clouds swallowed the moon again. It was very dark. Corin tried to keep his mind active. He saw to his horse and then ignited a small pile of faggots he'd gathered in the dark.

After a light meal of dried beef (courtesy of Burmon) and biscuits (Kyssa), Corin warmed his hands by the blaze, but food and fire did little to improve his mood. Corin had spent too many nights alone in the wilderness, without home or companion. Usually it didn't bother him, but this part of Kelthaine always dampened his spirits.

It was a desolate, melancholy place, the sort of joint a troll or ogre might frequent if such things existed. Corin told himself they didn't, but after the last few days...

Corin watched the flickering flames, trying in vain to find sleep. His mind wandered down dark paths, and despite his determination not to, Corin began thinking about the witch at the ford and what she had said.

His parents had rarely spoken to him of his birth on the night of the great storm in Finnehalle, thirty years before. Corin had never given much heed too it. Yet now he recalled how often folk had commented on how different he was from his brothers, in both looks and manner.

Corin shook his head. He had always felt slightly removed from the rest of his folk. His father had laughed whenever he broached it with him, which wasn't often. The fisherman had told him not to worry, putting it down to an independent spirit and a restless nature.

Corin brooded as the fire crackled lazy. Time drifted. Then the freshening night wind extinguished Corin's struggling flames, scattering ash over his blanket and scolding his face.

Pox on it.

Corin rolled over and sighed, dreaming of the soft bed in Silon's far-off villa. Then his thoughts drifted upon the merchant's sultry daughter and her naughty little fingers, and that didn't help him at all. It was nearly dawn before Corin managed a shallow sleep. And when he did, the dream stole upon him...

***

He lies in a bed, his young body bruised and battered. Outside, gulls assail the morning. A woman kneels beside him, her face beautiful in the lamplight. "My father is dead! My brothers!" Corin's throat is sore from rasping.

"They are at peace now," the woman replies, her voice soft and husky. Her breath hints of rain on summer meadows. She leans forward, rich copper hair framing a perfect oval face. Eyes of green and gold smile down at him.

"What of my mother? My sisters?"

"They were taken." The woman's eyes turn sad. "The brigand's ship struck a rock. They too are lost, I'm afraid. But at least they were spared from slavery."

The boy Corin weeps, and the strange woman consoles him until, exhausted, he is claimed by sleep again....

The scene shifts.... He is older, and this is the future—somehow Corin knows this. In his hand an alien sword glistens with uncanny white light.

Callanak... A name comes to him then fades from memory.

At Corin's back an army waits in apprehension as ahead a horde approaches to confront them. Corin's force is dwarfed by the dark horde. It surrounds his army, encompasses it.

A hooded figure with doglike features emerges from the dark mass calling out his name with mocking laughter. This leader brandishes a tall spear. Dream Corin recognizes the spear. Fear radiates from that ebony shaft. Other names enter his mind...

Morak, The Dog Lord, Golganak.... Then they too fade into blackness. Behind their leader, the Groil legions sway trancelike, and drumbeats echo in the valley beyond. A booming fills the sky. He glances up. There are giant figures in the clouds watching, the Gods awaiting the outcome. The scene shifts again ...

Corin hears a woman call his name in fear. He turns to help, but his arms are held fast in iron manacles. He tries to speak, but no sound passes from his lips. Corin sees the woman's face and knows that he loves her.

Shallan... another name. She pleads to him, calling out his name, but he is held fast. She screams. Dark figures seize her and drag her away from battlements. Corin struggles to break free of his bonds. Helpless he watches in paralyzed horror as his army is crushed close by and the city burns behind him, its people consumed by dark flame.

From somewhere behind, a canine voice whispers...

At last the way is clear for our return....

The scene shifts a final time. Behind him, there is laughter. Corin turns, sees the blonde girl-child smiling down on him from the tree branch above.

"Your father," she giggles. "Remember your father...."

***

Corin woke with a start. What in the gibbering nine worlds had all that been about? The evil tree faerie again, he suspected, or else the witch at the ford. But why pick on him? Corin rubbed some life into his veins then stared blearily at Thunderhoof, who watched him nonplussed from beneath the shelter of a tree. Sometimes he envied that horse.

After a lean breakfast, Corin saddled up, wearily launched his stiff bones onto Thunderhoof's back, and set out once again eastward along the road. There was no need to rush. He'd made good progress yesterday and expected to arrive at Waysmeet sometime before evening.

Hopefully the Queen and her companions would be waiting for him and they could get on with this business, and he, Corin, would be closer to getting rich—or at least better connected.

It wasn't what you knew but who you knew in this life. A discreet dalliance with said Queen could do wonders for his prospects. One has to focus on the positive, however elusive it may prove. At present it was almost invisible.

The day wore on hour by dreary hour. Above, the sky cleared and the full moon watched them as it followed their path through a line of firs. On they wended, horse and rider over hill and under wood.

Hours later Corin spied movement on the road ahead. He waited under cover of trees until the two mounted strangers approached. They both looked like merchants and were dressed in the gaudy fashions of Morwella.

Corin rested his hand on Biter's pommel and calmly emerged from his hide. The two men eyed him warily, looking about to see if he was accompanied. Corin held out both hands to show he meant them no harm, but the men glared at him with suspicion.

"I'm no highwayman, just a simple traveler!" he called across to them. "What news from the east?"

"A good deal and none of it pleasant." The nearest scowled, still eyeing Corin with distrust. "Vangaris is crawling with spies and there are mercenaries scouting the lands hereabouts. Whom they seek we do not know."

"Who are these mercenaries?" Corin enquired, but they didn't reply, passing him by with an unfriendly glance at his sax and longsword. Corin spat at the ground as he watched them pass. But then Corin didn't like Morwellans.

By afternoon a dark line smudged the horizon. Corin felt a familiar chill in his bones, recognizing the southern fringe of the Forest of Dreams. He pressed on, heavy hearted, eyes scanning the way ahead. He reached a fork in the road and reined in, allowing Thunderhoof brief respite under the shadow of some lofty pines.

Corin remembered this place from his earlier visit. It was here that the road veered south toward Kella and Kelthara, Kelthaine's largest cities. A smaller track branched off from under the shadow of the trees. This was the original route that passed through Waysmeet. It was badly pitted and very overgrown in places.

In the corner stood a gibbet, its chains creaking despondently in the wind. The cage that hung from it was rusty and ancient; the bones of its last unfortunate occupant long since turned to dust.

Corin glanced up at the gibbet with a sour expression. This place made him shudder. Nothing stirred except the wind in the pines and the dismal creaking of the cage. A flutter of wings above him caused him to start. Glancing up, Corin saw that a raven had settled on the iron cage above. Greedily it watched him as it preened its midnight feathers.

Corin swore under his breath. Those black eyes probed into his soul. They reminded him of the hag at the river.

"Go away, bird." Corin hurled a stick in the direction of the raven. Unruffled, the uncanny creature glared at him from the safety of its perch. Corin cursed under his breath and hastily spurred Thunderhoof away from both gibbet and crow.

Taking the old way, Corin was soon forced to dismount so that he could pass through thickets of blackthorn and hazel. Thunderhoof clumped faithfully behind him. This way was scarce more than a worn out path corroded with potholes and puddles. Horse and rider stumbled on gloomily for some hours and the landscape changed little. In the distance, the dark line of trees drew nearer. Corin felt the tension growing with every step. He cast a professional eye back along the road behind him, but there was no one to be seen.

His progress was becoming slower all the time. Once or twice he had to stop to assault the undergrowth with his sax. Corin grumbled to various deities as thorns and brambles tore at his exposed forearms.

It was some time before he realized that the wind had ceased altogether. No birdsong broke the heavy silence, and no scurrying creature crossed his path. The ominous shadow of the great forest reared scarcely a mile to his left. Corin was close; he loosened Biter in its scabbard.

"What's that?" Corin heard a rush of wings swoop over his head. He turned, glimpsed the raven and something else half hidden behind bark and leaf. An old man, hunched and huddled, crouching on a stick with his features hidden.

The raven settled silent on his left shoulder, and both man and bird faded from view. Corin trudged on, sweating.

Minutes later Corin glimpsed the first ivy-strewn stones of a building buried beneath a mass of undergrowth, and beyond that what looked like the remains of an old wall trailed off toward the trees.

Waysmeet, at last.

Corin guided Thunder under a clutch of blackthorn. Both horse and rider stopped suddenly. Somewhere close by a weird howl shattered the silence and lasted three long seconds before tapering off and fading into distance.

Corin felt Thunderhoof tug against his reins in sudden alarm. "Steady boy. I know what you mean! That didn't sound like a wolf." There it came again, closer this time. A doglike howl—weird and unsettling.

Something hunted.

"Wait here, I won't be long." Corin looped Thunderhoof's reins to a small tree before sliding Clouter free of its scabbard. Whatever was out there sounded big. Big weird beasties called for big swords. None came bigger than Clouter. Corin gripped the longsword with both hands and sloped forward through the thicket.

There were more chilling howls, and they were nearer, a co-ordinated series of snapping, barky, growly, whines that set Corin's teeth on edge. Whatever was out there didn't sound friendly. It didn't sound natural either.

Slowly and warily, Corin approached the ruins of the village. His eyes narrowed when he spotted the broken gates of Waysmeet through the gloom. He waited for several moments, listening, testing the air.

Corin thought he heard a soft voice whisper over to his left but couldn't be sure. He tried not to think about the many rumors he'd heard concerning this place.

Prizing himself carefully between the broken gates, Corin ventured into the grass-covered streets of the ruined town. Nothing stirred. Warily, Corin approached the old inn. Its shadowy tumbled mass showed beneath tall trees, luring him on from its place at the edge of the crossroads.

A shriek sliced the silence. Corin froze, sensing sudden movement to his left. Instinctively he ducked low. A sharp hiss whistled over his head followed by a soft thud, and the quivering shaft of an arrow embedded itself in a nearby tree.

Corin jumped to his feet, longsword ready, wishing that he hadn't left his new bow and steel coat with Thunder.

Too late now. Corin pitched himself into the undergrowth hoping to spot the archer as he half ran half stumbled forward, but there was no sign of his assailant. He cursed as a cacophony of weird howls erupted from all directions. From somewhere closer, a man's angry shout was joined by the sudden clash of steel.

Corin took shelter behind a ruined wall. He listened, gauging numbers and distance. The sound of fighting echoed through the ruined houses. Close to his right was the old inn; a half-open door hinted at shadows.

Corin waited as seconds passed and the ringing peel of steel grew closer, accompanied by another series of dreadful howls. From somewhere behind the inn a woman's voice yelled something obscene. There was no fear in that voice, only outrage and disgust.

Corin waited no longer. With a yell he hurled himself through the door. Shadows leapt up as he ran headlong through the building finding nothing but another door through which he crashed amid a shower of splinters. The inn was empty, but outside, the sound of fighting rose higher.

Chapter 12

The Groil

Roman cursed and spat in disgust as he dispatched another hooded Dog Face with his broadsword. To his right the Queen held her own, cutting and thrusting with consummate skill. Roman was glad she'd bid him teach her swordplay.

Her Highness had proved an able student, after only several months proving a match for most of his men. After a year they couldn't touch her. Even Roman got a sweat on when sparring with the Queen.

He heard Tamersane curse as a fiend lashed out at him. Instinctively, Roman spun on his heels, launching a dazzling riposte into the dog-creature's back. The thing howled and crumpled as Roman's sword tore into it. No meat—just teeth and gristle. Roman looked horrified, and the stink of the thing almost made him retch. Sorcery—it had to be. These things were way too ugly to be naturel. Roman gagged, took out another one with a back sweep.

Whatever these dog-things were, they were not difficult to kill, which was just as well for there seemed no end of them. They were everywhere, howling and shrieking like rabid wolves, ema-ciated bodies veiled behind long cloaks, with snarling snouts and lolling wet tongues, the brown-yellow teeth snaggled and long.

Roman was a seasoned warrior; he'd crossed swords with many strange folk. But what these dog-things were he had no idea. The odd glance he got beneath a hood wasn't encouraging, revealing canine yellow eyes and pointy hairless ears the color of freshly spilled blood.

Their skin, when visible, was blackened and burnt. Worse than any of that, the things stank like Kella's sewers in high summer. Roman blocked a wild blow from a creature and slit its belly open with a back sweep. No guts—just foul yellow gas venting out. Roman wretched. The stench was beyond description. The creature crumpled like folded paper in a fire, but others clustered and snarled around Roman until he was surrounded.

Die you honking howlers!

Roman hewed and hacked, sending skinny blackened limbs in all directions. Then something struck his head from behind and he pitched forward into darkness.

Ariane saw her champion fall and cried out in fury, thrusting her rapier into the dribbling snout of a dog-fiend. Tamersane leapt to cover her right, and behind her Galed babbled in panic and swung about wildly with his woodman's axe.

The Queen fought on in grim defiance. It was obvious to her that they had been stalked for days, that these dog creatures were the same devils that had scared their horses. Caswallon must have got word of her movements despite their efforts at secrecy.

Now they were trapped, and more of the creatures emerged from the woods beyond the village. There seemed no end to them. Ariane thrust her free hand up at her hood, freeing her dark locks. She could see better, but what she saw wasn't encouraging. Roman lay motionless to her left, blood oozing from his head, and the enemy surrounded the group of them. Snarling barking, some stood on two legs and others four. She felt Tamersane's back ram against her own as the howlers closed around them.

Elanion, make it quick! Ariane shut her eyes, waiting for the inevitable searing pain.

It never came.

Instead she heard a heavy crash and thump. Someone shouted something obscene. Ariane opened her eyes and blinked. A severed dog-head flew past her ear, spraying her face with stinking ooze. She gagged at the stench then gaped in surprise.

A stranger had entered the fray; hacking and slicing like a man possessed, with a massive sword. Ariane had never seen such manic violence. Yet for all his lack of grace, the longswordsman was lethal.

Wild eyed and shaggy-haired, rangy and tall, he ploughed into the back of two dog-heads, dispatching them with a savagery she'd not witnessed before. Three more lay motionless at his feet before the others realized they were being attacked and turned in snarling rage to confront this new antagonist.

Ariane found her strength again. She launched herself at a hooded hound with renewed passion. Silon's mercenary had arrived just in time. And what a warrior he was!

***

Corin felt the familiar rage soar through his veins. He slew and slew, venting his wrath, hewing the hooded dog-creatures surrounding the young woman. There she stood, small and defiant, shouldered by a fair-haired warrior. A second fighter lay motionless on the ground and a third, smaller man, flailed about with two hands gripping a small ax.

They were garbed as Silon had said they would be, in the tattered green robes of Elanion's travelling priests. The Queen was pretty in a sharp-nosed angular sort of way. Her body (those bits showing, which weren't many) seemed well put together, her motions fluid, lithe like a dancer's, and her dark eyes hinted at a hellcat temper.

Corin had managed a quick study whilst awarding a warped grin in her direction, just before dispatching another fiend with a backhanded sweep from Clouter—a practiced blow, that one. It caught most his enemies unawares.

But the bloody things kept coming.

It was proving monotonous. Corin sliced and stabbed,

lunged and clubbed. Dark stinking blood and doglike limbs flew everywhere, but it was useless. They kept coming out of the trees. Thirty? Forty? Hard to tell. Lots, anyway, and every one reeking like last month's leftovers.

More of the creatures turned toward Corin, demanding his full attention. These newcomers carried curved, serrated blades in their claw like hands and commenced swinging them hungrily, aiming for his throat. Corin dived and ducked, lashed out and kicked, whilst Clouter claimed two more bodies.

And still they came—some on four legs some on two. It didn't seem to matter. Corin could see the smaller man, clearly no fighter, was panicking as he tried vainly to protect his Queen. The fool actually appeared to be more of a hindrance to her. The fact that he was still alive was something of a miracle. The Queen fought on in desperation whilst the fair-haired warrior battled skillfully beside her.

The ground beneath Corin's feet was slippery with the stinking blood of the dog-fiends. He'd lost count of the dead. Corin cursed under his breath. He was tiring fast, and his brief glimpses of the others showed the exhaustion on their faces.

Clouter whirled full circle, cutting clean through three dog-things and spraying gore in all directions. Mid-swing Corin stole a glance at the Queen. She looked shattered, and her priest's cloak was covered in dark blood.

It's not ending like this.

Corin channeled his rage and tapped into his reserves, ramming his wolf's-head pommel hard into the snarling face of a dog-creature. He jumped back, blocked a clumsy thrust from another one with his forearm. Then one grabbed his leg from behind. Corin swung round, reaching for his knife with his left hand, but he lost his footing in the slippery mud.

Dog Face stooped over him, snarling and dribbling with serrated blade held ready. Corin winced at the foul stench of the creature's rancid breath.

Get on with it, you pile of dog shite!

Dog Face obliged, closing in to finish him. Corin's desperately searching left hand eventually freed the dagger in his boot. He stabbed upwards hard in the general direction of Dog Face's groin, hoping that region actually housed something worth puncturing.

The fiend shrieked as the knife tore into its blackened flesh. It fell backward, but then another took its place, towering over Corin, a double-headed axe grasped in its leathery paws.

Welcome to the party, stinky.

The weapon rose up and Corin strained to lift Clouter, but it was useless.

Bugger you, Silon....

Corin tensed for the deathblow. But the creature let out a strange grunt and dropped the axe, pitching snout first to the dirt. Protruding from its back was a grey fletched arrow.

Corin rolled free, seizing Clouter with blood-slippery hands, his strength renewed with having cheated death yet again.

Gercha! Corin hewed and hacked, skewered and sliced, driving the creatures back; he was happy—in his element.

More arrows whistled from the trees, striking the hooded dog-things with deadly accuracy. The creatures howled in fear, gaping about in search of this new foe. Corin felled two more, pausing when a gruff voice barked approval and another sword joined with his own.

It was the wounded man back on his feet. Corin grinned, recognizing Roman Parrantios, the famed Champion of Kelwyn, who he'd once seen at tournament in Wynais.

The champion still bled profusely from his earlier blow, but he fought with skilled tenacity. Within moments most of the enemy lay butchered at their feet. A remaining few fled on all fours into the woods, but the arrows followed them with mortal precision. Soon the yapping and howling ceased. None survived. This archer, whoever he was, was thorough.

Corin wiped his sword on the nearest creature's cloak. Breathing heavily, he looked around for a sign of the hidden archer. He saw nothing. There was nobody there. Even the bracken and nettles around the old path lay undisturbed. It was as though the archer were a phantom from the forest.

"Whoever you are, thanks!" Corin called out breathlessly,

scanning the trees. His new companions were panting and sitting a way off, nursing aches and bruises. They were worn out, but Corin had got his second wind. He stomped about for a moment and then wandered over to join his new friends. They viewed his approach from the inn's drafty courtyard as dusk settled in the glade.

The woman caught his eye as she fastidiously wiped filth from her cloak.

"You must be Corin an Fol," she said, her voice clear and confident. "We are in your debt, longswordsman. I thank you, sir."

"A pleasure," Corin mumbled, awkwardly aware that this was the first Queen he'd encountered. She didn't look like a Queen in his opinion, more like a hell-catwith fierce black eyes and sharp feral features. Pretty, though, in a hungry, pouncy sort of way.

"May I introduce Squire Galed," the young woman continued, gesturing toward the sweat-soaked, balding man who still gripped his tiny axe with both hands as if he expected to see at least another twenty dog-fiends re-emerge from the murk. The man blinked at Corin, who grinned back.

"And these valiant fighters are two of my finest warriors. The noble Tamersane of Port Wind, my cousin." The fair-haired warrior grinned as if he'd heard something amusing.

"Hello mate." He smiled at Corin and thrust out a gloved right hand. Corin shook it. "That's a big tool you carry." Tamersane's eyes were on Clouter.

"And my stalwart champion, Captain Roman Parrantios," the woman said after awarding Tamersane a pained expression. Corin turned to where Roman stood leaning on his broadsword. The champion's bearded face was streaked with blood, most of it his own. Roman grinned horribly at Corin.

"Greeting, longswordsman," Roman said. "Good fight, eh? I was just breaking into a sweat!"

Corin grasped Roman's hand in friendship. "Me too," he replied, eyes smiling, and Squire Galed looked at him with a mixture of disgust and bewilderment.

"Warriors," Galed grumbled under his breath. "You're all mad as bats."

"And I," continued the woman, flashing her fierce dark eyes in his direction, "am Ariane san Kelwyn."

Corin nodded. He sank to his knees before her, not quite knowing the right thing to say or do. He eventually managed, "I have been asked to aid Your Highness, to find the Oracle in the forest."

"On your feet, good fellow. Kneeling doesn't suit your kind." Her tongue was sharp, but an impish smile accompanied it: Corin realized he was going to have problems with this Queen. He felt a fart coming on and held it back betwixt his buttocks, now not being the time.

"Here we are and in one piece, though barely." Ariane wrinkled her nose with distaste at the mass of doglike bodies strewn around the inn. Corin was impressed by her calm manner; she appeared unshaken by the fight.

The Queen was not very tall, quite short in fact, but she carried authority as one used to commanding armies of men—very confident for one so young.

She was, he decided, very pretty, if one could describe a Queen as pretty. Not beautiful but definitely worth a go were he to get the chance—unlikely as that surely was. But you never know. He'd got off to a good start, showing up when he did. That had to count for something.

Her face was oval with a slightly pointed chin, and her pert, sharp nose showed a faint dusting of freckles. It was her eyes that demanded Corin's attention. Those wicked jets could render a man witless.

Queen Ariane's hair was cut at shoulder length, black as raven's wing and glossy thick. She caught his questing eye, and her small mouth tilted upwards slightly. Corin reddened, feeling a stirring below.

Ease back, trigger...

"We need to decide our next move first," Roman Parrantios was saying. He was on his feet again and restless. He stooped to kick the lifeless body of one of their attackers. "There may be more of these dog-things about."

Corin reached down and pulled the hood from the nearest figure. The canine face beneath was hideously scarred and deformed, with twisted snout and gaping yellow dead eyes.

"What manner of beings are they?" Corin asked, incredulous that such things actually existed. They reminded him of the thing in the courtyard the other night.

"They are called Groil, if I remember my history correctly," answered Ariane. "They were servants of the Urgolais who used to haunt these lands before the coming of King Kell. Caswallon must have grown powerful indeed if he sent these creatures to slay us."

"That bastard has a lot to answer for," growled Roman. He thanked Galed. The squire, finally convinced that their enemies were all dead, had stowed the wood axe back in his belt and stood wiping the champion's bloody face with a damp cloth.

"You'll mend," he ventured after fussing and tutting for a nonce. "Your head's as thick as an ox."

"Thanks," replied Roman dryly.

"Caswallon has been given great powers by the Urgolais," the Queen was saying. "These Groil creatures must have been awakened by their dark wizardry. May the Goddess curse our enemies!"

Galed finished with Roman's face and sloped off weary. Corin exchanged glances with Roman. The big fighter appeared a cheerful soul, perhaps forty, darkly bearded with broken nose and three missing teeth. Despite that, the Champion of Kelwyn was still a handsome man, and Corin, like many others, had heard of his colorful exploits among the ladies of court at Wynais.

Tamersane appeared rather aloof and distant, a bit in love with himself. And this Galed character was an irritant, Corin decided. The scrawny squire had more hair on his face than on his head. He seemed to be constantly complaining, and Corin took an instant dislike to him.

"We must flee from here, Queen!" Galed was whining. "Let us make for the forest; it will be safer under cover."

"No!" snapped Corin with a sudden venom that turned all faces in his direction.

Even the bored-looking Tamersane raised a quizzical brow.

"Why ever not, friend Corin?" he asked with his winning smile. Tamersane was much too handsome for Corin's liking. Beneath his green cloak, he was garbed like a peacock. He wore a superior look on his patrician features, and a mop of thick yellow hairas blonde as his Queen's was darkthatched his broad shoulders. Those clear blue eyes sparkled with sardonic humor. A smug git, this one, Corin thought.

"Squire Galed here can get overexcited upon occasion, but for once his words appear sensible enough." Tamersane studied Corin with shrewd eyes behind his easy smile.

Corin shook his head. "Evening is upon us. The forest is dangerous even in daylight, but in the dark it is perilous indeed. Let us stay within these crumbling walls tonight and regain our strength. Tomorrow at first light, we will enter the forest."

"But this is madness, Queen!" Galed tugged at her sleeve like a pleading puppy. "Who is this wild man to advise us, this mercenary from the backwoods." Corin's eyes narrowed dangerously at that. "We could be attacked in the night," Galed continued, "and this place has a very bad feeling about it. I—"

"Shut up, you little prick!" Corin cut in. "We stay put tonight. I may be a northern lowlife, but I know this country, 'Squire' Galed. And I know that friggin' forest! So shut up. Please."

Both the Queen and her champion were looking at Corin curiously whilst Tamersane grinned like a tomcat.

"He's a smooth talker, this longfellow."

"Shut up, Tamersane." That from the Queen.

"But the enemy knows we are here!" grumbled Galed, refusing to quit, his face furious with being addressed as both "prick" and "little." To his right, the Queen was smirking slightly. Galed saw her expression and looked wounded. He persisted as one under siege.

"We only survived the attack because of that mysterious archer. Who is to say he will return to our aid next time?"

"Enough, Galed, I'm tired of your bollocks." Ariane waved him to silence. "Corin an Fol knows this region better than we do. Silon trusted his guidance and so shall we."

She appraised Corin with a quizzical eye. He nodded awkwardly in return—a bit shocked by her language, if truth be told.

"I would guess this place defendable as anywhere hereabouts," she continued. "If the enemy knows we are here, then so does our friend the archer. I am most grateful to him!" She lifted her voice to the wind.

That was the end of the matter, and despite Galed's continuing protestations (most under his breath), they made a rudimentary camp under the shelter of some oaks at the edge of the village.

They stayed well away from the inn, as the interior was filthy and the common room stank with the urine of wild beasts. Corin left to retrieve Thunderhoof from his tree whilst the other men set about cooking the evening meal.

"That is a fine horse," said Roman, glancing up from his task as Corin and Thunderhoof joined them by their hastily assembled fire. "Where did you acquire him?"

"Raleen, during the Permian Wars," replied Corin. "A gift from Silon in Port Sarfe for work well done."

"I am impressed," responded the big man, and the horse pricked up his ears. "He is a splendid beast."

"He has his moments," responded Corin as he led Thunderhoof into the overgrown gardens, leaving him to feed on the long grasses.

The Queen insisted they share their rations with the longswordsman from Fol. Corin gratefully accepted some dried pork from Tamersane.

As he munched, Corin eyed the darkening trees suspiciously, and the others said little. They were all exhausted from the fight and very hungry. At least it was a dry night. Dry and still. The shadow of the forest loomed nearer as night deepened. Corin watched the fire cast weird shapes along the ruined walls of Waysmeet.

"The Groil came upon our scent two days past," the Queen told him. "We escaped their net by leaving our mounts behind as bait. We travelled across country, covering our tracks. To scant avail. They must have followed our scent to this creepy place." She shuddered, suddenly chilled.

"How long will it take to reach the Oracle of Elanion?" Queen

Ariane asked Corin as the others watched in silence. Galed's dark eyes flickered about nervously, and when somewhere close an owl screeched, he jumped in alarm.

Beside him Tamersane laughed and patted Galed on the back. "There, there, old chap—'tis but a hooter." Galed glared at Tamersane but refused to reply.

"If we get a good start, we should be there before sundown tomorrow," Corin replied, unsettled by the Queen's keen gaze. Those black eyes were shrewd and penetrating. Corin had that urge again and felt his color rise.

Shite...

"I thought you said that we should avoid the forest after dark," muttered Galed, chewing on a dry bit of crackling and eying Corin suspiciously.

"If we can avoid it, yes!" blurted Corin, wishing that he could do something unpleasant to Galed. "Tomorrow we will have no choice. Tonight we do!"

"What do you know of yonder wood, Corin?" enquired Tamersane, leaning over to pitch another faggot on the flames. He prodded Galed affectionately in the ribs.

"Not much," replied Corin truthfully. "I've been through it once before after falling foul on a wager. It's a strange place, not evil exactly but very peculiar. There is a presence there, a hidden warning of danger." Corin shrugged. "Thankfully, I didn't encounter anything myself. I've met some who have, though, and there are rumors concerning a green lady said to dwell deep within."

Corin stopped, and they watched him in silence. He looked up at the pale moon, feeling suddenly weary; the silver satellite stared down at him uncaring from its lofty perch above the trees. The owl called again, and Corin wondered what the bird hunted.

"My intentions were for us to skirt the forest's eastern side and follow the Morwellan road for some miles, then cut across to the Oracle," Corin explained. "That way would be shorter, but after this attack, the sooner we enter the cover of the forest tomorrow the better. I'm sure Caswallon has other spies. I encountered two merchants who hinted there were brigands about." He was going to use the word mercenary, but he knew that would draw an acid comment from Galed.

"This whole area has a strange feeling about it, and the old inn at Waysmeet has also many stories to tell," added Queen Ariane with a shudder. "I cannot say I feel comfortable here."

"Indeed it has, Your Highness," nodded Corin. "Even now I can feel the watchful eyes of the ghosts that dwelt here long ago. They are said to wander hungrily under the moonlight seeking fresh souls." Corin could feel no such thing but just wanted to spook the already jittery Galed. The little man glowered at him, and Roman guffawed, slapping him on the back.

"What's the matter, Galed?" he asked. "You've gone a bit pale, lad!"

"Piss off," Galed managed between bites.

"What do you seek at the Oracle, Your Highness?" Corin asked, ignoring the banter. "Silon spoke to me of the Tekara's ruin and the fearful events concerning stupid Prince Tarin. But what can you gain by this trip?"

"Prince Tarin is my distant cousin," she answered tartly, her eyes disapproving of Corin's description of the Prince. "I would save him from harm if I can, whether he deserves it or not.

"But to answer your question, I seek knowledge from the Goddess on how to deal with Caswallon the usurper. I have dreamt of Her—only at the Oracle will She share Her wisdom with such as I.

"The Forest of Dreams is the very heart of Ansu, Corin. Our Goddess, Elanion, is this green world's guardian and Her influence greater here than anywhere else on this continent, that I'm aware of. In my recent dreams, the Lady of the Forest bade me into Her realm." She studied Corin's face for a few moments then closed her eyes.

"So, here we are."

"What do you know of the Huntsman?" Corin asked her suddenly, after he had sat gazing at the firelight for some while.

"The Wild Huntsman? Very little," replied the Queen, looking hard at Corin and wondering what lay behind this question. "Only that he is a harbinger of war who is said to appear in times of great need. Why do you ask? Have you seen him, Corin?"

Corin nodded. "Three times, Queen. Once watching me from a ridge a few days back, once up in the sky with his hounds, and the last time earlier today—only this time he looked to be an old man leaning on a stick with a raven on his shoulder. Silon thought it significant, but I'm not so sure," he added.

"Maybe it is significant," Ariane replied. "He has two ravens, according to myth. They say both contain the souls of great warriors who died in battle in ancient times. They also say the Huntsman only shows himself to those of royal blood."

"I think in my case he must have made a mistake!" snorted Corin before staring hard at Galed, daring him to speak.

But the Queen continued to look at him for a while, her expression strange. "You have a certain look about you, longswordsman," she mused. "You remind me of someone...I once knew. It is strange."

Corin shrugged, lost for words. He wondered where this was going and turned his gaze awkwardly toward the fire. Corin thought again of his uncanny encounter with the witch at the ford, and his expression grew cold. *Who is my real father?*

"What of your horse, Corin?" asked Roman, changing the subject and breaking the troubled silence. "Thunderhoof will impede our journey through the forest."

"I was going to stable him at the nearest village in the morning," replied Corin. "There's a place some miles south, and the folk thereabouts are trustworthy enough, despite their rough manners." Corin glanced over to where the horse could just be seen looming out of the night. "But now I fear Thunderhoof will have to take his chances in the wild. He'll be fine. He knows his way about and will probably head back west again. Won't you, Thunder!?" Thunderhoof remained unimpressed.

"Not necessarily," cut in Ariane, raising her hand. "I need to get word back to Silon in Port Sarfe. He has business in Permio and was heading down there after seeing you. Silon must be informed of our attack, and I'd rather not trust to pigeon—even if we could source a trained bird out here. Tamersane, here, is a fine horse-man," Ariane said. "Undetected, he could be in Port Sarfe within three weeks." She placed a slender hand on Corin's shoulder. "Only with your kind permission, of course."

"I will look after yon beastie. Have no fear." Tamersane showed that winning smile again.

"I would advise it," responded Corin with a short laugh, "for he will bite you if you don't." From over in the shadows Thunderhoof stamped his foot and snorted in derision. They all agreed this made sense. And so it was decided: Tamersane would depart with Thunderhoof in the morning.

An hour later and wrapped cozy in her blanket, Queen Ariane's mind was working overtime. They had been lucky today—damn lucky. If it hadn't been for Corin and the mystery archer, they would be corpses greying on the ground.

She hadn't showed it, but Caswallon's ability to reach them up here had shaken her badly. How had he known she was here? Spies? His own sorcerous questing? Either way, it was highly disturbing.

Ariane had thought that once they were north of Kella's vicin-ity they would have free rein. But somehow Caswallon had outma-neuvered them. How? A frightening question. And what else did the Usurper have up his sleeve?

Ariane hated Caswallon. She had known the High Councilor for years, had seen first-hand how he played on Kelsalion's frailty and bought followers in the council with gold.

And Caswallon loathed her. Worse, he lusted after her. Her father alone had stood up to him, and Caswallon didn't like that.

Sorcerer and Queen, they were cat and mouse. The clever mouse had got away this time, but the cat was patient and had help too: Groil, creatures fashioned from low sorcery, resembling crude hollow forms of their masters, the Urgolais. So the rumors had to be true. Caswallon had sold his soul to the Dog People, the evil ones that Kell had helped scourge from these lands.

And now they were back. How many and just how power-ful they were she could only guess at. But they were able to aid

Caswallon, and that was blackest news.

But not everything was against them. Ariane cast an eye in Corin's direction, where he sat hunched by the fire. First impressions, she liked him. He played the bad-arse mercenary 'I don't give a shite' role well. But Ariane could see more to him than that.

This Corin was bitter, certainly. He had small respect for authority, which made her smile, she, who had always been surrounded by courteous men like Yail Tolranna and his brother Tamersane. Even Roman had some courtly skills when he chose to employ them. Corin an Fol was not a subtle man. But he was interesting.

And what a fighter! Ariane had never seen a longswordsman in action before. Quite a spectacle. Though he lacked all grace, Corin possessed a demon's skill with that massive blade.

She studied his features as he brooded into the fire. This one, she decided, would scrub up well. His face was comely in a rough, rangy sort of way, and the scar only added to his raffish charma charm this Corin didn't realize he had. Ariane yawned. She needed to sleep, so she closed her eyes and eventually drifted off.

Meanwhile, night deepened and shadows hung low.

Darkness shrouded the inn. The silver moon slipped behind a wall of heavy cloud, and a bitter chill entered the weed-covered gardens of Waysmeet. They had set watch, Corin taking the second two hours after Tamersane.

As the others slept, he stared out into the blackness, his thoughts troubled. The inn beckoned from the gloom, and Corin's gaze was drawn toward the nearest window. He felt a shiver creep along his spine.

She's back....

There was a face in that window, watching him. A sad and beautiful face. It was the face of a woman, her hair a copper spiral and her eyes green and gold.

I don't know what Vervandi sees in you....

Tongue-tied and shivering, Corin stared back at her, but then something moved in the bushes. He turned sharply to see what it was. Some prowling beast perhaps? Silence. Nothing.

Corin returned his stricken gaze to the window. There was no one there. From the old inn at Waysmeet there came no sound. Corin shook his head with a silent curse. Ghosts, Groil and witches. And now *she* had returned to haunt him after all this time. That beautiful mystery woman who had stalked his dreams since the time of the raid.

Vervandi...

Whatever was happening to him? Corin slung Clouter across his knees and commenced working his oil cloth along its steely length. Once done, he honed edges industriously with his whetstone. It wouldn't do to dwell on such uncanny things, least of all here in Waysmeet amongst the tumbled ruins. They passed slowly, those two hours.

Eventually Roman relieved him. Corin curled up in his cloak, stealing a glance at the sleeping Queen before slipping gratefully into dreamless oblivion.

***

Shadows drift across deserted streets. Pale eyes watch from empty rooms as night deepens further. The Silent Ones stir from their rest to wander as they always do on moonlit nights, their pale shapes shimmering beneath the racing cloud. Time passes so very slowly here, where dimensions cross and worlds collide. A slim figure rises effortlessly to his feet in one smooth fluid motion.

Bleyne the archer smiles watching the shadows dance. Bleyne has no fear of such things. He too is a creature of the forest. He has reclaimed all his arrows, so it is time he returns to his mistress. The archer glances at the shaggy figure hunched low over the fire and smiles that knowing smile. Let them enter the forest tomorrow. If they survive the test, his mistress will await them in the Sacred Grove.

Chapter 13

The Forest of Dreams

The taproom stank of beer and sweat. Stale tobacco stung his eyes as he watched the cockroach skitter into range. Just a few more inches and he would have it. One... two... Cale struck, seizing the insect between thumb and forefinger and ramming it into his mouth. He crunched loudly. It didn't actually taste that bad. After four days grubbing at earthworms and beetles, it was almost diverting, and he was so very hungry.

Things had not gone well for the boy since his flight from the smithy four days ago. He was half starved, soaking wet, and trying to shake off what promised to be the foulest of head colds.

He missed the twins. It wasn't that he'd liked either of them. Who would? But at least they'd got him fed. Cale scanned the filthy floor for more grubs. He should never have left Kelthara. Cale was a city boy. He belonged in the grime and grot of the back streets, not these bleak windy hinterlands. Still, he was alive, and out of the rain for the time being.

Cale cast a wary eye at the soldiers who sat dicing at a table near the fire. They were a rough lot, mercenaries, he suspected, Morwellans by their speech. They drank sparingly, casting the odd glance toward the door as if awaiting someone. No one paid heed to the boy. The grubby proprietor had let him shelter from the rain for a copper coin. One of the three he still retained.

Cale's return to Kelthaine had not been without event. That first night, he'd found a homestead, located the kitchens, and was almost away when the yeoman returned with his dogs. Cale escaped empty handed. Worse still, he dropped most the coin he'd lifted from the smithy in his panic to get away.

It was a close call. He'd scaled the wall of the garth inches ahead of the dogs. The nearest one bit a fist-size hole in his pants, exposing a pink buttock. Since then he'd dared two more garths, to scant avail. Folk were wary in this region, it being border country.

He'd crossed the river at the ford, following the old road east until he reached this cluster of hovels with its tawdry tavern. Last night had been unpleasant, for weird howls had echoed from the hills beyond, and it had turned bitterly cold. Cale didn't have much of a plan. He'd head for home, try and take up with some of the crew he'd known in his pickpocketing days. It would be all right. Cale was a survivor.

The door swung open with a groan. A stranger entered, tall, lean, his hard features scanning the gloom and finally resting on the soldiers at the table. He glanced briefly at Cale then stooped into the taproom, shaking the rain from his shoulders.

The boy shuddered. This fellow reminded him of the man called Corin an Fol, but he was leaner in build, with eyes the grey of granite. They were just as cold too—those eyes. Snake eyes, thought Cale.

This was one scary bad-arse. The men greeted this newcomer, hailing him as their captain. Stone-eyes took seat beside them, downed a flagon in one, wiped his mouth, and belched loudly into the fire. The proprietor was hovering at the bar, looking greasy and nervous. The captain stared hard at him, until hint taken, he vanished behind doors. They ignored Cale. Asides from the boy, the inn was empty.

"We can talk here," the nearest man said as Cale's ears pricked. "What news, Captain Hagan?"

The captain didn't answer at first. He watched the flames crackle and dance as his men shuffled in discomfort. Cale could tell they feared their leader, which wasn't surprising. They looked tough, but he looked tougher

"They are at Waysmeet near the forest." His voice cut through the gloom with a surgeon's precision. The words were crisp, abrupt, and slightly sardonic. "I am informed they mean to enter said wood in search of the Oracle."

"Are they mad?" gasped another soldier. This one sported a horned helmet that looked welded to his head despite the close proximity of the fire. Slung across his back hung an iron crossbow and a score of quarry bolts. He had very few teeth, the boy noted. Cale forgot his hunger as he listened intently.

"Mad or not, Borgil, we cannot let them slip our net," the captain answered. "The Lord of Crenna was most adamant, as only he can be. The Queen is not to be hurt. The others we can slay." He glanced at Borgil (horned head), who nodded back.

"Best put an arrow in Parrantios. He's a dangerous bastard." The captain leaned closer. "The men can draw lots. The six losers will enter the wood at dawn. A dozen more will block all roads beyond. I will join the rest at Kashorn to await our royal prisoner and the pirate ships of Crenna. There are to be no mistakes. Is that clear? I want that fucking gold Caswallon promised. Every shiny sovereign." He spoke on in whispers, and Cale's ears strained to listen...

"Some kind of conspiracy," the leader was saying, "Belmarius and Halfdan are part of it. Caswallon means to crush them all." Cale spied another cockroach within range. He tried to resist but his stomach grumbled. He pounced, narrowly missing the creature and slipping from his bench with a thump. All eyes turned toward him.

"Have you been listening, you little shite?" The leader's granite stare pinned him to the spot. Cale gaped stupidly. The crossbowman smiled evilly and brandished a curved knife in his grubby fist. He thrust its point into the table.

"Let me silence him, Captain," Borgil ventured.

"You can kill me, I suppose," gulped the boy, "but you'd be wasting a lot of talent. I could be useful to you, Captain Hagan." He watched the cockroach scale the table leg and winced as an iron-clad fist splattered it to oblivion. What a shame, Cale thought. The leader laughed, breaking the silence.

"Do tell me," he barked. "What possible use could be gleaned from a guttersnipe like you? Speak, gobshite, while my patience endures!"

"I'm a trained thief and cutpurse." Cale puffed his chest out amid hoots of derision from the men. He ignored them. "Academy of Kelthara. I recently travelled with two renowned brothers. They trusted me, and because of my skills I won their respect. Unfortunately, my contract expired four days past. My partners were murdered by an unpleasant character called Corin an Fol. Hence..." Cale sighed theatrically and dusted his sleeve. His dignity and gravitas were lost on this audience.

"I'm seeking new employment and am ready to negotiate terms. I" Cale stopped, noticing how the captain's stony eyes had narrowed dangerously.

"What business led you to cross paths with Corin an Fol?" Captain Hagan demanded. "Speak quickly!"

Cale blanched. This Hagan bastard made the twins seem like nursemaids. Hurriedly he recanted his tale, telling of the raid at the smithy, the twin's bloody demise, and the fury of the longswords-man from Fol. Hagan nodded thoughtfully as Cale's tongue dried and his fingers fiddled beneath the table.

"So..." Hagan sighed. He winked at Cale and smiled the sort of smile you'd see on a lazy snake, were you to look hard enough. "Corin has returned from Permio. Interesting. Last I heard he was working for that oily bastard, Silon. A cushy job down there in the sunshine. Wonder why he quit?"

"Gold?" suggested Borgil.

"Aye, probably, but gold from whom and for what? Silon's not big up here, and I know most the players who are. They don't offer contracts to lone operatives—not without my permission. No, I think our boy's got in with Kelwyn."

The captain watched Cale's bug eyes twitch nervously for a moment, then yelled out for the landlord.

"Feed this sweet boy and dry his cloths by the fire," he ordered. "Oh, and give him a hot toddy—the little fucker's half frozen." The innkeeper emerged red-faced and flustered but rushed to obey.

Hagen turned to Cale again. "Maybe you will prove useful, boy. You've certainly got pluck. What's your name?" Cale puffed his chest (not much of a chest, but one had one's pride).

"Cale an Kelthara," he offered, feeling rather pleased with himself. The crossbowman glared at him beneath his helmet, Cale would have to watch that one, he decided.

But hey, things were on the up! After a steaming meal and a hesitant wash, the boy felt that at last his luck had turned. The future looked suddenly very bright. Who needed arseholes like Ulf and his brother anyway? Cale had found his niche. He would become a leading member of Captain Hagan's mercenary band.

***

"What hour is it?" Corin enquired, rolling from his blanket and coughing into the grey morning.

"Almost dawn," replied Roman. "I'll wake the other beauties and the Queen." He grinned. Corin stifled a yawn and rubbed the sleep from his eyes. Close by, the others were stirring as Roman stomped about.

Ariane, already up and sorting her stuff out, appeared bright and fresh with the determined look that seemed her constant companion. Tamersane and Roman were soon busy breaking camp, whilst Galed sat dreaming, bleary eyed, over a cold cup of tea. Corin managed a wry grin. It seemed the poor fellow hadn't got a wink of sleep throughout the whole night.

After a swift breakfast and more tea, they bade farewell to Tamersane and the horse. Corin patted Thunderhoof's chestnut flank. "Take care of him. We've been through a lot together."

"Do not worry," replied the younger man with his winning smile. "Thunderhoof and I are already fast friends!" Thunderhoof snorted in derision but didn't complain when Tamersane heaved

Corin's saddle across his back. "Your bow, Corin, you had best take that."

"Keep it for now. You need speed, and a well-placed arrow might get you out the shit. I'm a crap shot anyway, it would just be more clobber to carry."

"Thanks, I'll look after it." Tamersane awarded the bow a critical eye. "Yew, the best for length and strength. You carry good weapons, Corin an Fol." He turned to Ariane. "Any particular message for the merchant in the south?"

"Just inform him of our plight," she responded. "Silon needs to know how powerful Caswallon has become. He'll need to keep watch on the Usurper's movements within Kelthaine. Go with speed, cousin, and watch your arse. There might be more Groil lurking about."

Tamersane saluted her and waved farewell to his companions. Moments later he was off, easing Thunderhoof down the lane. Corin watched horse and rider fade into the morning.

Farewell, Thunder...Corin straightened Clouter on his back and turned to face the forest.

Queen Ariane's quick mind was racing this morning. Yesterday's attack had shaken her worse than she'd thought. Last night she'd hardly slept. The Queen shuddered thinking of the power wielded by the ruthless new ruler in Kella City.

Caswallon. A man steeped in dark lore, whose obsidian eyes had followed her so rapaciously last year during their visit to the High King's court. And what of Tarin, her stupid, idle, distant cousin? Corin was right, the Prince was an idiot.

But lived he yet? Most likely not. Ariane knew this quest to be a desperate gambit. It was hard to hold positive, but one thing assured her. She studied their guide with professional interest (and a hint of personal, too, were she to own to such) as his long strides led them toward the forest.

This Corin an Fol was a strange one. There was such an air of resentment about him, as if he begrudged his lot in life. But he was arrogant with it, which spoke to her of breeding.

And he had a good face—strong. Ariane sensed a rebellious

streak that didn't take well to authority. She imagined him in court and smiled. This Corin had attitude, though she didn't like the way he goaded Galed. But then Galed needed to toughen up, and Silon had spoken well of Corin. Ariane perceived that somewhere beneath that roguish exterior resided a noble heart. Buried deep, admittedly.

And this Corin was pleasing to the eye, she decided. Not like Tamersane, who was actually ridiculously handsomeprettier than she, if truth be known. The girls back home, they all loved Tamersane. And Tamersane—he loved them all right back, did old silver spoon.

Corin an Fol was not remotely pretty. Rather he was ugly in a very attractive way: his too-long nose, curling lip, sulky gazeand that nasty scar. All made for a weather-beaten, wintery kind of look.

Their guide's long face loomed from one scowl to the next. Despite that the Queen found him fascinating, and she wondered what went on inside that cloudy head. Corin was attracted to her, that much was blatantly obvious. She could read him like a poster. She'd caught him gawping last night. The impudence! What a savage! Ariane smiled invisibly. The days ahead would prove interesting, at least!

Corin paused beneath the canopy of trees. He adjusted the priest's cloak over his steel shirt. He'd recently acquired it from Tamersane.

Give away horse and bow, get this sack of shit instead.

This additional cloak was an encumbrance, and together with his own practical one and weapons, Corin felt weighed down and rather idiotic. The Queen had insisted he dress like the rest of them. He had reluctantly conceded to her wisdom but felt hot and irritable beneath the woolen garment. He turned to face the others.

"Here we leave the road, follow what tracks we can into the forest. We had better tread carefully, people. This is a strange place."

"Best get on with it, then," grumbled Galed, following the others beneath the creaking boughs.

At first they made good progress. The forest felt warm and sheltered after the bleak region they had left. Late autumn sun shimmered through branches of beech and oak. The feeling was one of peace. But as they drew deeper into the wood, the trees closed in on them and it was hard to follow any defined path.

It grew stuffy. The air felt oppressive, and they struggled beneath the weight of their green cloaks. The atmosphere was strange in this wood; a cloying, watchful silence. They felt hidden eyes on their backs, unfriendly eyes. The companions glanced nervously from side to side. Every now and then, Galed jumped at a noise that only he had heard

"I don't like this wood," he grumbled. "There's something uncanny about it. I feel naked beneath these trees despite this heavy cloak."

"There is a presence in the forest," agreed Corin, for once abandoning his dislike of the squire. "But as we mean it no harm, it should leave us be. I hope," he added with a wink. Corin glanced up. The light was dimming every step, for now the leaf-laden branches formed a solid roof above. The track ahead narrowed to scarce more than a deer run. Corin paused for a moment, listening. Beside him Roman wiped sweat from his brow and fingered his sword hilt.

"Fuck this heat," he muttered.

"Corin, are you sure this is the right way?" asked the Queen, sensing his doubt.

"Aye, Queen...Your Highness...ladyship...madam." Corin felt awkward under that acerbic gaze. The Queen raised a brow and revealed the faintest glimmer of a smile. Corin straightened, manfully summoning a confidence he didn't feel.

"The heart of the forest lies to the northeast. As long as we proceed in that direction we can't go far wrong. Besides, most these tracks will lead us to the sacred grove where the Oracle lies. No problem."

"Good," the Queen replied. "I don't want to become lost in this place. These ancient trees dislike our presence here, and I sense other beings dwelling in the darkness." She smirked slightly at his awkward expression.

"Plain Ariane will be sufficient from now on, Corin an Fol. We are all friends here." Corin grinned and winked at Galed, who for his part looked outraged at his Queen's familiarity with this rogue.

"Ariane it is," Corin answered, hoping his face didn't look as red as it felt. It was so damned hot in this wood. It was all right for the Queen and Galed. They weren't wearing steel coats. He and Roman were struggling beneath steel, weaponry and double cloaks. They squished and stooped like soggy bears, with grumpiness to match.

As the day wore on, the stifling heat drained their energy. There was very little air. Here and there a mighty oak, or a tall forbidding ash, blocked their way, and they had to scramble through the thicket of briar and thorn before they could regain it. They struggled and swore, particularly the Queen, Corin noted with surprise. He recorded every expletive, and glanced at Roman in alarm. The big champion grinned like a shark as he squelched on through the gloom.

"She spent a lot of time with my men in the barracks, learning sword craft and strategy," Roman explained. "That and colorful language, too. She's like her old man. The King. Nogel had little time for the niceties of court."

Corin wasn't sure what to think about that. This Ariane wasn't quite what he'd expected in a Queen. He'd imagined a whimsical floaty beauty with lofty airs and graces. Instead, here was someone who could teach Holly a few tricks. That said, she was definitely worth a go and she seemed to like him. And you never know...

Their cloaks were becoming a worsening hazard; they caught on branches and got punctured by inch-long thorns. And drowsiness assaulted them, sapping their will. Galed held back a yawn, looked ready to drop off.

Corin was about to suggest they stop and have a bite to eat when he heard or rather felt a rush of wings above. Cursing, he looked up and saw a raven settle on a low branch a dozen paces away. Its beady eyes watched them pass beneath with silent scrutiny. Corin scowled at the bird, resuming his pace, and the others followed in morbid silence. Roman hung back for a minute eyeing the raven suspiciously.

"I don't like that bird," he muttered, sensing something odd about the creature. "Something's amiss here," he whispered rejoining the others. Roman glanced back, eyes narrowing. There was movement behind them—just a flicker of light but enough to alert Roman's seasoned eye.

Someone follows.

He stared for a moment longer, then he caught it: movement, a figure flitting silently from tree to tree. Roman caught up with Corin and placed a warning hand on his shoulder.

"We are being stalked," he said." We'd better hide up for a while and see if we can find out who it is!"

Corin nodded, cursing under his breath. The last thing they needed was another attack by Groil or any other doggy horrors Caswallon could muster against them. Roman whispered in the Queen's ear, and she nodded. Galed looked on with sweating, creased brow.

They abandoned the track, mindful not to leave footprints and faded like ghosts into the darker trees to their left. These were great evergreens, and their dense resinous blanket wrapped the companions in darkness. The air was even closer here, and their speech was muffled. They stood motionless, listening, waiting...

Long moments passed. The forest held its breath. Then Corin heard it. He nodded slowly at Ariane's champion, who bulked beside him in the silence. The sound was closer, easier to define. Corin recognized soft patter of footsteps hastening along the track.

He looked out carefully from behind the stump, saw six figures dressed as hunters hurrying passed the spot they had just vacated. The leader shouldered a heavy crossbow. His features were hidden beneath a large kettle helmet. Corin recognized him immediately.

Borgil of Leeth, Hagan's brutal lieutenant.

He shot a warning glance at Roman "I know these men," he hissed "They're fucking mercenaries down from Morwella."

"In Caswallon's pay, no doubt." Ariane's dark eyes penetrated the gloom. "Can we lose them, Corin?"

"Aye," said Corin, nodding, "if we journey deeper into this thicket and steer clear of the more obvious tracks. But be on your guard, Quee—Ariane. We are deep inside the forest. It doesn't bode well straying from paths." She nodded and bit her lip in silence.

They crouched uncomfortably for several moments as late flies buzzed in their ears. One settled on Roman's nose.

"Bugger off," he hissed, but the fly ignored him. They waited for several minutes after the last soldier slipped from view. Corin was the first to move. He signaled they follow and with practiced silence weaved a way forward beneath the cloying firs.

For over an hour they struggled at snail's pace. Invisible branches whipped their faces, and roots trapped their feet. The heat was almost overwhelming. It was hard to breath. Their feet felt leaden, and their eyes itched from the resin and bird shit.

"Are you sure we are going in the right direction?" Galed demanded of Corin. The squire resembled a walking sack of sweat. He looked worn out, and Corin could tell he'd almost reached the end of his tether.

"I know what I'm—"

A man's scream sundered the silence.

"That was a death cry," whispered Roman grimly. "Someone else is hunting!" All thoughts were on the mysterious archer who had come to their aid.

"Best we keep moving. Come on, people!" Corin urged. Even Galed needed no further prompting, finding some energy from somewhere and launching himself in the opposite direction from the distant cry.

Minutes passed, maybe half an hour. The squire started grumbling again. Then Corin grinned, feeling a rush of relief flood through him. They'd stumbled across another path.

"I think I know where we are," he told them. "I recognize this track. If followed, it will lead us to a large lake at the other side of these pines."

Corin paused, taking a grateful sip from the water gourd Roman handed him. He wiped his mouth on the priest's cloak before continuing. "If we skirt around the lakeshore and then turn right again, we should come across the Oracle in several hours' time. Follow me."

Corin led them on in haste. The hours were passing and they still had a way to go. It wasn't long before they glanced water shimmering through the trees. Moments later they emerged at the shore of a wide serene lake.

A vision of tranquility, it shimmered before them. Polished by sunlight, the blue expanse caressed emerald swards and tapered into a narrow point at the distant northern shore. From there the rhythmic chime of a tall waterfall could be heard cascading ceaselessly into the perfect blue beneath. Birch and maple framed the shoreline, their gold and crimson mirrored in the water. Nothing stirred; it was as though they'd wandered into a dream.

It was beautiful, like the canvas of a giant watercolor crafted by a joyful god. They felt like trespassers, rude, grubby intruders. They stumbled on, lost for words. Light spilled from clear skies overhead. They forgot the stifling firs and the enemies that stalked them. There was something about this place. Was it witchcraft? The water promised serenity. It called out to them, soothing fraught nerves, quelling fears.

As one, they hurried down to the lake edge. Nothing else mattered. They had to touch that beguiling water, had to bathe in that golden light. They approached the lake, not noticing the slight ripple that stirred in the distance.

"Such beauty..." Ariane sighed. She reached out to touch her pale reflection with a shaking hand.

"Be careful, Queen!" warned Corin, his voice sounding uncouth, uninvited. "Best not touch the water. There's enchantment here. I can sense it."

"Oh, but it's so beautiful," she leaned closer. "A little time spent here will revive our aching limbs and tired minds. Surely"

"Corin is right, Queen; I too feel bewitchment here!" Roman was struggling to stay alert as drowsiness lured him down to the shore. "I think we'd best continue and regain out wits," he urged. She nodded reluctantly; but at her side Galed was lost for words.

Corin quickened his pace. He too felt the lure of the lake but clenched his teeth together. He kept his eyes stoically on the path ahead. He'd heard stories about this place but couldn't recall their content. One word came to mind: *peril.*

They trudged on doggedly, skirting the southern side of the lake. Every footstep was an effort, each breath a heavy chore. Sleep beckoned, promising kindly dreams.

Beneath their feet perfect pebbles chimed in tune with the distant voice of the waterfall.

The surface of the lake was calm perfection. Its depths hinted something else. Something intangible. Danger perhaps? Here and there pale tendrils of mist drifted up like wraiths before vanishing in wan autumn sunlight. Silver arching birches and golden maples fenced the path, casting shadows over water. Occasionally a gentle breeze would stir their limbs, and leaves of crimson and gold would glide and dance before settling silent on the path.

At the far side beyond the birches stood a dock, a small jetty constructed of slender wood, its weed-strewn stanchions lapped soothingly by the water. Moored neatly alongside was a golden barge of eldritch beauty. It rocked gently, bidding them board, promising rest and deep contentment. A dozen golden oars straddled the narrow decking. At its beam, saffron drapes formed a pavilion, concealing hidden wonders within.

The golden barge had a voice. It called to them in watery whispers, bidding them board. Cast off and be free, it told them. Each traveler had an overwhelming conviction: One had only to clamber on deck to be at peace forever. Galed groaned longingly, commenced stumbling his way down toward the jetty.

"Stop, Galed!!" Corin croaked. "The lake is bewitched you idiot. We must be wary!" He cursed as the diminutive squire paid him no heed, hastening down toward the waiting barge.

"Begging your pardon, Ariane," Corin hurtled after her man. He grabbed Galed from behind, dragging him backwards by the cloak pin at his throat. Galed coughed, spluttered, and cursed but at last regained his composure just enough to mutter a rancid 'Thank you.'

"I just wanted to see what was inside that tent," Galed assured the Queen. "I wouldn't have entered." She raised an eyebrow at that.

"Death," muttered Corin. "That's what's inside there. This whole place is a trap."

Reluctantly they left the barge and jetty behind. The shoreline was more open on this side, revealing a sizeable part of the lake. A mile or so from the bank was an island. They hadn't noticed it before. Its gentle slopes were peppered with cedar and spruce. Smoke columned skyward from somewhere in their midst.

Corin looked closer, entranced. He saw a cottage walled by apple blossom, trapping the last of the evening sun. Inside, a fire was under way; the embers glowed with warm invitation.

Then he saw the woman.

He knew her in an instant, of course. *You again...* She looked up and smiled across to him. She seemed very close—almost in arms reach. She called out, her voice warm and rich like liquid amber.

"Corin, my young love. It has been so very long. Have you forgotten me?" The words were carried on ripples approaching from across the water. She stood there beautiful and smilingimpossible yet true. "Come join me. Abandon this foolhardy quest. There is much I could give you, my only love!"

"Corin, do not listen!" Ariane's shrill bark snapped him back into alertness. The Queen's voice was crow harsh compared to the sultry tones of the woman on the island. Corin froze. He had unwittingly been making his way back to the distant barge behind them.

Shite—me too... Corin glanced back across the water, but a sudden mist veiled his vision. He could no longer see the woman. Both the homely house and the island it had stood upon had vanished. Perhaps they had never been there. *But I saw her...*

"BEWARE THE LAKE!" thundered a voice that seemed to come from everywhere at once. "DO NOT DREAM. STAY ALERT!"

Corin and Roman exchanged worried glances, whilst Galed cringed and covered his ears.

"Who are you that speaks?" Ariane called out, wild eyed with hand on her sword hilt. "Declare yourself, spirit!"

There was no answer. Corin suddenly pictured an old man

in a cloak shouldering a bright spear, features occluded by a wide-brimmed hat. He cursed enthusiastically. Beside him, Galed wept openly. Corin was not the only one that had seen a vision of wonder. Roman's face was bleak, and Ariane looked deeply troubled. The Queen said nothing of what she had seen, but her expression was sad, as if recalling a tragic event from her past. She tried to smile.

"I believe we are getting near to the center of this wood! It becomes stranger by the minute."

"Aye, Queen," responded Roman wearily. "It's as if the ancient Faen are among us, stealing our very thoughts!"

"Faen?" Corin looked puzzled. "What are Faen? He vaguely recalled Silon's mentioning that word on Barin's ship, but the wine had occluded his memory.

"The forgotten people. The faerie folk," said Galed, finding his voice. "Do they know nothing of history in Fol? I know it's remote up there, but I'd have thought"

"Enough, Galed!" snapped the Queen. "You were educated in the High Academy at Wynais, a privilege granted to few, even among the wealthy in Kelwyn. The faerie folk have all but disappeared; few of our people remember them now."

"Have they anything to do with the Aralais and the Urgolais?" asked Corin, grinning nastily at Galed. "That lot are quite well known in Fol. I've even met "

"The Faen are different." Ariane paused, glanced around the lake. The music of the waterfall was louder, compelling. It boomed thunderously as they resumed their tread and made hastily toward it. Almost it drowned out Ariane's voice as she explained what she knew.

"Legend says that when the Aralais came to this part of Ansu they found the Faen already here. They paid them scant heed, for these were a secretive folk, dwelling quietly in woods and caves, revealing little of themselves. It's widely suspected that some had dealings with the Urgolais warlocks and became evil.

"Dark Faen, we call them in Wynais. There is a place in the mountains close to my country, a very bad place. Ulan Valek, it was called..." she turned her head as if afraid to utter more. It was

Galed that picked up the tale whilst trudging behind his Queen.

"Many Faen were lost in the terrible war that raged between the Golden Ones and their shadowy brethren. They were caught in the crossfire. Those that survived became even more secretive and were seldom seen.

"To this day the Faen shun the open lands where men dwell, preferring to stay in the forests and groves where the mantle of Elanion, their patron, still partially protects them. Little more is known about them, save that which is written in the ancient records of Arollas the Golden."

"Aye, they lurk and creep about in the shadows," added Roman with a scowl. "I know men who've seen them on the morrow of battle. Grey ghosts walking among the dead, stealing their souls."

"That's just stupid superstition, Roman," retorted the Queen. "Come on." She quickened her step again. "We're nearing the northern shore. Let us heed the voice's warning, be rid of this lake and its fell spirit!"

They hurried. Ahead were tall pines, the ground rising steep on this side of the water. It was strewn with rocks they would have to climb. Beyond these crouched more firs, their dark canopies reaching out toward the setting sun.

The waterfall loomed to their right, deafening their senses, its churning force cascading down in frothing torrents. The booming voice thundered like an angry god descending in wrath.

Corin thought he heard voices in that song. Cold voices. Angry voices. Voices full of hate and resentment. Voices that threatened to engulf the companions, trip and snare them; break them on the rocks, or else drag them beneath cold water and drown them.

"Hurry!" he yelled "Let us be free of this place!"

They reached the jumbled rocks at the edge of the fall and ascended alongside the torrent. The four of them clung desperately to wet moss-covered stone, hauling themselves up as icy spray buffeted their bodies and soaked them to the skin. Corin cursed the heavy priest's cloak yet again. It weighed him down and trapped his ankles, and Clouter's scabbard kept catching on the rocks.

"This sodding waterfall, it's trying to drown us and throw us back into the lake!" yelled Roman. "Hang on, and keep bloody climbing!"

They struggled tenaciously hand over hand, heaving their soaked bodies from rock to rock. Ariane led the way up—she was lighter and spritely on her feet. Galed struggled miserably behind her, whilst Corin and Roman panted and swore as they strained beneath their heavy garments and clanking clutter.

Water lashed their faces with icy spears and battered their tired bodies in its hunger to drag them down. Corin could hear the voices clearly roaring in his right ear, promising him a watery grave below. He shut them out and heaved mightily his strong limbs, carrying him passed Galed and Ariane too.

At last he reached the stony ridge that basined the head of the waterfall. Cursing and gasping for breath, Corin turned to see how his friends were faring. He leaned down, offering his hand to the Queen, who grabbed it gratefully.

Beneath her, Roman pushed an exhausted Galed over the edge and rolled onto the bank with a relieved grunt. There they remained for a time coughing, cursing, and eventually regaining some composure.

Corin was first on his feet. He studied the terrain in the fading light, trying to discern an opening in the wall of forest ahead. They were trapped on an island outcrop, a slippery rock assaulted on all sides by the rushing stream.

Corin scratched his ear and farted. "We'll have to wade through that," he said, not relishing the idea. No matter. They were wet through already.

"What if it drags us back down?" Galed moaned.

"Well, don't fucking let it," answered Corin. "What do you suggest, we fly over?"

"Oh, piss off."

"Men…" Ariane plunged into the water and led the way into the rushing stream. Corin gaped stupidly at her and then followed, gasping, for the water's touch was even colder than the waterfall's spray had been.

It was hard to draw breath. They linked arms, stepping carefully, as the stones were weed covered and slippery underfoot. Corin stumbled on a sharp rock that grazed his leg. He swore, then glancing up, froze in astonishment. Beside him Ariane and the others gasped in wonder.

On the bank of the stream watching them calmly sat the strangest being Corin had ever seen. She looked like a young girl, but her skin had a pale blue tinge to it, and the long hair that scarce covered her nakedness sparkled like silver. She attended that hair with a fishbone comb and watched them silently—as a cat watches birds feeding at table.

"A Nix!" exclaimed Ariane in wonder. "Be on your guard. She is most dangerous!"

"Is she Faen?" whispered Corin, fingering Biter's hilt. They waded over in haste, anxious to distance themselves from the strange girl on the rock.

They were almost at the far bank when several things happened at once. The Nix rose up laughing, her mouth revealing perfect pearls of razor-sharp teeth, all neatly filed into points.

To Corin's left, Ariane screamed in horror as a pale sinewy arm grasped her leg, pulling her down into the icy water!

Corin had Biter out before he knew it. He hacked down viciously at the arm, severing it, and noticed with horror how it was covered in scales like a fish. He had scant time to dwell on that fact. Other arms erupted from the water, tugging at their drenched cloaks.

The water churned and tossed in whirling eddies. The four had their weapons free. Even Galed had mustered the wits to grasp his axe and was chopping down in frenzied panic.

Corin sliced and stabbed with Biter, Roman swore and hewed, whilst Ariane skewered fishy arms with her rapier in silent fury, and all the time the Nix's cruel laughter echoed across the bank.

"Corin an Fol," she called, her voice sounding like it came from deep underwater. "Brave, sweet Corin an Fol. Would you fight so desperately to save me? Don't I deserve love as much as that Queen you so want to fuck?" She laughed out loud seeing Corin blanch as he sliced a fishy arm from Galed's leg.

"And Roman, steadfast captain loyal and soooo strong, love me. Fuck me. *Love meeeeee!*" Roman ignored her, just kept hacking.

"Come, both of you. Join with me! Forget the stupid little Queen and her doomed mission. I will take you beneath the lake to my wondrous home, show you pleasures you cannot begin to imagine. Forget this foolish quest. You will fail. Join me instead beneath the water, and love me. I need loving! I hunger for it!"

The Nix stood up to reveal her naked body. Corin stole a sly peep between swipes. It was cold and perfect, if a little too blue for Corin's taste. Still she was lovely, and he wouldn't rule out a quick one should chance allow. Then he cursed as something bit into his leg.

"Argh!" Corin stabbed down with fury at what seemed to be a fish with a human head. The thing just gulped at him as it clung tenaciously to his thigh. Corin tore it off in disgust and fought his way over to the bank where the others, exhausted, joined him, Roman having finally dispatched the last of the fish things with his broadsword. Behind them the stream settled, resumed its natural course as if nothing had happened. Corin looked across at where the Nix had been. She had vanished from sight, although he thought he heard her voice calling from far below the lake.

"Come back, Corin, my love. There is still time. Do you stir beneath that cloak? Deny your destiny. It will ensnare you. Love me instead. Fuck me. Taste me..."

Corin focused on the forest ahead.

The light was fading fast as they distanced themselves from the lake of the Nix. They trudged on in silence, minds tired and confused, bodies battered and bruised. At least no one had been badly hurt by the attack in the stream, but that assault had left them all shattered and drained.

Once again, the desire for sleep tugged at them. Corin was worried. Time was passing quickly, and he wanted to get to the sacred glade of the Oracle before nightfall. He found a new track; this one was broader, allowing good progress, and their spirits revived for a time. Corin led the way in long strides, the Queen and Galed behind him, whilst Roman's bulk guarded their rear.

As evening deepened, the forest opened out. The trees were bigger hereabouts, allowing more light. A welcome breeze carried scents of wood mold and fungus. The path showed deer tracks, and once briefly Corin locked eyes with a fox. Birds chattered above then grew silent as light faded. They gained a small ridge and stopped in sudden surprise. Corin's hand rested on his sax hilt.

Blocking their path was a man dressed from head to foot in green leather, small in build, raven-haired and whip lean. A single braid travelled the length of his back, and his features bordered on swarthy.

Coal-black eyes calmly appraised them. His age was hard to judge, but there were thin lines on his weathered brow. His hands and cheeks were engraved with faint spirals: tattoos, intricate and complex. Covering his shoulders was a magnificent russet cloak that seemed to shimmer in the gloom.

None of this Corin noticed. Instead it was to the great longbow his eyes were drawn, and the quiver of grey-fletched arrows accompanying it. The archer!

So you show yourself at last.

Chapter 14

The Goddess Speaks

The archer watched them in silence for a moment, but when Ariane made to step forward he raised his left hand, bidding her wait. This she did with a flushing of cheeks, not being used to such imperious gestures from strangers.

"I am called Bleyne," the archer announced in a cool musical voice. "I serve the Mistress of the Trees. She awaits your arrival at Valen-Durannin."

"Where is that?" Roman asked. Beside him, Corin kept two eyes on the archer, appraising their chances should this turn ugly.

"It is the sacred glade in which stands the Oracle of Elanion," Bleyne replied. This archer had an annoyingly arrogant air about him, as if he knew everything and they knew nothing. Corin was becoming vexed. He commenced surveying the stranger with professional distrust. He was skinny and hard, quick and dangerous, and they all knew how well he used that bow.

"It was you that came to our aid yesterday, was it not?" he demanded of the archer.

Bleyne shrugged. "I have followed your noisy trek through the forest," he responded elusively. "You people have more enemies than you think. There are creatures far worse than Groil seeking to thwart your passage." Ariane raised her eyebrows at that, and Galed paled visibly, but the archer changed the subject before they could question him.

"The High Goddess desires you pass through her domain unhurt. She deems you carry a candle of hope against the growing dark. Old Night stirs beneath his mountain, and his legions fester in their charnel pits. Dark spirits return to reclaim their lands from mankind, who usurped them long ago."

"How wonderful," muttered Corin under his breath. Not only was this Bleyne patronizing, he was evidently cheerful too.

Ariane tried again. "We are hunted by mercenaries in the pay of Caswallon the Usurper. Have you encountered any?" the Queen enquired.

Bleyne shrugged. "Three are dead, three more fled. There are other footpads lurking at our fringes. They'll not enter the forest again." The archer's eyes were faintly ironic; it was another thing that irritated Corin.

"It was unwise of you to stray so close to Vaniel's lake," Bleyne told them. "She is a vengeful spirit. She remembers how Kell and his sons cruelly pursued her kin with their long spears, driving them ever further from their realms, slaying them at will. Kell believed they were wicked kin of the Elementals he knew back in Gol, and he trusted them not. Faen have long memories, and Vaniel still hates the sons of men. You would have been undone had not the Goddess bid her let you pass."

"She didn't exactly let us pass," countered Ariane with a frown. "We were attacked by her...things."

"She was merely being playful, Queen," responded the archer with a slight raise of an eyebrow. "Nixes like to play before they eat."

"Eat," muttered Galed looking horrified. "Eat what?"

The archer neglected to respond to so stupid a question. Corin felt a cold shiver grip his bowels. He glanced at Roman. The big man's face looked pale in the fading light. Better not to think about it.

Bleyne surveyed them for a minute further then urged them forward with another imperial finger. "Follow me." Bleyne turned without waiting for a reply. Within moments he'd vanished from view up the track.

"He's a bit up his own regions," muttered Roman and Corin nodded. Ariane silenced them with a look.

"He saved us, remember." Reluctantly they nodded whilst Galed just looked miserable behind them. "Let's get moving," Ariane said. "I don't think this Bleyne is one to wait around."

They followed in haste; eventually spying Bleyne's shadow flitting through the trees ahead. They hurried to join him, matching their pace to his. Galed needed to skip and jump to keep up, panting and issuing wide, gulping stares.

This Bleyne character appeared to glide effortlessly along the path without stirring so much as a leaf. Even Corin was short of breath after half an hour at this pace. The Queen was holding her own, though her cheeks glowed and she stumbled once or twice. Roman looked like a furnace. Bleyne held the pace, indifferent to their discomfort.

Finally the track broadened, and great old trees filed their flanks. Something caught Corin's eye down among the roots and rotting leaves. A motionless shape, half hidden in the bracken on the side of the track. It was the body of a man. Embedded in his throat was a grey-feathered arrow.

"You need not be concerned about pursuit whilst in the forest." Bleyne stooped gracefully to regain his shaft. "No man may bring evil here and live!" He resumed his pace with fluidity and animal grace. Galed groaned, and the others set their teeth and stomped on behind.

Dusk settled among the groves. Bleyne led them on for two more hours without once checking his pace. Corin wondered how much longer Galed could keep this up. He had been surprised by the squire's resilience but could see that the little man was fading fast. He'd thrown up twice and looked half dead.

Bleyne, glancing back now and then, appeared not to notice, or if he did, he certainly didn't care. Corin glared at the archer's back. He didn't like being indebted to this bastard. Bleyne had good timing and could shoot a bow—so what. It didn't mean he was on their side.

Corin glanced up, saw a lone star shining above the trees. It was getting dark and the atmosphere eerie. Corin felt edgy and sensed they were being watched. Now and then he caught furtive movement beneath dark boughs. Movement on two legs, not four, and not human legs, of that he felt certain.

He said nothing, just tightened his lips and kept walking. Woods. Corin vowed to stay clear of them from now on. They were a breeding ground for all manner of goblins and spooks, of late most of which seemed to cherish an unhealthy interest in him. Why? Better not to know. Corin ground his teeth and muttered obscenities under his breath.

Night fell silent, and the trees closed in. High above their weary heads, the stars glinted and the full moon winked through latticed branches, casting witchy light on the forest floor.

It was deathly quiet. They had entered the region of the Oracle. The night air hung heavy with beguilement. Far away, an owl called out. Seconds later, another answered.

Silence again. Corin shivered, pulling the still partially damp cloak around his shoulders and adjusting Clouter's scabbard on his aching back. He could feel the thud of his heartbeat.

Tight lipped, he followed the archer, who at last had slackened the pace. Corin, glancing back, was pleased to see Galed still in the land of living, though he didn't look well. Corin grinned at him and Galed squinted back.

Ariane's sharp features were enhanced by the moon's silver sheen. She looked driven, inspired, and hungry for what awaited them. Corin could not help but admire her. This Queen was match for any fighting man he'd known. Again he wondered at his chances of pulling her. Slim, but then his odds had never been good with posh women. She caught his roving eye and turned away, a faint smile hinting the corner of her mouth. Beside her, Roman panted like an ancient hound.

All around, silence hung like a headsman's axe: tangible, suspended in air, and waiting to fall. The track ran smooth and level beneath their feet. Above their heads, the branches refused to stir. Corin thought he heard whispering voices in the darkness. More wood goblins, he suspected, and refused to listen.

After a final steep climb that left them again breathless (and Galed almost on his knees), they entered a broad open glade, a grassy sward that sighed beneath their feet. The air was cooler here, fresh and clean. After the dense canopy of the trees, it felt welcoming and pure. They were revived by its clarity. Even Galed managed a faint grin. Far above, the sky painted a patchwork of stars. The moon rode free from the treetops, its face filling the glade with silvery blue light.

They stopped at Bleyne's signal. Corin glanced ahead. At the center of the sward stood a circle of standing stones that seemed to float beneath the moonlight. Tall and ominous, they loomed. Blue light glistened upon their surface. Ariane sighed, drinking in the enchanted air. Roman coughed, and Galed tried to slow his rasping breath.

Bleyne approached the circle of stones. He turned to address them in a quiet voice.

"You are come at last to Valen-Durannin," Bleyne told them. "Within this ring of stone resides the Oracle of Blessed Elanion, high Goddess of Ansu, Queen of the Faen, and Mistress to the Trees. Approach slowly, and speak no word. This is hallowed ground!"

Corin felt the small hairs stiffen on his neck. Again he was faced with something he didn't understand. He didn't like it—not one bit. Fear tugged at him as did a desire to run.

He steeled his nerves and scratched his scar, glanced at the others, who looked as worried as he did—all bar the Queen, who was rearing to go. Bleyne waved them forward, and Ariane didn't hesitate. Corin, less keen, glanced at her back. He took a furtive step forward and then another and more still, at last joining the archer at the stone circle and glaring uneasily about.

The other men followed close behind, moonlight illuminating their pale worried countenances. Poor Galed's face was a mask of fear, and Roman Parrantios' expression grim, as if he drew near the hour of his doom. Corin scowled and glared at the tall stones, expecting one to reach out and grab him.

But Queen Ariane approached the stone circle with ill-disguised eagerness. Here at last she hoped they would gain knowledge of Prince Tarin, the Tekara's whereabouts, and how to stop Caswallon. Here too, mayhap they would glean an insight into the darkness aiding the sorcerer.

At Bleyne's word they entered the stone circle, eyes wide with amazement. The ring was huge, appearing much larger than it had from without. Bleyne led them through a maze of stone towers, sloped inward facing each other. Each stone sloped twelve feet tall, culminating with a jagged point, like so many hounds teeth, a seemingly endless circle within a circle.

A spiral of confusion. Within minutes they all felt disorientated and confused. Corin, glancing back, could see no way out. It was as though the stones were closing in behind them whilst they stood frozen to the spot.

Corin felt an icy sweat run down his back. He glanced down at his feet.

Bad mistake. The ground was moving and the stones rotating in a most alarming way. Corin wondered whether he was under some spell and would wake relieved in some sleazy brothel down in Raleen, with a lively wench sitting on his chest. No such luck.

Round and round the tall stones went, whirling faster and faster. Corin's head felt giddy and sick. He heard a soft thud beside him and saw that Galed had stumbled to the ground. He lay still, his hand covering his spewy mouth. Corin reached down and dragged the squire back to his feet.

"Don't throw up here," he urged Galed. "You'll anger the Goddess!"

Galed looked at him daggers but said nothing, keeping his hand over his mouth, stoically biting back the nausea that was almost consuming him.

Then miraculously the spinning stopped. They were in the very center of the circle of circles. Before them loomed a large round well, domed by a roof of silver that glistened and sparkled beneath the moon and starlight. Corin was first to approach it. He peered over the rim and grabbed the sides in panic as vertigo seized him.

Shite and buggerations...

The well appeared bottomless and empty. Corin could see his reflection encased by stars, yet there was no water to reflect it. He was about to tell the others, but they were all looking at someone standing behind him.

Then he turned and saw the woman.

Oh, it's you again.

Corin's jaw dropped in astonishment. Was this another illusion? Some foul, cruel trickery? But no, she was real this time, standing serene in the moonlight, the breeze lifting the hem of her long green-gold dress.

The woman from his dreams, hers was a face Corin would never forget. Tall and stately she stood before him, with hair like burnished copper and shimmering dress of emerald, with golden trimmings at cuff and hem, loose and flowing, yet clinging to her ample curves. It had been she he had seen on the island in the lake, and at the window in the ruined village. That same beautiful mysterious face had haunted his dreams since the terrible day in Finnehalle when the raiders had come. She hadn't aged at all.

Who are you really?

She turned toward him with a smile.

"And warm greeting to you, Corin son of Fol." Her voice was bittersweet, honey-coated lemon. "So you have taken up the challenge of your destiny. Good. You will need all your strength in the weeks ahead." Corin gaped at her stupidly, his tongue rendered silent by her beauty. She smiled again and turned away.

"Come!" The woman addressed them all. "The Goddess awaits you!"

"Who are you?" Corin croaked, and she turned to him again. Her gold-green eyes tugged at his soul. They always had. He'd known her kindness for scarce minutes very long ago, and no other woman had ever come so close to unlocking the troubled confines of his heart.

She'd stalked his dreams pitilessly through the years, and she had returned. Whole and earthly. It was almost too much. Almost. "I saw you on the lake," Corin floundered. Women had always been his weakness, particularly this woman. His dream woman.

"You saw what you wanted to see on the lake," she answered quietly, her words flowing like liquid amber. "That was another's design.

"My true name cannot be revealed in this place. Like my sisters, I have many. You, mortal, may call me Vervandi. It was a name I bore long ago, and will again in days to come. You have heard it mentioned before, and it will suffice here."

Vervandi... Corin remembered the words of the witch at the ford. He wanted to enquire further but felt tongue tied and confused. She turned to address the others again. "Come now! Time marches. Elanion is waiting!"

She bade them gather around the stone well. Corin noticed that Bleyne was nowhere to be seen. He shrugged. The archer must have business elsewhere. No great loss.

Corin watched Vervandi lead the Queen toward the yawning chasm of the well. Ariane's dark eyes shone with excitement and fear. Her hands shook, and she shivered. The other woman towered over her. She looked like a child beside Vervandi.

"Come Queen of Kelwyn!" The woman called Vervandi beckoned. "It is time. You must summon the spirit of the Goddess!"

Ariane nodded. She'd waited so long for this moment. She braced herself and leaned over the well wall, staring deep into the bottomless void, her heart racing and chest thudding.

Answers, I need answers.

Ariane sank to her knees with only her head showing above the rim. Her hands were taut as they gripped the cold stone of the Oracle's edge.

"Goddess of light!" Queen Ariane called down in a clear voice while the three men watched silently behind. "I have lived to serve you all my life. You and no other. I beseech your help in this your hallowed grove! Dark days have fallen on our lands, High Lady. King Kelsalion is dead, the Four Kingdoms in disarray. Our enemy, the sorcerer Caswallon, grows stronger. He threatens your people too. The land is in peril!"

Corin and Roman exchanged worried glances while Galed's eyes bulged in dread. Vervandi said nothing but still leaned over the Queen like a willowy sentinel.

"Come, Mistress of the Trees!" Ariane's face was rigid with concentration. "We need your guidance, Earth Mother, I seek knowledge concerning Prince Tarin and the remnants of the shattered crown, the Tekara. Goddess, help us, I beseech thee!" Her words trailed off into the night. Nobody moved. The air was fused with potent silence.

Then sudden lightning speared the cobalt sky, striking a stone and splitting it deafeningly in two. The violence of that noise blasted their ears and set them ringing. The men gasped and stumbled, but Ariane was locked in trance. She alone held to her task.

Then Vervandi spoke: "Behold the Goddess. Elanion comes!"

***

Still. So very quiet and still in the glade. Deathly hush. Even time has stopped in this hallowed place.

At first Corin sees nothing. Then he notices a smoky substance taking form above the stone well. He watches, entranced. The smoke fills his lungs like heady wine. Corin feels tipsy, confused. He is unable to move, his breath frozen in time. The substance takes shape before his dazzled eyes.

It becomes a woman. Myriad whirling colors parade her essence. She shifts from blue to emerald, carmine to golden yellow. Changing always, drifting in and out of vision. Corin watches in dream state. Forgotten his silent companions, forgotten the Queen still kneeling at the well, and forgotten the woman Vervandi leaning over her. He watches and believes that he dreams.

She rises from the well in smoky spirals, a towering figure filling the night sky until the stars and moon crown Her shrouded head and shoulders. Corin watches, his mind weird, a cocktail of perplexity and fear, hope and excitement. She manifests before his eyes.

The Goddess Elanion. She is a paradox, solid but quicksilver, motionless yet shifting sands. One moment She appears serene and beautiful, beyond the ken of mortal beings. Then Her face melts away, becoming hideous and wrinkled like that witch at the ford.

Her body changes constantly, from young to old, plump to gaunt. Only the eyes are constant, great golden orbs with violet centers. Alien and merciless is that gaze, immediate yet distant, ice cold surmounted by fire.

She speaks. Her voice is everywhere and nowhere. It's in the trees, beyond the skies, and down beneath the crusty earth.

The Goddess speaks...

"...The one you seek is far from here. In Crenna shall you answers find. Upon that isle in dungeons dark, he that awaits you will appear.

"Southward then must your journey lie, beneath the deserts burning sun. Beyond Ty-tander's searing flame, in mines of crystal shall he be found: the Blinded Smith to aid your cause.

"To that Great Cavern three must go. The tortured one will crown re-forge. Then shall war begin at will.

"And when crown again is wrought anew, then shall the true King be revealed..."

The voice fades. Corin shuffles his feet. No one else moves. Corin hears a squeaky sound and registers it as the Queen speaking at the well. He tries to listen, but his mind is wandering through foggy corridors.

"So Tarin is imprisoned in Crenna?" Ariane's words are excited, rushed.

The voice of the goddess fills the night again.

"Where the Prince is found, there too the crown. To Crenna must you sail."

"What of Caswallon?" Ariane's voice is barely audible. "How can we defeat him?" she asks, and Corin strains to listen.

"He is but a servant of what comes behind. They will weave a web to trap you. In yourselves you must believe, to overcome the growing dark."

The voice changes, softens. It reaches out, touches them all, warming and comforting. Corin smiles like a man just released from a heavy chore. He feels tired but refreshed, worn down but happy—a strange emotion for him, that.

"Go with our blessing. Rest in the arms of the forest tonight. Tomorrow make haste to Kashorn by the sea.

"Courage shall you need in the weeks ahead. The game commences. Soon shall more be revealed!"

That hypnotic gaze falls on Ariane crouched below.

"Young Queen, your father's strength flows deep within you. The men by your side shall not let you down. Even the least of them shall prove his worth in time."

Then the violet golden gaze turns to the others standing there, speaking words that only they can hear.

To Corin she says this, her voice filling his head like the tolling of a bell.

"Wayward wanderer, your destiny approaches! My daughters will aid you when they can, though others seek to trap you.

Hold to courage, not self-doubt. In you rests mankind's central hope. Seek your father on the High Wall. Among the outlaws shall you find him, when snow is falling fast.

Beware of Darkvale and She who weaves her midnight webs. Undeyna is His creature. She will snare you if she can..."

Corin's face is deathly pale—gone is the warm peaceful feeling, replaced by trepidation and worry.

"I do not understand," he croaks up at the shifting entity in the sky. "My father died long ago, and who is this Undeyna person?" He feels lost, weighed down by something he cannot comprehend. "Why am I stalked by otherworldly beings?" Corin asks, then dares a bigger question.

"Who am I?"

"These answers shall you find in the months ahead. Perhaps."

There is kindness in her voice; it is something he hadn't expected. Kindness laced with sadness, the ageless sorrow of an immortal doomed to watch the Weaver's dance—to see things of beauty fade to ruin.

"I knew one like you once when I wore a mortal guise. Erun Cade I loved for a time, though he knew it not."

Corin made to speak, but the goddess's face hardened and she addressed them all.

"Peril paves your road. Yet friends you have and more shall meet, before the war commences. We are at the quickening again. The pendulum swings wide; Golganak wakens, thus Callanak too.

"Sword and spear will play their part. Seek the sword at rainbow's end when the time is right. In Laras Lassladan can it be found, within the caves of morning.

"Old Night is waking, shaking his bonds, and gathering his sundered limbs. He knows his window of chance draws nigh. Our brother the Huntsman rides out laughing, on this the eve of war...."

The towering image of Elanion is fading. The stars shine through her raiment. Her essence still fills the night sky, but even as they watch with crooked necks, it disperses like smoke on a windy morning.

She speaks a final time.

"Go forth with Our blessing. Bleyne I give you, for his destiny lies alongside yours. Go, my children. Our love goes with you..."

The voice trails off far beyond the trees. The Goddess fades to smoke and mist then is gone. Only her eyes remain. They flicker twice then vanish too. Then the spell breaks and the forest breathes once more.

***

Corin's mind was racing. Was he some kind of freak? He wondered if the goddess had spoken similarly to the others. Judging by their expressions, it seemed likely.

Galed was pale and troubled, even Roman looked decidedly glum. Only the Queen appeared infused, vindicated by what she had heard. Corin scratched his ear and yawned. He could only take so much of this weirdness and was feeling hungry and grumpy again.

Vervandi broke the silence with a brisk clap. She beckoned the travelers follow. Corin blinked up at the stars.

More bloody walking. He felt sluggish and befuddled, like he was awakening from a deep sleep. And perhaps he was.

"Come," Vervandi urged them again. "There is some way to go before you can rest. It is not wise for mortals to remain too long in Valen-Durrannin. Bleyne has scouted the forest for footpads. He will await us near the northern fringes. Once there, you can rest. We must make haste! It is some miles off and the night is passing!"

The companions shook themselves into weary motion. Galed groaned noisily at the thought of walking again. The ethereal presence of Elanion had left them all stunned and speechless. They felt exhausted, worn out by the rigors of their day. Even Ariane failed to stifle a yawn. Bleary-eyed they shambled into motion, following the willowy redhead into the gloom.

Vervandi led them through the stones, thankfully motionless and grey, out into the glade beyond. Once there, they joined another path beneath the trees. All was silent save the distant hooting of another owl. Night deepened in the Forest of Dreams.

Queen Ariane walked in silence, her thoughts solid on the journey ahead. Behind her, Roman's strong face was set with resignation. He fingered his sword hilt and glowered up at the trees. The Queen's champion was eager to leave this forest with its mysteries and strange beings. Tomorrow they'd return to the lands of men. Not before time, he thought. Galed shuffled and groaned behind him, somehow still keeping to his feet.

Last came Corin an Fol, wrapped in gloom, his heart full of foreboding. He didn't understand many of the Goddess's words, but that seemed to be the norm of late. Hints and innuendoes. His mind felt like a witch's kettle, cloudy, churning, and full of nasty things.

He scratched the vivid scar on his brow. It was itching again. Elanion's words echoed through the tired corridors of his mind. He thought about Vervandi, half hidden in the gloom ahead.

Corin shook his head and focused on the moonlit path. He felt alone, haunted by shadows that stalked his every move. Like a drunken fool Corin watched the swaying hips of the tall woman in the gloom. Strangely, he drew no pleasure from the sight.

It was quite late when they topped a round hill, its green

dome high above the trees. Strewn about its northern base was a tumbled cluster of rocks marking the entrance to a large cave. They clambered down, Galed stumbling and falling twice.

Bleyne awaited them at the entrance to the cave mouth. He stood impassive and unmoving, his silhouette casting long shadows in the moonlight.

"Here we are at last," announced Vervandi. "These caves are sacred to the Goddess. No evil will come to this place. Rest for what is left of the night. Sleep without dreaming. There is fire for warmth, and Bleyne will have prepared a meal."

This last proved true, for the smell of roasting meat had greeted them at the cave's mouth. Corin felt his stomach rumble. They hadn't eaten since breakfast. The thought of hot food revived his flagging spirits greatly.

Once inside, they gaped at the beauty surrounding them. The cavern was huge. Moonlight flickered off its many walls, revealing hidden passages leading deep beneath the forest floor.

Weird twisted stalactites reached down like frozen lovers to the waiting stalagmites below. Water chimed out of the darkness within. Ahead lay a deep pool. Its crystal depth reflected starlight from a hole in the cavern above.

Corin shook his head in wonder, his hunger and weariness forgotten for the moment. He thought he heard soft music emanating from somewhere below. It sounded like a harp. Perhaps it was the running water. He couldn't be sure.

"Where is this place?" he asked Vervandi. "I've not heard of it before."

"It is called Caromanya. The Cave of Wonders, in your tongue," she replied. "It is a place of peace and contemplation. Come. Time to eat!"

She led them to where the archer sat roasting a large deer on a spit. He nodded curtly before cutting them tender chunks with his hunting knife. The meat was flavored with wild garlic and rosemary, and they consumed it with enthusiasm.

Finally sated, they tossed their green cloaks on the cave floor and made ready for welcome sleep. Behind them Bleyne's fire roared and flickered, casting wondrous shadows on the cavern walls.

Corin yawned and stretched. He shut his eyes then opened them again. His restless gaze fell on Vervandi. He studied that beautiful face as the firelight burnished her hair. She caught his gaze and smiled. But there was sadness in her eyes, and Corin turned away, unsure as what to think.

Who are you, Vervandi? Why have you returned after all this time?

The fire flickered and crackled, and the weird harp-song sound of water echoed in the distance. Corin rolled deeper into Tamersane's cloak, mercifully dry. Vervandi was talking to the Queen.

Vervandi. The name meant nothing to him yet was so familiar. Another riddle, but he was too tired to dwell on it. Corin felt sleep steal upon him. He glanced one last time at the copper-haired woman whispering to the young Queen.

In the morning Vervandi was gone.

Chapter 15

The Valley

The girl stood naked and shivering by the door. He glanced her way, his hooded eyes taking in her pale breasts and sliding down to briefly acknowledge the dark thatch nestled between her thighs.

She was raven haired and perhaps nineteen. He didn't know her name—not that that was relevant. The parents had been taken by Perani for questioning. Once proud nobles, they would be Groil feed now.

His Groil, a gift from the Dog Lord himself. More had arrived last night with more still promised, though he'd sent three score up north to scan the wilderness and sniff out any sign of Ariane san Kelwyn. No word on that yet, and almost a week had passed.

That little bitch-minx alone thwarted his authority. He'd chosen this girl partially because her dark hair and eyes reminded him of the Queen, and he'd had her locks cropped to shoulder length, in Ariane's boyish style. Later, when he was plowing her, Caswallon would scrape her back bloody with his sharp nails and bite her flesh—his need for the Queen bad.

It was a power thing, control, as if by hurting this creature he could somehow undermine his enemy. He'd let the girl go when spent, send her out broken and bleeding to walk the streets alone, prey to whatever predators lurked out there. And there were many.

She wouldn't last long, poor thing. Kella City was a place of terror now. Perani's secret police arrested any with the faintest hint of loyalism. Perani was proving an asset, efficient and reliable.

He'd had his doubts about the veteran general initially. But the man was greedy and a social climber. He'd do well in Caswallon's world, until he became expendable and met an untimely end. Keep them close, and never trust them.

Caswallon turned his attention to the hearth, which even now crackled and hissed like a grouchy hound. It was here that the Dog Lord chose to appear before him. Three times the old one had come—each visit leaving Caswallon edgy and covered in sweat.

The Dog Lord was evil incarnate. But the gift of power came with a price. No matter. He was more than willing to pay. Caswallon was *their* ally now (the word servant had been used, but he'd brushed that aside).

They needed a clever mortal with spell craft to help enable their return to power in these lands once theirs. In return Caswallon would be given knowledge and power beyond mortal ken as well as the gift of immortality were he to prove useful enough. There was much to be gained by this ghastly union.

Caswallon allowed himself a thin smile. Rael Hakkenon had the boy to play with, and his sub-contractor Hagan of Morwella would soon apprehend Ariane and the others, should they miraculously evade his Groil hounds, which of course they wouldn't.

All was going to plan. He would have Ariane brought before him, whipped and servile. She would be his puppet, his toy. His smile deepened, anticipating that future joy. He turned to the girl.

"Come here." She shuffled across, her eyes glazed as deer brought low by archer's arrow. Caswallon thrust his left hand up under her chin, forcing her head back, whilst his right slid down her belly and eased into the soft flesh between her thighs. She said nothing—even her breathing hardly changed. She was like a dead thing. Caswallon scowled.

"Your parents dared challenge my authority," he told her,

lowering his left hand to squeeze a breast. "They were spies for Kelwyn." He lied. "After long torture they told all. Now their bodies are Groil feed, the bones crunched and gnawed and the marrows sucked clean." Still she didn't respond.

Patience exhausted, Caswallon struck her hard across the cheek, sending her sprawling on her face. He took her then, hard and fast from behind, and once done hurled her out the door. The bitch had given him scant pleasure. It had been like shafting a corpse.

He called out and the retainer came—the new retainer, the old (human) one having been eaten. This Groil had arrived with the new batch. Like Drol it had a brittle command of words, but unlike Two-Heads, this one had certain special qualities.

Flail, Caswallon called this current favorite (Drol having been demoted to second Groil, and not happy about it), though he had no idea if the creature had a name. Flail was bright for a Groil. It could speak in longer grunts than Drol and was dependable.

Unusually (even for a Groil) Flail had six arms and four legs. A large belt housed the six serrated blades clanking at its waist. Another interesting feature was the third eye in the back of Flail's hairless head. Even with its slow brain the creature missed little.

Caswallon addressed his retainer.

"Cast that pitiful creature out on the streets. Do not touch her, leave her to the night. And summon Perani. I would speak with him!"

Flail nodded stiffly, saluted with all six claws and then shuffled and stooped out the door and commenced clonking and scraping back down the stairs.

Caswallon leaned back in his chair, he opened a flask of brandy and took a long pull. It would soon be time to summon the Dog Lord, and he'd prefer not be sober.

***

They awoke refreshed, as bright fingers of sunlight filtered into the cave from without, warming their limbs and banishing sleep. Roman rubbed his eyes and grinned. The cut on the side of his face was starting to mend. He felt good this morning and was more than ready for the day ahead.

"Well, I don't know what the rest of you think," he announced after dunking his bearded face in the cool, clear water of the pool. "I'll be glad to leave this forest. However, I cannot say that I relish the thought of visiting Crenna overmuch."

"Good luck with that," said Corin. He had no wish to travel within a hundred miles of that cursed island—the occupants having murdered his kin. He balked at the thought of the Queen's journeying there. "Bad idea, I think," he said. "Goddess's advice bit dodgy in that area." Roman nodded and looked thoughtful. Corin, feeling awkward, stared at the cave entrance.

It's not my concern. Once I've been paid, I'll slip away.

Corin had no intention of boarding Barin's ship. He'd see them safe from Kashorn Harbor, watch them set sail into the sunset, and then return to Fol with some financial recompense for his efforts. That was all he had promised Silon. But he still felt like a deserter leaving this Queen and her men to deal with Crenise scum.

Roman looked at him thoughtfully for a moment.

"Did you say something?" Roman asked.

"I was only thinking out loud."

"Well there's certainly plenty to think about, but not before breakfast."

Corin consented readily to this opinion. He unsheathed Biter, gave it a critical eye, and then ran a whetstone down its steely length. He felt uneasy and edgy. It seemed like betrayal leaving these new companions to their fate.

Bloody Crenna of all places—why didn't she let that little shite Tarin fester and rot on that island? Morals and valiant deeds—they got you nowhere in this world. Cunning, coin, and an edge with a blade, that was what kept a fellow ahead. Simple, really.

But despite his self-assurance, Corin was confused. The words the Goddess had spoken to him were like flies buzzing in his head. Though he couldn't really recall what she had said, he felt somehow compelled to continue in this fruitless voyage.

And what would returning promptly to Finnehalle gain him

save a good romp with Holly (which was close to reason enough, on reflection).

Still, he was troubled. Corin glanced around for the woman Vervandi, hoping he could question her further and was disappointed when Roman told him she'd departed sometime during the night.

"Some woman, that!" said Roman with a grin. "There's strangeness about her, though. Rather aloof, don't you think? What did you say her name was? Oddly I cannot recall it."

Corin looked up from his sax with a frown. "Vervandi," he replied and was about to say more when Queen Ariane cut him short.

"She's a daughter of the Goddess," she told them, "one of three sisters who call themselves the fates. I am wary of her. She appears a friend, but what her involvement is with our business I do not know. I shied from asking her last night. I'm not sure if we can trust her. She has her father's blood in her veins, after all."

"Her father?" Corin was puzzled.

"Oroonin the Crafty." Ariane's dark eyes pinned him. Corin felt transparent and ashamed. This Queen was so sharp, perhaps she'd guessed what he'd been thinking just now. She turned away from him, her jet hair glistening with the morning sun.

"Legend says they are estranged," Ariane continued, "that Vervandi favors her mother but the other two follow him. The gods have their own quarrels, Corin, just like us, only they sulk for centuries. Oroonin has not spoken to Elanion in uncountable years."

Both Roman and Corin were captivated by this latest revelation, but knowing whom Vervandi sprang from did little to assure them. Of course, Corin had heard of Oroonin—everyone had. One of the great old gods. He'd even heard somewhere that this Oroonin and the horrible Huntsman were the same entity.

Corin considered that total crap. The Huntsman was a freak. Why would one of the gods, however grumpy, dress up in cloak and silly hat and charge about in the skies curdling milk whilst blowing his horns and wagging his spear about? All a bit unnecessary, in Corin's opinion.

"Vervandi is wise, however," continued the Queen, sipping

the tea produced by a grinning Galed, who looked almost human again this morning. "I learned much from her concerning our enemy and the ancient evil that aids him, none of it good. It seems we are beset on all sides." Her shrewd eyes measured Corin thoughtfully for a moment.

"Vervandi mentioned your name more than once, Corin an Fol. Apparently she has watched you with interest for some time. Why would that be, I wonder?"

Corin glanced up from honing Biter again. "I do not know, Queen." He feigned indifference with a shrug. He wasn't enjoying this conversation. Such things travelled better on a full stomach. *Vervandi? A Fate? This is getting worse. Why would one of the Fates watch over me?*

"She informed me that you encountered one of her sisters at the river Fol, some nights ago." Corin averted her gaze and attacked Biter's edge with renewed zeal. "Well?" Ariane pressed him.

Corin disguised his growing alarm with an awkward laugh. "How could that foul witch be Vervandi's sister? She was ancient, a hag!" Even as Corin spoke, the words of the witch at the ford returned to trouble him.

I don't know what Vervandi sees in you.

"Her name is Skolde," continued the Queen, measuring his reaction as if weighing his resolve. "She represents the future. Vervandi deals with the present and the girl child Urdei, the past."

Corin recalled the pretty child in the tree by the smithy. He winced. *The bog faerie was related to those two? This was getting worse by the minute.* Corin slung Biter in its scabbard and eased his hunting knife into his palm. He commenced oiling and wiping—anything to avoid those sharp, coaly eyes.

"I don't understand any of this," Corin muttered after a few minutes at the knife.

"Nor I," Ariane agreed. "Mystery surrounds you, longswordsman."

Corin was about to respond when Bleyne suddenly appeared at the entrance of the cave. The archer stood calmly watching them with his impassive gaze. The great wooden bow was slung diagonal across his back, together with a full sack of grey fletched shafts. His tattooed right hand rested on the bone handle of his long curved hunting knife. He'd traded his sumptuous cloak for one of faded fur-capped leather.

"We had best be leaving," Bleyne announced. "I've scoured the lands north of the forest for brigands. I found several tracks leading away. Hopefully, they're spooked enough and will return to Morwella." Corin raised an eyebrow in the archer's direction.

Not if I know Hagan, they won't.

They snatched a hasty breakfast and broke camp quickly. Within minutes, they'd reassembled outside the cave. Ariane sighed as she left the Caverns of Caromanya. She doubted she would ever encounter such beauty again.

Outside, autumn sun spangled through the russet mantle of the forest. Corin glanced up. A strong breeze stirred the trees, and crusty leaves whirled and danced to the forest floor. It felt colder this morning. He wrapped the heavy green cloak about his shoulders, for once grateful he had it. The air carried the pleasant odor of leaf decay, and Corin shivered. Winter was approaching fast.

Bleyne guided them north throughout that cold morning. The archer had resumed his punishing pace, but after their rest they had no trouble keeping up. Even Galed was relatively cheerful. This part of the forest was rockier, more open. Great pines crested ridges, wuthering in the chilly breeze. They thinned like old man's stubble as the terrain grew steeper.

At noon they topped a final ridge. The forest broke ranks behind them as if held fast by invisible bonds. The companions studied the new landscape ahead. It wasn't a cheerful sight. Their way was blocked by brooding hills, stark to the eye after the lush canopy of the trees.

Corin turned on a whim, whispering farewell to the forest and she who resided within its demesne. For a moment he stood watching the multitude of trees swaying in the breeze and fading into hazy distance. He rubbed his scar and turned away.

To the north reared flinty hills. These were the grim heights that skirted Morwella. Beyond that troubled country heaved the

Gulf of Leeth until it met the vastness of the country it was named for. A wild region that was rumored to be, a huge country ruled by bloodthirsty kings. Barin's enemies. Leeth. Legend spoke of giants and trolls and of terrible dragons that guarded stolen gold in long forgotten caves. A few days ago Corin would have scoffed at the existence of such beings, but not now.

At least they were not going that way! Their journey led northwest, to the sea. It was only a half score miles from the northern fringes of the forest to Kelthaine's rocky coast. The town of Kashorn lay hidden somewhere beyond those hills. They studied the road ahead for a while. In the middle distance a gap yawned between two hills. Through it showed a faint glimmer of water.

"That must be the Gulf of Leeth," announced Corin. They had decided to stop for a brief lunch, and he had taken over as guide again from Bleyne, the archer having lost interest now that they had left the forest.

Corin was baffled and irritated by Bleyne's attitude, his acceptance of everything and fey belief that the Goddess warded his every step. It wasn't a consensus Corin subscribed to.

"Kashorn cannot be far," he added, frowning at Bleyne. "Let's hope the road isn't watched." He turned to Roman. "Do we dare it or else stab out across country?"

"Why not chance the road?" replied Roman. "That way we can be in Kashorn before evening settles. Hopefully Bleyne's arrows have driven the mercenaries away for the moment. Let's hope also that Barin's ship is waiting. We can vacate port without much ado." He rubbed his beard thoughtfully. "We had best be careful, though. Kashorn might be watched."

Ariane nodded in agreement. "We must be wary, yes. Those cutthroats could still be around." She turned to Bleyne, who was leaning on his bow and scanning the hills with mild disinterest. "Did Elanion reveal anything about our journey to you?" she asked him.

The archer shrugged his shoulders. "The Goddess speaks in riddles. It is not my place to question her wisdom but rather to obey her."

Corin and Roman exchanged skeptical glances, but neither

spoke. Doubtless, the archer had his reasons for joining them aside from the Goddess's wishes. They didn't really swallow that devout stuff. They were fighters. They trusted cold steel more than riddles. Corin coughed. Enough conversation. Time to get moving again.

He set the pace, striding through tussocks of couch grass, leading them on toward the stark slopes ahead. Alone with his thoughts, Corin recalled his former life. Wenching and fighting had covered most of it, not much of a legacy, really. And now this trip...

"Come on Galed, keep up!" Corin turned back to vent his grouchiness on the squire, who as always was struggling several yards behind them. Galed muttered something obscene beneath his hood but quickened his pace nonetheless.

They reached the road. It was well trodden but in reasonable repair, and so their progress was good. To the north bulked the bleak hills of Morwella. This open country felt uncomfortably exposed after the security of the forest. Southward, the smaller hills of Kelthaine hurried to meet their bigger cousins, forcing the land into a narrow valley pierced by the grey twisting ribbon of the road.

Something about that valley felt wrong.

An invisible menace resonated from its stone-piled slopes. The way looked clear as far as they could see, but that did little to reassure them. Large boulders lay strewn and disorderly close to the path; each one could hide a dozen men. Smaller stones were scattered and piled across the ground like broken toys. These they would have to clamber over. It was not a comforting thought.

Corin and Roman exchanged a look, neither liking this place. Ariane looked worried and Galed stressed. Only Bleyne looked indifferent, casually content with his own thoughts.

As the five approached the valley's entrance, their uneasiness grew into trepidation. Corin felt his skin crawl in a familiar way. He pictured a big ugly dog slavering over his sleeping body and shivered.

It were though they'd entered the invisible web of some insidious spider. Nobody spoke, their faces taught with tension. Galed's teeth rattled noisily. Only Bleyne appeared relaxed, infuriatingly so, Corin thought.

Bastard isn't afraid of anything.

Stone faced, Corin led the way into the valley's cleft. Behind them the Forest of Dreams had dwindled into smudgy distance. Corin looked back that way, feeling a sudden compulsion. He started as movement caught his eye at the forest hem.

What's that?

It was no more than a glint, but Corin knew they were being watched. He shielded his eyes and stared harder. Then Corin saw him. Hardly visible beneath the tree line—an old man wrapped in a billowing cloak, features shrouded by a wide-brimmed hat. The afternoon sun glanced off the polished tip of a spear. Corin turned away, muttering.

"What is it?" Roman had joined him and looked back at the forest. "Are we being followed, Corin?"

Corin shrugged. "I don't know—just a feeling."

The valley yawned to greet them. Through it the wind strengthened cold, accompanied by a new sound, the distant roar of breakers. The sea! Once past these hills they would arrive at the ocean, providing they got through these hills, Corin couldn't help thinking.

The terrain was rough, the vista remote, and that bitter wind whistled down from the hills, whipping cloak, numbing faces, making eyes water. The oppressive feeling grew with every reluctant step they took.

It was a tangible thing, like the enchantment of Vaniel, only far more sinister. Each traveler, save perhaps Bleyne, suspected a hidden threat waiting nasty around the corner. Corin lead the way.

They entered the valley. A hostile cold hemmed them in. Galed swallowed incessantly as he struggled to keep his teeth together, whilst Corin and Roman scanned every nook and rock barring their way.

To their right towered the heights of Morwella, resembling cruel, crooked giants of stone. No one said a word. Roman and Corin kept their hands on their weapons, whilst Bleyne, his dark eyes alert and body tuned, calmly notched arrow to bowstring.

Behind him, Galed fingered his small axe and muttered obscenities. Ariane loosened her rapier in its scabbard. She stole cat-wary, now and then glancing anxiously up at the menacing slopes to either side.

A sharp cry, remote and cold. Looking up the Queen saw strange birds circling high above, their alien voices pitiless in that place.

"Those don't look like eagles," grumbled Roman glancing up.

"Come on!" Corin said. "Let's keep moving."

The atmosphere grew even colder. The wind's icy fingers probed deep beneath their garments, chilling them to the bone. Stronger and stronger, it whipped through the rocky valley, howling painfully in their ears and sapping their resolve.

"This is no natural wind!" yelled Roman with a curse. "Something works against us!"

"Aye," groaned Galed. "I don't like this place."

"Shut up!" yelled Corin without glancing back. "We've not far to go! Just keep your mouths shut and move faster."

They quickened their pace to a trot. The wind heightened its pitch, drowning out the distant grind of the sea. To either side, the valley had closed in with sheer sides forcing them into single file.

Bleyne raised his voice above the wind's din.

"There is someone blocking the road ahead," he said, catching up with Corin and tugging his sleeve. "Who or what it is I cannot see!"

"No point seeking cover here!" shouted Roman, crashing into Bleyne's back and knocking the smaller man off balance. Annoyance flashed briefly in the archer's eyes but vanished inside a second.

Roman was straining to see through the twisting jumble of rocks. The wind tore at his face and his eyes streamed salty rivulets. "It has probably spotted us already!" Roman announced helpfully.

But Corin knew what *it* was. He pictured a snarling dog on two legs, and unslung Clouter from its scabbard. He also freed the knife beneath his sleeve and eased it into his left palm but almost dropped it, so sweaty was his hand. This feeling of dread was horribly familiar to Corin. The others looked terrified. Even Bleyne's face appeared blanched.

Urgolais.

It was an Urgolais, for sure. Perhaps it was Morak himself. Corin felt certain this was the same ghastly entity that had been driven off by the Wild Hunt outside the inn.

Corin's loathing replaced his earlier dread. Once again he was being confronted. This time his new friends were in danger too. They didn't know this shithead, but he did. Anger boiled up inside him, fury at the hold this creature had had over him that night. And rage, witnessing the fear it wielded over his comrades.

Time to die, Dog Face!

With a shout Corin ran forward and, glancing round, was pleased to see Roman Parrantios close at his heel.

"Be wary!" hissed Bleyne, matching their pace with arrow ready and bowstring taut. "I fear this is no natural foe!"

"You're fucking right there!" Corin told him.

They came close. Corin recognized the thin shape cowled in its black, lifeless cloak, the famished, scarred Dog Face with its long snout half protruding from the deep hood. The spook's substance was hard to define; it shifted like smoke, seemed to crawl and cluster like an ants nest spilling open on a hot midsummer's day.

Corin's skin crawled too. He ignored the icy worms eating into his veins, shut out the mocking voice in the wind. He would not be overcome a second time. Corin an Fol would master this creep or die.

He controlled his breathing with practiced discipline and slowed to a walk, leveling Clouter at his tormentor's exposed snout.

"Yes," Corin said with a snarl. "I remember you, courtyard lurker! Morak is it? Who cares? Giant dog turd you are. This time you don't spook me. This time I'm ready!"

"Is it Groil?" gasped Roman, now at Corin's side, his heavy blade gripped in either palm. The champion's beard was coated with frozen sweat and his eyes were wide and staring.

"Something much worse." Corin fingered the knife in his left hand. "Look out. Here it comes!"

They fanned out to confront the creature, the path being just wide enough for the three to stand abreast. Behind them forgotten stood Galed and the Queen. Ariane, steeling her nerves, ran to join them, followed by the terrified, panting Galed, who didn't want to be left on his own. The squire's teeth rattled in time with the wind.

"Your Highness, get back!" snapped Roman as Ariane pushed alongside. "We need room to swing!" Roman blocked her path with his big sword, stepping between her and the spook. Dog Face was scarce yards away, approaching fast with weird jerky movements.

"What the fuck is that thing?" Ariane hissed in Bleyne's ear, ignoring her champion's protestations."

"An Urgolais, one of the witchy people," replied the archer, pulling back his bowstring until the arrow's fletch brushed his right earlobe.

"Here it comes!"

As Bleyne spoke, the creature's smoky essence congealed before their eyes. It was weirdly tall and thin, emaciated even. Black cloak and hood clung to its brittle frame like a bat's broken wings, and the dog snout twitched as though hungry for their scent. It halted a score of feet away, blocking their path.

It spoke something then, a guttural unpronounceable word. Then the hood slipped back from its head, revealing sickly yellow eyes and curved jagged teeth beneath that wolf-like snout.

The face was horrific. It didn't resemble a dog at all, Corin realized, but a thing beyond description, with blackened scabby skin, human ears pierced with spikes and needles, and whirls and scars and pockmarks burnt deep into its flesh. Worse than that it stank like rotting road kill on a blazing hot day.

Fear assaulted them all. Ariane gasped as her fingers failed to hold her hilt. She watched silent as her blade clattered on the rocky earth. Galed weeping sunk to his knees, retching and puking, and Roman cursed as both callused hands failed to stop his broadsword from slipping from his grip.

Dark clouds smothered the valley. The hills shook with sudden thunder, and the wind shrieked and bludgeoned them with invisible fists of iron.

"I'm done with this," announced Corin, facing down the creature with an iron will he hadn't realized he possessed. He stepped forward, hurled his knife. Beside him Bleyne's bowstring snapped taught, the shaft bolting free.

Roman, yelling expletives, regained his weapon and ran forward to confront their foe. He stopped short, momentarily blinded, as lightning struck the road ahead.

A wailing shriek trailed off down the valley followed by distant hollow murmurings. They froze, mouths gaping, unable to speak over the din. More lightning bolts speared rocks and stone, searing grass and scorching shrub; one struck Roman's cloak, singeing his collar and sending him spinning.

Thunder boomed in their ears, and icy hail whipped their faces raw. *Boom, boom*, the thunder deepened. The valley shuddered and quaked. Rocks broke free from the steep sides of the hills. A stony torrent, they cascaded down upon the stricken mortals, some coming to rest scarce feet away. Of their tormenter there was no longer any sign.

Corin was the first to recover, his rage giving him strength.

"Come on!" he yelled as the rocks crashed and rolled, threatening to cut off their escape. The thunder deafened them. It creaked and crackled overhead like a massive chariot driven by a reckless god.

Corin lifted Galed to his feet, shaking the witless squire back to life. He could see that the poor fellow had soiled himself. "We will be crushed to death!" he told him. "Quickly man. Get your arse mobile! Kashorn cannot be far!" Galed blinked up at him, then nodded.

"I'm all right," he said.

Behind him Ariane rocked on her knees, her hands covering her ears.

"Are you all right, Queen?" asked Roman amid gasps. He helped Ariane regain her feet.

"I'm fine, Roman," she lied. "Don't fuss me! Just let's get out of here!" Her jaw dropped. "Look out!" she cried as a great rock thundered down and her champion barely hauled her out of harm's way.

They fled.

Above and behind, the hills boomed and echoed with the roar of tumbling stone. They ran like hunted game. Corin glanced skyward, braving the hail. He thought he saw faces carved in the hills. Cruel faces, stone giants stirring from timeless slumber, furiously seeking to crush the pathetic creatures that dared scurry like beetles below.

And up yours, too!

Breathless, drenched by melting hail and sweat, they reached the end of the valley as a final rock crashed behind, exploding on the road and blocking any possible return.

They left the valley behind, found sanctuary in the lee of a low rise, its heathery crown ringed by stunted trees.

As they panted and glared, the wind eased back, the clouds departed, and a pale sun reappeared, raising their rattled spirits. The hills still glowered at them, daring them return. A tepid but welcome warmth returned to the land, and a lone blackbird chided bravely in the twisted pines above.

They had escaped the valley, but Corin couldn't help but wonder what was next.

Chapter 16

Kashorn

They took stock, regaining breath and calming racing nerves. Galed couldn't control his shivering. He looked thoroughly wretched. Corin felt some sympathy for the squire, recalling the first time he had encountered that horror and how it had given him the willies too.

The Queen, though, was hiding her fear magnificently. She looked thoroughly pissed off but not scared. Royalty or not, she was a fine woman Corin thought. He flashed an optimistic grin her way, but she glared back, dismal.

"It has gone." Bleyne stated the apparent without hint of irony. He seemed almost disappointed. A slight flicker of annoyance creased his normally impassive face. "I wasted an arrow for nothing."

Beside him Corin grumbled agreement. He'd lost a good throwing knife. He'd tried to regain it when they fled, but like its intended target, it had vanished into mist. Roman coughed, adjusted his cloak, noticing with a start that it still smoldered. He patted it angrily and then licked his fingers in pain.

They resumed their journey, pressing harder. The renewed

need for urgency weighing on all of them.

"What in Elanion's sacred name was that thing?" Galed had only just recovered his voice. He still trembled like jelly but just managed to persuade his teeth stay together long enough to form a sentence. When no one responded, he asked again, this time aiming the question at Bleyne.

The archer's face revealed nothing, but his answer chilled them to the bone. "Urgolais," he said. "One of the Shadowy Ones—no doubt about that. They have our scent." He grinned.

"You don't have to be so cheerful about it," Corin told the archer.

Bleyne ignored him and instead glanced almost longingly behind at the sunlit valley. "A nightmare being banished to the far side of Uffarn. It is as the Goddess has told us. Old Night awakens, and his servants muster. War is coming to Ansu. Come on!" Corin shook his head in resignation.

Oh, do shut up...

"Let's hope that bloody ship is waiting for us," muttered Roman from somewhere behind.

"Barin will be there," Corin replied.

"He better be..."

The air was still chilly, not the menacing cold of the valley but raw nonetheless. It was accompanied by a sharp tang of salt carried on the wind. Corin couldn't suppress a smile; it felt good to smell the sea again. It reassured him. He'd never been to Kashorn but guessed they were very near.

He led the way with eager strides. The afternoon sun passed overhead, and evening beckoned. The sound of the waves crashed and boomed somewhere below. Ahead lay gorse and heather brushed by wind, beyond that, nothing but air.

They cleared the furze break and as one stopped and gaped in wonder. The scene before them had dramatically changed.

They stood poised at the knife edge of a great cliff, sheer and flawless, flanking to right and left as far as the eye could see. Below, sea birds shrieked. Corin spied fulmars, kittiwakes, and puffins, their small shapes swooping and diving amongst the towering cliffs.

Beyond the birds, the Western Ocean churned and heaved its rhythmic dance. White horses rode upon its wide expanse, cantering across from the sun-drenched horizon. At last they had reached the ocean!

Corin leaned out precariously. He glimpsed a stone harbor far below, its arm thrust seaward like a broken finger. Beyond that, torchlight flickered amidst smoky roofs.

Kashorn.

There it lay. Far below where they stood and mostly hidden from view, sheltered from the sea's wrath by a huge shoulder of rock. Corin gazed seaward. He cursed silently. *The Starlight Wanderer* was nowhere in sight. Perhaps the water was deep enough for her to moor hard against the quay and out of their field of vision. He prayed it was so.

"Any suggestions on how we get down?" Corin asked Bleyne. He assumed the archer would know, as everyone else appeared blank, and this was new territory for him.

Bleyne nodded. "It is not as bad as it looks," he replied with his customary casualness. "There is a path hereabouts, cut deep into the rock face. It's very steep and slippery but manageable, with care."

"Oh wonderful!" exclaimed Galed. "Now we're to be eagles. I think I'd prefer a pit full of snakes!"

"That comes later," said Corin with a smile.

A short search revealed Bleyne's path. A sharp wedge, it chiseled into the cliff face and descended at an alarming pitch. One slip and they would be broken like twigs on the rocks below. Shallow and treacherous steps were cut into the rock, weathered smooth by wind and salt.

After some hesitation, mainly on the part of Galed, they commenced the descent. It was painfully slow. They clung to the rock like limpets, descending at slug pace. Vertigo tugged them. They felt exposed and vulnerable as they tenuously made their way down toward the town below.

It seemed to take an age. A moment's lack of concentration would prove fatal, sending them spinning down into the crashing waves. Corin, in front and below, paused to allow his friends to rest. He took a look around whilst the others caught up.

Westward, the sun slid bloody into the ocean. The sky too was flushed with violent crimson, promising a clear day tomorrow. It was beautiful, but they were not really in appreciative mood. Reluctantly, they resumed their descent at Corin's word. Bleyne brought up the rear, his expression bored again.

Two thirds of the way down was a wide ledge. Here they paused again, rested a while, and regained their sense of balance. Galed sat pale faced in the corner, whilst the others stood surveying. All about, seabirds swooped and dived, their harsh cries deriding these impostors to their craggy domain. Ariane took a seat on a lump of rock and shut her eyes for a minute, gathering her thoughts.

Corin, Roman, and Bleyne approached the rim of the shelf with care. Lying on their stomachs they looked down at the harbor. Much nearer. The sea chopped and battered the granite wall, but all else seemed calm. Of Barin's ship there was no sign. Corin swore under his breath then looked up as Roman grabbed his arm.

"Look!" he said, pointing to the southern side of the harbor still partially hidden by cliffs. "Do you see them?" Roman hinted at tiny figures standing on the harbor wall. They were gazing seaward, clearly waiting for a ship to arrive, their hoarse shouts borne up on the wind.

"Your mercenary friends are down there," announced Bleyne, whose eyes were sharper than the others. "Look, there is old kettlehead and the tall grey-eyed captain that leads them." Corin followed the archer's gaze, then scowled when he recognized Hagan and the helmeted Borgil. A smaller figure at their side seemed oddly familiar too. Corin cursed their ill fortune.

They continued the painful decline, grateful that the path angled behind a huge rock, concealing their whereabouts from anyone looking up.

Down they struggled until they reached another ledge. This time they had a clear view of both town and harbor—and were filled with dismay. Kashorn was awash with soldiers.

"Captain Barin must have got wind of them," Ariane swore heartily. "Perhaps he will slip into the harbor at nightfall," she hoped.

"Those men await something," said Roman, watching keenly. "I fear we are expected, my Queen. Are you certain these are the same rogues that followed us through the forest?" he asked Bleyne. The archer nodded in silence.

"I know that man." Corin pointed to the tall leader of the mercenaries. "Hagan Delmorier," he spat into the wind. "I fought alongside him in the desert. He's a bastard."

Corin remembered the tall Morwellan from the Permio wars; Hagan was an accomplished swordsman and a ferocious fighter. He was intelligent and ruthless, caring for nothing but gold coin and easy women. They hadn't got on. Hagan played with weighted dice.

"Well, it seems that the villain serves Caswallon now," said Roman with a snort of derision. "Come, we had better get ready for trouble!"

"Are you mad, captain?" Galed was aghast. "There must be thirty of them!" He shook his head in horror. "You fighting men, you're all bloody daft!"

"Look!" pointed Ariane suddenly. "There is Barin's ship!"

Corin felt a flood of relief as *The Starlight Wanderer* emerged at last from the gloaming. Twin masts and proud, the brig was a valiant sight. The last crimson rays of the setting sun burnished her fourteen sails, the main emblazoned with the great Sea Eagle.

She rounded the harbor arm. Below, the soldiers were shouting and waving their arms in surprise and alarm. It was apparent now they'd not expected this vessel. That at least was good news.

Corin could make out the towering bulk of Barin minding the helm whilst his men hurried about deck, hauling sheets and making ready for docking. They appeared agitated, and Barin's voice boomed orders like a man possessed. The ship tacked landward. She stole into the harbor like a fox entering a hen pen. Hagan's men waited with swords drawn and spears held high.

"What is that out there?" asked Roman in sudden disbelief.

He shielded his eyes and cursed in realization. Another sail had appeared beyond the harbor wall, followed closely by two more. Pirate ships! They were Crenise pirate ships.

"He is being pursued!" shouted Corin. "We must help him! Hurry!" Without waiting for an answer, he reclaimed the steps. The others seemed not to hear. They watched in growing despair as three sleek black-sailed ships rounded the harbor wall. These were much smaller than Barin's vessel; they were faster, though, and would be able to tack easier in the limited space of the harbor.

They glided landward, quickly gaining on *the Starlight Wanderer*. These were the Assassin's sharks, his raiding ships, and terror of the western waters. Narrow hulls painted black as jet, they glistened like oily serpents, sinuous and lithe.

Corin remembered the last time he had seen a craft like these. All too well he remembered. He knew the narrow hulls were built for speed. He knew their short keels allowed them to enter shallow waters. He knew how swift and deadly they were.

Once again, he was fourteen years old on that beautifully brutal morning. His old scar twitched, and he fingered Biter's hilt hungrily. Each ship bore a single square sail of black cloth emblazoned with a red fist clutching a hapless bird by its broken neck. The emblem of the Lord of Crenna, feared and dreaded throughout all decent lands.

Bastards...BASTARDS! I'M COMING!

Corin slithered down at speed. His mouth frothed as the battle madness seized him, the old rage reaching boiling point within. Again he saw his father cut down, witnessed his brothers' greying corpses, heard the terrified cries of his womenfolk dragged by their hair to waiting ships whilst their cottage burned.

Corin quickened his already reckless pace, slipping more than once but somehow regaining his feet. Gulls yelled obscenities at him, and below men shouted. Corin cared not. His mind was a lit fuse, sparking, eager to explode. Other voices mocked him as the hard stone bruised his reckless descent. He heard the hag laughing at the ford.

You ride into peril, Corin an Fol!

Images of the Huntsman and the hooded Urgolais melded into the contorted faces of murdering pirates. Hatred fuelled Corin with strength, channeling his wrath. He plunged down, heedless of the yelling soldiers that witnessed his descent. *Bastards! Bastards! Bastards!*

*****

Hagan Delmorier, mercenary captain, renegade, and ruthless brigand—recently banished from his homeland, Morwella, for unspeakable deeds, so the Duke said— surveyed the harbor with cold, grey eyes.

Twats were late again. Crenise not known for reliability. But then Hagan was dispassionate this evening. He wasn't interested in the politics and obsessions of that twisted usurper back in Kella City.

And he had no love for Rael Hakkenon, either. Who would? The Assassin was an evil whoreson. Hagan smiled slightly at that thought. What did that make him? Cruel, cynical, and brutal— certainly all of those. But he wasn't sadistic, not like the Lord of Crenna.

Rael Hakkenon gave Hagan the creeps, and Caswallon unnerved him in a most unmanly manner. The sorcerer was warped and depraved, made Hagan's skin crawl. Truth be told, Hagan wanted no part of any of this Queen-kidnapping business.

He had no quarrel with Kelwyn's leading lady—and she was a fine-looking woman besides. He'd spied her once whilst on contract work in silver Wynais. No, this wasn't really Hagan's province. He preferred a good old ambush or skirmish—like those halcyon days down in fly-stinky Permio.

But who could refuse the gold Caswallon had promised him—and Rael too. Hagan would be rich once this little job was done. And it shouldn't prove that difficult. There was only Roman Parrantios to worry about, and a crafty crossbow bolt would put paid to him. And then there was Corin an Fol...

Hagan had been stunned, though he hadn't shown it of course, when the tyke Cale had mentioned the name of his former companion. Corin and he had had some fine old times during the Permio conflicts. But nothing lasts in this life.

Corin an Fol was a total shite. He'd cheated at cards and blamed it on Hagan. There had been a fight—Corin had carved an exit with that horrible sword of his, leaving Hagan to mop up the rest, very nearly skewered by a half score vengeful Permian merchants.

Hagan had sworn he'd kill Corin when next he saw him. But he hadn't seen him for three years, his work taking him up into Leeth, where Daan Redhand was carving a name for himself. But now Corin was here in northern Kelthaine, and if Hagan's scouts were to be trusted, approaching this very spot.

Hagan grinned—a rare thing that, he seldom smiled. Cale looked up at him and grinned too. The boy worshipped Hagan, and for his part, the captain was fond of the lad. Cale was bright, a survivor. He would do well, providing Borgil didn't kill him.

Cale had pissed off Hagan's second with his gobby cheek. Borgil—not the sharpest instrument, though loyal and usefully viscous with that axe of his—had been the butt of Cale's wit the other night. Something about losing six of his men to wood sprites and bog faeries.

Borgil, being a touch sensitive about the subject, had taken umbrage and vowed to gut the lad there and then. Hagan, laughing, had intervened. But Borgil wasn't the forgiving type, and Hagan feared for the lad's future. Not that he gave a fuck, really. The only thing that mattered to Hagan was gold, lots of it coming his way soon. Oh, and Corin an Fol of course.

"Captain, they're here!" Borgil's gruff tones came from further down the quay. Cale paled a touch and muttered something inaudible. Hagan ignored him.

"'Bout bloody time!" Hagan shouted back. He shielded his eyes against the setting sun and gazed seaward. The Northman's ship had arrived, as Caswallon had promised it would, and so had the pirates hot on its tale. Another shout reached him from a fellow minding the back streets.

"People up on the cliff! Coming down, Captain! The idiot in

front's in some hurry."

"That'll be Corin," replied Hagan. "He owes me money and cannot wait to pay."

"And I thought he needed the privy!" laughed the fellow up the lane.

Hagan smiled a second time that evening. This was going to be some fun after all. He ruffled Cale's ginger mop and eased his broadsword in its scabbard.

"Come on, Master Cale—it's time to settle an old score."

Chapter 17

The Starlight Wanderer

Roman shook himself into action. Corin had vanished below, and they were standing gawping like fishes washed ashore.

"Come on!" he barked at the others. "We have to reach Barin's ship before those pirates do! Follow me!" Ariane nodded, her dark eyes defiant and angry.

"Let's get this done," she said. Meanwhile, Bleyne hoisted Galed to his feet and bade him follow.

The squire gulped. "What about those mercenaries?" he asked as they vacated the ledge.

"We'll have to crash through them!" shouted Roman without glancing back. "Stick close to me, my Queen! Don't worry Galed, boy. I will protect you!"

"That's a great comfort," muttered the squire, adding, "wait for me!" as once again he was left behind.

Corin yelled as he ran hopping and skipping down the treacherous stair. The battle rage had claimed him again. The berserker-gang—a rare thing that gave him terrible energy for a while then left him worn and shattered.

It was useful, though, had got him out of countless scrapes.

His former weariness was blown asunder and days of brooding washed away. Crenna, those pirates he so hated, were down there.

I'm coming. Get ready!

Corin grinned. Fighting! Hack and slice! Stab and hue, and kill the bastards!

This is what I do best!

At last he could vent his fury on a tangible enemy below.

Down he stormed, Clouter in right hand, mindless of the slippery stone beneath his feet. Down and down, until he reached the tumbled slate roofs of the smoke-wracked town. The soldiers' shouts were closing. He could see them rushing through the narrow, twisting streets. Corin didn't care. He'd cut through them on his way to the pirates.

"Corin! Please...we're coming!" A women's voice up above. The Queen's tones eased into his rage. Corin slowed and for the first time in his life controlled that awful anger boiling up inside him.

Ariane—she needs me...

He stole a frantic glance behind, only now remembering his friends. Corin saw that Roman was leading the others down the cliff. They too were hurrying, and even Galed had a sprint on.

Corin struggled to master his rage. Every nerve in his wiry body urged him leap down, start the killing. He channeled that rage with a new-found discipline and hung back, regaining his breath.

I am more than just a killer—and she needs me.

Corin leaped onto the roof of the nearest building. He crouched there with Clouter angled over his back and waited for his friends to catch up. Below, the streets were full of angry shouts. Corin assessed the situation. He wished he'd kept the bow and not given it to Tamersane.

Still, he was cooler, the rage brought under control by his haphazard decent and Ariane's worried shout. But it was still inside him, latent fire awaiting its chance to reclaim him. But he wouldn't let it, not this time. For the first time in his life, Corin an Fol was thinking about someone else.

She needs me...

Corin glanced up wild-eyed as Roman and the Queen landed beside him, followed by a crashing, arm-swinging, and sweating Galed. Last to arrive was Bleyne, cool and casual as though he were off on an afternoon stroll. Arrow on the nock, he sprang lithely onto the slippery roof.

Close by and below, the sound of steel-shod feet resonated through the cobbled streets. Corin glanced at his companions: Ariane looked worried, Roman resolute, and Galed manic. Bleyne looked like Bleyne.

"Ready?" Corin asked. They nodded. At Corin's signal he and Roman dropped silently to the dusky floor of the street below. They waited for a minute and then signaled up to the others. Bleyne remained perched on the roof, scanning all approaches.

Still maintaining his new-found calm, Corin studied the town with professional precision. Kashorn appeared much like Finnehalle, though starker, the grey cold stone awarding little cheer.

Beyond the low thatched roofs stood the stone harbor, larger and squarer in shape than that of his town, no doubt built for defense against the winter swells. Ariane had her slim rapier clutched in her right hand. To her left Roman crouched wary, whilst just behind them Galed pawed nervously at the handle of his axe.

Kashorn seemed an uninspiring place, cold and comfortless as the dark cliffs looming above it. The spray-washed streets were empty, excluding the odd dog that nosed at discarded waste.

It was evident the town's folk had shut themselves inside, sensing trouble. That ploy wouldn't work with Crenise pirates. They would be dragged out and gutted, all save the comeliest women, who would service the crew on the long voyage back.

Occasionally Corin glimpsed movement from within a house and caught the wary eye of a frightened villager. He did not blame them. What else could they do? There was nowhere to run, and soon blood would be spilt on these streets.

Bleyne joined them. "They're in the next street," he whispered, pointing to their left. "Best we lose ourselves in this labyrinth before they are on us." The archer oozed cheerfulness. Galed shook his head in disbelief. Corin and Roman were bad enough. Bleyne was something else entirely.

I'm glad you're on our side, though...

Galed launched a practice swing with his wood axe, narrowly missing Roman's left ear. Ariane glanced his way, her face flushed with anticipation. Galed felt for her then. It helped him to be brave. He tried another swing, stronger and better this time. Ariane smiled, and Galed was filled with pride for the woman he loved.

Corin turned and stared at his friends. "All right, let's do it," he said.

Into the dusk-gloomy streets of Kashorn they ran, flitting in and out between the buildings. Corin stooped, waving them back. He slipped a throwing knife under his sleeve, then led the way again. The sound of running feet was very close, but the street in front was empty.

"Hold together!" Roman growled. They regrouped at the corner of a fishing hut. Beyond that, barely a hundred yards away, loomed the harbor's arm, twelve paces broad and ninety feet in length. Here a tense knot of Hagan's men waited with swords and spears ready to intercept the brigantine drawing alongside.

The Starlight Wanderer's sails billowed in the stiffening blow. Her crewmen yelled curses, cast lines, and leapt ashore. Within moments, noisy shouts and the sound of clashing steel resounded through the streets. Above that, rose a booming voice that could only be Barin of Valkador.

"Now is our chance!" urged Corin, only just keeping a lid on his rage as the sound of fighting stirred his blood. "A brave dash and we'll make it to the ship! Come on!"

"Let's hope this Barin character stays alive long enough to sail it," grumbled Galed as he took the rear again.

"Chin up, Galed," said Roman. "You've never seen a northman fight!"

"I can't wait."

Corin led the way, sprinting through the streets toward the harbor. It wasn't far. The four followed hard on his heels. Bleyne pushed Galed forward and half turned, so his bow could cover them from any pursuit sure to follow.

They reached the last street, hurdling scattered nets and flotsam. Rats scurried out from under feet. Behind, someone shouted. Corin stole a glance back. Armed men had entered the street and were giving angry chase. Bleyne's arrow took the foremost in the throat, but the rest closed the gap.

"Keep running!" Corin yelled, "Let Bleyne deal with those bastards!" They urged their legs on, nearing the end of the street, heedless of the shouting behind and the sound of clashing steel ahead. Then something hissed and thudded. A crossbow bolt. It whooshed over Galed's head, embedding itself in the oak timber of a post, with a quivering thud.

"Fuck," said Roman. "That was close."

"Why me?" Galed grumbled. "I was never meant for this!"

More bolts buzzed over their heads. Corin managed a wry grin. At least Hagan's boys were crap shots. One quarrel passed clean through Roman's cloak before embedding itself in a wall. He swore again but kept running.

Close ahead, the crash and boom of breakers assaulted the harbor wall, accompanying the desperate sound of fighting.

Nearly there! They reached the end of the street and paused for breath. "One last push!" Corin said. Ariane nodded while the Kelwynian men panted and puffed. The threat of Bleyne's arrows kept Hagan's boys lurking at safe distance.

But then a tall figure blocked their passage. A swordsman, lean and long, garbed in black, silver-studded leather, face scarred and eyes cold grey. Other men strode out casually from behind the last house on their right, led by a huge, ugly brute sporting a kettle helmet.

A boy followed. Corin recognized Cale. He looked scrawny and unwashed, and his ginger mane was a twiggy matted mess—so no change there. The boy stood gawping at the Queen as if he'd never seen a woman before.

The grey-eyed leader was smiling broadly. Corin knew how rarely Hagan smiled. His old comrade/adversary appeared in good shape. The captain's tunic and gauntlets looked expensive, trimmed as they were with those silver studs, as was the scabbard that carried his heavy blade.

Hagan appraised them calmly, coolly eyeing each in turn. His smile widened when he saw the Queen. Lastly he looked at Corin and fondly patted the shaggy head of the boy at his side.

"Well done, shithead," Hagan told the boy, and Cale beamed scarlet. Compliments were rare from the captain—though he'd prefer being addressed by his correct title now and then. "So," continued Hagan, "the wayfaring Corin an Fol has returned north after long in the sun. How strange we should meet again in chilly Kashorn, of all places."

Corin didn't respond, just spat in Hagan's direction.

Cale felt nervous. He'd been hoping one of the lads would skewer Corin an Fol with a crossbow. He hadn't planned on meeting this evil bugger again. It was hard enough keeping Borgil at bay. He locked eyes with Corin and winced as a wet fart won free from between his buttocks.

Those steely eyes clocked him briefly before turning to Captain Hagan. There was fusion in the air, the atmosphere tense as midnight murder. Cale couldn't guess this one. He shuddered, turned away, and gaped at the woman again.

Not a woman, a Queen, though she was probably both really. He couldn't stop looking at her, but she scant noticed Cale's affectionate attentions. Her dark eyes were locked on Hagan and Corin. The big bugger beside her caught the boy's eye and growled. Cale stuck his tongue out and farted again.

Up yours...

Cale resumed his inspection of the Queen. She was small and dark and very pretty, in Cale's expert opinion. Brave too. Cale noticed how she gripped her expensive sword with angry confidence, noted how her elegant royal hand hardly shook, though her knuckles were white where she gripped the hilt.

Behind her loomed Borgil. He ratcheted another bolt and leveled his crossbow. The kettle helmet hid all save his bloodshot eyes and crooked, grinning toothless mouth.

Cale didn't like Borgil very much. The man was a weirdo with a humor transplant and stale lingering aroma. Kettle-head was bad enough before, but since his escape from the forest and harsh berating from the captain for losing three good men (with Cale's humorous input as salt in the wound), Borgil had been oozing vengeful menace at every given opportunity.

And he hated everybody, did Borgil. But he hated Cale more than anyone else. Big Ugly was jealous of the new affection Hagan had for the boy. Cale ignored Borgil, kept his gaze on the Queen and commenced reconsidering his options.

He liked Captain Hagan and respected him. But if he got in with her royal gorgeousness and won her favor (which of course he would, what with his winning charm and good looks, panache, and so forth), who knew what he could aspire to? She might make him an earl or something important. Cale rather fancied becoming an earl. He decided to watch and wait, review the situation as events unfolded. He wouldn't have to wait long.

Hagan grinned as he ruffled the boy's ginger mane. Corin had recognized the lad at once, though he was baffled by how the guttersnipe had mingled successfully into such a renowned bunch of freebooters. A survivor, this boy.

"So here we are, Hagan." Corin readied Clouter. Roman and Ariane marked Hagan's men, whilst Bleyne put Borgil in his sights and kept an eye on the others still lurking down the street. Close by, the sound of fighting intensified. Barin roared like a bear beset by wolves.

"It's ironic, don't you think?" Hagan ignored the din. He stroked the boy's hair as if Cale were a cat. "Strange how fate brings the Scourge of Permio to this remote corner of Kelthaine? And in such a hasty hurry, too?" Hagan shook his head in mock concern, then gave a small sardonic bow to Ariane. She rewarded this with contempt.

"Your Highness," Hagan continued, his cold grey gaze never leaving Corin. "I beg your indulgence. I was forgetting my manners. But Corin and I are old friends." Hagan dusted his shoulder with sudden irritation. "Perhaps *acquaintance* is a better term."

Corin counted the men filing their captain. There were seven.

Five waited behind, two carrying crossbows. It would be close.

"You appear unchanged since I last saw you in Cappel Cormac," Corin said. "But you surprise me, Hagan. I didn't think that even you would stoop to this level. Who pays you, Caswallon or Rael Hakkenon of Crenna?"

"Actually, on this occasion, both. I am most fortunate." Hagan grinned. He was relishing this reunion. He signaled to his men to relax their guard. No need to rush now they had their quarry cornered.

Beyond the street, new shouts were added to the sound of fighting. Hagan's men on the quay whooped in delight as the Crenise warships bore down on Barin's ship. It would all be over soon.

"You know me, Corin, I serve the best payers," Hagan continued with a shrug. "It's nothing personal. You of all people will understand that. I wonder, is her Highness aware of what a total bastard you actually are?" Hagan winked at Ariane, who glared back. "You, pretty lady will make me a rich man."

"Fuck you!"

Hagan feigned shock. "My goodness, Queen, wherever did you learn such language?" Beside him, the boy Cale looked even more impressed.

A swearing Queen. Awesome!

Hagan shrugged, feigning disappointment. "Time presses, however. Perhaps you would care accompany me to the harbor, my pretty one. My lads and the Assassin's boys hopelessly outnumber your Northman friend and his band of tossers.

"Now then, my patience wanes," said Hagan, still pinning Corin with his eyes whilst the other glared back in silence. "If you would be so kind, those Crenise warships await us."

"You streak of Morwellan shite!" spat Roman, no longer able to contain his rage. His sword arced toward Hagan in a blur of steel. "I'll slice you down the middle!"

"Wait, Roman!" shouted Corin.

Hagan leapt backwards, signaling to his crossbowman to fire. One raised his weapon, then screamed in agony as a raven, appearing from nowhere, tore hungrily at his face, plucking out first one eye then the other. The man fell screaming and rolling, the raven a blood-soaked blackness raking his ruined face.

Borgil fired, but Bleyne's arrow pierced his arm and his shot went wild. He fell back, clutching at the grey-fletched shaft protruding from his bicep. The man by his side spun round in alarm, then gurgled as Bleyne's next arrow ripped into his throat.

The raven had vanished as swiftly as it had appeared, leaving its weeping victim fruitlessly trying to staunch the scarlet drops spilling from his sightless sockets. Hagan's men were frightened, and the boy Cale pale as a sheet with a bad need to void his bowels.

No one liked sorcery, and that had been no natural bird. Something untoward was at work here. They hesitated, uncomfortable and at odds with how best to proceed.

Corin and Roman seized their moment. With a whirl of steel they bore down on the mercenaries, killing three. The Queen skewered a fourth, while Bleyne put paid to the final pair. The three left standing behind in the street hung well back, waiting their chance, but Bleyne arced high: his arrows found them one by one.

Only Hagan and the boy remained. Cale grinned lovingly at the Queen. He tore loose from the captain's grip and bolted down the quay before anyone could react.

Hagan shrugged. "Such loyalty." He calmly stepped out of reach of their blades. "This is foolishness," Hagan said. "Come Queen!" he ignored the others with distain.

Panther swift, Hagan reached for her, only to be confronted by her leveled blade. He raised an approving brow and stepped back again. "A swearing and fighting Queen—gosh! Fancy a quick one before we board, My Lady? You rather excite me."

"Fuck off!" Ariane hissed. "I'll not have my plans foiled by the likes of you!" She thrust her sword hard toward Hagan's throat, forcing him off balance. He recovered his step and lopsided grin simultaneously.

"How I envy Caswallon. Your resistance is hopeless though. I—"

"Oh shut up," Corin, having seized the initiative by slipping behind Hagan whilst the other regained his balance, rammed his shoulder hard into Hagan's exposed back, throwing the captain off balance. "Run for that ship, Ariane, before it's too late!" he yelled. "I'll deal with this bastard."

Hagan rolled, regaining his posture with catlike ease. His heavy sword blurred toward Corin's throat. It was Corin's turn to retreat and wait his chance. Corin was wary. Hagan was cunning fast with a sword.

They circled tentatively, testing each other, probing, seeking an opening. Both were canny veterans with their steel. Corin thrust out with Clouter but was blocked by Hagan's parry, and then the mercenary captain let fly a dazzling riposte that Corin barely stopped.

He lunged again, a difficult thing to do with so big a blade, forcing Hagan back. Corin was dimly aware that the others hadn't moved yet when a voice he knew interrupted his fight.

"Valkador!" came the shout. Barin had joined them. "Hurry behind me! We are beset on all sides."

Hagan jumped back, eyed the huge axeman in alarm. "I think I'll depart for the nonce," he told them. "I'm sure we can finish this some other time." Hagan ducked under Bleyne's questing arrow and vanished down a side alley before anyone could move.

"Bastard!" Ariane spat at his departing shadow. "I wanted to see you gut him, Corin." Corin was about to give chase.

"Let him go!" shouted Barin, his huge fist grabbing Corin's shoulder and forcing him back. "That rude fellow can wait. We must board my vessel while it still frigging floats! Come on!"

At Barin's words they raced into the harbor. The first of the Crenise fighting ships had closed with *The Starlight Wanderer*. Sinewy raiders massed on deck, seeking to clamber on board Barin's brig. His crew fought them off with fury, but they were heavily outnumbered.

The skinny Fassof was yelling at Barin to hurry. He had his knife held ready, waiting to sever the bowline. More of the crew were battling Hagan's mercenaries on the quay. Soon they would be surrounded and trapped.

With a bear-angry roar, Barin was on them, wielding his horribly huge axe like a windmill sail caught in a gale. Heads flew in all directions. Sundered limbs splattered the sea-washed stone with gore and gristle.

Barin's face was a mask of rage. None could withstand him. The others followed in his wake. Corin and Roman slew with precision. Bleyne had shouldered his bow and now favored a long knife. The Queen's rapier was dripping scarlet, and Galed screamed as he stuck a pirate between the eyes with his axe.

The last of Hagan's men rushed to confront them, fury written on their faces. Barin swept them aside like harmless bugs in a bloody whirl of furious steel.

They reached the vessel! Barin hurled himself aboard. Growling profanities, he set about swatting pirates who had dared leap onto his deck. Corin and the Queen followed close behind, whilst Roman pushed Galed onboard and dispatched a final mercenary in the throat with a backwards sweep of his broadsword.

Last came Bleyne, bow in hand again. He'd recovered most of his arrows, and these he loosed at the screaming pirates leaping down onto the blood-soaked deck.

Fassof cut the bowline.

The brigantine lurched free of her mooring. Barin wrenched the wheel from a pirate, butted the man's face, snapping his neck like a rotten branch, and then pitched him headfirst overboard to float like a discarded rag doll. The brig's stern crushed two others as she scraped along the quay, their screams lost in the waves.

A score remained on deck, but their clumsy cutlasses and belaying pins were no match for the heavy swords of Roman and Corin an Fol, let alone Barin's terrible axe.

Within minutes they were all dead, tossed overboard for shark bait. The pirate ships cast off in keen pursuit, leaving Hagan's few surviving men (including Borgil, now with right horn missing from the crest of his kettle helm) jeering and lewdly gesticulating from the safety of the quayside.

But the chase was on!

Barin worked the wheel. "Get a grip on those oars, and reef

the sails!" he shouted. "Let's win free of this harbor, lads!" As one, his men sped to carry out his orders. Barin's blue eyes scanned the deck. They narrowed when he noticed Roman leaning out over the gunwale.

"What's he doing?" he asked of Corin, who was industriously cleaning Biter on a pirate's scarf. Clouter was stowed, the last pirates having called for close-quarter work. His face was a mask of blood from this latest scrap.

"Methinks we've caught a fish," said the Queen's champion, grinning. Roman heaved a soggy, wretched bundle of bones onto the deck with a heavy grunt. Corin scowled, recognizing the boy Cale.

"I think we have a new recruit," laughed Roman as Barin and the others watched on. Behind, the nearest pirate ship was gaining fast. In moments it would be upon them.

"I'd throw that little shite back in," suggested Corin, who was awarded by a black look from the Queen. Needless to say, Corin's advice was ignored on this occasion. Cale had survived yet again. The boy winked at Corin and went to hide behind Barin.

Little shite...

"Hold steady, lads," urged Barin, frowning at the closing ship. Then something hissed from above, and the leading ship floundered in sudden confusion. Barin hooted in delight. Bleyne had shot the helmsman through the throat, and the sleek vessel lost ground as other men struggled with the tiller. Bleyne shot two more, and the ship swung wide. Barin's crew cheered, putting their backs to the oars with renewed vigor.

The gap widened again.

Behind the struggling craft, the other two changed tack. The furthest beat a course through the choppy water to cut off *The Starlight Wanderer's* escape from the harbor. The second vessel was swinging past its stranded sister. This one's deck seethed with screaming pirates, furious that their prey had sprung the trap.

Corin glanced above. Brawny sailors wrestled with cloth and line, cussing and shouting in the rapidly fading light. Within moments, all fourteen sails were under control, and the ship lurched hard to starboard.

Corin scanned the deck and scratched at a cut on his forearm. He frowned when he saw the Queen assiduously drying the scrawny boy as Galed watched on with a bemused expression.

Corin turned and spat on the deck. He felt drained and exhausted. He'd killed a dozen pirates at least, his berserkergang released at last. Every one had been a pleasure, but now he felt lost and forlorn, as he always did after such exertions. Sometimes it was hard to go on hating every waking hour.

"What are our chances, Captain Barin!" Ariane asked the northman. She'd told Galed to take the boy below deck and shove some food inside him. Corin looked at the Queen. There was blood on her face and clothes. It did nothing to mask her beauty. Rather, it enhanced it. She was a cracker.

"Hard to say, Queen," replied Barin with a shrug. "Those Crenise war sharks are faster than my ship, but they are coast huggers. Their keels are shallow. Once at sea we can lose them easily enough, providing the wind holds in our favor. But first we must vacate this harbor, and that could well prove tricky."

Corin turned. The second ship was gaining on them fast. The third one had nearly reached the harbor's gateway, blocking their passage. Hearing noises, he looked shoreward. A furor had erupted from the town; figures could be seen emerging from the buildings where they had lain hidden.

Amid shouts, they manned skiffs that soon bristled like water hedgehogs weighed down with their rusty pikes and poleaxes, hoes, and fish hooks (the only weapons they had to hand). They rowed madly toward the stranded vessel that still struggled without a competent helmsman.

Corin grinned. The townsfolk of Kashorn had found their courage at last. No doubt they also had old scores to settle with the hated pirates of Crenna. There was no sign of Hagan Delmorier. Corin assumed he'd slipped away with his surviving men. Doubtless that thorn will scratch again.

He caught Ariane's eye. She smiled once then turned away. Corin was relieved she'd suffered no apparent hurt. He felt ashamed again. In his hunger for vengeance during this last fight, he'd given scant thought to her welfare.

He felt strangely protective toward her; it was not something he had expected. Attraction certainly—but protection...? Corin shook his head. Something within him was changing. Life was becoming more complicated. Women—it usually had something to do with them. But this time it was different.

When he looked at Ariane, Corin felt a soft side to his nature he never knew he had. This worried him. Corin was chary, sensing the emergence of a word he'd long since neglected: *responsibility*.

What was happening to him? Things used to be so simple. Kill or be killed. Drink, wench, win at dice—or else lose and leg it with the money anyway. A part of him knew those days were gone. Long gone, driven away by dark eyes and lashes.

"They be closin' captain!" Fassof's shout returned him to the immediate. The second pirate ship was almost upon them. Its crew waved cutlasses and spikes in anticipated glee.

"Hard on those oars!" roared Barin "Bend those backs, lads! Let's keep in front of this tub of shite; we can tackle the other one in due course. Row hard!"

Barin had lost three crewmen in the melee on the quay. Corin and Roman took their seats at the benches. Each grasped a vacant oar amid the heaving and groaning. The brigantine gathered pace, lurching toward the open water ahead.

But not fast enough.

Their foe was bridging the distance. In a few moments they would be assailed again. Barin doubted they could win through against such numbers this time. He struck the rail with his mallet-sized fist. Despite everything, they were caught in the web. It was depressing. Then he noticed Roman was gawping at the topmost yardarm, high above them.

"What's he doing now?" Roman pointed skyward like an excited schoolboy. "He's like a bloody human fly."

Corin looked up at the gloom. Bleyne the archer was perched precariously at the very top of the mast, his bow and sack of arrows slung askance across his back. Standing poised with admirable balance, Bleyne bent the bow and notched a shaft in place.

He held bow and arrow with his left hand while his right wrapped a dark cloth around the arrow tip. Corin saw the archer pour dark liquid onto the cloth. His eyes widened when the arrow blazed with sudden flame.

In one fluid action Bleyne let fly his fiery shaft at the enemy ship. It cometed over the water, an amber jet of flame lighting the near darkness around it, striking the helmsman in his chest, pinning him hard to the gunwale. The pilot yammered in horror as his body erupted in flame. Within seconds the deck caught and men scurried back and forth in panic.

A great roar of delight went up from the crew of *The Starlight Wanderer.* "Way hey! Whoa!" They shouted. "Way to go, archer fellow. Well done!" Corin and Roman traded a friendly head butt, while Cale cartwheeled soggy along the deck. Ariane clapped whilst Galed just belched in silent wonder. The brigantine surged ahead, thanks to Bleyne once again.

That only left one.

"That was some impressive bowmanship!" Barin beamed as Bleyne rejoined them on deck. "That was an impossible shot. The finest I've ever seen! What are you, a bloody elf or something?"

"I don't know what you mean," replied Bleyne, looking annoyed for once.

Barin looked puzzled, and Corin, seeing his friends baffled face, waved him relax.

"Bleyne doesn't say much about his past," Corin told Barin. "Come to think of it, he doesn't say much about anything."

The archer shrugged, already bored with the banter, and nodded gratefully when a sailor offered him a flask of wine to quench his thirst. "That fire should keep them busy for a while," he acknowledged after a moment's reflection.

"I did not know you were a sorcerer, Bleyne!" Ariane hugged the archer in delight. Galed and Cale stood gaping on deck. Cale's face was flushed with excitement. This was good stuff.

"What was that uncanny liquid, Mr. Archer?" Cale asked wide-eyed and watching the flames crackle and hiss on the rapidly shrinking ship. "It burns like dragon's breath—if such things exist,"

Cale added quickly lest they thought him gullible for believing in such stuff.

"I'll shove a dragon up your arse," muttered Corin, but Cale ignored him.

"It's an ointment of the goddess," replied Bleyne matter of factly. "Together with a few holy words in Faen. That is all—nothing special."

"Well, whatever it was it certainly surprised our friends back there!" guffawed Barin. "Now it's my turn. Let's look to this last fellow!"

Night fell. Ahead bulked the harbor wall's crablike arms, a gap showing narrowly between them. White water crashed and spumed through the gap, promising a choppy crossing should they win through. The ocean beyond heaved wintry grey-black in the rapidly fading light. The last enemy ship bridged the gap, blocking them off from the open sea.

"What do we do now?" Corin asked Barin, who was scratching his ear.

"Wait and see," responded his friend. He winked at Cale and spun the wheel. *The Starlight Wanderer* pitched to portside, nearly throwing a startled Galed overboard, and then rounded hard on the smaller pirate ship.

Waves parted like torn cloth as the brig ploughed ahead, eager and hungry for her prey. Ariane and Roman watched with open mouths, and Corin's eyes were wide, but Barin laughed out loud.

"WA-hey! Don't you just love this?" Barin yelled. Corin, startled, glanced up at his hulking comrade, wondering if he was possessed by some random demon. The giant's blonde braided locks lifted in the wind, trailing behind his craggy face. Barin resembled a war god out of the fables of the distant northlands.

"Full ahead, lads. Wind and oar!" Barin roared in glee. "Let us put an end to this carrion filth!"

Corin watched, stunned. He didn't notice the shivering Galed just behind him or the boy. Cale's hair stuck out like ginger snaps and his gaping mouth gave him the appearance of a hooked guppy.

"Surely we're not going to ram that ship?" the boy asked in

horror. Beside him Galed covered his face with both hands.

Corin turned, witnessing them both vanish below decks. He turned back. The gap was closing fast. Three hundred yards, two hundred, one...

Shite... Corin grabbed the rail and locked his arm around it.

Too late the Crenise realized their peril. They swarmed and stumbled, heaved on the tiller, panicking, realizing their folly as the great ship of the north reared terrible above them.

The iron eagle-head ram (hitherto hidden beneath the waves) tore into the black ship with a wrenching, scraping, horrible groan. Men screamed, crushed and torn limb from limb. Others were pitched into the pitiless swell to drown.

"Come on, you worms!" boomed Barin, his face florid with rage. "Feel the kiss of *The Starlight Wanderer!*" The brig's bow engulfed the pirate ship, consuming it utterly, splitting the narrow hull in two with a final sickening crack.

Within minutes the cold sea had claimed it, both decks and ragged sail. The crew cheered as Barin of Valkador expertly piloted his ship through the churning gap, out of Kashorn harbor and into the open sea beyond.

Behind, the last desperate cries of drowning men were soon swallowed by the night. Shoreward, the first ship had torn itself loose from the vengeful fisher folk of Kashorn. It limped across the harbor, manned by scarce a dozen crew (the rest fish bait and a few unfortunates dragged ashore alive and kicking for retribution long unpaid). The ship passed its fire-ravished sister still burning readily and casting an orange glow in the darkness behind.

Against all odds, they had won free, thanks to Bleyne the archer and the seamanship of Valkador.

As night closed in, Kashorn's folk cheered on the quayside. The men stripped the captives naked and sharpened their fish hooks and flensing knives, whilst their wives brought ale for their celebration.

Their enemies were vanquished; once again the town was their own. They watched spellbound, as the blue and silver sails of the great ship faded into the darkness of the Western Ocean.

Where the brigantine had come from, or why, they couldn't begin to guess. But they would never forget her. Neither would they forget the terrible giant with the windmill-huge axe, the wild-eyed murdering longswordsman, and the fighting dark-haired beauty accompanying him.

The few surviving mercenaries had fled into the night. No, the people of Kashorn would not forget this day. Not for many years. They had sent their enemies packing.

Time to do nasty things to those prisoners...

An hour later, Corin watched wistfully as the harbor slipped to stern. He could see the lights of Kashorn's taverns twinkling into life.

Looks like I'm going to Crenna after all. Thank you, Elanion. Thank you very much.

A gruff voice shattered his train of thought. "Well, that was a good afternoon's work." Barin's reckless, gleeful rage had been replaced by his habitual good nature. The ship's master rewarded Corin with a broad grin.

"Well met, again, Corin an Fol. Good is it seeing you hale, laddie. I look forward to a rematch at dice and hearing all the news of your journey. That Queen is some looker, eh!"

"That she is," Corin acknowledged without expansion. Despite everything, he felt relieved to be on board.

She needs me...

Within earshot, her small hands gripping the starboard rail, Ariane pretended she hadn't heard those last words. She smiled impishly. They'd sprung the trap! Whatever perils lay ahead, they had done well up to now.

The boy who called himself Cale was staring at her with adoring eyes. She liked the lad despite Corin's misgivings and general disgust that he'd joined them. Corin was wrong this time. Cale would prove a good companion.

He'd mixed with ill company thus far and just needed the right guidance, she deemed. She brushed salty locks from her face and smiled at the starlit sky engulfing them. Behind, Barin stood guffawing with Corin and Roman her champion. For an hour she watched them dice away the night beneath a diadem of stars. At least she had good men beside her. No, not good, never good. Magnificent!

Corin watched the Queen of Kelwyn retire below deck. The boy followed, eyeing him warily, clinging to her shadow like magnet to metal. That boy was trouble, but Corin had to hand it to him, the lad knew which way his bread was buttered.

I was trouble at that age, too. I still am trouble. As long as he stays out of my way we'll get along just fine.

Corin nodded to Roman as the big swordsman bade him goodnight. He liked Roman. In fact, he liked all his new friends bar Cale. He was even warming to Galed, who had shown rare courage today.

Corin questioned his new emotions again. Was he becoming soft? He needed a beer certainly; he'd not had one in days. He glanced above. The sky's tapestry filled the night, its cast of pearly billions dancing on the water. Corin shivered. It was chilly and the hour late. Sighing, he turned to his hulking friend lounging at the wheel. Together they watched the distant lamps of Kashorn harbor dwindle into yesterday.

"Any word from Silon?" Corin asked his friend.

"I set him ashore at Fardoris, on Tarin's trail," replied Barin, "then turned north again. He plans to hold council with Belmarius in southern Raleen but has business to attend in Permio first. Belmarius's army is camped somewhere near the river Liaho. His Bears still remain faithful to Prince Tarin. Silon remains optimistic for our chances."

"Glad someone does."

Barin turned and waved a curt thanks to Fassof, who had handed the two friends a cold mug of ale each. Corin scarcely disguised his delight.

They sipped in silence for some time, listening to the lapping water, each wrapped in their own thoughts. Barin was thinking of his honey-haired daughters and his blue-eyed busty wife. As ever, he missed them.

Corin's thoughts were on the journey ahead. A journey he'd not intended to undergo. Crenna. Of all places he was going to

Crenna. It was almost morning when Barin broke their silence. His face was thoughtful, rather sad.

"I feel that we stand on the brink of war," he sighed. "A war more final and terrible than any that have preceded it." He drained his ale mug for the twelfth time that night. "Caswallon has become powerful in Kelthaine," Barin continued. "Far too powerful. Kella is a hostile place these days."

Corin nodded, saying nothing. They had survived Kashorn, but Caswallon would be aware of that soon enough, if not from Hagan then from his other spies. Meanwhile they were sailing into even greater peril, to the island of his childhood enemies. The people who had butchered his family.

So be it.

Corin shrugged, finally relinquishing his battle with whatever fate awaited him. He would have made a hopeless farmer or a fisherman anyway. He turned to Barin with a sudden grin

"Let's go below for another ale and a final game. I swear I'll beat you sooner or later."

Barin chuckled deeply. "I doubt it," he answered. "You're too impatient, laddo." He turned to the mate who stood close by. "Fassof, mind the helm and keep a skeleton watch. Let most the lads sleep." The mate nodded. "Oh, and Fassof," added Barin.

"What?"

"Set course for Crenna, old chap."

***

Hagan watched from the cliff tops as the brigantine slipped into the night. He was left with nine men only. Even worse, one of them was Borgil. Things had gone badly awry.

No matter. He'd still get Caswallon's gold. It would just take longer than he'd expected. His face stung from a shallow cut he'd received from Corin. Another debt to pay, he acknowledged.

Hagan smiled. Next time, he would be the victor. One of his sharper-eyed men had informed him Cale had been hauled on board Barin's ship. Hagan admired that lad. He'd still slit his throat for deserting him.

Hagan never forgave. He would journey south at first light. He wasn't relishing explaining things to the new Lord of Kella, admitting that his mission thus far had failed.

But Hagan was no craven. He would have his gold, sorcerer or no sorcerer. Then he would recruit more men, seek out Corin an Fol, and finish him with sharp steel, leaving him bleeding in some rat-infested gutter. Then he'd capture that feisty bitch of a Queen and drag her in chains to Caswallon.

He'd get a few sly pokes up her arse before the warlock had his wicked way. The Morwellan killer smiled that crooked smile. Smiling—it was becoming a habit of late. The new Hagan, jocular and urbane. In his mind he'd already formed the blueprint to a plan. He would be rich within a month or two. It was all that mattered.

End of Part One

Part Two

Island

Chapter 18

Schemers and Dreamers

Night crouched on Kella like a brooding beast. Nothing stirred. The twisted cobbled streets were deserted. Even the skinny dogs scurrying about for scraps of food seemed furtive.

It was almost tangible, a mood of foreboding lurking and creeping outside the smoke-clogged houses whilst the city folk shivered within. The dark hours were very dangerous in Kella these days. There were things prowling out there in the streets—shadowy things, creatures that even the wildest dogs gave a wide birth. From whence they came no one knew, though everyone suspected.

Out on the walls, the guards paced back and forth, as restless as the rest. Occasionally one of them would glance up at the high tower of Kell's golden palace and shudder. A sorcerer dwelt there now.

Soft footsteps announced the arrival of the Captain of the Citadel, the newly appointed Lord Perani. Formerly the High King's champion, he had thrown his lot in with Caswallon and held the city under curfew.

The two guards sprang to attention as their captain's burly frame emerged from the night. "All is quiet, my lord," said the nearest man, a slight quaver in his voice. "The city sleeps."

"That is well," responded Perani with a growl. The deep voice fitted well with the captain's ferocious appearance. Perani was a big man, broad of shoulder and strong boned. It was said none had ever bested him with the sword. The heavyset features were scarred from his many fights.

Once, he'd been Lord General of the elite Tigers, but the Tigers were gone, disbanded on Caswallon's orders after the disgraced Belmarius had fled with his Bear Regiment following the failed coup two years back. Belmarius and Halfdan had both become alarmed at how Caswallon's influence was clouding all the High King's decisions. They had approached Perani to gain his support and, after council, the three agreed to act against Caswallon, using their influence to banish him and his followers from the realm. But Perani was already in Caswallon's pay. He betrayed his fellow generals. The Tigers turned on the other two regiments, and so the coup failed before it even began.

After that, Perani's first task had been to smash the Wolves, the only regiment still openly defiant to Caswallon. Those Wolves not put to the sword had vanished with their outlawed leader, Halfdan, rumored dead.

Since that pathetic insurrection, Caswallon smelled treachery everywhere. Hence, the "loyal" Tigers were no more. The coup had been quashed under the High King's orders, but even back then everyone knew who was behind the action.

Caswallon had been cunning, working on Kelsalion's paranoia until the High King ordered the swift execution of many notable loyalists, his staunchest supporters. So two years later, when Caswallon seized control in Kella, most his enemies were already dead. Perani, shrewd and forward thinking, had made his choice then. Live or die—simple really.

Perani looked up at the high tower, from whence there shone a single yellow light, the only glow allowed in Kella after the midnight hour. Caswallon forbade illumination, as it compromised his alchemy.

Despite his stoic nature, Perani shuddered, feeling the growing menace emanating from that light high above. What transpired up there no one knew, or at least lived to say. Perani shook his head, wondering what price he would have to pay for serving this new ruler. Power always had its price.

"Keep alert!" he snapped at the two men. Relief showed in their eyes as he curtly left them to their cold duty. It had been a bloody business, the remolding of Kella City. Initially there had been a lot of resistance among the noble houses, those still alive after the coup the previous summer.

After the initial shock of the High King's assassination, many had suspected Caswallon's involvement. Only a week ago a few of these had sought to bring him down in various ways. They were foolhardy, brave men. They—and their families—had died horribly. There were few of Kell's noble descendants left, thanks to Caswallon—and Perani.

A scream was cut short somewhere deep in the city.

That'll be the Groil feeding.

Perani still struggled with the Groil, creatures of sorcery summoned in the depth of night. The city was crawling with them.

But what choice did he have? To remain neutral was no option. And he was ambitious, seeing his own rise to wealth and power written in the new order.

It had been easy, really. Those two great lords of Kelthaine were both far away now and no threat: Belmarius in the south, sulking on the Permian border, awaiting the war with the Sultan that would surely come. With him, the third army of Kelthaine, the displaced Bears. They would die down there in the heat and dust.

Of Lord Halfdan's whereabouts no one was certain, though Perani suspected he was still alive. The High King's brother was fox cunning. Perani didn't go with the rumor of his death and instead suspected Halfdan was walled up in his mountain fortress, Point Keep. Halfdan could hold out for months there, as Point Keep lay hidden in the deep folds of the High Wall itself. Together with its sister castle, Car Carranis, Point Keep guarded the Gap of Leeth in the northeastern frontier of Kelthaine. Both strongholds remained loyal to the dead High King. Halfdan, were he alive, was doubtless plotting revenge with his surviving Wolves.

Let him rot there for the meanwhile—they'd flush Halfdan's wolf pack out in due course, once Caswallon had dealt with the other rebels down in Kelwyn. Besides, they'd probably kill each other out of sheer boredom.

The Wolves had ever been a band of drunken ruffians, commoners recruited mainly for their violent nature and reckless courage, despised in Kella even before the coup. But during that fight most had died defending their city whilst Belmarius had slunk away and Perani sold out.

Another scream—this one closer. The Groil were busy tonight.

A year back Craggon, the last Lord Captain of the Citadel, had met with an unfortunate accident. Caswallon had given his commission to Perani, together with certain other rewards.

After the High King's murder, Perani had seized the heads of various noble families and dragged them before the council, claiming they were Permian sympathizers involved in the assassination of Kelsalion—ridiculous notion though that was.

The unfortunates had been swiftly tried, tortured, and beheaded. Those heads still rotted on spikes above the South Gate, a warning to General Belmarius should he rediscover his courage and return.

The nobles' homes were burned down, those not taken by the sorcerer's people, and their families were executed or sold into slavery—all save the young girls and boys. These went to Caswallon, whose appetite was large in such matters.

It had not stopped there. Perani had almost lost his nerve when he witnessed Caswallon's full wrath descending on the city. The memory of that slaughter still hung in the air.

All suspected supporters of the renegade son of Kelsalion were put to the sword, which meant anyone not in Caswallon's pay. Perani, battle hardened and ruthless, had never witnessed such carnage. His hands were bloodied too, for he'd needed to show his commitment. It haunted him at night. He hadn't slept much since then.

Regret? Too late, much too late.

Besides, Perani stood to gain much. He had replaced his officers with men as ruthless as himself, the foremost the brutish Derino. Perani adjusted his fox-fur cloak to keep out the night chill. Deep in thought, he continued his walk amongst the granite battlements fencing the troubled city from without.

More screams. Perani turned in time to see three shadowy misshaped figures dragging what looked to be a body down a side passage into gloom. The nearest shadow, as though sensing that Perani watched, turned and gazed up at the walls. Perani shuddered when that canine snout snuffled in his direction. Then they were gone, off hunting for yet more flesh.

What choice did he have?

***

The Astrologer's Nest was the highest room in the tower, a lone chamber hundreds of feet above the main palace. Once, it had been full of maps of strange lands, orbs, crystals, star charts, and other marvelous things.

Like his forbears, the High King had come here often with his councilors in earlier days, before the darkness had seeped into his soul after the loss at sea of his wife and first born. Many times, Kelsalion had stared out on cold nights like this one, counting the stars that surmounted the sky.

That was then.

Now the High King was dead, conveniently murdered, his son fled, feared lost. Like the Palace, this tower served a new master. Those human servants still alive stayed well away from this lofty place unless summoned hence by the sorcerer, or else his chief retainer, the Groil called Flail.

Caswallon glared into the glass orb, another gift form his new "mentor" but one which today awarded small pleasure. He'd been scrying for half hour, seeking the appointed place. At last he found it. Within the globe's midst Caswallon saw a field, broken stones, and ivy-strewn masonry.

Waysmeet Village.

Staring closer, Caswallon saw the Groil, and his eyes narrowed. Two score lay scattered there, hacked and bloody, strewn about the ruins.

So, she got away.

He had underestimated the rebels. Maybe they had help too, but who and why? Not to worry. There was still the Assassin's man, Hagan Delmorier—very dependable, so Rael had told him.

Caswallon ran his lean fingers over the crystal surface, and the scene shifted north. He found the cliffs and ocean, but Kashorn was veiled by mist. Frustrated and disappointed by the Groil's inexplicable failure, Caswallon stood, walked over to the lone window, and gazed out into the night.

A knock on the door, then a scrape and thud. Flail bringing another girl.

Caswallon turned, saw Six Claws drag the half-naked, weeping wretch into the room. The Groil slung her on the carpet, where she remained like a dead thing. She was younger than the last one had been.

Caswallon liked them young—and the boys too, when the mood took him. He ignored her. She was less than nothing. His mind was on higher matters.

He'd always been ambitious, even in the early days when his shrewd council had won him high favor with Kelsalion. He'd risen above his peers, who came to fear the feverish glint in his eye.

As the High King aged rapidly, after his consort's death, Caswallon saw the change in his ruler, witnessed his ebbing confidence. He fed that doubt, sowed seeds of malcontent among the nobles at court: *Kelsalion has become weak, the Tekara's power is waning* were but two of the rumors he started years ago. He could rule better, Caswallon told those first confederates.

The land needed strength. Fresh blood was what was required, a new regime. So Caswallon bought followers with gold and cunning, allies to his cause. He placed them in high places, bidding them watch and listen, keep him informed. Through the years those spies swelled in number. Fear grew, as subtle whispers led to midnight knives.

After Lord Halfdan's son—the High King's nephew and only

heir—was lost at sea together with his beloved Queen, the desperate and forlorn Kelsalion clung to his chief advisor as though Caswallon alone could put paid to his wretchedness.

And from thence came his rise to power.

The bastard Tarin, mostly ignored by his father, became spoilt and vain, a foolish boy and not popular. Caswallon worked on Prince Tarin, too. He studied the night skies and awaited his chance. And then, after crushing the coup three years ago, Caswallon was strong enough to summon the Dog People out of the dark places.

At first he was terrified. He'd studied the dark crafts for years, learning much of lore, but that didn't prepare him for that first visit. His mind's eye had wondered far, yearning for knowledge. And far beneath the earth Caswallon found them waiting, the custodians of all the knowledge he desired.

The Urgolais, they were called. The ancient Dog People, whose blood had been corrupted by the stain of Old Night in millennia past—or so it was said. Caswallon was challenged. The Urgolais leader, Morak, questioned him long and hard in that dark place.

Though long ago defeated and driven underground, Morak's surviving kin still retained some of their latent power. Morak had been a servant of Old Night during the Second War of the Gods. He'd been burnt horribly during that time, his features twisted and warped and his skull misshapen. The Dog Lord, his enemies called him after that.

A dark soul, Morak craved vengeance on those who had helped his enemies, the Aralais, also necromancers of yesteryear. For his part, Morak, a shadow of what he had been during the bitter war with the Aralais, saw in Caswallon a way of destroying those that had aided his enemies, the descendants of Kell.

So the Dog Lord and his kin made a pact with Caswallon. They would give Kelsalion's councilor dark new powers in return for service to their cause, the seeking out and final obliteration of the Aralais people and the allies they had, for Morak believed there were Aralais still thriving in the far corners of the nine worlds. And so started the unholy alliance between mortal sorcerer and alien witch lord.

Caswallon turned to the fire, which crackled but awarded little heat from the mantle. He felt tense, nervous. He had delayed this moment long enough. Procrastinating and dwelling on past achievements would gain him nothing. He couldn't put it off any longer.

Time to summon his mentor. Caswallon prepared his mind for the contact, summoning inner strength and banishing fear to the furthest corner of his mind. It was never easy speaking with the Dog Lord. Caswallon stared into the fire, filtering away any random thoughts. He commenced focusing, channeling...

***

That same night, away north, moonlight spilled on dark shapes, a fleet of galleons one hundred strong, all sailing south, gliding downstream toward a sleeping city. Before now, it had only been raids, but that had changed. Everything had changed.

This was the commencement—the start of it all. The iron-crowned King stood tall on the prow of the leading vessel, two of his sons beside him.

In silence they stood there, until morning rose wet and cold and the city was in sight just ahead. All three grinned as the docks shadowed into view. Minutes later they disembarked—a host of shaggy men, ten thousand strong.

Most would range south east for Car Carranis, but a few would stay put, linger just long enough to leave this proud city in ruins. The King gave the order and the carnage began. Too late the watchtower guards saw them.

At last, after long preparations, the real invasion of Morwella had begun.

***

That night Shallan, first lady of Morwella, dreamt she walked the woods again, the branches creaking and the questing moon patrolling high above. As she approaches the ancient grove, her feet cold and bare, she sees him standing there.

The Horned Man, he of the sad, quiet eyes.

Shallan watches him as the night air tosses her cloak, and cascading leaves float down around her. He is very tall and, despite the icy chill, clad only in leggings of woven dun. His face is ageless yet chiseled by time.

The Horned Man's skin is nut brown, lined and scarred with those fine tattoos spiraling on forehead and cheek. The horns are long and twisting, thrusting out from the shaggy hair, ashen grey and wild, that tumbled well below his back.

He was broad of shoulder and deep of chest, hirsute and powerful. But it is the eyes that make her wonder. Those huge eyes told a thousand tales. They are the color of oak bark and are moist in the moonlight.

They are watching her.

He is a fearsome sight, but Shallan feels no dread. Rather she feels familiarity, a link from her past. But what and how? Somehow she knows this being is her friend and wants to warn her of something. As before, she tries approaching him, but he shifts back into the trees, furtive and wary, shy even—strange for so fierce a being.

Who are you, what purpose your waiting here?

But even as Shallan speaks in her dream voice, the Horned Man turns away, head bowed and broad shoulders hunched, and walks silently back into the forest, his sinewy frame brushed by gossamer and moonlight.

Shallan knows she can't follow, not yet.

She woke then.

The predawn grey paled her bare walls and ceiling. Shallan rolled free of the heavy covers and shivered, reaching across for her wolf-skin cloak and then taking a seat by the lone window, as was often her want.

From there, as the wind tossed rain into her face, Shallan gazed out on the city far below. Beyond those glistening roofs, the slatey river showed sluggish and mournful. Shallan saw ships down there, their hulls and masts rocking in the young day's gale.

Vangaris, a city beset by storms. Morwella, a country on the brink of ruin, overrun by brigands, and threatened by invasion on all fronts.

And no word from Kella City. It was apparent the new ruler of Kelthaine cared not for the fate of its northern bastion. For years Vangaris had kept at bay the Crenise menace and those barbarians out of wild Leeth and beyond.

But now it seemed they were expendable. Once, they'd been the jewel in poor Kelsalion's eyes, Shallan's long dead aunt, the High Queen, had been Morwellan, after all. How times change, and this Caswallon was rumored a tyrant. They would receive no aid from that quarter, not now.

A soft knock at the door. Her father—who else.

"I am awake," Shallan told him without turning her head.

He entered, a small man, neat and precise, garbed in heavy cloak and gilded cloth and with slender blade at waist.

The Duke Tomais, noble and kind, but lost without his lovely wife, her dear mother gone so many years. There was just the two of them now that Shallan's brothers had set out to put down the uprising in the north, that rebellion caused and fed—Shallan had no doubt—by the brutal renegade Hagan Delmorier.

"We must speak, daughter." The duke looked tired. He hardly ever sleeps these days, the worry eating into him. Shallan frets for his health.

She nodded and he entered, taking a chair across from where she still gazed winsome out the window.

"You'll catch chill, child," Tomais told her, and Shallan shrugged indifference. He rubbed his troubled eyes and fidgeted.

"You are leaving Vangaris, Shallan, tomorrow at first light."

"No."

"You must!" The duke's left hand thudded into his right palm, and Shallan almost cried at the pain so evident in his face. "I will not be challenged in this, girl."

"I'm not leaving you, father, not with the wolves gathering hungry outside."

"And what can you do to assay the storm, child? Your heart is strong, as was your mother's, but you are young yet and naïve."

"I've seen twenty-seven winters, father," Shallan answered, the determination setting her mouth. "Most noblewoman are long wed at my age, with several bairns at their feet. And those poor common folk, well, they are often old and bent by toil and strain when they reach my years. Young, no father, I am not young."

Shallan knew she was beautiful, had seen it in men's eyes for years. For most of her adult life, she had endured the trite poetry of vain suitors and smiled politely whilst receiving shallow flattery from stupid, idle troubadours. There were no real men left in Morwella these days, not since her brothers had departed.

Shallan of Morwella, lady of the flowing chestnut locks and blue-grey gaze. Tall, graceful, and serene. That perfect oval face with skin of flawless ivory. She of the full red lips and winsome smile. That was how they saw her, those fools at the feasting hall. She might look serene, but inside Shallan, a fire raged. How she hated this world!

"Stop dreaming!" The duke slammed his palm again. "I'll brook no argument, daughter. You will leave on tomorrow's tide, bound for Wynais, where your cousin, the Queen, will doubtless be happy to receive you."

"Ariane?" *That little bitch. Father, you have no idea.*

"Of course Ariane." The duke was becoming annoyed. "I will leave you to your morning peruse, beloved. Don't catch a chill, you need be fit for the journey."

"I'm not going, father."

He didn't hear her, had already left the room. Shallan shrugged, turned back to witness late-autumn sunlight waken the city streets below. Her dreamy gaze followed the river north, and it was there, at its wide marshy mouth, that she saw them.

A fleet of ships.

Five score at least, baroque and savage in design. Raiders or invaders for sure! Shallan watched the distant vessels emerge into the morning. She gazed down with morbid fascination as the following wind guided them down like so many gaudy, swaying towers toward Vangaris's docks.

Shallan smiled a bitter smile then. She'd got her wish and wouldn't be leaving tomorrow. She wouldn't be leaving any time soon.

Chapter 19

The Gift

The room in the tower fell deathly cold. A tangible silence emanated from the walls. The air shimmered then congealed. The fire spluttered once, then went out. His lone candle did the same. The forgotten girl wailed by the door. She turned, tried to flee into the corridor beyond.

"Stay!" the tiny part of him that noticed her ordered. Caswallon's face remained fixed on the smoky essence, creeping like canker from the shrunken fire. She froze, the girl, caught like a lamped rabbit, her pale skin glistening with icy sweat.

A peel of smoke lingered in the hearth. That smoke took form, became a face, a horrible face scaled and blistered by ancient burns, the skin like wintry leaves. Two yellow eyes gazed out like frozen lanterns above a long hairless snout terminating in wide nostrils, flaring and moist with odor.

The girl screamed, but no one heard her. Caswallon controlled his urge to run. This was always the hard part. He stared back at the face hovering above the mantle.

Those yellow eyes saw the girl and raked her naked flesh. She crumpled, her prone, lifeless form blocking the doorway. The Dog

Face turned away. Outside, dark cloud occluded the stars. Fear stole silent into every corner of the city.

The Urgolais had come.

"Lord Morak." Caswallon bowed stiffly, trying to keep his dignity and not show any fear of this creature, who fed so hungrily on that emotion. "Forgive my urgent summons. I believe our enemies have help from some unknown quarter. There is doubt in my mind on how best to proceed. What must I do? I seek only to serve, aid your cause, so I seek your help in this."

The eyes flickered once, then narrowed to feverish slivers. The voice, when it came, was remote yet resonant. It carried within it the stench of the gallows.

"We are aware." The voice slithered like invisible slime. *"Our enemy seeks to block our return to power. It is to be expected. He will fail. He is nothing to what he once was, whereas we are many. He stands alone, for his brethren are scattered wide and far.*

The ravages of time have worked hard upon him. Like us, he must rely on the strength of petty mortals to do his work. Mortals that you will destroy, Caswallon."

"The rebels' time is short, if they're not dead already, then they soon will be." Caswallon's hands were shakin. "There are none dare challenge the Urgolais' return to Ansu. I will personally deal with this upstart Queen."

"The Queen is of no consequence to us, fool." The voice crackled like fire sticks in rain. *"You may do with her what you wish."* A weird sound followed, like a dog laughing, were such a thing possible. *"You are transparent, Caswallon. You seek the girl as a plaything. That does not concern us, but something else does."*

The eyes blazed wide suddenly, making Caswallon start in his chair. He gripped its wooden arms and clung on.

"One mortal does interest us. This one the Huntsman has chosen for his conduit. The Huntsman is our enemy. His puppet must be destroyed. We have tried twice, but he is protected, and without Golganak, our powers are too weak for us to manifest fully."

"Who is this man? I'll send word have him brought here in chains."

"No need. His name is Corin an Fol. He accompanies your little Queen. Even now, they sail to Crenna after overcoming your useless snares. You wasted my Groil, Caswallon. Don't waste anymore. It takes work fashioning such creatures in our form."

"They escaped the trap at Kashorn?"

"Of course they did, fool. I know not what the Huntsman plans with this man. Maybe he intends to use him as a pawn against Old Night. The Huntsman is wily. He alone of the gods our master cannot read."

"I know nothing of the man that you speak of, lord," replied Caswallon, embarrassed and annoyed that his lust for Queen Ariane had been so easily detected. "But I vow to you, this Corin an Fol will soon be dead, together with his companions, all save the Queen. I will send word by pigeon to the Assassin in Crenna so he can prepare for their arrival."

"There is no need; I have brought one that will serve you better than birds." The dog laugh again—it put Caswallon's teeth on edge.

"More Groil will be arriving through the coming weeks. As my powers return I will fashion more still. Other beings will follow. Soon shall your army swell with griffins and trolls, ogres and shadowstalkers. And then there is Vaarg. He may pay you a visit soon.

"Vaarg?" Caswallon paled. "I thought the dragons all dead."

"The time for Old Night's return draws nigh, mortal wizard. We must serve him in absolution or be foiled by our enemies again. Like our master, the Huntsman never sleeps!"

Those yellow lamp eyes probed the room for a moment, and the snout sniffed at some hidden scent. Then Morak's gaze tore upon the prone figure of the girl, much like a hawk espying a mouse whilst hunting high above.

The maw opened, revealing grey broken fangs. A fleshy liverish tongue lapped between them, slavering pinkish phlegm on the floor. Caswallon gagged at the stench.

"We sense a challenge on the island of Crenna. Your Assassin has not been as wary as he thinks. Someone transpires against him. Someone familiar..." The serpent eyes wavered for a moment. *"But that cannot be... he was lost."* The dog-snout snarled then, as if some hidden enemy had entered the room.

"Send word to your servant in Crenna," the Dog Lord told Caswallon. *"These rebels must be caught and destroyed. You can keep your Queen for a while, but kill this Corin an Fol! And that fool Prince Tarin, he too must be slain.*

"It was most unwise of you to let him flee the city with the shards of the Tekara. Whilst they remain, our enemy still has a chance—and he is wily, Caswallon!

"You have not served us well in this and must prove sharper henceforth, if you are to reap your reward. You have much to gain, mortal. Once reunited with Golganak, we Urgolais will make you our foremost lieutenant here in this region of Ansu."

"And now for my gift."

Morak's sickly gaze shifted to far the corner where another dark shape was taking smoky form. Caswallon watched with wary eyes. Again he shielded his fear, though only just.

"I have a new servant for you." Those yellow eyes showed something that might be interpreted as humor as they fell on the steaming, stinking lump manifesting ugly beneath the table.

"What in Yffarn is that thing, lord?" Caswallon gulped before daring another glance at the evolving pile of brown-grey flesh to his right.

"This is Gribble," Morak told him. *"He is a Soilfin, an ancient creature newly awakened by our spell-craft. You will find him useful. Gribble can fly fast and hidden. He will act on your fargaze."*

Caswallon recalled hearing somewhere that creatures known as Soilfins had been involved in the long struggle between the Urgolais and the Aralais. Like the dragons, he'd believed them extinct. After another brief glance at the bubbling mess on the floor, he wished they still were.

"Do not fail us again, Caswallon. Your reward will be great

when we reclaim our heritage, but fail and your soul will be sent to Yffarn. I depart and leave you this Soilfin. There were many of his kind once. Most died in the last War between our people and the golden ones.

"Look after Gribble well. He will be of great use as a spy. Soilfin's have large appetites and require regular man flesh for sustenance. See that he is well fed before you send him to Crenna!"

When the Dog Lord stopped speaking, silence claimed the room, apart from a horrid scraping sound by the thing lurking under the table. Morak's yellow eyes were fading, and his ravished face and blackened snout dwindled back to acrid smoke. That smoke trailed off and vanished up the chimney. Caswallon breathed a sigh of relief and then dared look under the table.

That is disgusting...

Beneath the table the gurgling nastiness was taking shape quickly. Caswallon watched in horrible fascination, his nose twitching. The emerging creature stank of age-old sweat and stale detritus.

The Soilfin, Gribble. He saw the thing clearly now that the deeper dark of Morak's essence had departed. The size of a large cat, its face resembled that of an ape with small blood-red eyes. The foul smell clung like resin to its hairless hide.

The creature Gribble eyed him evilly, baring pointy, narrow teeth. Some were missing. The Soilfin's skin was a wrinkled leathery brown. Sinewy arms led down to bony fingers, each tipped with a cruel filthy talon. Sprouting from its stunted back were two leathery wings. Bat-like and large, they cocooned the ugly body beneath.

Gribble crawled out from under the table. The Soilfin hopped and flapped and winked up at Caswallon, who reached for his kerchief to quell the stench.

The half-conscious girl stirred, looked up, saw the goblin thing, and screamed in utter horror. The creature called Gribble watched her with greedy eyes, mouth dribbling, until once again she sank to the floor in merciful oblivion.

Caswallon regained his feet with a shudder. He felt wobbly

and a little sick, if truth be told—the Soilfin's stench not helping that. Caswallon paced to the window, levered it open, and got a blast of cold air.

A voice spoke behind him, the creature Gribble.

"I'm famished," Gribble announced. The voice was a squeaky, creaky unpleasantness. It set Caswallon's teeth on edge.

"So! And you must be fed often it seems," Caswallon answered, hiding his revulsion under duress. "Eat well. Then I've work for you, my new small friend," he added.

"I will serve you well, Mr. Caswallon," responded Gribble, dribbling and depositing resinous pools of foulness on the floor, "so long as you keep feeding me." Gribble's ape gaze fell on the girl, and he dribbled again.

"I am sure that you will." Caswallon turned to the terrified girl.

Not her...

"Go below," he told the girl, now awake, on her knees and sobbing. "Inform a servant send word to Lord Perani. I would speak with him at once. Oh, and get Flail or Two heads send a prisoner up here, no one of consequence. Gribble is hungry!" Caswallon laughed at the horror on the girl's face as she fled, weeping.

"Return to me soon!" he called after her fleeing form. "I too have an appetite for fresh meat."

***

Perani watched suspiciously as the palace servant hurried toward him out of the gloom. "My Lord Perani," panted the man. "You are requested to join the Sorcerer Caswallon in his high tower immediately."

"I am coming," replied Perani with a brief nod. He had anticipated this. He wondered what new atrocities he would be compelled to commit in the dark days ahead. His jaw was set with grim resignation; his lot was cast. There would be no turning back.

So be it

But as Perani turned to leave the battlements he paused, feeling cold eyes watching him from behind. Glancing over, the general noticed a raven had settled on the wall of the keep. The bird watched him in silence with those cold black eyes. There was something very unsettling about that stare.

Perani shuddered and turned away. Just a bloody bird. Trouble was, nothing was as it seemed in Kella City these days. Perani didn't like sorcery more than anyone else, but it was better to be on the side of he that controlled it.

And now to the palace and the long climb up that draughty tower. Only the gods knew what new horrors lurked inside that building.

Perani set his teeth together and squared his shoulders. Grim-faced, he made his way purposely toward the palace gates and his approaching doom. The raven swooped low and croaked insults over his head. It settled on a roof close by and again watched him with those canny eyes. Perani ignored the bird. He walked on but as he passed, the raven's cries mocked him.

Krani, krani, betrayer of the realm!

***

Dawn lit the rimy fields of Kelthaine. Above them flew the Soilfin on his new master's special orders. Freshly fed and invigorated, Gribble had swollen to the size of a large cow then shrunk again as he digested the dead High King's former head gardener.

Gribble needed food often, preferably humans, though cats and dogs were tolerable sufficing as a sandwich. He hated vegetables. Children were best. Very tasty. He could eat a dozen in one helping.

It was a paradox, so small a creature eating so much. But food was fuel and Soilfins had always been hungry. It was part of the reason they became extinct. There was never enough to eat—back then.

In good times, when he had served the Urgolais during the endless war, there had been plenty of food. The Urgolais were always torturing things and dismembering them, and the Soilfins always got the scraps.

Then those pale-eyed foreign men came from overseas, his

masters fled, and Gribble's kin were left to forage for what flesh they could find. They had been hunted ruthlessly until only a score remained. One such was Gribble. For a thousand years he'd clung to life, festering in his underground freezing cot, waiting for his old boss, Dog Lord Morak, to summon him again and then feed and succor him.

Gribble dribbled as he flew, thinking of juicy meat to come, winging high, an ungainly speck staining an otherwise flawless chilly sky. His destination was Crenna, the Island of Thieves.

First, though, he would wing north to the coast hard by Kashorn village. Mr. Caswallon wished to know his enemy's whereabouts. Gribble studied the land below as he flew, marking hamlets and farms in case he needed sustenance on his way back.

North of Kella the country rose in wooded hills, becoming increasingly rugged. He glimpsed the moonlit ribbon of road, followed its course until it met another by a deserted village at a crossroads, a bleak place showing no sign of life.

He swooped low, saw the creaking gibbet of bones nearby. Not much meat there. Beyond the crossroads filed a dark forest. Gribble skirted wide, sensing danger within those shadowy groves. He reached the coast, swept down from the cliffs, and swung low over the roofs of the harbor town.

How Gribble laughed when the weary drink-fuddled folk of Kashorn looked up in horror and swiftly took to their cups again.

Yes, it's me. I'm back!

Far out to sea soared the Soilfin, seeking a vessel: a trader, a brigantine with two sturdy masts and fourteen sails.

The Starlight Wanderer...

Just before dawn Gribble spied the vessel, resplendent in her rigging. He winged low, circled three times, his keen goblin eyes scanning, making sure these were his new master's quarries. They were dangerous terrorists, apparently, led by some Queen Mr. Caswallon wanted to poke. Bit of a shame that—Queens were usually rather tasty.

Gribble wheeled low again, showed the ship his arse, and then satisfied, the Soilfin turned skyward up into the blue, hurrying, needing to reach Crenna before the sun rose full. Soilfins shunned the daylight hours mostly, and besides, he was becoming hungry again.

Chapter 20

Into the West

Cale watched the sun rise over waves as the great creaking ship pitched toward morning. He stood at the stern, Queen Ariane at his side. Cale loved the Queen. He'd not known her a full day but had fallen for her big-time, from the second he'd seen her defiant, lovely face, had witnessed bug-eyed the way she stood up so feisty to nasty Hagan and his men.

Cale felt a bit guilty about Hagan. He had been genuine in his offer of loyal and useful service. But situations change. You have to keep your options open. One look at mountain-sized Barin had left him no doubt which would be the winning side, outnumbered or not.

Cale realized it had been rash to swim out in hope he could board the ship, rash and foolhardy. He'd just wanted to be with the Queen, though. And now he was. And when she smiled that sassy smile of hers, well, he would slay armies for her. It was love, unrequited, but he didn't mind that.

Cale didn't know much about their plans, his new comrades. That wasn't important. He was sure that things would work out. They had him with them, anyway. Cale was a great believer in providence. Sometimes things get rough, but you know, in the end you always win through. Just gotta keep an eye out for the hazards. He breathed deep, relishing the salty air, reveling at the pitch and roll and the sparkle of the wintry water below.

Aside the Queen, Cale liked Roman. The big gruff fighter had been kindly to him and had put him at ease. Bleyne was a strange one; he kept to himself and shared little. What an archer, though! Cale was in awe of his witchy skill. He did comment to the bowman once, but Bleyne hadn't responded. That one would take a bit of working out.

Of Barin he was in total awe. Who wouldn't be? The man was gigantic, his fists like dinner plates, and that shaggy blonde beard gave him a hulking haystack appearance. He'd winked at Cale, though, and grinned through those grizzled whiskers. Heartily relieved, the boy realized he'd found another ally.

Fassof and the crew ignored him totally, but then they ignored everyone. They were fine sailors, in Cale's evaluation of such matters. Not that he knew anything about boats—rather, ships. He knew the difference now. The northmen exuded vulgar confidence when they vaulted about the rigging and did the stuff that sailors do.

Cale hadn't warmed to Galed much, the balding squire being highly critical of his manners (which weren't the best he had to admit) and appearing rattled at the obvious affection Queen Ariane had for him. Squire Galed was a nitpicker who had taken it upon himself to criticize Cale at every given opportunity.

Corin was different. Alone of the party he kept his distance from Cale, except to scowl at him once or twice. There was something scary about Corin's eyes. Cale knew that his inherent charm would never work with that one. He caught his eye, and the long-swordsman turned away to talk to his friend Barin.

"He doesn't like me," Cale muttered trying to hide his nervousness. "It wasn't my fault back there in the smithy. I didn't hurt anyone." The Queen turned in his direction. "Why does he hate me?" Cale asked her.

"Corin doesn't hate you, Cale." Her words were soothing,

kindly. "He's just a troubled soul. He's been through a lot, and something about you reminds him of his past. Besides, you need to shape up." Her words were sterner. "You are lucky I didn't skewer you for siding with Hagan and his gang."

"I didn't know you back then."

"Hmm."

Ariane knew the boy's presence on board rankled Corin. She also knew those steely eyes held no hatred for the lad: rather sadness, and a haunting self-doubt.

"He'll come round. Just wait and see." she awarded Cale that dazzling smile, and Cale's eyes lit up. He was happy again. The Queen liked him, so nothing else mattered. He was her sworn man, Cale decided, now and forever.

Hagan's mercenaries couldn't match up to this sort of company, particularly Borgil the badger eater. Cale was meant for better things. He was on the up. He smiled warmly up at his Queen as the great ship fled the rising sun and charged glorious into the west.

Barin had kept a constant watch throughout the remainder of that night, choosing to take the helm himself and let grumpy Fassof get some sleep. Corin had joined him at first light, grumbling about Roman's virulent snoring, which had easily eclipsed the boom and thud of the waves.

He'd reached over to a bucket of seawater, immersed his head, and swore profusely at its icy touch. For an hour he took turn at wheel, greeting the others as they emerged amid sleepy eyes and yawns.

To stern, the sky washed pinkish grey. Corin glanced up as a skein of geese wended south, their honking cries low over water. Bleyne was already up, watching keenly from the prow. Corin glanced at the diminutive archer, then adjusted the borrowed priest's cloak to rebuff the chilling wind.

"A fine morning," Barin gave out. He looked fresh and alert despite his denial of sleep. Corin wished he felt the same.

"Any sign of pursuit?" he croaked. He studied the distant cliffs away to port and some miles off but saw nothing.

"I doubt our friends will trouble us again on this voyage," replied Barin. "They've little to gain, and if they return to their island without booty they will be a laughing stock among their peers." Barin rubbed his beard thoughtfully, shaking small chunks of three-day-old cheese loose from its knotty curls.

"No, I expect they'll lurk near Morwella and lie in wait for a fat, unsuspecting merchant ship on its way east to Vangaris Port!"

"How long will it take us to reach Crenna, Captain Barin?" Queen Ariane joined them. The boy Cale stayed put. Corin noted Ariane looked tired, her eyes betraying shadows of a restless night.

"Four or five days, Your Highness," responded Barin, "depending on the weather. The swell will grow as we enter the Western Ocean's expanse. Storms are common out there, particularly with winter approaching.

"Excuse me a moment." Barin yelled up at a bleary-eyed member of the crew. They were rather grumpy this morning. They'd drunk profusely last night, celebrating their victory over the pirates. Thick heads abounded. "Oi... shitehead!"

"What?" groaned the crewman, a stout bearded fellow with a jewel-encrusted dagger hanging from his belt.

"You look like a dog's breakfast, Cogga! Cease ya friggin' in the riggin'. Go below, tell that idle slug Ruagon get some food on the way for the Queen and my friends!" ordered Barin.

Stout Cogga grumbled his way below deck. Half hour later, the rotund galley master surfaced with a huge steaming plate of fresh mackerel. This was consumed gratefully by all.

Corin picked his teeth clean, then turned to Ariane.

"What are our plans on arrival?" he asked her.

Ariane didn't answer at first. She sipped her herb tea, needing time to think. She recalled a visit made to the island long before.

"I came to Crenna as a child accompanying my father, the King," she said eventually. "That was just before Rael Hakkenon seized control. In those days the islanders were our allies, and the pirates kept at bay over on the wild western coast."

Ariane took another sip and winced slightly as the hot liquid found an exposed nerve in a tooth. She continued.

"The main city is called Kranek. It lies on the southern side of the island. Kranek has a huge harbor, where Rael Hakkenon keeps his fleet of Sharks. He doesn't term them ships. High up, behind the walls of the city, and under the shadow of the mountains, is the massive Keep, where he and his loathsome minions reside. Beneath that tower of stone is where Prince Tarin will be held prisoner, of that I'm certain.

"We have two choices," she added. "We can either moor up on the north side of the island, which is more rugged and unin- habited so we are unlikely to be noticed. Or... we can sail round to the western side, which I do not know. That way is longer but not so mountainous, thus would prove less rigorous than crossing the island from the north."

"There is a third way, Queen," interrupted Barin with his mouth still full of fish. She chose to ignore that fact, but Galed's frown was evident, the squire having just surfaced green-faced from below.

"We could sail into Kranek harbor," Barin urged, oblivious of their horrified expressions, "and moor alongside our pirate friends!" He grinned, the idea amusing him greatly. Galed rolled his eyes in disbelief. He glanced sharply at Cale, who joined them in breakfast and was currently grinning up at Galed like an un- hinged cat. Galed swatted the boy's ear.

"I've been to Kranek many times," Barin was saying. "Valkador has no quarrel with Crenna. I am sure we can pull it off if we keep our heads. Err...maybe that's the wrong terminology."

"Oh, and there's every chance of that," mumbled Galed.

"That was before yesterday," said Corin, thinking of their clash in the harbor. "But it might work, Queen, if we pretend to be harmless merchants!"

"There is no such thing," cut in Roman, who also joined them, smelling breakfast.

Ariane sipped her tea. "I like not this suggestion," she told them. "Nevertheless, I shall consider your words. How about we fare below, escape this chill? I need warmth to think clearly, and we need to know exactly what we are doing."

Barin nodded. He bade scowling Fassof take the wheel whilst

he join the Queen in the comfort of his master's cabin. The others followed except Bleyne, who still watched hawk-like from the prow.

Cale shadowed the Queen. The boy took a seat nearby, keeping a wary eye on Corin, but the longswordsman was busy laughing at Roman Parrantios. Ariane's champion was swearing prolifically, having cracked his head on a beam. Corin marveled how Barin put up with all this low, bone-crunching timber. He must have to go about on his knees. Roman looked pale as he nursed his sore head, much to Corin's amusement.

"It's this northern ale," he complained. "They put something evil in it."

"Enough wining, Roman! Go get Bleyne," snapped Ariane. She frowned at her champion, irritated by his banter. "Clarity in this is crucial. I want everyone present. So get your bloody act together!"

"Sorry." Roman made a hasty exit.

By the time a subdued Roman returned with the archer, the others were already deep in conversation. Galed spoke out vigorously against Barin's bold plan. He favored crossing the island by foot. But Barin shook his head.

"It is too mountainous, squire, too treacherous and steep— particularly for your short legs!" He poured himself a large flagon of ale, gulping it down in seconds. "Ah, this is my proper breakfast." Barin wiped his mouth and belched. "What do you think, Bleyne? You haven't said much to date. What would Elanion's servant advise?"

"I have little knowledge of Crenna," responded the archer with his habitual half smile. "But there is need for haste, therefore I believe we have no alternative but to go with your plan, master Barin."

Corin yawned. "Personally I think we should let him rot on that bloody island—no offence, Highness." Ariane glared at Corin, but he persisted. "I mean, this seems a reckless venture just to rescue a wayward Prince."

"Did you not listen to the Goddess, Corin an Fol?" Ariane felt her face flush with emotion. "Were you asleep back there in the glade?"

"Of course not, and I'm on it—just think we're heading right for the spider's web. I've more cause to loathe Rael Hakkenon's boys than anyone here. Doesn't mean I want to throw my life away."

"We need to locate those shards, Corin," Barin intervened. "In their recovery lies our only chance of victory. Prince Tarin will know where they are."

"Barin's right, Corin. This isn't just about Tarin." Ariane placed a hand on Corin's shoulder, making him jump slightly. "The Goddess wouldn't send us to our deaths. I know this. The Tekara's remains are not in Caswallon's hands. Neither do the pirates possess them. If they did, the game would be over already."

"How can you be so sure?"

"Call it royal intuition." Ariane smiled at him, and Corin noted how her hand remained on his shoulder. Cale noted that, too, and curled his upper lip. "I know we still have a chance," she said. "Elanion will protect us."

"A fool's chance," muttered Corin. "But since we've got to do this, let's sail right on in, get the job done, and bugger off again."

"My sentiments exactly," added Roman whilst Cale announced this the best plan he could think of on such short notice. Roman cuffed the boy's ear, but Cale just grinned at him.

That left only Galed, but as usual, the squire was outvoted. Ariane ignored his protestations with an imperial wave of the hand.

"Time is against us, Galed. That much I concede," she said. "We must rescue Prince Tarin before it is too late!"

"But, Highness—

"Shut up!" Resigned, Galed did as he was told whilst Ariane studied each of the companions in turn, measuring their resolve.

"Do we concur, gentlemen?" Ariane asked then. They nodded, all save Galed, who was sulking, and Cale, who was scratching his ear. And Bleyne, who wasn't really doing anything. "Good. That's settled, then. We will take captain Barin's advice and sail openly into Kranek harbor. Then it's down to luck and the Goddess."

"And good sharp steel," Corin added.

"That too, should we require it."

That day passed bright and cold. To the south, distant cliffs smudged the horizon. Corin stared at them wistfully.

"The north coast of Fol," he informed Roman as they watched from the port rail. "My home lies beyond those bluffs. I would be retired there if I hadn't become embroiled in all this... excitement."

Corin wished his path lay that way instead of ahead to the island of his enemies. Roman didn't respond. He seemed lost in thought. After a while he made his excuses and went below.

Corin watched Roman leave before venturing aft and claiming a bench. Here for a time he moped silent in the sunshine, his mind troubled and wandering. Crenna—they were sailing to Crenna. Why was this happening to him?

A soft sound caused Corin to look up suddenly. The Queen folded neatly beside him.

Where had she come from? Corin had had no idea she was above deck. Caught off guard, he grunted hello and shuffled along the bench to allow her more space. He noticed she shuffled after him, closing the gap again.

Behind them, smiling-boy Fassof worked the wheel. Aside the mate and the odd crewman, Ariane and Corin had the aft deck to themselves.

"I'm sorry you've been caught up in all this," Ariane said softly, her eyes on the watery horizon.

Corin shrugged. "I was between jobs."

"Silon hinted at gold, didn't he?"

"He did...but,"

"You will receive it. I promise." Ariane's eyes were unsettling him in a most peculiar way.

"That's not why I'm here." Corin felt awkward now gold had been mentioned. "Coin was what got me moving, but now I've met you all, I—"

"No need to explain. I understand." Ariane awarded him a look that could have meant anything. She was tough to read, this Queen. But then, he'd never been good at understanding what went on inside a woman's head. He generally left that region alone and focused inside their skirts instead. A woman's mind was a danger-ous place. Evidently Queens were no exception to the rule.

"You are a good man, Corin an Fol. But you undersell yourself."

Corin frowned. Where was this going? Was she coming on to him or just being nice. For once, he edged toward caution.

"I've never done good things, Queen, only bad. I'm no worse than most of my kind, but no better either. I just am."

"And what exactly is your kind?" Ariane's lip curled slightly, hinting at amusement.

"Oh, you know, brigand, mercenary, general ruffian. I was in the Wolves after all."

"Thrown out, I heard. Quite a legacy." It was Corin's turn to gaze out at the ocean. So nice of Silon to mention that to her.

"Mine is a checkered past, Ariane."

"Aye, but an interesting one, I'll warrant." Her gaze fell toward the horizon again. "But the past doesn't concern me, longswordsman. The future, on the other hand..." Ariane sighed and made an odd gesture with her left hand. Apparently he wasn't the only one feeling awkward here.

"I'm glad you're with us, warrior. I need strong men beside me. And I appreciate how hard it must be for you to visit Crenna."

"I've always felt guilty I haven't visited before."

"What could you have done? Nothing can bring your kin back, Corin."

"I know, but killing a few Crenise would sure make me feel better. And I worry for you, Queen. I lack your total faith in the Goddess. It's not that I don't believe Elanion will help us, but sometimes shite just happens anyway."

"Then believe in me instead. It's love that keeps us strong, Corin an Fol."

Corin struggled to reply to that last sentence. By the time the words came, the Queen had already got up and left him.

I will always be there for you, Ariane.

Corin blinked and gulped air. What had all that been about? Had he missed something? He thought about following her, but she'd already vanished below decks.

Idiot.

Confused Corin blinked again and resumed his survey of the water. He found he could no longer concentrate. Damn that Queen. Was she playing games with him? Corin fidgeted and glared at the horizon. Were they bound for anywhere else, he would smile, but the thought of Ariane trapped on Crenna gave him scant room for joy.

Ahead was nothing but sea and sky, blue on blue. Clouds raced above, hurrying in from the west, and white horses crashed and foamed at either side of *The Starlight Wanderer's* wake.

Chapter 21

The Challenge

Days passed without event. Barin's crew, moody and sober, drove the ship on apace. The travelers amused themselves as they could. Corin played dice with Barin and laconic Fassof.

Cale watched dolphins chasing the bow whilst keeping as close to the Queen as she'd let him. Roman drilled the eager boy and reluctant Galed in the use of the broadsword, whilst Ariane watched pensive from the prow, her thoughts on the days ahead, on Prince Tarin, and the kingdom she had left behind. And on Corin an Fol.

Perched close by, standing permanently at the prow, was the solitary figure of Bleyne. What he was thinking no one could guess. Far behind, the rocky cape marking Fol's western tip dwindled into wintry distance.

On the third day out from Kashorn, they lost sight of land. All around stretched open water. "We have made good progress," announced Barin to his guests. "We should make Crenna on the eve of tomorrow."

"What's that?" Corin's eyes were on the ocean ahead. He pointed out to sea, slightly off to starboard. Dark jagged shapes could be seen jutting out of the water; they resembled the broken teeth of some ancient leviathan.

"Those are the Teeth of Croagon," replied Barin. "We will pass them shortly. They are a harbor for seals and seafowl."

"That is no seal," said the sharp-eyed Bleyne, pointing to the furthest rock. A figure stood there silhouetted against the sky. Soon they all saw him, an old man bent and stooping, shrouded by cloak and hood. On his left shoulder a large black bird perched silent. Corin cursed under his breath.

The Huntsman again.

He exchanged a worried glance with Ariane. Neither spoke.

They passed the rocky eyelets to port, their eyes fixed ahead, avoiding he who stood watching them in silence. The crew took to oar with grim faces, eager to be away.

Above, sails flapped, filled with sudden wind. It felt much colder. Racks of lowering cloud had swallowed the sun. Corin alone watched as they cleared the strange rocks and their silent witness dwindled to stern.

What is it you want with me, old man?

A sharp cry shattered his thoughts. Corin looked up, shielding his eyes with his right hand. He saw Fassof waving his arms about amid the blanket of sail.

"West away!" the mate yelled from his perch. "Dark sail on the horizon!"

"Friend or foe, I wonder," muttered Roman, who stood at Corin's right. Together they saw the square shape of a sail emerge above the waves. Barin stared hard at the sail for several minutes, his craggy face tense. It was coming straight toward them, swelling in size. Barin, at last recognizing the banner, swore a succession of colorful expletives. He knew that emblem well. He had good cause to. It was a golden boar snarling from a crimson background.

"Who is it, Captain Barin?" Ariane's pale face was taught with anxiety.

"It is the ship of my enemy," replied Barin. "See you. It bears the emblems of Leeth, of King Haal the Filthy." Barin spat over the gunwale.

"May he rot in the churning pits of Uffarn!" Barin looked closer at the vessel and his scowl deepened. "It's Daan Redhand himself, the King's firstborn and my sworn enemy. He is sailing directly toward us!"

"Will he attack?" Cale squeaked from somewhere behind. The boy's bravado was fading fast as he valiantly struggled with a necessary trip to the head below. He'd wedged himself between Roman and the Queen and scratched his ear nervously.

Cale had heard all about Leeth, heard what they did to their enemies in that horrible country. Kelthara wasn't far from the border, and there were many stories. The twins had told him that they ate babies in that land and waged war starkers, even the women. He tried to hold his teeth together as he watched the square bulk of the ugly vessel pitch angry toward them.

"It is unlikely, boy." Barin relaxed his gaze, seeing the worry in Cale's eyes. "The men of Leeth prefer to fight on solid ground. They lack the maritime skills possessed by those of Valkador."

Barin tugged his beard, pulling off a sizeable chunk. "I do wonder though," he continued in a voice meant for all of them. "What would bring Redhand this far from his homeland? He was never one to roam far from the coast of Leeth, not like his brothers."

They watched the ship approach. It was huge and bulky, sitting high on the water like an ungainly, swaying tower. Corin suspected it would be slower than the brig; it appeared unwieldy, arrogant in its construction, roughly square in shape, sporting four wooden turrets like a floating castle.

Corin had never imagined such a monstrosity. Later, Barin told him the craft was nothing more than a giant raft, the huge single sail dragging it across the ocean as though it were on skies.

Barin didn't rate the construction, but then he didn't rate anything about Leeth. It was gaudy, the timbers striped in yellow and red. They sprouted oars with haphazard abandon.

In silence they watched the monstrous vessel loom toward them, a menacing hulk pushing against waves and trailing foam in its wake. Shaggy men swamped the single deck, brandishing spears and axes, shouting and chewing their dirty beards. Corin exchanged a worried glance with Roman—not an encouraging sight.

They looked to be a grubby lot, their long hair stiff and spiky or else tied in wagging pleats. Cale's eyes bulged; he pictured this lot seated round a campfire farting and cavorting whilst cooking their parents. A part of him wondered whether he should have stayed with Hagan, then he looked up at the Queen and set his jaw. Cale would not let her down.

The hulk loomed nearer, threatening to engulf them. At the last moment it passed to starboard, scarce thirty feet away, its broad beam awash with jeering tattooed faces. Corin was relieved to see no archers on board. Rather, they sported long spears and heavy bladed axes.

Below, waves churned and eddied in the narrow gap between the ships. Fassof held steady at the helm. In minutes the ships would pass each other's wake and the danger would be gone. In the meantime, they must needs keep their heads.

A huge man shouldered his way through the throng. He was yelling at and punching anyone who didn't move fast enough. This must Barin's buddy, Corin thought.

Daan Redhand, warrior Prince of Leeth. He was huge, was Daan, towering over his men, who were also very big. The Prince was garbed in silver fur, his bare sinewy arms snaked with golden bands and rings. A gold circlet held his greying shaggy mane in place.

He looked arrogant and cruel. He alone of the company wore no tattoos. He grinned across the waves, sneering at them with massive arms folded and relaxed.

"So that's the infamous Daan Redhand." Ariane's jet orbs sparked defiance. "This encounter should prove interesting."

The Prince pulled back his rich fur cloak, revealing a long golden-hilted sword belted to his waist, together with a great twisted horn of some unspeakable beast. Gold hoops adorned the horn. He rested his ringed fingers on the rail and yelled across.

"Oi, Barin!" Daan's voice was crow-raw, guttural and harsh. "The hour draws near when we meet in battle. My sword, Icefang, longs for your neck!"

"Why not now, Redhand, you piece of shite!" countered Barin with a shout. He hefted his huge axe, his face flushed in anger. "Wyrmfang is hungry!"

Prince Redhand laughed cruelly at his enemy's defiant gesture. "I would sorely love to, as would my men!" Behind him his warriors roared and spat in agreement with their Prince. A few cast spears, which sank several feet short of the trader.

"Stop that, you morons." Redhand's eyes flashed with sudden anger, then he smiled again. Cale thought of a cat dismembering a mouse with a pair of small tongs. He was heartily glad the ship was already passing them astern.

"Unfortunately, I am somewhat pressed for time," shouted the Prince. "My father, the King, and my brothers have recently departed Grimhold to invade Morwella and Kelthaine's eastern borders." He laughed at the horrified looks on their faces.

"I can see this is fresh news. I so like being the bearer of joyful tidings. In the coming weeks, the Boar banner of Leeth shall crown the parapet of Point Keep. Car Carranis will follow this winter."

Redhand spread his brawny arms wide in a sweeping gesture. "I must hurry to join them for the slaughter whilst there is still plunder to be had and soft southern woman to be ploughed!" He made an obscene gesture with his fingers.

"You're a fucking liar!" Ariane couldn't contain her fury any longer. "Lord Halfdan holds Point Keep with his renowned Wolves; he will never surrender the city to shite like you!"

The Prince turned his attention on Ariane. He looked both surprised and amused to see her there. "I marvel at you, Barin, permitting a woman board your ship and letting her speak out of turn!"

Ariane, livid, was about to shout back, but Roman clutched her arm. "Careful, my Queen," he urged. "We don't want your identity revealed to this bastard. You'd best remain silent." Ariane nodded, but her look could have filleted the laughing Prince into edible chunks.

Redhand was still laughing, but he was further from them, standing haughty at the stern of his ship.

"When the last city in Kelthaine is reduced to ashes, I will come seeking you, Barin an Valkador," he shouted through cupped hands. "Be patient until that day. It will not be long in arriving!" Redhand's shouts faded from earshot. He raised the golden horn to his lips and blew three long blasts.

"Farewell, Barin!" Prince Redhand called after them. "We will meet again soon, and I shall drink from your skull!"

"Piss off!" Ariane yelled back, making the Prince roar with laughter.

"She's a feisty bitch, Barin. You all taking turns?" Barin, lost for words, was chewing his beard and snarling.

Corin watched the vessel slip astern. Beside him, Bleyne notched an arrow to his bowstring.

"Leave it, Bleyne, not this time," he told the archer. "This feud is a matter of honor between Barin and that barbarian shite. We dare not interfere." Bleyne shrugged as if the concept of honor was a thing both alien and absurd. He stored the arrow and unstrung his bow.

"Anything to keep the peace," Bleyne answered, then returned to his perch at the prow as if nothing untoward had occurred. Corin rolled his eyes. Bleyne wasn't easy company.

Corin watched Redhand's ship shrink with distance. Close by, the Queen and her champion were locked in deep debate. Redhand's news had caused a deal of alarm. Corin found it hard to swallow. He recalled those halcyon days in the Wolves serving under Lord Halfdan. The Queen was right; that one would never let Point Keep fall into the hands of its enemies.

"It cannot be true!" Ariane was saying as Corin joined the debate now unfolding. "We heard no news from the east before I left Wynais. Point Keep is the second greatest castle in the Four Kingdoms, well able to withstand a long siege. Even from those bastards."

"Do not believe that blackheart," said Barin, whose face had almost returned to its normal color. "I doubt there was any truth in his words." Ariane responded with a bleak smile. She then accompanied the ship's master below decks. Cale followed, grinning with relief. Once below, they were joined by Galed, who still sported a greenish hue, evidently feeling the ill effects of the rolling waves.

Corin remained on deck for a time. He needed to think, and seeing the Huntsman again had unnerved him.

"I wonder what is really occurring back in the Four Kingdoms," he pondered out loud. High above, the great Sea Eagle of Valkador swelled and billowed on the flapping lower main.

"I suspect we will know soon enough," came a gravelly voice. Corin turned. Roman stood beside him. "Those devils have surely come from Crenna."

"Think you the King of Leeth has formed alliance with Rael Hakkenon?" Corin's eyes probed Roman. If so, then things were rapidly getting out of hand.

"We must assume so." Roman looked despondent. Far behind, the tiny speck that was Redhand's ship faded into sky and water. Once again they were alone on the ocean.

"What is it, my friend. Does something ail you?" Corin looked hard at Roman, concerned by his pensive expression. He was usually the one that moped. Roman had proved a good-natured robust companion. Corin liked him greatly, but there was something about the way he looked that troubled him.

Roman shook his head slowly before replying. "I don't like being on this ship," he owned. "It gives a man too much time to think, especially fighting men like us." Corin nodded in agreement. "Something bothers me beyond the words of that bragging Prince. Something deeper, more profound."

Roman stared hard at Corin; his bearded face lined with worry. "I think we are being used in some vast cosmic game, played out by gods whose dark purpose lies far beyond our comprehension. I fear that we are pawns to their whim."

"You mean the Huntsman?"

"He is certainly part of it." Roman paused before saying something very odd. "I will die on Crenna, Corin. I have dreamt it."

Before Corin could think of a suitable reply, Roman left him to join the others below deck. Apart from Bleyne's solitary shadow, curt Fassof at the wheel, and a few terse crewmen, Corin was alone on deck. He braced his legs against the rolling motion of the ship, letting it null his emptiness.

Corin felt gaunt, trapped by his emotions and helpless as a deer cornered by an unknown hunter. He didn't like the feeling. Roman's last words had alarmed him. He worried for his friend, hoping that it was just a mood brought on by their journey, a part of Roman he hadn't seen before. He watched from the deck, his own mood dark as the mass of cumulus trawling the skies. Corin felt remote and lost, out of his depth. He thought of Ariane, of Crenna ahead, and of Finnehalle, lost in cloud and distance behind. What will be will be.

We are all pawns in a cosmic game...

Throughout that day the swell picked up. The oars had long since been racked and stowed, no longer needed, for there was plenty of wind. With so little to do, the companions brooded away the hours. Cale cheated at dice, and green-faced Galed cuffed him often, to scant avail. Barin talked at length with the Queen, whilst Roman avoided Corin's eye, embarrassed by their earlier discussion.

Fassof minded the helm and yelled at his duty crew. Other crewmen diced and slept amongst coiled ropes and well-oiled cleats. Serene and silent as ever, Bleyne scanned the horizon from his perch on the bowsprit. Toward dusk the wind strengthened to gale. Waves mustered, formed ranks, and reared up high before them.

"Looks like storm coming," said Ariane, observing their gloomy faces. Galed's resembled pea soup. "Well at least it will shake off this melancholy mood that's descended on all of us," she added, frowning at Roman and Galed. "You two miseries are getting on my nerves."

Barin was oblivious of the evident gloom resonating from his cabin. His craggy face loomed, grinning from the hatch above

"We're nearing Crenna," he beamed. The Queen nodded, smiling faintly. Everyone else ignored him. "With morning's light we should raise the island's snow-clad mountains," added Barin, infused. "We have done well! Get what sleep you can. This night may prove a rough one."

"Marvelous, that's just bloody marvelous!" Galed grumbled. "I cannot sleep on board this churning bucket anyway!" He felt like he'd been turned inside out, his head thundered, and his stomach heaved in outrage and rebellion.

"I thought this already rough," he complained to Cale, who appeared, much to Galed's disgust, immune from any effect of the swell. The boy just grinned at him in that oh-so-annoying, spoilt-puppy way.

Little shite.

That night, nobody slept. The wind roared like a wounded beast. Towering waves crashed against the hull, immersing decks, battering and drenching the struggling crew as they wrestled with sheet and sail.

"Master Fassof, take a firm hand on that wheel, old chap!" roared Barin. "Steer her into the wind —there's a good fellow. This breeze will have us in Crenna in no time!"

"I'm already fucking doing it!!" responded the fiery redhead, swinging on the helm like a demented monkey.

"Thank you!" Barin smiled. "He gets a bit stressed now and then," Barin explained, though none were currently in earshot. Corin staggered across the cabin, cursing as an overripe melon bounced free of its precarious perch in a net and exploded pink in his face. Cale, watching from a corner, laughed at that. The boy covered his mouth when Corin glared across at him.

Beneath the table, Galed vomited furiously into a copper bowl. Both Ariane and Roman looked pale and unwell. The master's cabin was awash with misery. Corin rolled his eyes in disgust.

He ventured out, gasping as a solid wall of salt water rammed into his face like an iron fist, drenching him in icy brine. He lost his balance then, tumbling back into the storm-tossed cabin below. Galed glanced up from his bowl, and Cale sniggered into his hands.

"Don't say anything!" Corin glowered at the boy. He nursed a bruised head to accompany his wounded pride. Ariane, glancing up, managed a wan smile in his direction, evidently finding humor in his predicament. Enough. With a great yank, Corin heaved his bruised, soaking bulk onto the deck.

Barin shouted orders. Sails were reefed and the wheel lashed to port rail. Crewmen toiled aloft with curses whilst their fellows, with more curses, labored at oars, struggling valiantly to weather the storm.

Voice ragged from barking commands, Barin took hold of the wheel, freeing it from its lash. Skillfully he steered a course into the raging night. Timber creaked and groaned. Cold salt-laden wind lashed faces raw, colder water soaked their straining muscles, sapping their strength.

High above, Bleyne, having stowed his bow, was helping with the sails, cheerfully immune to the deluge. Corin seized an oar, waging his own private war with the storm. It was very dark. Spray and spume flew about, washing decks. Ropes came loose, were re-tied only to work loose again, and the great Sea Eagle of Valkador flapped wildly in the giddy blackness high above.

Toward dawn Corin joined Barin at the helm. Laughing, he took a turn on the wheel. His grin was unhinged, fuelled by adrenaline, wildly exhilarated by the storms wrath. It didn't matter that icy rain pummeled his face blue. The storm raged through that long exhausting night, only abating with the onset of dawn.

Chapter 22

The Island of Thieves

Morning's light revealed a calmer sea. Clouds thinned, and both timbers and voyagers groaned with relief. Sensuata, that notoriously capricious sea god, had wearied of His game and let them be. Barin's men slumped motionless over their oars. Most were already asleep with exhaustion.

Corin was cold and tired. He managed a grin as his companions surfaced, all of them bleary eyed and shivering, except the boy, who looked like he'd enjoyed the rough and tumble night.

Barin was untouched by the storm's fury. His cheerful eyes sparkled in the morning sunlight. He alone appeared eager to greet the coming day.

At mid-morning they spied land. It was Fassof who saw it first.

"Hoy, land ahead!" came the hoarse yell from high above as the freckled mate perched tenuously on the crow's nest. "We've raised the Island of Thieves!" Nobody clapped.

Corin joined the somber gathering at the prow, hungry to see what the horizon revealed. He focused and at last spied dark peaks.

"Crenna," announced Barin with a grunt. "Last night's blow

has helped us; we will be in Kranek harbor by sundown." He stuck his head below deck and growled. "Ruagon, you worthless bilge barrel, get lunch on the way. Everyone's famished!" It was true, even Galed had recovered enough to eat.

"I'm already bloody well doing it!" Ruagon's grumble drifted up from somewhere amidships.

"Thank you."

After lunch the crew set about their duties with renewed zeal. Barin held to optimism. He aimed to reach port before dusk.

"Kranek has a busy harbor," he informed them. "Hopefully we won't be harassed when we enter." Corin glanced about ship. There was little damage from the fury of the previous night. His companions were in better spirits than the day before, despite their lack of sleep. Even Galed was almost cheery.

Roman interrupted his thoughts with an awkward cough. "The other night," he said. "It was just a strange mood brought on by indolence. Forget about it."

"I already have," lied Corin. He added nothing more, so Roman left him to his thoughts.

Afternoon brought the mountains higher. Great forests draped their shoulders with dark pines. The lofty summits were crowned with snow. Tiny shapes could be seen high above those peaks, circling and diving.

"Behold the eagles of Crenna!" announced Barin. As the day dwindled, the island dominated the western skyline. Pale sandy beaches stretched beneath dark trees. There was no sign of habitation. Corin felt the Queen brush against his shoulder. He shuffled awkwardly.

"There lies our destination," she said. Her hair was combed and immaculate despite the breeze, Corin couldn't help noticing. "Beautiful, is it not, Corin an Fol?"

"Very beautiful," Corin responded, not meaning the island. He changed the subject. "Were you very young when you visited before?" Corin asked awkwardly. He found it hard to look at those perceptive, dark eyes for more than a second or two. Instead he concentrated on the mountains ahead. A stunning vista—he had to admit that. Ariane continued to appraise him closely, he noted.

"Yes," the Queen answered eventually, after returning her gaze to the island. "Long ago my father and I accompanied the High King on one of his royal visits. Kelsalion was overlord of Crenna in those days. The island was part of the Four Kingdoms, though even then a tenuous, unruly part. That was before the Assassin seized the castle. I was only a young girl, but I remember it well enough."

"What do you know of this Rael Hakkenon?" Corin asked her. "His name is feared greatly throughout the lands I have travelled. People speak in whispers when they mention it. I heard a rumor he was born a noble, that something ghastly happened to him and twisted his mind toward cruelty."

"I heard that, too," replied Ariane. "Word is he was taken prisoner by the previous lord of Crenna and maimed in some most unfortunate manner. It would explain his ruthless reputation."

"Aye, that it would," Corin concurred, wincing at the thought. "I heard that he butchered the entire ruling house of Kranek."

"It's true." The Queen looked up at him. Their eyes met, danced for the briefest instant. She turned away, a small smile showing on her lips.

"Rael Hakkenon captured the fortress at night with his out-lawed pirate clan." Her voice was soft, and Corin was aware of how close she stood to him. "They slew the guards, then rounded up the occupants of the castle.

"They thrust them in a withy cage Rael had ordered constructed in the harbor. This they put to torch, burning to death all those within." Ariane shuddered picturing the scene.

"He made the citizens of Kranek watch the fate of their former lords. They say the screams were heard far out to sea by passing ships, and that the stench of burnt flesh lingered in the city streets for days. Can you imagine it, Corin? It must have been horrible. Those poor people...

"Since that day no one has dared speak out against the Assassin. Crenna became known as The Assassin's Isle after that grim event, although some still prefer calling it the Island of Thieves. We must tread very carefully, Corin."

"Aye, Queen, that we must," Corin replied. He so wanted to hold her, kiss those moist lips. He held back and turned away.

The sea was much calmer. They were protected by the island's lee. Barin gave the order to change course, spinning the wheel with his brawny arms. Slowly the great ship of Valkador turned southward and paralleled the shoreline, just a mile or so out from the rocky coves. Throughout the rest of that day they skirted the eastern coast of the island.

Corin watched the Queen follow Galed below deck, the ginger-headed Cale as ever at her hem. Strange emotions tugged at him. It was more than just attraction. He felt a need to protect her. He'd only known her a few days, but Corin cared about this Queen, more than anyone before in his life. Even his fondness for Holly in those early days was eclipsed by this new emotion.

It was just another thing troubling him. What went on inside that pretty royal head? Perhaps she just liked a bit of rough, now and then. But no, it was more than that.

Corin shrugged, unsheathed Clouter, and ran his wet stone down its long edges until the steel glistened diamond in the late afternoon sun.

He studied the landscape off to starboard. Ariane was right, the island *was* beautiful. Corin hadn't expected that, imagining a land as dark and cruel as its ruler's reputation. The mountains rose ridge upon ridge. Despite his prejudice, Corin felt awed by their towering majesty. He turned away and gazed seaward instead.

They steered south for some hours, keeping the shoreline hard to starboard. In their trail were mewling gulls. Eventually, as evening beckoned, they reached a rocky shoulder of the mountains where they split and jutted forth in craggy clusters, their rocky knees meeting the ocean in a great sweeping curve. Broken rocks, eyots, and skerries were strewn about, making the ship's way through difficult and hazardous.

But Barin knew these waters. He piloted a confident course through the skerries until they safely rounded the last outcrop of land. To south lay nothing but open water. Barin heaved heavy on the wheel, bringing the brigantine round to face the setting sun.

They had reached the southeast corner of the island.

Here the forests commandeered the rocky shore; there were no longer any beaches in view. Some miles west, framed by woods, a stone fortress could be seen, its walls rearing stark and gaunt beneath the mountain's mantle.

Sunlight reflected off granite. Below that shining tower was a city and a huge stone harbor partially hidden by the waves. Sailing closer, they espied dark sails gliding smoothly in the light evening breeze. The Assassin's Sharks, no doubt. High up and dominating the terrain stood the castle keep, frowning on the town below.

"That is Kranek," announced Ariane. "There's the Great Keep. Somewhere deep beneath the halls of that bleak tower we'll find Prince Tarin and learn what has become of the Tekara." The Queen's eyes shone with resolution as she spoke. "Or else perish in the attempt," she added under her breath.

As they approached Kranek's harbor they were amazed at its size. From east to west it stretched well over a mile. Moored within its perimeter were many ships. Sleek fighting sharks of Crenna there were but also merchant vessels, resplendent in the colors of many lands.

There were galleys and dhows from Permio and strange wicker craft from mysterious Golt. Bobbing between were the odd trader and brig, clinker-built trawlers, and myriad small craft. Corin now understood Barin's logic in coming here. It would not be difficult to mingle unnoticed amongst this multitude of mast and sail.

The Starlight Wanderer rounded the harbor arm. Sailors clambered onto yards, lashing gaskets and stowing sails, whilst their fellows took to oar, rowing to the eastern quay, where the merchanters and foreign ships were moored. Corin fastened his green cloak, concealing Biter. Clouter he had reluctantly stowed below in Barin's cabin. No way of hiding that.

They reached the quay and made fast to a wooden jetty. Within moments Fassof's warning yell announced unwelcome company. "Soldiers approaching from the town!" the mate shouted. "A score or so—the bastards are coming fast!"

Barin cursed in annoyance and then barked orders. Corin

slipped his hand beneath his cloak, fingering Biter's hilt.

"I'll handle this!" announced Barin. He turned to the approaching soldiers with a broad smile. "Greeting, Captain," he said to the leader, a thin man with drooping moustache and sallow, cratered face.

"What business have you in Kranek?" demanded the man, dark eyes suspicious and hooded.

"To trade, my friend," announced Barin, waving his arms expansively. "I have on board many furs and rugs from my homeland in far-off Valkador. Also jewels from the distant south to tempt your wealthy ladies!"

The man nodded slowly, clearly unimpressed. "Very well, but be warned, barbarian, weapons are banned in the harbor by the order of the Lord Assassin himself."

"As I said, Captain, we come in peace to trade." Barin's smile was swiftly replaced with a frown at the word *barbarian*. "Now, if you will excuse me," he added tersely, "I have work to attend to. Good day to you!"

The captain nodded knowingly. He glanced sideways at Corin, Roman, and the Queen, who kept her face well hidden beneath the hooded cloak. He smiled like a man with a perfect deck of cards.

"Good day to you, too, master merchant, but have a care." The captain turned briskly and, snapping his fingers, bid his soldiers follow him back up to the town. He stopped once before leaving the quay and called out.

"I did not realize it was the practice of northern barbarians to carry priests of the Witch Goddess on board. It will interest his Lordship a great deal." The captain spun on his heels again.

"That one means trouble," muttered Barin. Corin glowered as he watched the soldiers leave, his old hatred burning inside him. Ariane placed her arm on his shoulder.

"Be careful, Corin," she urged him. "Here is no place for hotheads."

"I know, but it's so fucking hard."

"Stay strong for me, fighter. I don't want to lose you." Corin looked up hearing that, but she'd moved on to bolster Cale and

Galed, who were looking very nervous. Corin stared after her. She was a bloody fine woman that Queen—a bloody fine woman. He wouldn't lose his temper. Not now. He had to stay alive to ensure she did, too.

It was agreed amongst them that Barin, Corin, the Queen, and Roman Parrantios would seek to gain access to the Great Keep after dusk. Bleyne, Galed, and Cale would stay behind to watch the harbor and placate any curious soldiers sniffing about. Fassof and the crew would keep the ship ready for a swift getaway, if needed.

"We will keep to our guise as priests of Elanion," said the Queen. "Ignore what that pompous twat said. He was just trying to unnerve us. The Goddess is respected amongst common folk everywhere, even Crenna," she assured them.

"Barin and I shall create a diversion. Once inside the gates, Corin and Roman will enter the keep while we two keep watch outside." She made it sound easy, Corin thought.

"The dungeons will be at the rear. They always are. All weapons must be well hidden beneath our robes, obviously. Remember this, all of you; I am a High Priestess of Elanion, here on the goddess's sacred business."

"We had best wait until nightfall proper and then enter the town under the cover of darkness," said Barin. "That oily worm of a captain will doubtless be watching the harbor, so we had better go carefully." He glanced up at the darkening sky. "It won't be long before we can slip into the city unnoticed."

Barin had reluctantly placed his massive axe in the safe keeping of Fassof, close by Corin's Clouter. Roman kept his broadsword, only just concealed under his shabby cloak. Barin stowed a short sword and a tiny crossbow in his belt, together with a small bag of bolts, his big woolen cloak hiding them from view; no priest's gown would fit him.

Corin had Biter and his five knives hidden beneath the green cloak. Ariane kept her rapier hidden beneath the folds of her own cloak. Those remaining on board made sure they had weapons to hand also. Tensely they all waited for night's cover and the general hubbub of the surrounding town to abate.

Just after dusk the chosen four stole silent along the jetty, taking care not to be seen by anyone, especially those soldiers still loitering on the edge of the town as if expecting trouble.

The heady stench of Kranek filled their nostrils as they filed into the narrow, oddly empty streets of the lower town. Ever upward coiled those streets, dirt strewn and rat ridden, hemmed by houses that tottered outwards from either side, almost meeting at roof height two (sometimes three) stories above. Ahead loomed the castle, a squat black beast watching them with torchy eyes. Through narrow windows the firelight flickered.

It was cold. Their breath froze as they walked. The night was tense and coffin silent.

Like four green ghosts, the companions shadowed their way up toward the high castle. At the rear walked Corin, grim of face and heavyhearted. He glanced often into the hidden alleys on either side of the street. Those houses spilt no light, and no sound issued from either tavern or inn. Beneath his priest's robe, Corin's right palm rested on Biter's bone hilt.

Into the dragon's den....

Chapter 23

The Dark Prince

Rael Hakkenon, Master Assassin, Pirate Prince, and Lord Protector of Crenna, watched the solitary candle flicker, gutter, and diminish. And so it is with men, he thought. A man burns brightly for his brief duration then is gone forever, extinguished like the candle flame.

No one is immune. Everything becomes ashes and dust eventually, even the gods cannot alter that. They burn brighter, with longer flames, but they too fail ultimately. They too are forgotten.

Rael had no fear of death. He courted it, rather, and sometimes yearned for it when the black walls closed in on him. Death alone was faithful, his constant companion, a pale, sleepless ghost that waited behind every corner. All one had was a brief flicker of time. It was enough. What mattered was what one achieved in the short time given.

What mattered was power.

His past had been a shadowy, bloodstained trail of revenge and ambition, of slow tortures of pain and pride. The future would prove more of the same until one day the pale ghost catches him at last. That day was long years away unless he should falter. Rael would not dwell on that day. His thoughts were on the present, his ambitions ruled the now.

There was little light seeping in through the heavy linen drapes that shrouded his high hall. That suited his mood. He often sat alone on the richly carved ebony chair. It was the throne and altar of this self-styled Prince. Here Rael passed his judgments, here he watched the fear in their eyes and fed on that fear.

Ahead, the great hall of Kranek Castle stretched silent, dark, and empty, a place of echoes and shadows, creeping draughts that bore cold whispers of feudal friction and sibling murder. Rael smiled thinly thinking of days gone by and of the blood spilt in this.

It had been thirty years since he first came to the island, a boy, half-starved and almost drowned, a lone survivor of the watery depths. Even at fourteen years he'd been cunning and cruel. Rael Hakkenon was a destroyer. It was his one great talent, his central reason for existing.

Violent youth, he'd stolen and cheated his way through the dirty back streets of Kranek. He'd killed his first man within a month of arriving. A brutal gang leader, Rael had stabbed him through the eye in one of the seedy inns. He'd taken control of the gang, fought the rival gangs, broke them one by one, and then welded them to his own.

At twenty-three Rael ruled the back streets, profiting from contraband and murder. His word was law among the gutters. Fear was his currency, corruption his profit. But Rael became bored. He was easily bored.

There had always been pirates in Crenna but they were no more than disparate outlaws in those days. They operated out of Storn, a craggy hidden harbor on the remote west of the island. Kranek's ruler had sought upon occasion to eradicate them, for they were an embarrassment to him. But he was fat and indolent and his efforts half cooked.

And so Rael Hakkenon took to piracy. He raided, raped and murdered his way along the coast, from Morwella to Golt, until his name was dreaded at every seaport. He returned to Crenna a rich man, built more ships, and took to the sea again. Rael had a large following of brigands and murderers, mostly Crenise but foreigners too.

For ten years he roved, and during that time Rael watched and waited too. He studied politics, read the signs, plotted and schemed. He entered Kelthaine, practiced swordplay in secret schools. Rael excelled beyond any other student in his talent for dealing death.

Then one day the High King's councilor, Caswallon, approached him. There were things they had in common, ambitions they could further together.

They formed a pact, a secret union that would serve both their purposes. Now and then the pirate chief was called on to perform certain functions for his ally. Murderous functions.

Killing excited Rael as no woman ever had. Known by everyone, feared by all, Rael took on a new guise, calling himself the Master Assassin. A silent phantom, he'd strike in the dark, anywhere at any time, extinguish life, and fade back into shadows. The legend grew and Rael fed its flames. He became vain, arrogant in his self-worship.

Then Rael deemed the time right to return to Kranek. He hatched a plot to bring down the current ruler but was betrayed. Rael had many enemies among those that feared him. He was brought in chains to the castle, amid bunting and regalia. A public holiday was awarded in Kranek. A high scaffold was erected to await his occupancy.

First he was punished.

In the dungeons below that monstrous keep, cruel things were done to Rael Hakkenon. One thing in particular, a terrible thing, warped and twisted him and shaped him into what he was today. The pain had been horrific, almost killing him, but his will proved greater.

The jailer was bribed by some of his men. Rael, broken and missing more than his pride, was bundled into a grain sack and smuggled out of the city a day before his hanging, drawing, and quartering were due.

In time he healed—his body anyway, as much as could be

expected—but Rael's mind was badly warped and twisted beyond any repair. He plotted again and orchestrated raids from his lair in Storn. Then on that joyful day nine years ago, Rael Hakkenon returned to the city.

He struck like an adder and this time succeeded. The ravens grew fat. Within three gloriously bloody days Crenna had a new ruler.

It had been a long road, but at forty-six winters Rael Hakkenon had reached the zenith of his power. His name was a stain on the face of Ansu. They would write sagas about him one day.

When Caswallon contacted him with the eerie new skills he'd acquired from his dog friends, Rael was only too willing to assist.

He stole into the royal bedroom, woke the High King, and held his mouth to prevent him from shouting. Rael wanted Kelsalion to see who it was that had come to claim his life.

Smiling, he'd slid the dagger across the old man's throat; watching as the crimson jet soaked bedclothes and floor, laughing softly at each feeble convulsion. Then, with black deed done, Rael fled into the night.

Rael's thoughts returned to present matters. He surveyed his hall with cold green eyes. Stone steps led down to a cobbled, uneven floor, and long wooden benches lined the walls at either side.

Central was the huge fire trench, spanning over fifteen feet across and more than four times the length, dividing the hall in two. Its embers glowed from the feasting fires of the night before. Beyond the ruddy fire pit, half hidden in the gloom, were two iron studded wooden doors. The entrance was guarded from without by the single motionless bulk of Graan, his personal bodyguard, he of the double axes and massive mace. Nothing stirred from within or without.

Rael Hakkenon was in a reflective mood today. His patrician face was impassive; his impenetrable, pale green eyes gazed into oblivion, delving deep among a maelstrom of black thoughts. The darkness suited his mood. Rael no longer liked the bright sun, for it brought on terrible headaches, part of the legacy of his torture, albeit a minor part. He rarely raided, being a creature of the night.

But his mind was busy. So much had occurred in the last weeks. It was difficult to contain the deep joy he felt, the rich vengeful satisfaction. Rael had the Prince, too, the bastard born of a whore. Tarin awaited his attentions in the cold dungeon below.

There was no need to hurry. Rael would arrange something specific, something novel and dramatic for the youth's demise. There would be mandolins to blend with the boy's screams. Rael liked to listen to soft music when he worked his hot knife into flesh.

Caswallon was in Rael's debt, and Kelthaine's new ruler had powerful friends. What these mysterious dog-beings sought to gain by aiding the wizard, Rael Hakkenon knew not. Nor did he care. What mattered was that Kelsalion the fool was dead and the Tekara destroyed beyond repair.

A new order had arisen in the Four Kingdoms that would always have need for killers of high quality. And Rael Hakkenon was of the highest quality. He smiled thinking of Prince Tarin trussed and turning in his cage, shivering, naked, and bathed in its own excrement.

The castle's dungeons were dark and cold, cut deep into the bedrock that housed the Keep's foundations. Many prisoners had died down there in various imaginative ways. More had been forgotten and left to starve, cocooned by terror, robed in their own misery.

Tales of what occurred in that oubliette sometimes reached the town. Nobody spoke of them, lest the Assassin's green gaze turn on them.

Rael had talked often with Tarin, goading the Prince during their westward voyage, horrifying him with hints of his impending fate. He hadn't frequented the dungeons though. He was already bored with that game, and besides, the stench was bad down there these days. He'd have to bring incense when he worked on the boy.

Rael mused: Should he flay the Prince's hide inch slowly, or hang him by hooks through the ankles above a vat of boiling fat?

It was a conundrum. The boy deserved certain theatrical attention. Maybe a harp should accompany the mandolins. It was only fitting. Rael would give it some thought over the next weeks.

He'd keep the fool's head, of course. Proof of the Prince's identity, should Caswallon or his dog allies demand it.

Rael Hakkenon had collected a number of heads over the years. He pickled them and arranged them neatly in order, as was his fetish. The Lord of Crenna despised untidiness.

Sounds outside...

Rael's cat's eyes narrowed dangerously, detecting the muffled sound of footsteps approaching fast. Moments later came a knock.

"Enter." Rael's voice severed the silence in the hall. He watched the doors open just wide enough to allow someone in. A man approached swiftly, nervously. He recognized the thin moustached features of his Captain of Guard, Pollomoi.

"Oh, it's you." The Assassin's voice was cultured, languid, and mocking. "Well...what?"

"My lord, forgive the intrusion," Pollomoi twitched like a cornered ferret. "There are strangers in Kranek."

"What... of... it?" Rael Hakkenon studied Pollomoi's sweating face. That twitch irritated him. Rael envisioned the captain without a nose. Maybe later. For the moment Pollomoi had his uses. Rael looked down in sudden disgust at his silver-trimmed perfumed cuff, spotting a small stain. He flicked at it. "There are always strangers in Kranek," he replied.

"These have a dangerous look to them, my lord," the captain said, coughing, then lowered his voice: "There is a young noblewoman among them, a priestess of the wood by her garb. She tried hiding her face from me."

Rael Hakkenon had no time for divine beings. Worship of any god was forbidden in Crenna, on pain of death and torture. It was a law he'd only just introduced. Rael would have no rivals, be they mortal or immortal. He studied Pollomoi.

"Stop that fucking twitching, you idiot." The Assassin's green eyes pinned Pollomoi like a fish wriggling on a hook.

"Forgive me, my lord! But I sense they mean trouble," Pollomoi persisted despite his evident discomfort. "Some of the others are also attired as priests, but two of these have the look of experienced warriors. I caught a glint of defiance in their gaze."

"How diverting." Rael was almost interested. "What manner of vessel?" he demanded.

"A trader, my lord, a bloody great brig," replied the captain. "And a deep-sea voyager from the northlands, by the look of her." Pollomoi failed to control his twitch and runnels of sweat were streaking his cheeks.

Rael raised a reflective brow. Most his men were ugly, but Pollomoi was particularly so. Rat on stilts was the image that came to mind. "Its captain is a huge bearded barbarian with an insolent tongue," Pollomoi said. "He claims to have visited your island before."

Rael Hakkenon was interested now.

"And the ships banner?" Rael demanded. His clipped tone cut clean through the drafty hall like a surgeon's scalpel.

"That of a sea eagle set silver on blue." Pollomoi straightened. "I have given orders that they remain onboard ship until I return with your wishes, my lord."

Rael Hakkenon thought for a moment.

"You will do nothing for the nonce," he ordered. "Watch them; keep me informed of any developments. And be vigilant, captain," he added, "lest your pathetic stoat head accompany the others currently feeding the crows above the city gates. You are dismissed for the immediate."

"Y— yes, my lord!" stuttered Pollomoi, his face white. He turned swiftly, hurrying from the mocking shadows of the murky hall. The doors shut behind him with a heavy thud.

Rael leaned back into the carved chair, resting his gloved hands behind his head. He yawned indolently as he listened to Pollomoi's fading footsteps.

"Graan!" he called out. The burly, shaggy shape emerged from the doors. "I'm not to be disturbed again. I've much to consider this morning." Graan nodded and withdrew. Rael smiled. Pollomoi's news was of interest after all.

So Barin of Valkador is here.

Rael smiled, his thoughts on the giant northman. Pity Barin hadn't arrived earlier. His meeting with Redhand would have proved most diverting. It was common knowledge those two brutes detested each other.

Northmen and their stupid grudges, particularly Valkador and Leeth. That had all started with that ice-witch. Rael had heard the tale in his youth. Turned her husband's son Bjarni (Barin's father) into a bear, she had, and then fled to Leeth with her lover—or so the story went.

Silence. Rael Hakkenon closed his eyes. He wondered what Barin was doing here and who it was accompanied him. Rael could guess the answer. Barin had contacts with Caswallon's enemies, rebels that plotted against the new regime. Silon and Belmarius were two such. Queen Ariane another. But then Hagan was on her case.

A woman, Pollomoi said. Perhaps the Queen had slipped through Delmorier's net. But Hagan was usually so very thorough.

Interesting.

Rael would send word east via pigeon. Caswallon would doubtless know more. But why would Barin carry passengers dressed as priests and come here, of all places? Why else if not to rescue that fool Tarin. Rael laughed out loud at their audacity. Such brazen folly! It seemed a new game had commenced and one he would truly relish.

***

An ugly scraping at the window broke his train of thought.

What is that?

Rael, irritated, turned in his throne and angrily surveyed the gap between the drapes. Something was outside. Not a bird—much too big. A cat, perhaps? A flying one, then.

Bloody nuisance.

Rael leaped to his feet. Whatever it was it would soon be skewered. He stole across to the curtained window and listened. The scratching continued, accompanied now and then by an odd hissing, gargling sound.

What the fuck is that?

Rael glimpsed a dark evil-looking shape crawling along the

ledge outside. He silently slid his silver-hilted rapier free of its jeweled scabbard with his left hand while his right pulled back the drapes.

Shite, that's ugly!

Rael gaped. It was a creature like no other, somewhere betwixt goblin and gibbon. It stank of putrefied detritus and was hairless with leathery wings. The horrid thing totally spoiled Rael's erstwhile enjoyable morning. He didn't doubt that the ugly had something to do with Caswallon's dog friends—they were always sending him weird shite these days, so his spies in Kella City told him. One day that wizard was going to overdo it and conjure up something really nasty that would gobble him up. Rael leaned out the window, poked the foulness with his rapier. It squeaked and squinted nastily at him.

"Fuck off!" it hissed. "I've got important contacts. Show some fucking respect!" The creature's voice set Rael's teeth on edge. And just what was that smell? He went to poke it again, but the thing hopped out of range.

"I've brought a message," it spat at him from the ledge, in that gurgling, noxious tone. "Most important. Can't wait. You're to listen and act immediately. I—"

Rael had had enough. He reached out, grabbed the obscenity by its wrinkly neck, and yanked it toward him through the window. It squeaked and dribbled and stared at him with vitriolic loathing. Rael's sword pinned it to the floor

"What manner of stinking atrociousness are you?" Rael crinkled his nose. "Speak quickly, little shiteling, else I cut your throat!"

"Get that fucking steel off me!" it hissed, tiny red eyes filled with hatred. "Don't you know a Soilfin when you see one? I bring word from Mr. Caswallon, my new boss. He has much to tell you."

Reluctantly, Rael withdrew the sword, and the creature showed what passed as a grin, revealing jagged greasy molars. It folded its leathery wings together, which made a sound like parchment torn in two. The thing resembled a giant bluebottle with a distorted monkey's face.

"What's the message?" Rael Hakkenon noticed with disgust that a gobbet of spittle had dared attach itself to his shirtsleeve. He flicked it off and wiped his fingers on his trousers. He would burn his clothes this afternoon and take a mile-long bath. "Speak, goblin shite! You affront my eyes!"

"I am Gribble," announced the creature, as though that explained everything. "A Soilfin, as I have already told you—indeed, the last surviving Soilfin, as far as I know. I served the ancient ones who now aid my new master, Mr. Caswallon. I am his special messenger."

"Well, get on with the fucking message and I might let you live, stinking creep that you are." A muffled sound revealed the shadowy bulk of Graan at the doors.

"I heard noises, my lord. Is all well?"

"It's just a flying goblin, Graan—nothing untoward. Leave us!"

"Yes... lord."

Rael's full attention was still on the Soilfin creature, currently scratching its left armpit with a long, curving claw. It bared its fangs again, this time showing a scabrous pinkish tongue.

"I'm hungry," it complained. "I'll need sustenance for the return flight." Rael's eyes narrowed to venomous slits of jade. Gribble noticed, saw just how dangerous this mortal could be, and decided on restraint

"Oh, very well," it conceded. "I can wait awhile yet, providing you nourish me before departure. I have come from Kella City, where Mr. Caswallon now rules in entirety, thanks partly to your assistance.

I know that, you winged twat.

"Get on with it." Rael wondered if he would have to torch the hall to banish this stink. The dungeons smelled rosy compared to this thing's honking hide.

"You're so friggin' impatient," complained Gribble. "You mortals, you're all the same.

"Mr. Caswallon has reason to believe his worst enemies are on this island—or else soon will be. A rough lot by all accounts."

Rael Hakkenon raised an eyebrow at that. "I had assumed that much, goblin," he feinted. "Pray continue."

"My name is Gribble, not Goblin. I'm not a friggin' goblin."

"You'll be a friggin' sliced goblin if you don't stop gibbering shite!"

"They seek Tarin," Gribble said, sulking. "Their leader is the renegade Queen of Kelwyn. My new master wants her for night-time nibbles, the rest you can slay. Especially the one called Corin an Fol. Very dangerous and nasty apparently."

"Who?"

"Mr. Caswallon also wants the shards of the Tekara returned to him at once. The Prince had them on him when you waylaid him, so you must have them."

Rael shook his head. "I know nothing of the remnants of the crown. I had the boy stripped once aboard my vessel. All he carried was a hunting knife."

Gribble picked at a flaring nostril. "Mr. Caswallon won't be pleased. He was most insistent. Oh, he also says a wizard is holed up somewhere nearby, some rival warlock that my former masters used to know. He'll stir up trouble. They always do. Mr. Caswallon wants you to smoke him out."

"I know of no fucking wizard. What nonsense is this?"

"It is no fucking nonsense," dribbled Gribble. "You must look into it, Mr. Assassin, and don't worry about taking on the wizard. There is one coming over that will assist you with matters of spell craft."

"Caswallon cannot fly yet."

"I'm not speaking of Mr. Caswallon but his mentor, Chief Morak Dog Face." The name meant nothing to the Assassin. "Chief Morak, too, has a stake in these matters. Heed my advice, Mr. Assassin. That one even you do not want to mess with!"

Gribble chewed his talons and resumed drooling. The Soilfin was very hungry. Rael watched the creature carefully, for once masking his disgust. He had a good deal to contemplate. He returned to his chair, gazed thoughtfully at the creature Gribble.

"What of Hagan and his men?" Rael asked the stinker. "I sent them to waylay the Queen at Caswallon's bequest.

"They were overcome at Kashorn some days ago. You need more efficient staff, Mr. Assassin. I would have been here earlier, but I got distracted," responded Gribble. "It was only a small town, but it took me a few days to digest all the occupants, so for a time I was too heavy for flight.

"Oh, that reminds me," continued the Soilfin, looking gleeful, if a foul-smelling, horrible, winged goblin could look gleeful. "I kept this for a snack." Gribble produced a be-ringed human hand from a deep fold of his left wing. He chewed on it avidly, crunching the bones with his yellow fangs.

The Assassin turned away. He decided to postpone lunch for a week. "Those little ships you sent for the Queen were outmaneuvered by the enemy vessel," crunched the Soilfin.

"Idiots!" snapped the Assassin. He pictured Barin of Valkador contorting in agony whilst hot irons scorched his flesh. If any of his men returned, he'd have them pickled. Their lives they could throw away as they wished, but his sharks were expensive.

Gribble looked up from his snack and grinned. "My sentiments exactly. I take my leave, Mr. Assassin, but I'm still hungry, so before I go…"

"What…?" Rael was relieved the Soilfin was leaving.

"I've a long flight ahead. Need fuel. That town I visited earlier, it was several miles inland. There could be one or two left alive, if I'm quick under the cover of darkness."

"Just piss off."

"Thank you. It's been a joy."

Rael watched with curled upper lip as Gribble goblin crawled back through the window and vanished from sight. "Revolting thing," Rael muttered, then he turned his attentions toward the doors. *Might prove useful, though.*

"Graan!" he snapped a finger and vainly waved his other hand in an attempt to banish the lingering odor.

"My lord?" The grizzled bodyguard was there.

"Summon my captains," Rael ordered. "Have the thralls slay some beasts and prepare a feast for tonight. We will have guests later, with royalty among them. They will be providing the entertainment!" He laughed, picturing the scene.

"Very good, my lord," growled the shaggy guard.

"Oh, and Graan," Rael added. "Bring me a flagon of expensive wine, and have my retainer run a scented bath. And get some incense sticks lit in here to dispel this fucking stench."

Graan withdrew. Rael Hakkenon ran a jeweled hand through his silvery hair, reflective again. There was much to contemplate. He would wait and see what followed. It should prove recreational. But first he would have that bath.

Chapter 24

Kranek Castle

Barin led the way up the steep cobbled street. High above, the Assassin's keep frowned down on them with foreboding. The night was moonless; clouds hung low, and no shadows followed in their wake.

They quickened their pace, feeling the tension fused all around. Corin stroked Biter's hilt and fingered the wolf brooch on his cloak. After half an hour's steady climb they left the hub of the town below, entering a more open, tree-strewn region.

The streets were wider up here, the houses wealthier, constructed of stone and not the wattle and daub of the cheaper harborside establishments. Up here was where the moneylenders dwelt, the Assassin's current favorites, and the people of rank, all of whom chose not to mix with the filthy rabble below.

Despite the chill, the companions were hot and breathless when they finally reached the top of the last tortuous lane. The harbor lights flickered far beneath them. *The Starlight Wanderer* was hidden in the gloom, somewhere beyond the empty streets. Corin wondered where all the people had gone.

He thought of Kashorn and scowled. Were they entering

another trap? It wouldn't surprise him in the least. He steeled his nerves. They'd won through at Kashorn, and they would win through here. They had to.

A watchful silence cloaked the city. Only the faint flickering of the newly lit torches showed any sign of life. At last the street opened out to a wider space. They'd gained the hill marking the end of the town.

Ahead reared the castle walls, looming like cliffs out of the murk. They stood on a large plateau of rock, a wide square flagged with marble slabs many-shaped and interlocking. To either side leaned tall stones, dim shapes that monitored their progress in silence.

A creepy place, sinister and silent. The plateau was smooth as though it had been scooped clean with a giant spoon. They made for the distant gates, keeping their profiles as low as they could. They stopped half way and scanned ahead, relieved that the gloom hid them from any prying eyes. All about, the marble slabs shimmered faintly in the dark.

Barin muttered something obscene into his beard. They were all getting edgy. Heavy cloud clung to the walls ahead, occluding the Assassin's keep from view. It had started to drizzle.

Barin regretted leaving his axe behind. He chewed his beard and grumbled to himself. Beside him Ariane's pale hands worked furiously beneath her cloak. Corin and Roman said nothing, but their eyes were fired with tension.

The marble plateau stretched into murky nothingness on either side. There was no growth of any kind here, just stone cut sheer and clean. Ariane glanced at the tall shapes to their right and left. She shuddered, recalling how this place had scared her as a child.

On closer inspection, she remembered the strange stones were baroque statues of beasts. Here was a snarling dragon, there a hideous griffin. All were mythical creatures from the ancient world fashioned by skills of long ago. This place was old. Older than the Four Kingdoms certainly, and no records shed light on the rulers back then. A cruel people they must have been.

The statues seemed almost sentient, appearing suddenly out of the gloom, watching silently as the four hurried by. Corin glanced at the statues in morbid fascination. There had to be at least thirty dark shapes, the bulk of which loomed close to the gates and would provide them with some cover should they need it.

Barin led them toward the gates, past the last statue, a thing with a fox's head—its granite eyes glared down on them as they passed.

The gates came full into view, their iron struts glistening in the wet night. These were fifteen foot high, comprised of dark oak banded with iron. They looked strong. Corin spotted the guards. Two figures huddled in stone portals either side of the heavy arch-way surmounting the castle entrance.

There were three severed heads hanging from the arch, tied by their hair. One still dripped blood on the marble stones. Ariane gagged at the sight, but Corin ignored the trophies. Instead he studied the guards. Each cloaked soldier carried a long spear. Their faces were hidden behind heavy helms.

Barin crouched low and watched for a time.

"Well, here we are," he whispered to the others. "Very inviting it is, too. I suppose we had better do something about our friends over there." He motioned to the guards. Roman nodded. He carefully began sliding his sword free until Ariane's pale hand stopped him.

"I can handle those with your help, Barin," said the Queen, her voice clear despite a slight tremor. A bead of blood showed she'd been biting her lip. "You will need to stay hidden close by," she added to the Northman, and then she signaled the other two wait."

"Be careful," muttered Corin.

She flashed him a quick grin. "Come on." She beckoned Barin follow.

***

The two guards leapt up in alarm when they saw the muffled figure of the young woman approaching them from the drizzly night. Eyes wary, they barred her way with crossed spears.

"None is permitted entrance here after dark by orders of the Lord Protector!" spoke the larger of the two. "Show yourself!"

Ariane smiled to herself. She pulled back her hood, allowing her sable locks to bounce free and caress her pale, elfin features. Her eyes were cold as she appraised the spearmen.

"I am a High Priestess of Elanion of the Forests. I would speak with your master on a matter both urgent and pressing. He has blasphemed, and the Goddess marked him as heretic." Her voice was cold and authoritative. "If you are wise you will open these gates and lead me to Rael Hakkenon immediately!" Though her manner was haughty, the guards were unmoved.

"I see no need to trouble himself with you, sweetness. It might prove hazardous at this hour, for you and us alike, what with his temper and all," chuckled the bigger man, who was clearly the leader of the two.

"Himself has no need of any goddess, nor does he care about any alleged friggin' heresy." The man flicked his head back in the direction of the castle behind. "He relies on cunning and the strength of his own sword arm, that alone." He smiled an ugly toothless smile. "So, it seems that you are out of luck, witchy-wenchy." His grin deepened. "You look comely, though. Methinks we'll keep you here instead, so you can entertain us two rough lads through the night. It's so quiet out here no one need know." He reached toward her with a gloved hand.

"Aye, take her, Gorrig!" hissed the other guard, his eyes squinting between the helmet slits like lusty currents.

Gorrig grinned. He grabbed the Queen's robe, then froze in horror as the hulking figure of Barin emerged from the night and towered above him.

"Shit!" Gorrig raised his spear, but Barin split his skull with the pommel of his short sword. The guard crumpled to the ground, dark blood smearing the already stained gateway. His accomplice reached for his own shaft. He was too late. Biter slid across his throat. Scarlet billowed and he fell across the body of his comrade. Corin grinned up at Barin.

"I hate missing out," he said and Ariane flashed him an angry glance.

They dragged the dead guards beneath one of the portals, though it was so dark they probably could have left them put. But best not leave anything to chance.

Roman reached down and snapped the chain that hung around Gorrig's neck. He carefully placed the heavy key in the gate lock and turned it slowly until the latch snapped back with a metallic clunk. A loud noise, that, in the silent mizzly dark.

They waited. Nothing. They exchanged hesitant glances. No one was looking forward to this. Roman shook the heavy drizzle from his cloak.

Time to get moving.

"Come on!" he urged them, between clenched teeth. Together with Barin and Corin, he launched a shoulder into the right gate and pushed hard. Corin winced as the gate rocked and groaned on its hinges, but it opened just enough for them to slip inside.

Bloody thing needs oiling.

Four grim, silent ghosts, they stole into Kranek Castle. It was even gloomier inside the walls, but once their eyes adjusted they found themselves in a cobbled courtyard, square in shape, perhaps forty feet across.

They took their bearings before moving forward. The rain was heavier now. Barin smothered a sneeze with his meaty palm. The courtyard glistened as water dripped on stone. Ariane shivered, once again recalling her earlier visit. Like the square outside, the courtyard was flagged with polished black marble.

A fountain chimed to their right, a welcoming sound were it anywhere else; here it just added to her trepidation. Grinning at them from dark corners were more of the gruesome statues. This time they were prowling beasts and cruelly beaked alien birds. Carved on the granite walls were hideous leering gargoyle faces from the realms of nightmare. Their dead stone eyes followed the Queen with hungry malice.

Ariane recalled the grim baron that had ruled here ten years earlier. He had paid reluctant scot to his overlord Kelsalion. Crenna was part of the Four Kingdoms then, it being a year before cruel Rael Hakkenon seized control of the island. She had been a girl of thirteen summers, high spirited and willful. Despite that, the castle and its forbidding statues had haunted her dreams often in later days.

Ariane thought of her father and steeled herself. She turned to the others. "This is where we must separate," Ariane told them.

"There are stairs on either side of the far wall. I remember a guard informing me that the one on the left leads down beneath the Great Keep to the dungeons far below." Ariane suppressed a shudder. "He hinted of what went on down there even in those days. Down there in the filthy stink is where Tarin will be held captive."

"Where does that other staircase lead to?" Corin enquired of her. He had spied it through the murk, a faint ruddy gleam of steps leading up to a torch-lit passage.

"That way is the great feasting hall of the Keep. It's where our enemy feasts his warriors throughout the long wintry nights. That way we do not go!"

They approached the other stair. Corin heard the crackling of flame and hiss of smoke exuding from dripping candles. The entrance yawned at them, revealing worn steps descending into torchy murk under another gothic arch. This too was carved with garish gargoyles, whose stony gaze dared they enter. Ariane stopped beneath the arch, her face pale and resolute. To Corin she looked very beautiful in that eerie forbidding place.

"Barin and I will stay here and keep watch on this passageway and the gate," she said. "Roman, you and Corin will seek out my royal cousin in the catacombs below."

Ariane paused to appraise the two warriors, her heart heavy. They were both so precious to her. Roman had always been by her side, a constant tower of strength and resolve, but Corin—this wild-eyed man of contradictions—had somehow crept inside her, stirring her blood in a way that she didn't understand. Ariane almost trembled as she looked up at his brooding features.

Enough nonsense.

"Be on your guard you two and don't piss about," she told

them. "They say the Assassin never sleeps!"

Roman nodded. Her champion was not happy about leaving his Queen. "You must take care also," he answered. "At some point they'll discover those two guards are missing."

"Take care of her, Barin," added Corin, looking up at his giant friend. "It will be a black day if we lose a Queen to gain a Prince!" He looked hard at them both for a moment. Ariane looked so tiny next to Barin's bulk Corin's heart lurched. Their eyes locked for the briefest moment, and Corin caught a glint of moisture streaking her left cheek.

I hate this.

Corin turned briskly on his heels and vanished in the gloom beyond the archway. Roman followed stone faced without further ado.

***

Barin listened to their fading footfalls. He turned to Ariane. "I think ours is the harder job, Your Highness," he said. "Sitting here and waiting."

"Yes," she replied, her thoughts far away. Barin marked how afraid she looked beneath her courage, how alone. He thought of his daughters her age back home. He wished he'd brought Wyrmfang with him. Something inside warned him he'd need it soon. He suppressed a fart—any noise could betray them. Time passed leaden slow. The fountain chimed, and the grinning gargoyles watched them from the walls.

***

Night deepened. Far below, beyond grim castle, past labyrinthine twists of street and low, thatched roofs, the harbor too was quiet. A light breeze drifted in from the sea. It buffeted the multitude of craft moored around the quayside, bobbing their hulls gently in slow rhythm.

The Starlight Wanderer's rain-slippery decks creaked and groaned. The bowline sploshed as it lapped water, and the wooden jetty dripped weed-covered slime. The earlier drizzle had lifted. A pale moon spilled out from dark cloud. Below deck the crew were tense and restless. Only the boy Cale was sleeping.

In the far corner of the cabin the gloomy figure of Galed could just be seen, huddled miserably beneath a blanket, trying to sleep but to no avail. He felt useless again. The ship's crew ignored him, and the taciturn Bleyne was difficult as always.

Cale was a better companion, although Galed failed to see why his Queen was so fond of the lad. He envied the boy's ability to sleep. Cale never seemed to worry about anything. He was almost as bad as Bleyne. Galed worried enough for both of them. He looked around for the archer, couldn't see him anywhere, and assumed Bleyne must have gone aloft. That one never seemed to sleep.

Galed was deeply worried. He knew the others saw him as a liability, a cumbrance to be endured. Nonetheless, here he was stuck on board this creaking tub, surrounded by enemies, fearfully awaiting the return of his beloved Queen, and desperately hoping she had not met her doom in that terrible fortress above. The hours dragged. Galed fretted and tossed before finally being rewarded by a restless sleep.

He woke cold and strangely alert. It was very dark, and the air in the cabin was thick with the flatulence of Barin's snoring men. A noise above startled him. Fassof's freckly image showed through the hatch, his red mane sparkling in the moonlight.

"What is it?" hissed Galed, his face creased with worry.

"The archer," responded the mate. "Bleyne...gone!"

"Gone? Gone where?"

"How the fuck should I know?"

***

Bleyne had felt the tension build as the night deepened. Suspense surrounded the harbor; menace lurked in the twisted streets beyond. His hunter's soul knew something was amiss. He could almost smell the deception carried on the breeze. His sharp black eyes pierced the night's gloom, scanning for movement.

Suddenly he tensed. There were shapes moving at the edge of

the town. Soldiers. Bleyne looked closer, saw four shadowy figures on the quayside, the wind whipping their bulky cloaks. They brandished spears that glinted silver in the moonlight. The city guard had returned to watch them.

Bleyne studied them in silence. He strung his bow and placed four arrows on the deck rail beside him. They were too far at the moment, but should they approach... He prayed Elanion will them forward, but they just stood silently as if awaiting orders from someone still hidden by the night.

Bleyne watched for at least an hour. Beneath him the deck timbers creaked, and the ship rolled gently from side to side. To his right the mooring lines tautened and slackened with the movement of water against the trader's hull. The wrongness in the air was almost tangible.

Silence. Bleyne watched and listened.

Then he heard it. A deep penetrating voice booming a defiant challenge from somewhere high above the town. That could only be Barin. Trumpets answered from the castle. Suddenly the night was full of shouts. They were in trouble up there! The time had come for him to act.

Bleyne quickly knelt and scooped up his arrows. He slung his bow and sack of shafts over his back, then straddled the guardrail. Clinging to the clinkered hull, the archer lowered himself silently into the water.

Bleyne ignored the icy kiss of the Sea God's daughters. He kicked out, swimming otter-lithe and swift toward the torch-lit quay, a score of yards beyond the waiting spearmen. Bleyne emerged silent and dripping. In moments, he vanished into the labyrinth of streets beyond.

***

Barin lurked beneath the gateway like a soggy bear. He fretted and cursed, fingered his short sword, and stomped to and fro. "It's too bloody quiet," he muttered under his breath. He glanced out at the silent square, grumbled again, and then rejoined the Queen, who sat waiting pale faced in the courtyard.

"It is very calm out there tonight," Barin said, risking a bluff smile that failed to conceal the worry in his eyes. "Perhaps the Assassin is abroad."

Ariane shook her head. "I do not think so," she answered, poking at a tooth that was troubling her again. She wished she had her flask. She could so use a cup of strong tea.

"Something is wrong here, Barin. I can sense it. They should be back by now." The Queen peered into the darkness beyond the arch, willing Corin and Roman to reappear. "I begin to doubt our wisdom in coming to this island. I pray the Goddess is watching."

Barin sat down beside her. He unsheathed his sword, fumbled for his whetstone, and then slowly worked along its already razored edge, keeping the noise to minimum. After a while he spoke, his voice quiet, consoling.

"Elanion meant for us to come here, Queen," he assured her. "We must believe in Her wisdom."

Ariane nodded. "You are right, but I feel we are being drawn into something bigger, much darker than we are aware of. I—" She stopped. Beyond the gates rung the clatter of steel-shod boots on stone. Soldiers were approaching fast!

Barin leapt to his feet. "Wait here," he told her. "It may be nothing to worry about. I'll go see."

Barin crossed the courtyard and eased his bulk through the gap between the gates. Once again he berated himself for leaving Wyrmfang with Fassof. This was a trap, Barin knew that now, certain as dawn following night.

Ariane was right. They had been fools to come here. The thunder of feet grew until it filled the night. Barin waited for them to arrive. He hoped there would not be too many, so he could finish them without excessive noise.

And here they were, ranging out of the night, shaggy guardsmen armed with spears and axes, their faces framed by kettle helmets, some sprouting horns. They froze seeing Barin's bulk at the gates. At the leader's signal they filed out, closing on the Northman with spears thrust forward.

Barin strode out to meet them. Too late he realized his error.

The gate creaked shut behind him. Iron bolts slammed into place, locking it fast. The sound of rushing feet and shouting filled the courtyard within.

Barin swore and kicked the gate. What an idiot he was. Ariane was trapped and he could do nothing to help her. He glared at the approaching spearmen and channeled his wrath.

"Come on then, shiteheads!" Barin roared. "It will take longer without my axe, but today you die!" Whooping defiance they rushed in, like so many snarling wolves attacking a great bear out of the fabled northern forests of Enromer.

"Valkador!" roared Barin. And so the killing began.

Chapter 25

The Cage

Ariane heard the heavy gate slam shut. She hadn't seen the men emerge from the other stairs and shut off her escape. Outside, Barin's thunderous battle cry shattered the night. Derisive hoots followed, announcing the arrival of the enemy.

Ariane had no time to think of her friend. A great clangor of trumpets split the air, deafening her. From the other stairs came the sound of rushing feet. There was nowhere to hide. She was undone.

Ariane watched in horror, mind racing, trying to form a plan. Torchlight flickered as the shouting grew nearer. Dark figures filled the courtyard, moonlight glinting off their spears. Ariane cursed. Her friends had no chance. And she was trapped. The Queen slid her rapier free and braced her feet.

At least I'll take a few of you with me!

Rael Hakkenon watched with mild interest as the young Queen valiantly fought off his men. He was impressed. She was good with that blade, better than most of his elite guard. Two of the clumsy idiots lay dead already, and a third screamed in agony as she hewed away his right hand after he tried pulling her down to the ground. The Queen fought with desperate precision, cussing and spitting like a wildcat.

It was most diverting to watch. Rael was almost disappointed when they surrounded her with spears and slowly, carefully forced her back against the wall. The spear points held her there. Rael Hakkenon, brandishing his beautiful smile, chose this moment to introduce himself.

Ariane watched the spearmen withdraw to let their leader through. She gasped deep breaths. She felt the cold stone at her back, and she angled along the wall, sword held ready for any attack.

Her body jolted into something hard, a stone griffin blocking her way, its sightless eyes hungrily triumphant as it glared down at her. Ariane almost quailed at that. Instead, defiant fury overcame her as she felt her doom approach. She lunged at the guards again, fast and hard, knocking spears aside, claiming two more lives before a languid voice cut in.

"Enough." Though lazy in its delivery, there was menacing power in that command. Ariane guessed who had issued it. The guards parted hastily to allow a man through. He was handsome and urbane, slender in build, immaculate from head to toe. This could only be Rael Hakkenon, hated pirate, lethal assassin, and scourge of the Four Kingdoms.

He was garbed in finest purple silk and shiny black, soft leather complimented by silver studs. A long, elegant rapier hung from a slender diamond-studded belt around his waist. Neatly combed shoulder-length silver hair framed his lean patrician face. His thin bloodless lips curved upward slightly in a sardonic smile.

About Rael's body clung a hint of musk. His sleeves were flared as were the trousers tucked neatly into doe-skinned boots. Over his shoulders was draped an ermine cloak the hue of freshly fallen snow. But it was the eyes Ariane noted, green as jade and twice as cold. They hinted keen intelligence and fast cunning and something else, a tortured blend of pain and expectation.

The eyes of a killer, the eyes of a cat. Rael Hakkenon stood before her, arms folded neatly.

Snake swift, Ariane's rapier leapt toward his heart.

"Die, Assassin!" she screamed. But Rael was quicker still. He danced to one side, grabbed her wrist, and twisted it painfully, forcing her to drop the rapier. Noisily it clattered on the flagstones.

"Elanion, help me!" croaked Ariane as two of the brutish guardsmen seized her and held her, spitting and cursing.

"The Witch of the Woods is no use to you here, my feisty little Queen." The Assassin's voice was elegant, his tone that of patient teacher instructing petulant child. Those green eyes mocked her, she felt naked and exposed.

"However," he purred, "I am deeply gratified you have chosen to visit my realm. Tonight I shall hold a feast in your honor. No! I insist. Least I could do! I would invite your confederates, but unfortunately they will all be dead within an hour or two. Shame...but there you have it, my dear."

Rael examined a manicured thumbnail and straightened his cuff. "It is a pity," he mused. "Soon the renowned Barin of Valkador will be rendered so much dog meat. A brute that size will keep them going for hours."

Rael cupped his ear theatrically as if listening in concern to the sounds of fighting beyond the gate. Evidently Barin was not dead yet. "As to the others, well, there is no escape from my dungeons, you see. It's only a matter of time before they are apprehended down there."

Rael spread his arms wide as if welcoming her embrace. "So with your kind permission we will retire to the great hall. The feasting is already underway. He grinned, showing impeccable teeth. "Going to be a long night. Oh, by the by," Rael added. "You, my sweet little hell-puss, shall be providing the entertainment!"

"Fuck you!"

Rael raised a brow. "Charming little cunt," he said, inspecting that thumbnail again.

"You bastard! What have you done with Prince Tarin?" Ariane hissed as they dragged her, feet first, up the gloomy stairway. The Assassin was examining her sword with professional interest. He poked a warrior's leather-clad buttock with it and giggled.

"No, I think you'll find young Tarin is the bastard, poor little whore's get. I had him slain some days hence," Rael added, sounding bored. "His rat-eaten body is rotting down there somewhere." Rael's hand vaguely gestured toward where the dungeons. "Soon your friends' carcasses will join it in communal festering." Rael shook his head slowly in mock concern.

"You were a goose coming to my island, Queen Ariane, and soon you will be cooked in your own silly fat. Did you really think I would fall for that priestess nonsense? Your pathetic goddess holds no sway in Crenna, my dear. Here, my word alone is law."

Rael signaled two burly guards carry her, lest she damage herself on the stairs. They hoisted Ariane up amid more spitting and curses. She kicked one guard in the face whilst poking another in the eye with a finger. Rael shook his head. Useless tossers, his guards.

"Get that bitch under control," he snarled." They did, eventually.

Brawly little madam.

No doubt this young Queen would keep Caswallon entertained for a time. But Rael would have some fun with her tonight. It was a shame: He didn't want to fall out with the new ruler in Kelthaine, so she would not be broken here.

They carried Queen Ariane through a maze of dark passages deep inside the fortress, finally reaching the great hall. Huge Graan opened the doors, and torches held aloft, they entered.

Ariane wept silent tears. The quest had failed. She doubted not that some grim fate awaited her too horrible to contemplate.

Elanion have mercy.

Walking just behind her, the Assassin's emerald orbs bore into her back like a cat eagerly anticipating its prey.

***

Corin and Roman threaded their way down the narrow stairway into the twisting passage. Down and down it led them into cloying darkness. There were no torches, but their eyes adjusted to the gloom enough for them to see.

Occasionally a cold gust of air revealed other passages on either side that then faded into the gloom. It was stuffy and damp down here, and a foul smell reached out to them, promising worse to come.

"We must be getting close to the dungeons. This stink offends my nostrils," gagged Roman. "Does this sodding passage go on forever? We must be almost underneath the mountains by now."

"Aye, it's clammy enough," agreed Corin. "I shouldn't think there are many that venture down here out of choice. Let's hope our idiot Princeling is still in one piece and not the cause of the stink." Roman grimaced hearing that.

Their pace slowed. The passage floor had become slippery with moss clinging to the age-old stones. Corin detested this darkness; he wondered how long it had been since they left Ariane in the courtyard. It felt like ages.

He hated the thought of her waiting in that awful place with only Barin to protect her, and him without his battle-axe too, the great lump. Perhaps Galed had been right. They *were* mad coming here. But it was too late.

After what seemed like hours but had probably only been a few minutes, the passage leveled out. Ahead, sticky with cobwebs, hung an iron gate.

They had reached the dungeons at last. A large bar held the rusty gate locked in place. This they removed and, gagging at the stink, they pushed open the gate. They had to heave hard as the hinges were stiff from disuse. The gate ground noisily.

They squeezed through, stopping for a minute to catch their breath. Corin, who had been looking back down the passage, heard something coming from that direction. He listened for a minute, then cursed

"Do you hear that?" he hissed.

Roman nodded grimly. It was what they dreaded most. Far above and very faint, the sound of marching feet echoed down the passage.

"We had better hurry," he said. Entering the dungeon, they noticed odd shapes in the murk. These on closer inspection turned out to be the bones of long dead prisoners. Some were chained to the walls, others spread over long tables. Most of them bore the gruesome signs of a horrible fate.

The two didn't dwell on that. They had a job to do—a shit one, but it had to be done. The further they went the worse the stench became. The corpses here were more recent; rancid flesh still clung to some in various stages of decomposition. Fat rats scurried beneath their feet, and cobwebs clung to their faces.

"Ugh, it's foul down here!" gagged Corin. He shuddered at the scene surrounding them. Here and there were racks, wheels, and clamps, all supporting what had once been men and woman. It was horrific.

He nearly jumped out of shock when he heard the voice.

"How very observant you are!" It came from somewhere in the gloom ahead. They exchanged quizzical glances. Whoever it was certainly didn't sound like Prince Tarin.

They hurried forward. Roman crashed into a spiky thing that sported an array of severed body parts. He winced and pushed it out of the way. Then he slammed into Corin's back. He too stopped and gawped.

A suspended cage creaked at them out of the murk. It was occupied, and this occupant was alive—very, by the way he was stamping his filthy feet and clucking at them. Corin and Roman exchanged glances.

What the...?

They approached warily. Closer inspection revealed an old man, emaciated and filthy, with matted beard and wild, staring eyes. The cage danced and rattled as he squatted froglike, gripping the sides and grinning at them like a lunatic.

"Who might you be?" asked Corin, looking up at the figure in disgust. "Speak swiftly! Maybe you can tell us where we can find the one we are seeking." He stopped to listen. Shouting could be heard from the passages above.

"Come, Corin, we had better hurry," urged Roman. "Let's try further on. Tarin must be here somewhere." Roman shook his friend's shoulder.

"It's too late, fools. You are already trapped!" The bony figure laughed from his rusty cage above them. He seemed oddly unconcerned about his predicament. "You had better free me fast if you want to see your companions again," he told them.

"Tell me where Prince Tarin is held and I will release you," barked Corin. "Otherwise you can fucking rot!" The sound of feet was close.

"How remarkably charitable of you, Corin an Fol—and so eloquently put, I might add." The prisoner chuckled slowly, a strange sound in that awful place. "It is difficult, however, to know exactly where Prince Tarin is at this precise moment," he continued, as if amused by the question.

"I would hope he is currently bound where I sent him, just a few days past. Before commencing his journey south, he has to reunite himself with the remnants of the crown, hidden in that graveyard a mile outside Fardoris."

Before Corin could respond and ask how this strange prisoner knew his name—and more, their business—a shout issued from the passage beyond the dungeon. Cursing, he unsheathed Biter and waited. Seconds later a score of guards emerged, crashing and cursing their way out of the gloom. The cage's occupant was right. They were already trapped!

Chapter 26

Sorcery and Steel

Corin and Roman met the Assassin's guards in a whirl of steel. Back and forth they fought, ducking low under unspeakable devices and lunging over tables stacked with filth and detritus, slashing and stabbing, lunging and hacking.

Three men lay dead on the ground before them, and a fourth stumbled gurgling as Roman's broadsword spilled his jellied guts on the dirt at their feet. But they were hard pressed and surrounded, and still more men poured angry into the dungeon.

"Release me, you idiots, before you get yourselves killed!" The cage dweller sounded peeved. "Release me, and I will get rid of these pests."

Corin parried a thrust from one man while lunging forward to finish another. Beside him, Roman hewed a guard's head from his body and blocked a spear thrust from another. But on they came. It would only be a matter of minutes before the two swordsmen were overcome.

"Hold them, Roman!" hissed Corin. Cat lithe he spun round and hacked the rusted chain above the prisoner's cage. Twice more he struck, badly pitting Biter's edge, until the cage crashed noisy to the floor, bursting open and disgorging its filthy inhabitant. The prisoner emerged grumbling from the wreckage and cursing Corin's clumsiness.

"At last," the wretch muttered. "I was beginning to despair at the obtuseness of mankind."

Corin and Roman were hemmed back to back; they hewed about in increasing desperation. Ignoring them, the emaciated prisoner grinned at the guards. He said something unintelligible under his breath.

The air shimmered and warped around him. There came a weird noise, a sucking, clicking sound, and the old man's thin body slowly altered its shape.

The Crenise warriors backed away in horror, terrified. The figure standing before them was no longer disheveled and feeble. He was very tall, broad shouldered and strong.

Gone were the filthy rags. He wore an embroidered cloak of sky-blue hue and gold trimmings that let off a sheen in the darkness surrounding them.

The stranger's hair was long and silvery gold. His eyes were large and impossibly blue. Weirdness emanated from him, a hypnotic will both powerful and coercing. That fusion reached out to the guards with smoky fingers. Their resolve melted like heated candle wax. They turned in panic, fleeing down the passageway.

"Be gone, and trouble us no more!" intoned the stranger in a melodic, resonant voice. He then turned to face Corin and Roman, who stood goggling, too startled to speak. This stranger, whoever he was, was clearly a magician, which though handy, was very disconcerting.

The warlock towered above them. He was nearly as tall as Barin. His skin emitted a faint golden glow. He looked down at the exhausted fighters with an enigmatic smile. The voice that spoke to them was urbane and rich, totally different from the earlier foolish cackle.

"You asked who I am, Corin an Fol." The stranger smiled expansively. "A moot question, I'll concede. I am called Zallerak at this time and in this place. In other places I have other names.

Zallerak will serve here. My present home is far away in the east, but once I had a dwelling in your small country—a wee cottage by the coast."

Corin shook his head. *This is bollocks.* He would not be hoodwinked, especially after all the weird shite of the previous week. He glared at the stranger, his expression grim. Corin had no fondness of wizardry, particularly now. Despite being saved by this Zallerak, he wasn't about to trust him.

"I once heard tell of a sorcerer that dwelt in a tower in the far west of Fol," he replied. "That was years ago, when I was a lad. He would be long dead by now."

"Indeed he would. Sorcerers do not live overly long in these troubled times," responded Zallerak. "Caswallon the Usurper has learned much of late. He won't tolerate rivals. Few can stand against him, bolstered as he is by the craft of Morak and his unpleasant kin."

"Who is this Morak really?" asked Roman, but Corin knew the answer.

"However, I am not a sorcerer," continued Zallerak, ignoring the question. "Not in the traditional sense. I merely know the odd trick and can occasionally, should the inclination occur, create an illusion to baffle the simple minded. I view myself rather as a travelling bard."

He parted his sky-blue cloak to reveal a small golden harp hanging from his belt. Corin's eyes widened. It was a thing of alien design and rare beauty.

"A way-blown minstrel," continued Zallerak, "wandering the wide realms, free and easy. I tell fables of long ago to indolent kings and lascivious queens, of which many...ah." He looked at the warriors with a conspirator's expression.

"Crenna is but the start of your adventures, my young friend." He was looking hard at Corin, much to the longswordsman's discomfort.

"A false start it has proved, but no matter. I knew you were due here, so I decided to wait for your noisy arrival in the dungeons."

Corin was painfully aware that this Zallerak was addressing

him and completely ignoring Roman.

"After freeing the young Prince I needed time to think," Zallerak said. "This dungeon proved ideal, apart from the smell, which got to me after a time. I thought that when my young, enthusiastic friends arrived they might need my help. I was right it seems. Thus I created the illusion of the cage."

"So you never were imprisoned?" Roman shook his head in disbelief. This was all beyond him and he was aware time was passing. He glanced toward the passage and nudged Corin's arm, but his friend was still locked in discussion with the stranger.

"Why did you not help us before?" Corin demanded. "We could have been killed while you were larking about in your pretend cage."

"I needed to be sure of your courage and competence," replied Zallerak. "I was curious of Oroonin's choice. I expect I would have intervened before you were dead but assumed it would look better on you if you rescued me first."

"What game are you playing, wizard?" Corin stared suspiciously at the self-proclaimed bard.

"Game! Game?" Zallerak's eyes blazed for a moment like great angry spheres of lapis lazuli. "This is no game, young Corin. I am not a wizard. Wizards are petty, meddling troublemakers.

"I am a bard, a mystic. There is much more to lose here than you know, boyo, or will ever know. Be content with the knowledge that Prince Tarin is free." He clapped a hand on Roman's shoulder, who recoiled as one stung.

"Come, you pair, follow me! You have wasted enough time in foolish banter. That nasty Assassin fellow has taken your little Queen captive, and even now your large friend Barin battles for his life outside the gates of this most unpleasant fortress!"

The two cursed angrily when they heard this news, vowing bloody vengeance on Rael Hakkenon should anything happen to Ariane. They felt useless and stupid, but short of options, they decided it best to follow the guidance of this mysterious, and clearly eccentric, bard. Corin thought ruefully of his friend Barin, alone as an island in fog, surrounded by a sea of foes—and without his war axe.

"Well then, lead on!" he snapped at Zallerak.

"Worry not," replied the self-styled bard with a reassuring wave of his hand. "We may yet have time to save them both. Follow me, dolts. We must make for the great hall of Kranek Keep where Rael the cruel is holding a feast for his chieftains. We will slip inside unnoticed, after a few dabblings on my part. I have, you see, already devised a plan that will enable us to rescue your young Queen, Roman Parrantios."

"What about Barin?" enquired Ariane's champion. "We cannot leave him to die unaided!"

"Oh, I believe he has help on the way also," responded Zallerak with a shrug. "Follow me, I know a shortcut through these passages!"

"Then lead us there and stop wittering," said Corin. He looked at Roman, who shrugged. What choice remained?

Together they followed the stranger called Zallerak up and out of the dungeon. As he led the two fighting men through the dark, Zallerak unraveled his plan. Corin questioned who this being really was and just what he was up to. What did he gain by aiding them? Time would tell. They caught up with the fleeing guards and slew them all.

***

Barin cursed and swore in frenzied fury. All about him, the slain bodies of the Assassin's elite guard lay strewn like broken dolls. Back and forth went his short sword, whirling ceaselessly, a deadly arc of steel.

He blocked a spear thrust with his forearm, whirled round to kick an axe man in the ribs, launching him back to take three others with him as he fell. The man lay still with his chest caved in.

"Valkador!" roared Barin, seizing the dead man's axe. "This hatchet will be better than nothing, I suppose." He glared at his foes from beneath the great archway, his vast bulk almost filling the space beneath. They had surrounded him and were swarming like wasps, with spears thrusting from every direction. Undismayed, Barin fought on, axe in left hand, sword in right.

Let them come; I haven't started yet!

As he hewed and stabbed and gutted, Barin thought of his friends. He hoped Corin and the others would be all right, that they would be able to save brave Ariane from Rael Hakkenon's thugs. Thinking of his friends gave him renewed vigor. He leapt forward, swinging the axe like a pendulum of death.

On Barin battled, breaking spear shafts with his stolen axe, piercing throats with the short sword, until bodies were piled high in front of him. But they kept coming. Others had arrived, and they pressed him back until he stood panting and sucking in gulps of breath, his back slammed hard into the shut gates.

Barin's time was running out.

A sword thrust got through his defense, slicing his forearm to the bone, then a spear struck his mailed chest beneath his cloak, bruising a rib, causing him to stumble sideways and trip on the blood-soaked stones beneath. Barin closed his eyes. He was spent and exhausted.

Time to die...

Yelling, the spearman leapt forward, his long weapon raised for the kill.

Instead, the guard pitched face first onto the ground. He twitched briefly then lay still. Protruding through his throat was a slender grey arrow. More arrows came whistling out of the night. The guards turned from their prey, alarmed by this new invisible foe.

Up Barin leapt, roaring like a wounded bear.

He was still alive! With a shout of pure joy Barin grabbed the collar of a stunned guard. He hoisted the shouting man high over his head, then hurled him down on his fellows to lie there limp and broken. Arrows buzzed past his ear, burying themselves in enemy flesh. Bleyne's arrows never missed. They found tiny gaps in armor and pierced eyeholes in helmets.

Snarling, Barin pounced and swung out with both weapons trailing blood in whirring circles of steel. Barin's renewed ferocity panicked the Crenise, as did the mystery shafts swooping in from the dark. They hung back and gaped about in the gloom, confused and crestfallen.

Barin strode toward them. The Crenise axe was blunt and his short sword pitted, slippery with blood. He let them drop to the ground with a clatter and strode forward bare knuckled and undeterred. Barin's dinner-plate fists pummeled one hapless guard to the ground. He laughed, hauled another off the ground and butted him in the face. Without a word, the man crumpled and joined his dead companion.

The Crenise warriors looked about desperately, searching for the murderous archer but to no avail. More shafts rained death.

How many did he have?

Then came a hoarse shout from across the square. Figures could be seen hurrying toward the city guards.

It was Fassof and the crew of *The Starlight Wanderer!* Wielding cutlasses and shouting in defiance, they entered the fight. Pale faced, the Assassin's guards turned to confront these new enemies. They were worried. Things weren't going as planned.

Bleyne the archer stepped out from behind one of the tall statues where he had been hiding, a slim dagger held in each hand now that his arrows were all spent. Barin yelled thanks, and the archer grinned in return. Then Fassof staggered toward Barin with the latter's battle-axe strapped across his straining back.

"I've carried this bloody thing all the way up that sodding hill," grumbled the fiery mate. He hefted Barin the axe. "I thought perhaps you might be missing it," he added with a lopsided grin.

Barin hugged the sweating mate, lifting Fassof off his feet.

"What kept you, shithead?" he gasped. "It's been hard work up here!" Barin panted, then waved the huge weapon at the surviving guards, who still outnumbered them two to one.

"Want some of this, weasels?" Barin chided them. "Now we can have a proper fight!" Barin grinned like a deranged beaver, and stepping forward, closed on the spearmen again.

The Assassin's guardsmen were starting to crumble despite their advantage in numbers. The ship's crew fought like demons, and their giant captain appeared unkillable. Only a fear of their lord kept them in their place. Should they fail and remain alive, their heads would grace the castle walls tomorrow. So they fought on but lacked their earlier enthusiasm.

Barin laughed as he slew, his joy of battle having returned. They were winning and fighting alongside him. His crew whooped as they cut down the enemy with their curved blades.

Somewhere in their midst were two figures who looked out of place and unsure of themselves. Cale had stolen ashore, leaving Galed no choice but to try and protect him. The squire stabbed about wildly with the unfamiliar cutlass, as much a hindrance to his comrades as a help.

Cale had persuaded Fassof to lend him a spare blade. He was fourteen, he'd told the redhead, old enough to fight. Galed had despaired at that.

"If my Queen is in peril, then my place is with her," Cale had announced to him with passion while the ship's crew was getting ready for the battle ahead. Galed finally conceded, deeming the terror of waiting alone on board ship more than either he or the boy could bear. And if the crew were lost —well, so were they.

And so they had followed the crew into the city and joined the carnage at the gates. Cale had watched in fascination when Fassof and Cogga silently dispatched the four guards in the harbor.

They had reached Kranek Castle just as Bleyne fired his final arrow. Without a moment's hesitation, Fassof had rushed headlong into the attack. The others followed, including the boy, hollering and waving his cutlass with both hands.

Galed gulped back bile, then he too entered the fray. At least they were winning. There were fewer of the enemy, and those remaining were clearly losing heart.

It would soon be over. Galed felt a flood of relief. He grinned at Cale, whose face was flushed with pride. Together they stole glances across the great square, where the pink hint of dawn revealed the snow-clad slopes of the mountains high above. Huge and majestic they reared, steep ridges burnished by a wintry sun that even now rose gold and dazzling, hailing the arrival of morning and the return of hope.

Movement caught Galed's eye as he watched the dawn awaken. He froze, rooted to the spot, an icy dread gripping his bowels.

He glanced at Cale. The boy had seen it too. Galed gulped, his mouth tinder dry.

This cannot be happening.

Galed felt his bladder loosen and his knees buckle. It wasn't over but had only just begun.

Across the square, marching purposely toward them, came the weasel-faced captain Pollomoi. Behind him tramped a hundred guardsmen, all shouting for their blood. But it wasn't these reinforcements that terrified Cale and the squire.

Across the granite square the gruesome stone statues were moving. As the cold early sunlight touched their weird shapes, they shook, contorted, and shuddered into ghastly motion.

It was horrible to witness. Slowly, the statues creaked and scraped toward the stunned fighters. The noise was unbearable, a groaning and grinding and tearing of stone on stone. Barin's sailors watched in stupefied horror, certain they faced death.

The surviving guards ran to join Pollomoi's men. They too gaped at the approaching stone giants, grateful but terrified of the dark power that had risen up to aid them, not knowing from whence it came. On they came, grim monoliths, stone scraping stone— a hideous mixture of deformed beast and skeletal bird, eyes glowing amber with a malice not their own.

"What sorcery is this?" Barin's face was bleak. Then he saw the hooded figure watching them from the shadows beyond. He glimpsed a ravaged face beneath that hood, a long snout and wide twitching nostrils.

The Dog Lord had come.

Barin shuddered at the numbing terror assaulting him. Almost he was unmanned by it. His mighty hands sweated as they gripped the axe shaft. This time there would be no one to aid him and his men. This time they were doomed.

He looked at Galed and the boy, both livid with fear. It was more than Barin could bear. Beside him stood Bleyne the archer as horror-struck as the rest. He'd regained some of his arrows, but they would be useless now.

"It is Morak," Bleyne muttered. "The Dog Lord, a servant of

Old Night! The Urgolais have returned. Elanion help us!" Bleyne's voice was swallowed by grinding, scraping granite. The stone beasts surrounded them.

Chapter 27

Vaarg

Dawn brought the urgent clatter of hooves on cobbled stone. The late autumn sun rose almost reluctantly to reveal a rider. Travel worn and drenched in sweat, he clung to his exhausted horse with stubborn tenacity. Relief flooded through him as he read the ivy-strewn marker showing that at last he drew near to his destination.

The rider willed himself on, pushing his struggling horse beyond exhaustion. He crested the final hill, saw the Sorcerer's tower piercing the sky like a finger of doom, casting weird shadows on the great city that clustered nervous below.

The rider saw a faint light high up in the tower and quailed. Did sorcerers never sleep? He steeled himself, approached the ornate gates, and then waited anxiously as they creaked open. Men coming toward him garbed in wool and iron. He spoke, and they waved him through.

Perani watched in thoughtful silence as the sweating horseman dismounted and ran up to join him on the battlements of the northern wall. The Captain of the Citadel waited for the man to regain his breath, before he raised a quizzical brow.

"What's the news from the east, messenger?" he demanded.

"I heard word the eastern castles are under attack. Is this true?"

"Aye, my lord," replied the rider. "I bring grave tidings from Car Carranis," he said. "There's rumor Point Keep has fallen to the eastern barbarians, although nothing is certain." He paused, wiped snot from his nose.

"Also, word arrived from Morwella just as I was leaving, dire news. Vangaris Harbor is under siege, awash with ships out of Leeth!" The messenger paused again, this time gratefully downing a flagon of offered wine in nervous gulps whilst Perani waited for him to continue.

"Our scouts have reported sighting a vast horde gathering in the eastern forests. It would appear King Haal is bent on invasion, my lord!"

"Yes, so it would seem," responded Perani, unsurprised by the news. "Get some food and rest man," he told the messenger. "Doubtless I will require your services soon enough. First I must consult Lord Caswallon. Await here for my return." Perani left the messenger at the wall without further comment. He barked a few curt commands, then made ready to leave.

The city was waking: Carts ground over cobbles, and market stores were manned by wan-faced vendors. Men spoke in whispers whilst women walked with heads kept low. Children were not much in evidence. Parents had learned to keep their little ones in doors soon after the arrival of the ghastly Groil. Several had gone missing. Cats skulked hungry and skinny dogs lurked mean in back alleys. This was Kella City of an early morn.

Ignoring all, Perani strode toward the palace, purposeful and grim, aware as always of the hate-filled eyes that watched him pass. Let them think what they will; his place of power was assured.

***

Caswallon reluctantly released his gaze from the crystal. He'd been transfixed watching the events on Crenna. He had tapped into Urgolais power on Morak's permission, recently renewing his fargaze skills so that he could easily control the glass orb over greater distance and watch events unfold in most areas—as long as he linked with the Dog Lords first and got their permission, which was, in point of fact, a bone of contention.

Morak had invited Caswallon to watch his show over on Crenna, and it was proving high entertainment indeed. Caswallon had witnessed in awe how the Dog Lord worked his spell on the stone creatures outside Kranek Castle.

If only he had such power. Well, he would in time. Then the Urgolais would be afraid of him, not the other way round. Patience. He'd learn all their tricks and then turn on them when the hour was right. The Dog Lord had been a fool to aid him.

Every day Caswallon's knowledge waxed. He had more Groil on loan, and other fell beings would follow as promised. Soon Caswallon wouldn't need the help of men. Soon... but not just yet.

Caswallon chuckled, his eyes on the crystal again. The stone ogres had surrounded the pathetic troop. Soon the fools would be no more.

Job done.

Caswallon's attentions turned to the walls below. With witch-tuned ears he'd locked onto the messenger reporting to Perani, heard the man imparting the "grievous" news. Caswallon smiled. This too had been part of his plan.

Only Perani knew the depth of his treachery, and the calculating general would play his part well enough. Perani knew where his loyalties need lay, thus was safe for the short term.

War was coming to Ansu. It would be Caswallon's war, and it would be as dark and dreadful as were his ambitions. Caswallon would guest the brutal King of Leeth and his violent sons here in Kelsalion's palace, whilst their savage men spread ruin throughout the countryside. He'd sent the King a letter promising a welcome once they brought Car Carranis low.

Let the barbarians have their time of glory. Once they had served his purpose they too would become his vassals. King Haal would swear fealty to the new Lord of Kelthaine. Caswallon's armies would swell in number and strength. Kelthaine was his, very soon Morwella would be reduced to ash, and the other two kingdoms would follow. Within a year Caswallon would become overlord of the western realms. He would seduce the neighboring lands with riches until they too were brought to heel.

It was all down to timing, that and careful planning. He rubbed his long bony fingers together in anticipation. His ascent to real power had only just begun.

Caswallon reached down to pat the crinkled head of his Soilfin. Strangely, he'd grown fond of the ugly creature. He'd fed Gribble by hand with the warm flesh of a prisoner after the goblin-ape had returned, famished from his foray out west.

Gribble grinned inanely up at him; the Soilfin liked his new guardian too. Theirs was a tenuous, peculiar friendship—twisted evil sorcerer and loathsome stinking goblin, perfect roommates in this drafty tower. Gribble thrived on the tasty morsels Caswallon had provided during their brief time together. The meat was always fresh. Better still, it was breathing.

Caswallon fingered his close-cropped beard. It was hard to conceal his growing anticipation for the power that would soon be his, and the pleasures that were sure to accompany it.

The Assassin would have the Queen caught like a wasp in a honey jar. For her Caswallon had special plans, dark and twisted schemes. He envisioned her naked and open before him. Little Ariane had given him a deal of trouble.

He would have her escorted to him trembling, her will broken and body no longer her own. There she would learn to please.

She would beg to please. Caswallon would use the Queen again and again until he wearied of her. Then he would feed her to Gribble as a special treat.

Caswallon released his fargaze from the crystal. It hurt to stare for more than a few minutes—even with Morak's guidance.

He stood, stretched, and paced across to the window. From there Caswallon gazed down upon the tiny figures scurrying about their petty duties far below. Like so many restless ants they hurried back and forth, driven by fear and uncertainty. Caswallon knew the people hated him, but that was irrelevant. Those that survived the coming war would become his slaves, or else food for his growing legion of Groil.

Only Perani and his second, Derino, knew of the Groil's whereabouts.

Two-Heads, Flail, and a few others dwelt here in the palace but most were hidden in the sewers below the city. Perfect place for them. At night they'd rise up through drains, pouncing on anyone unlucky enough to be in the vicinity.

Caswallon turned to see Gribble watching him warily. "What is it? What's wrong?" Then Caswallon gasped as a sharp pain lanced the length of his spine. He stumbled, almost fell.

Then the tower was rocked by sudden deafening noise. *Crack* and *boom!* The whole building shook and windows rattled. Caswallon was thrown to the floor whilst Gribble sped under the table and gulped. Caswallon groped, found his knees, and then fell flat again as the floor heaved beneath him. *Boom, crack—thud.* Caswallon covered his ears.

Light shimmered. There came a weird shrieking noise followed by another thud. The tower shuddered horribly. Then, just as Caswallon thought it would crumple and collapse, the racket and quaking subsided and were replaced by silence. Caswallon tried to quell the panic screaming through his veins. He knew what had caused this: a crack in the void. A fissure had opened from limbo, and something had got through.

Badly shaken, Caswallon regained his feet. For a time he leant against the table. He summoned courage, tentatively approached the window, and looked outside. Nothing. It was blacker than black out there. No atmosphere, no wind. Just emptiness.

Beneath the rocking table behind him Caswallon heard a squishy plopping sound. He turned, saw Gribble relieving himself in a jar. The Soilfin was shivering and grinding his filed teeth.

"That'll be Vaarg," the Soilfin muttered. "He has awoken then. They said he would at some point. He's bound to be hungry. Vaarg's appetite is much bigger than mine, Mr. Caswallon."

Caswallon's face faded to grey. Why hadn't the Dog Lord warned him of this? He glanced outside again. The blackness had dispersed into a mass of tawny cloud. These parted, and at last he saw it.

The hole in the sky.

A vast rent, jagged and distorting, shifting in and out of vision and hard to define. Beyond it was only void, the chaotic torn fabric of anti-matter, impossible to define, a wrongness that confused both eye and brain.

Through this opening sped the dragon.

A great winged beast, black and sleek like a fired crossbow bolt it arrowed toward the tower with impossible speed, swelling in size, the wing beats drumming like approaching thunder. Caswallon felt suddenly sick and frail. He staggered, gripped the chair again to steady himself.

Caswallon had quite forgotten about dragons.

***

For long centuries Vaarg had slumbered. It was the breaking of the crown that woke him, the echoes from which resonated throughout all nine worlds, reaching him at last in that cold dark place at the very edge of limbo.

Vaarg had stirred then, unfolded his great wings and opened wide his reptilian orbs. Vaarg had slept long enough—even by dragon standards. He was hungry for flesh; it was time to get moving. Time to see what had occurred during his enforced hibernation. He heard his old master's voice calling him from very far away. That voice sounded remote and weak—not what it once had been.

"I have need of you—It is beginning…"

"I AM COMING…"

And so Vaarg rose up; his coiled, iron-hard hide slithering and bulking as it gathered massive behind him. The cave shook as he hauled his scaly bulk to its icy entrance.

Vaarg's head gaped out into the dark. A mile behind and lost in the depth of the cave, his tail's tip whipped rocks free as it lashed to and fro in anticipation.

Vaarg launched his obsidian bulk out of the cave. For a brief instant he squatted horrible at the mouth, testing his wire-tough wings and flicking that cold tongue.

Then he lifted, soared high—reveling in the joy of flight after so very long asleep. Vaarg sailed majestic through midnight sky vacating that remote ledge on the edge of all worlds.

He tore up into the blacker black, cleaving through space, crossing alien skies and breaking through time dimensions as he had millennia ago. For it was told of dragons that, like the gods, they had the ability to move from planet to planet, whether by crossing space matter, or by secret wyrm holes known only to them.

Vaarg sailed passed blazing suns. As he sped the Firewyrm recounted the glory of the good old days: the wars of the gods, his allegiance with the Urgolais, and his master the Dog Lord hoisting Golganak high as he rode the dragon's back. Lord Morak and invincible Vaarg distributed death and obliteration on the Golden Folk, their enemies.

A glorious time! Throughout that endless war Vaarg ravaged and destroyed at his master's bidding. He'd torn down the Aralais towers with his kin. Together they had fed on the enemy flesh. But the Aralais were also strong. They'd countered, built flying craft, and set vengeful upon the dragons with laser guns and gases. Many of his brethren had been slain.

Then came the final battle and his master's fall. Vaarg witnessed the arrival of the mortal folk from overseas, rushing like fools to Aralais aid. Vaarg, seeing all was lost, had fled to his lofty eerie and vowed vengeance. But with the Urgolais power broken, he too became weakened and retired to sleep in hungry solitude.

Throughout the long millennia Vaarg slept, and the resonant Aralais power of the Tekara held his master's ghost at bay. But that time had passed. A new age of Chaos was beginning, and dragons had always been creatures of Chaos.

He approached the portal and spoke the word. The skies cracked open, allowing his shrieking passage into the green realm beyond and below.

And so Vaarg, last of the great Firewyrms, returned at last to the first world, Ansu, on the eve of war. And his hunger was great.

At Ulan Valek, the old Urgolais manse, deep beneath the mountain's shadow, Vaarg met the shade of his master. There amid the ruins of those haunted walls, Morak told him of his task, and Vaarg was content.

You will ally yourself with this Caswallon, my beloved. Watch him closely, he is slippery for a mortal.

And so Vaarg had come.

Caswallon clung to the table, his hair wild about his face. Outside, a metallic roar assaulted the morning as the dragon settled like a storm cloud on the tower. Vast and terrible, Vaarg clawed at the roof tiles beneath him, snapping them with his iron-hard talons.

The massively horned, tongue-flicking, nostrils-flaring, golden eyes-glaring, breath-burning triangular head angled down toward the pathetic figure of the wizard gawping stupid at the window.

Vaarg's long neck stretched forward like unraveling steel rope. His steamy breath scorched the thick glass of the window, shattering it and occluding Caswallon's vision. The warlock fell to his knees again and cried for mercy.

Vaarg spoke. "I COME ON MY MASTER'S BIDDING."

The voice was like splintering iron, profound and detonating, cold and ancient as the great glaziers of the frozen realms. Vaarg's voice cracked stone walls and split pavements in the panicked streets below. A few of the bravest folk dared glance skyward in stricken woe. Among these was Perani, as dumbstruck as the rest.

"MORAK QUESTIONS YOUR LOYALTY, MORTAL," hissed Vaarg, his steamy breath igniting the fire in Caswallon's hearth. "HE GROWS CONCERNED AT YOUR TRANSPARENT AMBITIONS." The long tongue trailed hot slime down the blackened, cracked surface of the window pane.

Caswallon's rattled reply was barely audible through the damaged glass, but the dragon's hearing was almost as good as his eyesight.

"Mighty Vaarg," Caswallon coughed. "Tell your lord I exist only to serve him and his master the Lord of Old Night," he lied. Beneath the table Gribble nervously sucked on a human thumb and stomped his feet.

The Soilfin was not enjoying this encounter. Dragons were unpredictable, none more so than Vaarg. Also they had been known to gobble up Soilfins when there was little else for them to feed on.

"THAT IS WELL," responded Vaarg. His whipping mile-long tail dislodged more stone to crash down on the palace roofs.

"MY MASTER HAS A TASK FOR YOU. HE HAS NEED OF HIS SPEAR. THE OLD ENEMY HAS RETURNED TO AID THOSE FOOLS YOU WOULD DESTROY. WITHOUT GOLGANAK MY MASTER CANNOT MANIFEST FULLY. THE DOG LORD GIVES YOU THIS CHANCE TO PROVE FEALTY, CASWALLON."

The dragon's claws exposed the roof's joists, and his tail sent them sailing down on the city below

"TO WIN MORAK'S COMPLETE CONFIDENCE," continued the dragon, "YOU MUST LOCATE GOLGANAK AND RETURN IT TO ITS MASTER, SO HE CAN RECOVER HIS EARTHLY FORM. ONLY THEN WILL OLD NIGHT HAVE TOTAL SUPREMACY. ONLY WITH THE BLACK SPEAR CAN CUL-SAAN BE FREED."

Caswallon had covered his ears. The room was spinning and his head hurt. He summoned his courage once more and looked out at the glaring single amber orb at the window, it being far too small to reveal the dragon's entire head.

"I will seek the spear, of course. But where to look?" he asked. Caswallon was playing for time, desperately trying to think a way through this.

"IN THE MOUNTAINS," answered Vaarg. He belched fire; it charred a roof beam. "GOLGANAK LIES SOMEWHERE BENEATH THE RUINS OF ULAN VALEK. MY MASTER HAS SEARCHED FOR IT TO NO AVAIL. STOUT HEARTS WILL BE NEEDED TO RECLAIM IT. THE GUARDIAN THAT STILL HAUNTS VALEK IS TERRIBLE INDEED."

"I know one that could be used and is dependable," replied Caswallon, thinking of the Assassin. He mouthed a quick spell to quench the burning beam above. "Leave this matter to me, Lord Vaarg, and please let Morak know I am loyal. But do tell me, valiant beast..." He shuddered, seeing the smoldering intelligence inside that amber gaze. It never blinked. "Who is this enemy, this warlock lurking in Crenna?"

"THAT NEED NOT CONCERN YOU, MORTAL." Vaarg's

baleful gaze froze the marrow deep inside Caswallon. "WHEN THE TIME IS RIGHT I WILL REND HIM APART. WE TWO ARE WELL AQUAINTED, AND I'VE A SCORE TO SETTLE."

The dragon tore off a capstone with his fore claw and tossed it down. Seconds later it crashed through the roof of a tavern, killing three souls within.

"FORGET THIS MEDLAR. HE IS MY PROVINCE," steamed Vaarg. "SEEK GOLGANAK. I MUST DEPART FOR A TIME. MY STRENGTH IS NOT AS IT WAS. I NEED SUSTENANCE AND MORE SLEEP. WHEN MY MASTER HAS THE SPEAR, I WILL RETURN—IF NOT BEFORE.

"DO NOT FAIL HIM, CASWALLON. THERE IS NO CORNER OF THIS UNIVERSE TO WHICH YOU COULD FLEE THAT I WOULDN'T FIND YOU—AND TEAR YOU LIMB FROM LIMB." Vaarg spread his huge wings wide. Their seven-hundred-foot span cast baroque shadows on the terrified city.

"I DEPART"

Those final booming words were accompanied by smoke and gas. Caswallon choked in the room—the dragon's noxious breath having seeped in through the damaged roof.

The dragon uncoiled his tail and took flight. His thunder-clap wing beats shook the walls and loosened Caswallon's bowels. Within moments the dragon had vanished through the rapidly shrinking hole in the sky. The rent closed behind him and all was silent for a time.

***

Caswallon felt numb from head to toe. He heard not the screams in palace and city, cared not that the people below were flailed witless by terror. On the city walls and at the gates, panicky guards blocked those hundreds seeking to flee the city.

Many citizens were slain in the carnage as were several soldiers. It was a mess down there—not that Caswallon noticed. Eventually order was restored with Perani's brutal efficiency.

A great many piled into taverns, seeking the oblivion of drink. Still more sought the usually neglected temples to Elanion, Borian, and Telcanna, the Sky God, much to their priest's delight. The sorcerer had forbade open worship, but terror of the winged horror had surpassed even their dread of Caswallon. The sun shone bright this morning heedless of the city's mood.

High in his tower Caswallon straightened his back painfully. His ears still rang with the metallic din of the dragon's thunderous voice. He struggled and shifted, leaning and panting against the wall. Caswallon felt exposed and outmaneuvered.

And very angry.

The bastards were onto him. He stood, thinking and plotting in silence, for most of that morning. Caswallon ignored both Perani's urgent request to see him and the Soilfin's grumbling stomach. Gribble had recovered quickly from Vaarg's visitation. Dragons were old hat to him. Besides he was hungry again.

By afternoon Caswallon felt better. Once again he had command of his senses. The dragon had nearly unmanned him, but he wouldn't be caught with his pants down again.

He formed a plan. Morak only suspected his treachery, so he still had time. Caswallon would find this Golganak, or rather Rael Hakkenon would for him. Then he would keep that terrible weapon for his own use, and with its help, he would put an end to Morak, turning the spear on its master and blasting him to cinders.

Caswallon well knew the power of Golganak. Vaarg would serve him once he knew how things were. With both dragon and spear onside, even the gods would learn to fear Caswallon. He laughed at that thought.

I shall be the Lord of Ansu...

He would summon Perani and inform the Captain of the Citadel of his wishes concerning the eastern defenses. They would have to kill the original messenger, of course.

Caswallon would send another man east. Handpicked by Perani or Derino, this messenger would inform Lord Starkhold of Car Carranis that aid would soon be with him. That aid would never arrive. Caswallon smiled. Car Carranis would fall prey to the baying hounds of Leeth. Point Keep would, too, for that matter— and with it Halfdan, if he lived yet.

He'd send Gribble back to Crenna, ascertain the outcome on that island. Caswallon's fargaze had been obliterated by the coming of Vaarg, and he would not find the strength to reclaim it anytime soon. Nor for that matter could he recall where the crystal globe had rolled off to in all the mayhem.

Mind made up, Caswallon summoned Flail Six-Hands to bring someone for the Soilfin to dine on. And to source carpenters to repair his battered roof. Caswallon was too exhausted to use spell craft.

There was much to be done.

A tapping at the scorched window pane distracted him.

What now! Movement caught Caswallon's eye.

It was a large raven, its beady black eyes mocking him from its perch on the window ledge, its hard black beak jabbing at the damaged pane. Caswallon sensed a supernatural presence in those pitiless coaly eyes. He was suddenly no longer so sure of himself.

Caswallon rapped the window hard, and the bird took wing with a coarse caw. It settled on an exposed roof beam above and watched him hungrily. Caswallon had a nasty thought. Maybe the raven served that other wizard.

It mattered not, he told himself. Vaarg would deal with that player. Soon he, Caswallon, would be the only sorcerer in the land.

Close by, the raven cawed again. Was it laughing at him?

A second later it was gone. Caswallon forgot the bird, began working assiduously on his plans. The first task was to feed the Soilfin. Caswallon heard screaming below. Now to the next job...

Chapter 28

The Bard

That night the great feasting hall was a splendor of firelight and roasting hogs. Claw-like sconces clutched candles flickering on the walls, casting light on the crowded tables.

There the Lord of Crenna's chieftains and premier fighters were seated in honor, all of them hard at feasting, amid swearing, farting and guffawing—with dogs scampering in between.

Rael Hakkenon had taken to his silver chair. There he held laughing court over the bruised and bleeding, spitting and cursing bundle of the Queen. He'd had Ariane chained on all fours to the leg of his throne.

Rael laughed every time he looked down on her defiant, wine-soaked face. He'd tossed the odd goblet at her every now and then.

Food and wine were in plenitude this evening, piled high on the long tables. The fire trench roared and crackled like a thousand hissing snakes. The skinny hounds chewed at cast bones, their lolling mouths slavering with spittle in the torchlight. Laughter and shouting eclipsed the roar of the fire.

Ariane looked around at the sneering faces. They were shaggy and unkempt, so unlike their immaculate sire. A false prince on his pseudo throne, Rael had changed into a silk robe that matched the icy green of his eyes.

Rael's fingers sparkled with rubies and sapphires. The left hand hung languidly at his side as if too lazy to stir. He looked down on Ariane now and then. She turned her gaze to the tapestry-draped walls. Each one depicted violent encounters, dark and disturbing, the products of a twisted mind. They gave her scant comfort.

"Left here by the previous tenant, my Queen," Rael said amiably, seeing where her gaze went. "Baron Gusher had a somewhat macabre taste and a pronounced sense of drama. He was neurotic, though, particularly after I extracted certain body parts from him with a hot blade."

Ariane spat up at him but missed.

"Your scum followers are almost as foul as you, Assassin!" Her voice was clear and strong, but deep inside terror was taking hold. Ariane almost lost it when she thought of her dear friends fighting for their lives, perhaps already dead or worse, being prepared for slow torture somewhere below. She reined herself in.

I'll not show weakness to such as these. She would not waver. Willow in a storm, she might bend but never snap. Ariane had King Nogel's strength of spirit, his passion and his pride. They would gain scant coin from her.

"Oh do call me Rael, Queen!" The Assassin was all smiles, his voice laconic and cultured, coated with a twist of venom. He radiated danger and was the most terrifying individual she'd encountered.

There was a wrongness about him. That perfect face was warped and marred by some hidden poison. He made her flesh crawl. No wonder the Lord of Crenna was feared in all four realms.

As Rael watched her, his smile vanished like rain on desert sand.

"I'm sorry we do not match up to your standards," he continued, "but we pirate folk don't often mix with such grandiose company as your royal self." His men were hooting and hollering, some banged the table tops with their eating knives and hurled food at each other.

Most were clad in furs and leather. Many wore gold bands around their arms and wrists. Their savage faces were covered with tattoos and ritual scars depicting their standing amongst their fellows.

They were the pirate captains of Crenna, scourge of the western waters, rapists and murderers everyone. Their greedy eyes blazed a savage lust. Ariane felt naked.

The eating knives were the only weapons allowed in the feasting hall. It was not uncommon for fights to break out among these chieftains, causing bitter feuds that lasted for years. After one particularly spiteful occasion, when a ship's captain gouged out his neighbor's eye and ate it, the Assassin had forbidden all altercation in the hall, on pain of public dismemberment.

Even so, one or two hadn't taken the hint and had fed the crows on the walls with their flesh. They were a rough lot. They leered at Ariane as they filled their bellies with stolen ale.

"Enough, lads. Calm down." Rael's jeweled hand waved them to silence. "She is a Queen, after all." He smiled his cat-cream smile. "We don't want to be disrespectful, do we?" The chieftains cheered and hooted their approval.

"Besides," continued their lord with a dramatic flourish of his right arm. "We must be wary. She is a biter. Quite nasty with a sword too, little bitch. I'm sure you'd concur. And what fool would teach a mere woman handle a blade. Their bitchy tongues are sharp enough as it is, no?" Some of the chieftains nodded at this last point, the rest just laughed.

"I wonder what I should do with her in the immediate. She has been most impolite, even for a Queen," Rael continued amiably. "Stealing inside my lovely castle, unbidden and uninvited, with her foolish friends, and slaying my guards too. Fortunate was it for them that none survived her blade. I would have had them flayed alive for letting themselves be overcome by a woman."

Rael wiped his sleeve with sudden irritated disgust. His expression was petulant. One of those idiot guards had managed to bleed on him.

"Well, then? What do you think we should do with her?"

"Let me take her, lord!" shouted a huge warrior, dribbling gobby torrents into his black beard. "Then I'll slit her throat, and we'll be done with her!"

"Feed her to the dogs!" snarled another, a thin toothless cross-eyed man with a blue spider tattooed on his forehead.

"Well, that is certainly tempting," purred the Assassin, showing his perfect teeth. "Regrettably, she is worth more to us alive and... undamaged," he told them. "Fret you not, though!" He held up his hands to quell their disappointed shouts. "We can still have a bit of fun, eh. Release her, Tolgan." Rael waved a languid hand at one of the chieftains on the nearest bench. "Let's see her crawl."

Grinning, Tolgan approached the throne, a big brute in his middle years and one of Rael's favorites, a total wild man, black beard speckled with grey and long, tangled ashen hair. A scar ran from left hairline to lower right cheek. Whoever had dealt that blow had removed the lower half of Tolgan's nose as well.

To say he was ugly was being polite. Not that anyone told Tolgan he was ugly, except the Assassin when the mood took him—and even that was a rare occurrence.

Tolgan grinned at Ariane. He reached down, worked the keys, and freed her arms and legs. "Here what the boss says? You're to crawl!" Tolgan kicked her and sent the Queen sprawling. Rael chuckled from his chair.

Ariane feigned submission. She lay on her belly, her fingers scraping the stone floor. Tolgan approached, made to launch another kick.

He was much too slow.

Ariane rolled. Roman had taught her this move years ago. She'd never thought she'd have to put it into practice. Her left leg shot up, blocking Tolgan's kick whilst she hopped effortlessly onto her right, rising slowly with controlled ease.

Tolgan cursed, launched another kick. She trapped his leg, swept the big man off balance, and then snapped out with her free leg, taking him hard in the balls. Tolgan groaned and slunk to his knees.

Ariane stepped forward, grabbed Tolgan's shaggy beard, and

yanked down hard whilst bringing her knee up, crunching into his half-nose and cracking it back. Tolgan slunk prone amid hoots of laughter from his comrades below. They were still laughing when he came to and staggered back to the benches.

Rael Hakkenon wasn't laughing. Ariane had turned her attention to the Assassin, her face a cold mask of contempt. "Call yourself a prince—do you, Assassin? You're no prince. You're just a pile of shite!" Ariane spat up at the lazy-eyed lord seated on his baroque throne. Rael watched her in silence. No one there could read his expression.

"Your days are numbered, bastard," she told him. "I have friends who will avenge any harm done to my person, either by you or that murdering usurper in Kella. I don't fear you, arsewipe, or those tosspots down there that pander to your clown's court!"

Several of the warriors drew back in surprise at these words. They were uncertain of what would follow. But the Assassin laughed out loud and clapped his gloved hands with pantomime delight.

"Isn't she a wonder, lads," he said. "What spirit she has—and so genteel a tongue! Is this really a Queen we have here or some common slattern? Perhaps naughty old Nogel was shagging some whore that spawned this little bitch, made a change from all the boars he used to poke."

They laughed at that, those chieftains. King Nogel had been famed for his love of boar hunting—a love that had finally cost him his life.

"Lucky old Caswallon." Rael was smiling. "She'll keep him occupied for weeks. What say you, lads?" Roars of approval came from the benches below."

Rael's gaze narrowed, the smile fleeing his lips. "You're bound for Kella, my love," Rael told her. "And to a warm reception from a most attentive Lord Caswallon. Little can I even guess what he's got planned for you. Sorcerers are said to have rather peculiar tastes, and I know this one's rumored quite perverse. I have heard that he likes hot tar and—"

"Fuck you!" Ariane wrenched free of the huge guard holding her arm (he having replaced Tolgan, who lurked at the back of the hall nursing his swollen bollocks). The guard cursed, groped for her.

Ariane jumped back out of reach. She caught the guard's questing arm at his wrist and yanked him forward toward her whilst sending her free elbow hard into his face. The big man fell back.

Ariane turned on the Assassin, still watching from his throne behind her. She kicked out hard and fast, catching Rael's shin above his ankle. He hissed like a tomcat and silence filled the hall. Tired of the game, Rael leapt to his feet, his hand on sword hilt.

"Time for a swift, fucking lesson, slut." Rael's humor had evaporated. He felt spiteful, vindictive. The little cunt had kicked him. He wanted to poke Ariane's arse with something hot and sharp.

But what's this? Rael strained to see through the smoke to focus on the far doors. A cacophony had erupted from that end of the hall. At last he spied two of his warriors dragging a filthy scrawny wretch out from a dark corner, where until now he had apparently been hiding.

"What the fuck is going on over there?" Rael snapped at the two guards. "And who is that idiot?"

"Lord, we caught him spying," replied the nearest of the warriors. This was a big ugly brute of a fellow who the Assassin didn't recognize. But Rael never took much notice of his guardsmen. "He claims to be a talented bard and a conjurer of tricks. I think he is a madman, my lord!" barked the warrior.

"I don't care what you think, twat. Silence your tongue lest I remove it!" In a calmer voice he added.

"Bring that pile of buggered bones here so that I can poke some holes in its useless hide." The chieftains laughed and hollered at this new entertainment.

The two guards and the wriggling wretch stopped a score of feet before the Assassin's chair. The wretch stepped forward. He thrust the guards aside as though they were but a bother.

"Unhand me, you knaves." He scowled at them, and they drew back, uncertain. The Assassin leapt to his feet. Beneath him

Ariane, on all fours again having been wrestled down by two fresh guards, stared wide-eyed at this weird disheveled newcomer.

The stranger spoke: "I am called Zallerak." He addressed the entire hall, his voice musical, clear, and compelling.

"I'm a teller of tales, some say the greatest bard in all Ansu!" Rael Hakkenon watched him po-faced. He took to his throne again and bid the fellow closer. This diversion had cooled his fire a bit. But it had better prove riveting. He fingered his rapier's hilt lazily, his hand itching to use it.

"So... you are a bard," Rael said lazily. "A boastful one, too," He looked hard at the stranger. Rael had his jeweled dagger out of its sheath and was deftly rolling the blade between the fingers of his left hand.

"I think actually that you are a spy," Rael said. "Caswallon's stinking goblin told me there was someone lurking about my castle plotting misdemeanors, although I can't think that he meant a ghastly decaying stick like you. Speak quickly. I am not known for my patience!"

"Oh, Gribble, yes I heard he returned." Zallerak's over-large eyes were everywhere. "You shouldn't listen to Soilfins, Assassin. They weld fact to fiction and fabricate duplicity. They are also rather vulgar," he added rubbing his long nose with a grubby finger. "And one does so detest vulgarity."

Ariane, forgotten for the moment, watched the strange scarecrow man. His apparel was shoddy and a cloying stink clung to his pale skin, but the stranger's voice resonated power. There was witchery here, of that she was certain. This Zallerak's eyes sparkled like sapphires beneath his shaggy brow. Also, those two silent guards at his side seemed oddly familiar.

"Enough fucking dribble!" Rael Hakkenon was angry again. "Who are you really?"

Zallerak didn't respond. His deep, clear eyes were still surveying the wall. He appeared distracted, unfazed.

Rael Hakkenon leapt from the throne, kicking Queen Ariane aside and jumping down until he held the dagger point to Zallerak's throat. "Speak, filth!" he snarled.

And Zallerak obliged.

As he spoke, his words drifted across the hall in rhythmic waves, lulling the atmosphere and easing the tension. The Assassin's jaw dropped a little. He looked puzzled. He withdrew the dagger from the vicinity of Zallerak's throat and re-sheathed it in silence. Rael listened to the incanted words and before he knew it, he too was caught in the web.

***

"I am the journeyman," Zallerak told them, as if they were children seated goggle-eyed before him, "the spinning wheel, once lost never found.

"I am newly ancient and recently old, returned and departed, both weak and strong." As he spoke, Zallerak's voice grew stronger and more resonant. It soaked into the tapestries and lulled the feasting fire's flames.

All listened in silence. Even the dogs had paused from their gnawing.

"I am the tool of fate," continued Zallerak, "the watcher at the gate, the paradox, the king's wise fool. I am the eye that sees four ways. I see within, I see without. I see past futures and certain doubt—and time long gone but yet to be.

"I am the maker of riddles but the solver of none. I came here when it ended. I left when it begun."

The words made no sense, but the voice was empathic and soothing. On either side of the fire trench the chieftains slunk back in their stools. Their eye lids were heavy. Even the Assassin let the words wash through him, unconcerned that he comprehended nothing spoken. Rael didn't often relax.

And there lay the problem.

Sorcery! Rael shook his head free of the words assaulting it. *This bastard's a sorcerer!*

Rael rejected the words caressing him. He rallied his iron will and shook off the spell. Furious, Rael paced the hall, enraged at being hoodwinked—if only for a few seconds. He kicked a slouching warrior to his feet and yelled at his drowsy chieftains.

"Seize this gibbering warlock!" Rael ordered. "Take the wanker outside and slay him in an unpleasant manner!" He kicked a second fellow, this time hard in his groin, but the warrior barely stirred. "Wake up you dopey fucking slugs!" The Assassin rounded on Zallerak. Rael would finish this bastard himself, he decided.

The witch-bard ignored him. He continued his dirge of riddles, oblivious to Rael Hakkenon's fury. Some of the warriors were responding to their leader's harsh command but found their limbs too heavy to move. The more they resisted the spell, the weaker they felt.

The chant echoed round the hall. One by one, the chieftains sank into a deep and troubled slumber. Only the Assassin remained conscious and, strangely, the two guards and Queen too. The rest, even the dogs, filled the hall with their snores.

***

The bard stopped abruptly, sensing the Assassin's proximity. Zallerak had a satisfied smile on his face. After all this time he could still do it.

He allowed himself a moment's self-congratulation and looked down at his body. Gone was the scarecrow. In its place stood a tall, powerfully built man sporting a magnificent cloak of midnight blue, draped over a turquoise tunic of softest linen.

His harp hung golden from the black lacquered belt at his waist. Zallerak hadn't even needed to use it. A yard or two away the dreadful Assassin fellow eyed him darkly. Zallerak wasn't quite sure why the spell hadn't worked fully on the Lord of Crenna. It had slowed him, but this Rael was a fighter. He was struggling hard to stay alert.

"Almost done," Zallerak announced, grinning at the Assassin. At his side the faces of the two warriors blurred and shimmered, and their bodies altered. Ariane gasped, then laughed in relieved delight. Before her stood a smiling Roman Parrantios and dour-faced but slightly bemused Corin an Fol.

"Sorcery!" Rael Hakkenon's fury severed Zallerak's hold on him. "Fucking sorcery!" Like a lightning strike, his rapier was free in his left hand. The Assassin lunged hard and fast for Zallerak's exposed chest.

But Roman was ready. The bearded champion struck the Assassin's blade aside and it clattered across the hall. Roman shouldered into him, knocking the smaller man to the ground. Roman stepped forward, sword held high, eager for the kill.

Snake swift the Assassin rolled out of reach. Rael leapt to his feet, a slender dagger balanced in either hand. He drew back his right arm but was hurled backward by an unseen force, pinned to the wall by the weirdly dreadful eyes of the warlock called Zallerak.

"Know this, Assassin," said the bard. "Your days of rule on this island grow shorter by the minute (an obvious statement but effective nonetheless), and your paltry plans are all but undone.

"Your cohort in Kelthaine will be most displeased when he learns of your failure to deliver him his prize!" Zallerak smiled maliciously. "Oh, incidentally," he continued, relishing the contorted rage on Rael's face as he tried to win free from the invisible bonds that held him.

"I freed young Prince Tarin a few days past, when first I arrived at this cheerful place. Your guards are very careless, murderous one. May I suggest you chastise them once we have taken our leave? Silly me, you're already planning that. You should try another hobby, man. All this bad attitude and butchery is most unhealthy. I mean, you can't have many friends, old lad."

Zallerak turned to the fire trench, his smile perfectly wicked.

"And...you really should take more care of the fires in your hall, Assassin; neglected thus, they could get out of hand!" In response to his words the flames erupted with sudden violence, soaring high above their heads, reaching out, licking hungrily at the macabre tapestries covering the walls, rendering them an inferno of crackling, hissing hatred.

Zallerak no longer needed his power to keep the Assassin at bay, the wrath of the fire had him trapped. His warriors were stirring from their stupor, some already ablaze and once aware, their horrified screams filled the hall.

Men choked and coughed, the dogs bolted for the doors amid

howls and whimpers. The hall was a cauldron of cooking flesh.

Time to leave...

"Hurry!" snapped Zallerak reaching down for Ariane's arm. He hoisted her aloft as though she were a child. The Queen was too stunned to speak, caught halfway between joy and horror at the furnace enveloping the hall

"It's time to run, my dear, don't you think?" Zallerak's head twitched toward the carnage at the tables. "Those not burnt alive will be mad with vengeance, and their master is not for dying just yet, methinks. Follow me, friendlies!"

Ariane hugged Roman amid tears and then reached up to plant a long lingering kiss on Corin's lips whilst throwing her arms about him.

"I knew you were not dead!" she cried while Corin got his breathe back, "though I fear that captain Barin may be." Corin blinked a yes.

As they fled the furnace, Ariane told them how Barin had been shut beyond the castle gate when she was captured. Corin said nothing hoping his friend was still alive.

"But I'm so happy to see you both," she said, kissing Corin again, who for his part looked a bit startled.

"You pair will be dead if you don't stop that stupid lip sucking and look lively," snapped Zallerak. "This is hardly the time for exchanging felicitations. Follow me!" His words parted the flames ahead. Tall and imperious, he led them from the burning hall.

Behind them the Assassin roared and spat bile. Free at last from Zallerak's coercion, Rael kicked and bit those fighters in reach. Some were only just awaking from their enforced slumber.

Rael's face was livid with rage, and his expensive robe was ruined, but he beat a way through the towering flames.

"You won't get far, wizard!" yelled Rael. "I'll roast your fucking head on a spit. I'll pickle and bleach it afterwards, then grow tomatoes in your hollow witchy skull. Escape from this fortress is impossible!"

"Impossible?" Zallerak looked back with a derisive snort. "Nothing is impossible, dear boy. In all the nine worlds and forgotten oceans, nothing!" He turned again, entered the great doorway at the end of the hall, then stopped.

The way was blocked.

Graan stood there, huge and hulking, clad in iron, his massive gauntleted hands resting on the heavy mace in front of him, the twin axes strapped across his back. Rael's bodyguard grinned, showing uneven teeth. His breath reaching them was rancid.

Zallerak yawned. "Will one of you buffoons gut this moron? We haven't got all bloody day." Graan stepped forward, swinging the mace, his huge arms bulging with sinewy, corded muscle.

Corin lunged for his throat. Graan knocked Biter aside and kicked out at Corin's groin, narrowly missing. Beside his friend, Roman let out a shout and swung his broadsword at the brute in a deadly arc. This too Rael's massive bodyguard deflected. Once more he raised his mace, going in for the kill. Graan stopped, grunted and looked down in sudden shock.

Ariane's rapier had slid beneath his ribs. Slowly, heavily, Graan crumpled. Roman swung his broadsword a second time and the bearded, shaggy head rolled free, trailing scarlet beneath the doorway. Ariane wiped her rapier on his cloak and ran from the hall.

"That felt good!" she said. "Come on, let's kill some more of these shitheads!"

They ran. Behind them, the Assassin's hell-cat yell announced his closeness. He'd survived with only a dozen of his war chiefs intact. These were baying like wolves on blood scent.

Down through the twisting, torch-lit passage, Zallerak led the Queen and her fighters until they emerged into the courtyard. Dawn's wan light paled the granite walls and arches. Panting, they stopped for a moment and regained their bearings, much to Zallerak's annoyance. "Come on, you loons," he scolded. "No time for recreation. That lot are almost upon us!"

Outside the gate the sound of fighting was clear. It seemed miraculously that Barin was still alive. Behind them, the passage resounded with the sound of many feet and shouting.

They vacated the courtyard.

Corin and Roman slew the new guards at the gate, unbarred the doors, and heaved one open. They leaped through just as the Assassin crashed across the courtyard, yelling and spitting obscenities. Corin slammed the heavy door shut in Rael's face.

"You can stay in there you little shite!" Corin yelled at the shrieking Assassin as he slid an iron bar through the handles. He turned and grinned at Ariane, and she grinned back. Now to go help Barin and get their arses off this island. Despite the odds, they had escaped from Kranek Castle.

But as things turned out, that was the easy bit.

Chapter 29

A Renewal of Loathing

Galed wanted to crawl beneath the pavers that covered the square outside the gate. Only Cale's petrified face held him to courage. He couldn't let the boy die. He was Ariane's squire (whatever that meant), had to do something.

Though the fear inside him threatened Galed's sanity, somehow he remained on his feet. The ogre-statues advanced slowly, inexorably, creaking and grinding across the square. They were in the service of the hooded figure in the shadows, of that there was no doubt.

Galed recalled the dog-creature near Kashorn. Urgolais—Bleyne had known back then. The Urgolais had returned, and one of them was here controlling these monstrous granite ogres.

The ground trembled beneath them, and strange alien lights glowed from the figures erstwhile lifeless eyes. From their gaping black mouths issued a sinister smokiness coupled with a high-pitched ululation.

In front of Galed stood Bleyne the archer, all his arrows spent. At his side were Cale, Fassof, and the sailors. Ahead of them, an island alone, stood Barin. What a warrior he was. Galed had never imagined, let alone seen, his type before.

Barin stood resolute and stern, the great axe gripped in his mighty fists. His defiance marked him as a demi god from a time of sagas and myth. Galed, despite the horror, was bursting with pride. If only Roman were here! And Corin an Fol. And my Queen! He couldn't die in better company.

But Barin was exhausted. He refused to show it, but he was almost done. The Northman's enemies lay hewn in heaps at his feet. His body was bruised blue-purple, the bleeding arm weakened him, and every muscle screamed rebellion.

Barin ignored the pain. He raised the heavy war axe, waited for the shrieking, scraping towers of stone to arrive. One thing Barin noted: they weren't overfast.

Here we go...

Barin spat blood and strode to meet them. He swung Wyrmfang two-handed, striking the nearest statue hard, a contorted troll-like creature, all craggy teeth and claw. Barin might as well have struck a mountain. The axe bit into the stone, but the creature didn't notice. The force of his blow numbed Barin's arm from finger to shoulder.

Ouch...

Barin squared his jaw, braced his legs, and swung again, ducking low as the monster reached toward him with stone arms the width of a fat man's belly. Again his axe blow faltered and the stubby claws reached slowly for his throat. Barin cursed the name of every god he could think of. His body was screaming pain.

Barin knew he was spent, but he summoned his strength for one last determined show of defiance. He could see that the other statues were closing on his crew and friends. It sickened him that they were all to die.

Barin hacked at the talons, severing a finger, but the other nine closed around his chest. He was hoisted high, helpless as a newborn lamb in that stone embrace despite his massive strength. The granite grip tightened like a tourniquet. Barin's broad chest burned like fire and his head spun. He fought for breath and vainly struck at the monster with his dinner-plate fists.

Barin knew he would soon be crushed to death. Slowly and inevitably, the ogre crushed him the way a great snake from the southern jungles coils around its prey, squeezing out life and resistance.

What a way to go...

Barin was seconds away from blacking out in his agony when the terrible pain subsided. Stars whirled in his head. He felt the air rush passed his ears as he was pitched to the floor.

Huge and baleful, the stone figure stooped over him then froze. A thin wail issued from its cavernous mouth. Barin gulped in air and grinned.

Convenient time to have a sorcery malfunction.

With his distorted but slowly restored vision, Barin saw smoky steam escaping the ogre's gaping maw. It didn't look healthy. Barin stood up and carefully checked all his bits were in place. He felt like he'd been stomped on by a herd of wild elk, but he managed a lopsided grin.

Someone's in our team.

As he watched it, Barin saw small cracks appear all over the frozen troll thing's rock-wrought hide, and it began oozing smelly green liquid. Then from somewhere close came the clear peel of harp strings, accompanied by a resonant voice singing words Barin didn't understand.

He didn't need to. Barin was from Valkador, an island once in thrall to the witch-lore of Helga Threebolts, his grandfather's spiteful second wife. She of the emerald eyes had turned his father into a bear when he spurned her lusty advances, Helga being bored with the old man.

Helga Threebolts had come from the far north, a place of weird skies, darkness, and cold, where shamans ruled the roost. Many such still wander through Leeth, casting death spells and witching up gales out of sheer caprice. Yes, Barin knew sorcery.

The words were compelling, challenging. Barin guessed it was some ancient song. There was power in the singer's voice but a positive stalwart power that challenged the malice radiated by the shadowy figure beyond. The singer mocked the statues with his lyrics.

Barin watched wide eyed as the ogre-statue's stone cast split with yawning fissures. It shuddered, belching steam and more of the foul green resin. The creature's wailing grew louder and higher in pitch.

Barin covered his ears from the din and saw that the other ogre-statues were also frozen and his comrades were recovering— Elanion be blessed!

The singer's voice filled the square, noble and pure above the hissing wails of the dying statues. His harp peeled chords of power, each one louder and more defined than the last. And every note assaulted the statues as no physical weapon had done.

Their fissured forms were swaying, tottering and rocking to and fro, brittle granite galleons at the mercy of a raging storm. Gaping rents were spreading across their stone torsos and limbs, yawning wider, oozing slime.

Beneath Barin's feet the ground was slippery. Dark vapor rose from the flagstones, lingering fetid for several seconds before the breeze took it away.

Barin saw the distant hooded figure had raised a claw-like finger and was pointing at someone he couldn't see. The mystery harper no doubt! Malice blazed from the Dog Lords' eyes, but this time it wasn't aimed at Barin or his men.

Like dominoes in a line, the Urgolais's creatures crumbled and groaned, crashing thunderous to the ground, exploding into powdery dust.

The singer had stopped and harp notes ceased. All was deathly quiet.

Barin, turning in a wary slow circle, saw a very tall man some yards behind him by the gates.

A strange sight to behold, he was garbed in midnight blue cloak thrown over a tunic of turquoise. The man's hair was very long and fine, silvery gold in hue. The breeze tossed it across his face so Barin couldn't see his eyes. In his gloved right fist, the stranger gripped a small golden harp, while the other was raised, palm in defiant challenge to the hoodie across the square.

The Enchanter stepped out from the shadow of the gatehouse.

The hooded figure, whom Barin assumed must be Morak Dog-turd himself, was flickering, shifting from substance to smoke, then to substance again. The atmosphere between these two was electric, and Barin guessed there were old scores he couldn't begin to imagine being settled here.

No one moved. Barin's men, his friends, the Crenise guard, the Assassin, and his captains lurking behind the gate—all who could watched for the outcome in spell-struck awe.

***

Zallerak had first sensed his enemy's return several months earlier. High in his windy tower he had often gazed out, unrest tugging at his ancient bones, a job not finished. For seven hundred years the bard had dwelt alone in that remote tower on the edge of the world, a spike of gleaming stone, soaring high above the cliffs of Cape Fol, a lone sentinel to wind and wave.

During that time the bard's only companions had been sea birds and porpoises, and now and then the odd siren soothed his needs and shared his bed. It was a time of study, a time of reflection, and above all, a time of much-needed peace. For the war had raged very long, the war he started with the Dog Lord.

They were two adversaries, both respected among their peoples, both seeking power. Throughout that millennia-long strife, they had battled each other with sword and spell craft.

Then at last he'd cast his enemy down and sent his soul screaming back to the void. His people had won. But they too were broken and their power all but gone.

Most fled to foreign lands: Some crossed the ocean to Gol before its fall, whilst others fared east into territories unknown. Zallerak stayed put, keeping his disguise. Men's memories are short, they soon forgot he existed at all. But he knew that one day his arch-foe would return for a re-match.

Then the day came when the Tekara shattered, allowing the enemy to break through from without. Since that moment he'd had to work fast lest the adversary outmaneuver him. That "fast work" concluded with his meeting the idiot Prince and journeying here to

Crenna to commence phase two: freeing the Princeboy and awaiting the arrival of the newcomers, those mortals who would help
him reach his endgame.

And so at last here in Crenna, Zallerak of the Golden People
faced the Dog Lord once again. It was just a test, they both knew
that, just a probe to see how strong the other was these days.

Morak's power lay in coercion and mind bending. The Dog
Lord manipulated fear in others and turned it against them.
Zallerak favored psychokinetic blasts and auto-suggestion. Both
used lightning when it was available. And both knew weather tricks,
summoning gales and torrents and fog and such. Elementary but
useful on occasion.

But both enchanters were weak compared to centuries past.
That said, Zallerak had the edge this time. He was here in body and
person whereas Morak was just a manifestation, a ghost of night
and shadows. And he'd lost his spear.

Zallerak could see his enemy's bad self lurking in the cave in
the void. Morak projected his power from that awful place. His real
essence was contained in jars linked by crackling cables, a magic
that had to be earthed else it would fizzle and fail.

From those bubbling jars the mind of Morak worked its malevolence, while his astral form guided it, sending up twisted jabs
of pain like arrows probing and lancing inside Zallerak's head.

At last it was his time to strike back.

***

Those watching knew nothing of the inner battle currently
raging between these enchanters, the very tall, blue-eyed one and
the sinister, twisted dog-snouted hoodie. Friend and foe watched
in awe awaiting the outcome. The bard contained the pain in his
skull, holding to his song until the last statue fell to dust.

The silence grew until it roared around their heads. The very
air crackled with latent thaumaturgy.

Then lightning struck the flagstones, deafening all and throwing
not a few from their feet, Cale included. Barin, looking up and, holding his ears, noticed the hooded dog creature had faded from view.

A cold wind had risen. It whipped the Urgolais's failing essence into nothing and sent his screaming shadow back into the void. On the other side, the harpist had slumped forward with head down and hair disheveled. Barin could see he was exhausted.

It's our turn again!

Barin shook his battered body into motion, cursing and grunting, forcing his tired bones across to where his wide eyed, slack-jawed crew and companions stood blinking in silence—apart from Cale, who was rubbing a sore knee and whingeing.

With a grunt, Barin rejoined his men and examined their situation. Not far away the Crenise were doing the same. Barin grinned seeing that boy, bowman, and squire had survived. However, he'd lost two more of his crew, and Fassof was nursing a broken arm. The mate's eyes were fiery as ever as he gripped the blade in his other hand.

Behind the castle the morning sun pinked the closest mountain's snowy upper slopes, casting golden shafts deep into its pine-clad timberline flanks. Eagles whirled in the thermals high above.

It was a brave morning. Barin couldn't really believe he was still alive to see it. The square ahead was littered with slime and ash, all that remained of the ogre-statues. Even as he watched, the filthy stuff turned to vapor and was scattered by the steady breeze.

Long seconds passed. Barin's party confronted Pollomoi's ashen-faced troop across the square. He laughed at the fear so evident in their eyes.

Your warlock lost, rat-face.

Pollomoi's boys were unsure what to do next. It was apparent none fancied chancing their luck with the giant axe man again.

A hand shoved Barin's shoulder hard, distracting him, and he laughed to see Corin an Fol had joined him.

"You took your bloody time!" Barin said. Corin shrugged, looking uncomfortable.

"We were a touch preoccupied," he told his giant friend, The Queen was there too, and Roman Parrantios. Barin was overjoyed to see them all in one piece. He was bruised, battered, bloody, scraped, crushed, and totally knackered but very happy.

But the joy soon passed. Barin looked up, hearing a shout.

The Assassin had broken through the gateway. Rael Hakkenon was spitting like a lynx in heat, yelling and kicking his dazed men into action. Behind him his captains swore vitriol and brandished their steel. It wasn't over yet. Barin gave Corin a wink and scratched his bleeding ear. Corin shrugged. Biter's steel was pitted and scored, but a few sharp bits remained. They would suffice.

Here we go again—round three!

Zallerak adjusted his cloak and fastidiously shook the ghastly ash from his gloved hands. He felt shaken and exhausted. He was so out of practice. He had to laugh, though, he'd certainly spoiled Dog Face's party.

Morak must have known someone with skill was over on Crenna, but to find Zallerak waiting for him—that must have been a shock for the old boy. It would put him on his back claws for a time. It would take Morak a good while to recover from the mind blasting Zallerak had hurled at him.

He heard a noise behind him and turned. The Assassin stood beneath the gateway; his spearmen and surviving chieftains were cursing and biting their nails. Rael Hakkenon said nothing, but his feline eyes blazed with emerald loathing. He stepped forward, signaling to his men to close in on Zallerak's newfound friends.

"Not you again," muttered Zallerak. "Can't you mortals ever take the hint and die?"

Zallerak, though weak and weary, was undismayed. There was no time for rest at present, too much at stake.

Just enough in me for a quick spell.

Zallerak scrutinized the gateway above Rael's head and mumbled some inaudible words. There came a resounding snap. The lintel split asunder and crashed, raining ruin and dust on the Assassin's men.

A dozen were crushed to death, but Rael vaulted clear. Most were still inside the courtyard. The dozen surviving chiefs having raised the castle guard, there were over a hundred men trapped in there, unable to get through. These cursed and yelled behind the wreckage, toiling at the rubble like bee-stung beavers.

"That should keep your minions occupied for a while." Zallerak mocked the Assassin with his sapphire gaze. Rael stood with Pollomoi, his face taut with loathing.

Rael was unable to speak. Froth dribbled from his mouth as he chewed at a knuckle. He was going to spend at least a month torturing tiny animals after this. First he would deal with this fucking warlock-musician cretin and his confederates. Rael awarded Pollomoi's men a thin horrible smile and signaled them attack.

Chapter 30

Escape from Crenna

Zallerak turned to Corin, who was presently making lewd gestures at the Assassin, whilst beside him Barin was still scratching
his bleeding ear. "We had better get moving, don't you think?"
Zallerak announced casually. "Come on, all of you. We've people
and places to see! Onwards!"

Corin nodded. He glanced at the Queen and Barin, and then
over at the enemy, who were reformed under Rael's sharp orders
and, with him at the center, were advancing in haste toward them,
spears thrust forward. Rael had bid them fan out pincer fashion,
block any escape.

Corin shifted his grip on Biter. They were surrounded, and
despite Zallerak's words, no one had moved. Corin was thirsty and
tired. He stole a fatigued glance at Zallerak as he waited for the
Crenise to close ranks on them.

Corin couldn't fathom this bard-wizard and it irked him.
Despite their perilous predicament, Zallerak was behaving as
if they were on an afternoon romp in the sunshine. This weirdo
might have saved them again, but Corin wasn't about to trust him.
He watched the Assassin's men with a discerning eye. Their cordon

was stretched too thin and they lacked precision. Corin winked at Roman. Both had spied the gap in their flank. It would suffice.

"Now!" Corin yelled, running headlong at the nearest spearman, Biter a steely blur at the end of his arm. "Swine array!"

The others followed, shouting. They formed a wedge at Corin's bidding, himself, Barin, and Roman at the head. Like a chopper splitting rotten wood, they smashed through the Assassin's line, and won free!

"Oh, well done!" said Zallerak as he neatly sidestepped a yelling guard and cuffed him with his gloved fist. "I can see latent talent beneath that obtuse skull of yours, young Corin. Come on, follow me!"

Shut up.

Corin and Roman held the enemy back with their blade skill while the others fled the plateau.

Zallerak and Barin led the way down through the streets. Behind them were Cale and the squire, Bleyne the Archer, and Queen Ariane and the crew. Ariane turned and yelled back. "You two, hurry up for fuck's sake!"

Corin hurled a knife at the Assassin. Rael ducked and lunged forward, but Corin and his friend had already turned on their heels. In moments they caught up with the others, the Crenise close behind.

The chase was on through Kranek town.

Barin grinned, ushering the others forward and joining Corin and Roman at the rear.

"Where did you find that magician chap?" Barin asked them, matching his huge pace with theirs. He turned and poleaxed a spearman who'd got too close, sending him spinning into the cursing Assassin behind.

Rael lost ground. He kicked and punched his way forward, but his men were bunched too tight. Besides they were all bigger than him and he couldn't see anything.

Get out the fucking way!

Another spearman closed on Corin, his weapon held high. Corin blocked the lunge and slid Biter into the guard's exposed belly before turning on his heels again.

"He was waiting for us in the dungeon," Roman panted to Barin. "Don't ask. I haven't a clue. But he's somehow involved with Tarin."

"Oh," replied Barin. Beside him Corin gutted another guard. "Well done," Barin told him.

"Thanks."

They gained the main street and careered toward the lower town. Barin relieved Corin at the rear, his axe purchasing them a few moments respite. Barin had swatted a few more guards and stood looming at them, the Assassin still lost in their midst. Corin tugged his arm.

"You planning on lingering here all day?"

Now it was Roman at the van. Ariane's champion swiftly put an end to several town folk that had just emerged to stop their flight, after hearing the Assassin's manic yells.

"He calls himself Zallerak," Corin was yelling up in Barin's ear. He gasped a breath before dispatching a burly axe man with a backwards sweep of his sax.

"That's a daft name," Barin said. He clipped another guard with his axe, sending the spearman spinning into a clutter of bins. Barin grunted with satisfaction before turning to address Corin again.

"Where is Prince Tarin?" Barin asked as they ran. "I do not see him. Wasn't he the reason for this little visit?"

"He pissed off a while ago. Zallerak let him loose."

"Oh, that's good."

"Is it?"

The street narrowed. They were in the lower town. The Assassin's men were gaining again. Barin grumbled. He was getting too old for all this stomping about. He turned, butted a tattooed guard, splitting the man's skull and sending him sprawling into his fellows behind.

"Yes and no," Corin was elaborating. "This Zallerak claims he freed the little twat from under the Assassin's nose and took his place in a homemade cage. Says he's sent him off on some quest away south, after picking up the Tekara shards he'd buried back near Fardoris."

"Sounds a bit complicated." Barin turned about, rammed his axe butt into the face of a spearmen.

"No doubt we'll hear more later," Barin added.

"No doubt," replied Corin. "Come on," he added. "Roman's reached the harbor. We'd best not be left behind."

"I'm sick of this running lark," groaned Barin as they loped through the town, vaulting debris and stamping on the odd rat. "No stomach, these bloody Crenise," he complained in Corin's ear.

Two pirates had emerged to block their way. They saw the size of Barin (worse, the size of his axe) and promptly bolted back from whence they'd came. "You show them a bit of muscle and they scatter like squirrels!"

Corin stole a glance back at their pursuit. "Himself is back. We'd best pick up our steps."

A few yards behind them the Assassin was screeching like an irate washerwoman. He'd forced his way through his men after stabbing their buttocks repeatedly with his rapier.

"Pollomoi!" Rael hollered, his voice hoarse from shrieking. "I'll have you fucking racked for this!" Rael turned to vent his wrath on the waking inhabitants of Kranek Town. They were emerging sleepy-eyed from their various abodes, surprised and alarmed by the early morning racket.

"Wake up, you tossers," Rael yelled at them. "Stop those impostors! Don't let them escape! If the bastards get away, I'll torch this town and flay the entire lot of you!

"Look, their escaping, Pollomoi!" Rael poked the lanky captain in his bony rib and bellowed in his ear. "I trust you left guards in the harbor, heh? It will be your miserable head if you haven't."

"Our men are there, lord." The captain twitched as they raced toward the harbor.

"They had bloody well better be."

Corin and Barin caught up with the others at the town end of the quay. Ahead down the jetty lay *The Starlight Wanderer*, her sails set and ready for a swift departure. Cogga and Ruagon had stayed behind but had not been idle. They stood waving and yelling encouragement from the deck.

Corin cursed. The wooden jetty was blocked by over a score of Pollomoi's guardsmen. They took them at a run, breaking through the soldiers' ranks. Corin yelled at the others to run for it. Zallerak and Bleyne were first to sprint for the ship. Cale followed but tripped. Roman shielded the boy from harm whilst Corin heaved him back on his feet.

"Bugger off while you've still got legs!" Corin told the boy. Meanwhile Ariane and her squire gained the walkway and ran to catch the others.

Roman turned, fended the guards off after allowing everyone through. He braced himself at the end of the jetty. At his side were Corin and Barin, weapons bloody as they dispatched the guards pressing against them.

Then Rael Hakkenon bounded onto the quay with Captain Pollomoi and three score warriors behind. Hard pressed and facing backwards, the three fighters withdrew along the jetty keeping the enemy at bay, with broadsword, sax, and massive axe.

Biter took the legs, Roman stabbed and sliced with his big blade, whilst Barin's axe wind-milled high over their heads tossing guards into the water amid trails of crimson and flying body parts.

Meanwhile, Bleyne, first on deck, sourced some arrows and began raining death on the Crenise from high at the trader's stern rail.

Still they came.

Barin pitched two spearmen into the sea. Bleyne shot three more. Nearer the brig, Galed tripped and fell onto the wooden planks of the jetty. Fassof, cussing, hauled him to his feet with his good arm.

Ariane and Cale had clambered aboard. Most the crew followed. Cale leaned down to help Galed up the ramp and Fassof leapt onboard. The remaining crew jumped on deck, at once running to aid the hard-pressed Cogga and Ruagon.

Corin and Barin were half way down the ramp, Roman a yard or two behind them. Ariane, watching anxiously, shouted a warning.

Too late Roman saw the crossbowman. A shaft pierced his thigh. He dropped to one knee. A second thudded into his shoulder. Roman slumped. From the quay the crossbowman was rewinding his weapon. Bleyne's next arrow took him out.

"Cale!" screamed Ariane. She was horrified. The boy had jumped back on the jetty and was rushing to aid Roman.

It was Corin who stopped him.

"Get back on deck ya little shite!" he yelled in Cale's ear. "We'll bring Roman." But even as he spoke Roman waved him back.

Ariane's champion was trapped, hemmed in by the Assassin's men. Roman knew he'd reached the end game. He smiled back at the weeping boy and Barin and Corin beside him.

"Look after my Queen, Cale," Roman winked at the boy. "You're a warrior now, lad. Don't fret about Corin; he's alright when you get used to him." Roman grinned raffishly at Corin and Barin.

"Farewell friends," he called, and as he spoke a fresh gobbet of blood trickled from his mouth. "Take the boy and be on your way. I will hold these bastards here for a while yet!"

"Don't be a fool!" shouted Corin. He thrust Cale into Barin's arms and raced back to help his friend. Bleyne was firing arrow after arrow from the quay, but his shafts were running low.

Corin had almost reached Roman, but the big man waved him back. "Dying beside me won't help, Corin an Fol. This wound is mortal." Corin slowed to a stop.

"Roman, I—"

"Go, they need you!" Roman spat blood. Another bolt ripped into his left arm. Bleyne shot the culprit, but there were more missiles coming. The town folk had finally rallied, many carried bows and slings.

Corin's heart sank. He realized there was no way out of this for Roman. His friend was right. Dying here would achieve nothing. Ariane would need him now more than ever before.

Agonized, Corin turned, ran back up the jetty, and leapt aboard behind Barin and the boy. Fassof cast off and Cogga took the wheel. Bolts thudded into the jetty and sank beneath the water behind them, but none reached the ship. Barin hauled up the anchor and *The Starlight Wanderer* slowly drifted from the dock.

Corin's knuckles were white as he gripped the stern rail. More crossbowmen had appeared and bowmen were firing from the harbor wall ahead. An arrow thudded into the timber inches from Corin's right hand. He hardly noticed it.

Beside him were Ariane, Galed, and the boy. All three were weeping, but Corin's face was set in stone. They watched the scene play out on the jetty, tormented, unable to turn away.

They saw Roman struggle to his feet. He stood alone, a noble a stag beset by baying hounds. Corin felt Ariane's small, cold hand seeking his. In silence he wrapped his calloused palm around her fingers, and she looked up into his eyes and sobbed. It was the first time he'd seen her cry.

They were jibing Roman now, the Crenise. Bleyne had shot over a dozen of them, but all his shafts were spent. Despondent, Bleyne took his place beside the others, his hard, brown, impassive face revealing little of the anguish he felt inside.

The gap widened from the jetty. They passed smaller ships anchored close by. Some bore crew that yelled at them and threw missiles, but the way ahead was clear, and Cogga skillfully worked the wheel. The archers fired from the wall but to no avail. Barin, after checking his vessel with Fassof, joined his friends at the stern. In silence they watched the scene reach its inevitable conclusion on the jetty.

***

Captain Pollomoi grinned, showing blackened teeth. He swung his sword hard to sweep Roman's head from his body, but the Champion of Kelwyn spun round at the last moment.

Roman had read the move. Smiling through his pain, Roman rammed his blade into the thin captain's belly. Pollomoi screamed in agony. Roman twisted the steel and pitched Pollomoi from the jetty into the reddened water below.

Roman stepped back, his face contorted in excruciation. He was exhausted. His arms and chest were covered in blood, most of it his, and his hands were slippery on the sword hilt. But he was ready to die and would take as many with him as he could. He gritted his teeth, refused to let the pain take hold.

Come on bastards, I'm not finished yet!

They came at him one at a time, probing with spears, jabbing with cutlasses. Others lobbed stones from the jetty and jeered.

Somehow Roman stayed on his feet, despite losing much blood. He fought stubbornly, heroically, ignoring the red agony pulsating through his veins. His broadsword cleaved the neck of a spearman. He twisted the blade free, ramming its pommel into the face of the man behind. Bones crunched. Roman grinned. Then he heard a lazy voice say,

"Get out the way. He is mine."

The Assassin stepped from behind his men, a slim rapier gripped in either hand. Rael's eyes were triumphant beads of jade. He smiled almost lovingly at Kelwyn's famous Champion.

Roman readied his broadsword

"At last," he spat the words, leaving a bloody trail from his mouth. "The lord of this shithole has come to meet his doom!" Roman stepped forward. "Die, bastard!" Roman lunged hard and straight for Rael Hakkenon's throat.

The Assassin leaped back, smile broadening on his thin lips. Rael was in his element. He played to the baying crowd on the quay. He was poised like a dancer, a death-wielding magician. Rael switched the blades in his hands, left to right and right to left.

Roman watched nonplussed. He faked a yawn. Then with dazzling speed Rael lunged, piercing Roman's broad chest through his ring mail with one sword, and then spinning on his heel, the Assassin sliced the other across the big warrior's neck. Roman fell.

At least my Queen is free....

***

So died Roman Parrantios, valiant Champion of Kelwyn. They butchered his body before casting it into the ocean.

"Let the sharks feast," laughed Rael Hakkenon. He waved at the figures watching in silence from Barin's departing ship. The brigantine had nearly cleared the harbor, but Rael could see them well enough to note their ravaged expressions.

"Hoist the chain!" Rael yelled across the harbor to where a group of workers stood by a squat metal building. They vanished inside at his word and moments later a harsh grinding, scraping noise filled the morning.

Barin groaned when he saw the heavy chain clear the surface yards in front of *The Starlight Wanderer's* bow. That thing would were tear his ship in two. He yelled to Cogga, who without hesitation joined him at the prow.

Each man grabbed an oar and slammed it down hard, checking the chain's advance. Barin's brute strength held the portside, but Cogga's grip was slipping.

The chain scraped the hull, a terrible sound. Corin grabbed an oar and thrust its blade down beside Cogga. Bleyne and Ruagon joined him, whilst another crewman aided Barin.

Scrape, slide, and groan. The brigantine's hull cleared the chain, breaking three oars in the process and nearly pitching Corin into the water. After it cleared the ship's keel the chain shot up six feet above water, blocking Rael's pursuing vessels, which had just launched from the harbor.

"Lower that fucking chain!" Rael yelled across the water. The idiots in the chain building didn't hear him, so the chain stayed up whilst the nearest sharks were forced to heave to and wait. "Morons! Bloody useless, morons!"

By the time the chain operatives had got their act together *The Starlight Wanderer* had won free of the harbor, allowing Barin some time to get ahead.

After ceasing his rant at the chain hoisters, Rael glanced moodily across to where *The Black Serpent* sat sleek and handsome at the other end of the quay. He would be boarding her soon. Then the chase would begin. His joy after killing Parrantios was forgotten. Those bastards had torched his castle and pissed on his parade. This was personal.

Rael watched Barin's brig slip from his harbor. He shrugged indifference. So what, they had a head start? The trader would be his by nightfall. He noticed that one fellow still watched him from the stern, the others having gone below deck saving the big straw-headed Barin at the wheel. Rael saw the lone watcher raise a fist at him in hatred. He smiled in return sensing a challenge.

I'll save you to last.

Rael reached down, grabbed hold of Roman's severed head by the hair. Laughing hysterically he held it high before tossing it across the water to splosh and vanish in the choppy waves. The lone figure watched him in silence. Rael saluted him with his twin rapiers before turning to Pollomoi's second.

"Get Cruel Cavan ready my ship," Rael told him. "Have the crew await my arrival. I will personally accompany them in putting an end to this scum."

An hour later *The Black Serpent* left the quayside at the head of thirty ships. Rael stood at the prow of his *Serpent*. Looking back, he raised a hand to acknowledge the city guard, whose spear points ensured those watching cheer loudly from the quay.

Rael had just emerged above deck after washing and changing his apparel. The Lord of Crenna was clad in matching black diamond-studded leather tunic and trousers.

He sported a silver blue headscarf, trimmed with pearls, and a broad scarlet sash girdled his waist. It was a trifle flamboyant, but then one must needs look the part. His cutthroat crew roared approval. Rael awarded them a lopsided grin. He was sort of happy. It felt good to be at sea again—as long as his headaches didn't return.

Chapter 31

Loose Ends

Corin stood silently watching from the stern of Barin's ship, his face resolute. He had locked eyes with the Assassin. Rael Hakkenon would not forget him. They would meet soon and Rael the cruel would die. He owed Roman that much.

Ariane joined him. The Queen said nothing, but her face was rouged by crying. She had wept openly when she saw her champion fall. The Queen seemed very young, almost a girl, not the survivor he'd become accustomed to.

"I will avenge him," Corin vowed to her. "I swear to you, my longsword and sax won't rest until I have sent the cursed soul of Rael Hakkenon back screaming to whatever shithole it surfaced from!"

Ariane didn't respond, just looked up at him with those dark, sad eyes. Corin couldn't stand it. He wanted to hold her, kiss her, and run his calloused hands through her hair. Instead he showed her his back, making briskly for the bow, his head clouded by a thousand doubts.

Ariane watched Corin's awkward departure in silence, her face pale and lost.

You're a bastard, Corin an Fol, walking away from me when I need you so much. Ariane shook her head and slammed her white knuckles hard into the rail. *Turn around, damn you!*

But he didn't, so she cursed him again and went below.

Barin stood by Cogga at the wheel. With them was Zallerak. The bard had just emerged on deck. He alone hadn't witnessed Roman's fall. Corin joined them and ignored the bard. Instead he greeted Barin and Cogga. The three watched the Assassin's sharks vacate the harbor and gather in pursuit behind them. The chase had begun again. No one on deck seemed to care.

Barin broke the silence. "How are you, lad?" Corin shrugged an answer. "My heart grieves for the loss of our friend," Barin continued. "But Roman died well and sits amongst his forefather's with head held high in honor."

Corin nodded slowly.

Yeah. Maybe.

He glanced over at the bowsprit where the small huddled figure of Galed sat weeping amongst a large coil of rope. There was no sign of Cale. Corin assumed the boy had gone below deck, too.

"He was a brave man and a loyal friend," Corin said to Barin after a long pause. He turned to the squire, who was looking at him in wretched silence "I shall avenge Roman, Galed," Corin told him. "I have sworn to do so."

"That won't bring him back," replied the squire, his eyes reddened with tears.

Barin nodded. "It's a sad business," he said. "I think, however, we have more immediate matters to deal with. Roman wouldn't want us moping and lolling about like stranded seal cubs. Those sharks back there are among Rael Hakkenon's prime raiders. They're a deal swifter than those others we outran at Kashorn. And then there's *The Black Serpent*. She's in a class of her own."

"Hakkenon's flagship, think he'll sail it himself?" Corin hoped he did so they could resume their recent courtesies.

"Aye, most likely, or else it'll be the *Serpent's* skipper, Cruel Cavan. That bastard's second to none at sail craft. He alone the Assassin trusts. But I think we've pissed Rael off just enough to get him back on board again. They say he doesn't sail much these days, preferring to lurk in that castle of his."

"That was before Zallerak torched it."

"There is that, too," Barin rubbed his chin after searching for it through his beard.

"And there they are." Cogga pointed back to the harbor now small with distance. He counted thirty dark sails perhaps an hour behind them. That was ignoring the three following their wake a mile to stern, gaining very slowly.

"*Serpent's* said to be the fastest craft on the ocean," Barin said, "and Cavan the canniest pilot. He'll soon catch those other three up, us too if we don't get some decent wind soon. Even if we do it'll be a long run. They're not likely to give up the chase this time. Not with himself on board."

Bleyne joined them. The archer nodded when he heard Barin's last comment. "The nearest three are gaining on us already," he said calmly.

Barin nodded. "It will be tight, but once we get into deep water and pick up some good blow, we should be able to hold them off until nightfall. I hope," he added with a wry smile.

Corin turned to Zallerak. The bard was still watching in silence and seemed lost in thought. "Can you aid us again, wizard?" Corin asked him.

"What, heh?" Zallerak looked hard at Corin "Aid you!" Zallerak snapped in irritation. "I have done little else since I happened upon your jovial acquaintance, Corin an Fol. And received small gratitude thus far, I might add."

Zallerak's expression softened. "I am not a tap, Corin. The use of sorcery, as you youngsters call it, has its price. That encounter at Kranek wore me out. I am not immune to fatigue."

"Sorry I asked," said Corin and turned away. "It's just that if we get shafted, then you will too—unless you can fly, of course. But I am not sure that's one of your skills?" Zallerak ignored him.

Corin shrugged and gazed astern. The nearest shark was almost upon them. Arrows sped over the water. Most dropped short, but one or two struck the deck.

"Luckily these pirates are crap archers, unlike the city guard" said Barin "The Assassin considers the bow a peasants weapon." Bleyne raised an eyebrow at that. "But unless we get a helpful wind soon we're buggered," continued Barin, looking up at the sky and mouthing the word *please.*

"The next twenty minutes might prove challenging. I—" Barin stopped. He scratched his beard in sudden consternation. "Where the frig did she come from?"

Corin turned just in time to see the little girl, Urdei, blow him a kiss from the bowsprit. "Mind the rocks!" Urdei called across to them.

"Rocks? What rocks?" Barin gaped at the girl.

"Those rocks," said Cogga, pointing to where a row of teeth-like islets showed just above the water. Corin didn't understand why they hadn't seen them before. They were making straight toward the bloody things. He suddenly had that nasty feeling something untoward was about to happen. He turned to glare at Urdei, but she'd disappeared from sight. So no change there.

And he wasn't wrong, for when Barin swung the wheel and turned the brigantine, Corin noticed that the rocks turned with them. Corin frowned. Rocks shouldn't do that. And then just at that choice moment, the kraken chose to reveal itself to them.

***

"So you let them get away?" Caswallon's cold eyes glared down at the tall man standing below.

"We were unlucky, milord. I—"

"I was informed you were reliable, Hagan, that you could be trusted for any task however challenging. Yet you stumble at the first fence and then have the gall to come creeping in here and ask for gold. Why shouldn't I have you flayed, fed to my Groil or Gribble the Soilfin?"

"Because you know I'm useful." Hagan shifted his feet. He hadn't wanted to come here but needed to.

"Not lately."

"And I know the brigand, Corin an Fol."

"What is that to me?"

"Lord Perani told me you had an interest in such a one."

Caswallon leaned back on the Glass Throne and sighed. He didn't often come here, preferring his high tower, but it was a fine day outside and the sun filtering through the windows warmed his bones.

Aside Captain Hagan the palace was empty and eerie, his Groil standing guard outside. Caswallon had over two hundred of the creatures now, all primed and ready for his planned move against Kelwyn next month.

"May happen I do." Caswallon tossed a wallet down on the floor at Hagan's feet. "In any case he is one of the terrorists. I want them all dead, captain, all save Queen Ariane. But then you know that, don't you?"

"Last I heard they were making for Crenna, milord."

"Well, they've escaped," said Caswallon. Hagan looked startled hearing that. Caswallon waved a hand. "They had help. It's complicated. And the Assassin is in hot pursuit. Gribble arrived back half an hour ago with the news."

"The Soilfin creature?" Hagan had glimpsed the foul goblin thing in a side room. It had winked at him whilst crunching on something unspeakable. He hadn't lingered in the vicinity.

"The very same. At least I can rely on him to do a good job." Caswallon's dark gaze flicked at Hagan in contempt. The mercenary stood his ground and didn't flinch. After a moment Caswallon relaxed his gaze. This Hagan had sand. Maybe he should reward the mercenary with a personal commission, providing he didn't screw up again, of course. Caswallon waved a dismissive hand.

"The Assassin will most likely catch up with them at sea, but I want you as back up. This lot have an uncanny knack for avoiding my nets."

"What would you have me do, milord?"

"Ride at speed down to Port Wind and Calprissa. You and your men need to cover both cities. If that little slattern does evade the Assassin, she'll be making for one those ports. Don't engage unless you have the advantage. They're dangerous and I might need you for other contracts. Groil are useful but lack a certain initiative. Besides, once Ariane has landed, we can pick our place for ambush.

"And Corin an Fol?"

"Kill the bastard when you get the chance. But don't do anything rash, Hagan." Caswallon made a dismissive gesture. "Take the coin. There will be more when you return."

"Milord." Hagan reached down warily and plucked the wallet from the mosaic floor. He saluted Caswallon and made to turn.

"One last thing."

"Milord?"

"Fail me again and I will feed you and your men to my new army. They're always short of fresh meat. Now go, captain, and make haste south."

Hagan saluted again and vacated the hall. "Bastard," he muttered under his breath and then louder when he saw how tight Caswallon had been with his coin.

Borgil and the lads joined him in the tavern an hour later. Once informed, they made their way grumbling to the stables and got ready.

They left Kella City that afternoon. For his part Hagan wasn't sorry.

***

Left to his thoughts, Caswallon folded his lean hands and took to gazing idly down from the throne. The Glass Throne, it would never seat a king again. Those days were over, thanks to him. Caswallon smiled his thin smile. He had done well, in the main.

The dragon's visit had proved a shock, but he was over that. Things were in hand, his roof was repaired, the Queen and her fools would be dealt with shortly, and whoever aided them would be finished by Morak.

The Dog Lord had been quiet of late. Caswallon had tried to summon him but to no avail. But that happened now and then when the lines got blocked between here and limbo.

In any case everything was planned out meticulously. All that remained was trimming loose ends: the Queen, Kelthara City, and Duke Tomais of Morwella (missing and on the run). The two strongholds Point Keep and Car Carranis were still in the hands of his enemies, Starkhold and Halfdan. But they too would be dealt with by Leeth, so he didn't have to worry there.

From his crystal, Caswallon had been watching the satisfying events over in Morwella earlier today. Vangaris had fallen. Bodies lay everywhere, but Caswallon, scrying, saw no evidence of the duke and his daughter among the well-born corpses lined up in neat rows outside the castle wall. He had specifically asked King Haal to kill every noble and assumed duke and daughter had fled the city as refugees.

No problem, his Groil would mop them up.

Perani had been out east holding a secret meeting with their new ally, the King of Leeth whose main force was camped along the river south of Vangaris harbor. The general had got back just in time to interview Hagan and inform Caswallon of a mutiny over in Kelthara. That city had always been trouble. Another job for Groil. That left just Ariane.

Caswallon leaned back in the throne and poured a large class of claret from the crystal decanter. He felt fairly content. He'd achieved most of his goals and was ready for the next stage, the invasion of Kelwyn and Raleen, Morwella having already fallen. Caswallon smiled again: By next year all Four Kingdoms would be his.

"Gribble, you there?"

"Never far away, Mr. Caswallon—unless I am far away, of course." Gribble emerged dribbling, from the corridor outside. "Always happy to help."

"Yes, yes. Go get Drol, Two-Heads, I need to speak with him." The Soilfin departed and moments later returned with the huge shambling Groil.

"Gather a unit together," Caswallon told Two-Heads. "Lead a foray east into Kelthara. Root out the trouble makers, and make your presence known in the city. I will not be gainsaid by upstart nobles."

Kelthara had long been a thorn in Caswallon's side. Most survivors from his recent pogrom had fled to that city. Kelthara was a nest of stewing malcontents he needed to pour hot water on fast. It was past time he cleared things up over there.

"Oh, and Drol." Both heads gaped at him, the one on the right had its tongue lolling out. "Send a party north east. Duke Tomais of Morwella and his daughter are at large. They are harmless, but I'd sooner see them dead, if you take my meaning." Two-Heads grunted and shambled away.

Caswallon sipped his wine. He remembered Lady Shallan, Tomais's aloof daughter, Ariane's cousin. Killing Shallan was yet another way to get at the Queen.

"What about me, Mr. Caswallon?" Gribble had that hurt, left out expression.

"Ah, I was just coming to that." Caswallon smiled at the goblin whilst sipping his wine. "I've just the job for you, goblin."

"I'm not a bloody goblin."

"Yes you are, but I like you, so come on over and I'll let you know my very special plans."

"Do they involve eating?" Gribble enquired whilst hopping across to gaze hopeful up at the Glass Throne. You never knew your luck these days. Don't ask don't get.

***

Shallan gazed down at the fires raging through the city below. She wanted to ride back, sword in hand, kill the raiders single handed. She and her father had fled Vangaris several hours earlier. It felt like betrayal, but Duke Tomais had insisted.

"We need seek help!" he'd told her. "Forget Caswallon and Kelthaine. We'll fare further south to Wynais or Raleen."

"What of Vangaris, your city, and Morwella, your country, father?"

"It's too late for both. Those who could fled this morning. As for the rest..." The duke's face was ashen. He didn't look well and the loss of his city had hit him hard. But they had no choice. Must survive, if only for Shallan's sake. Tomais would have gladly perished alone in his library where his beloved Elenia passed away so very long ago.

Shallan didn't understand him. His daughter tossed her haughty head and spurred the horse up the rise, her long chestnut hair wild and carefree in the wind and her rich velvet cloak billowing behind her. Tomais watched her crest the hill with bleak expression.

So beautiful, so headstrong, so like your mother.

The duke kicked his steed forward, following behind at a more leisurely pace, his heart heavy as a lodestone. They had a long, perilous journey ahead. Brigands and mercenaries were everywhere in these hills, and when they reached Kelthaine they'd have Caswallon's spies to worry about—not to mention the Faen and other beings. Their journey would take them close to the Forest of Dreams, not a comforting thought. Best not dwell on it. The ride south to the Kelwynian border was through the wildest country. No time to tarry.

Evening found them far from the city. They set camp in a wood, ate dry beef, and dared not light a fire despite the bitter chill. Father and daughter took turn at watch. At some point Shallan slept despite the cold biting through her cloak and blanket. She dreamed...

Shallan walked the old wood again, through the creaking willows up toward the great oaks where the shrine showed dull between their knotty trunks. The Horned Man was waiting there, as she knew he would be.

Who are you?

"Your friend," he said and turned away.

Wait...

The Horned Man stopped, his shadowy bulk framed by creaking trees.

Can't you help us?

He turned slowly, gazed across at her with sad big eyes.

Perhaps. In the meantime heed my advice. Forget Wynais, child. Instead seek out the merchant's villa in Raleen. Silon will help you if he can. But avoid the man called Corin an Fol. I see his shadow fading into yours...

Dream Shallan wanted to enquire more, but at that point a

noise woke her and she opened her eyes. Her father stood there.

"I heard voices," Tomais said, his tired face troubled.

"I was dreaming, father. I cried out, that's all."

"It's more than that, there was someone here. I saw a shadow under the trees."

"It was the Horned Man. He was in my dream again. He wants to help us."

"The Horned Man doesn't exist!" The duke's face was angry. He looked guilty too, Shallan couldn't help noting.

"You'd best stop this dreaming and moping, daughter. We've a long tough road ahead." The duke turned and made his way toward where the beasts were tethered.

"He said we should make for Silon's villa, father, somewhere in Raleen." Shallan didn't mention the other thing the Horned Man had said. Not that that mattered. The duke wasn't listening.

Father and daughter said little throughout that day or the evening that followed. Tomais's face was haunted by guilt and failure, Shallan's confused and dreamy. Nothing seemed real to her at present.

Shallan wondered whether her father was right, that the Horned Man was some crazy creation of her imagination. If so, what did they mean, all these dreams? She envied her brothers and their swords, no matter how stacked the odds against them. For all Shallan knew, they might be dead. She still envied them, though. At least they were striking back. What could she do aside ride and mope beside her father?

Her brothers were warriors, not like Shallan and her father. They were just shadows fleeing shadows. That night Shallan dreamt of nothing and was oddly relieved it was so.

Duke Tomais didn't sleep at all. His mind was a whirl of contradictions, and now his daughter was dreaming of the Horned Man. The Duke recalled the conversation he'd had with the duchess the day he'd found her in the glade, the Horned Man lying naked beside her. Elenia had been so distraught he could still picture her face, pale and weeping. Because he loved her he'd let her keep the child.

Our daughter must never know.

And now the horned one had returned to haunt Shallan's dreams.

"You cannot have her. She is my daughter, not yours, Cornelius."

A rustle in the trees, the duke turned, glimpsed eyes watching in the murk. They winked twice then disappeared. Tomais groaned and rolled over. Doubtless just a trick of the light.

That following morning Shallan and her father crossed the border into Kelthaine. Behind them the hills of Morwella were ringed with fires. The barbarian army was on the move. Soon the whole country would be reduced to ashes.

They didn't look back. Father and daughter rode hard, skirted the dark forest, and continued ranging south for three days without event. Then on the fourth morning just before breakfast, the Groil decided come visit.

Chapter 32

A New Dance

The head was the first part to break surface, if a triangular, slant-eyed, scaly, slippery, fishy-stained, teeth-gleaming acre of ugliness could be described as a head. Then came the neck—long, sleek and metallic blue-green. After that appeared the snaky, oily body, over a mile in length showing as isolated loops above the water.

Behind them, the Crenise had begun turning their craft, but it was too late for the brigantine.

Thud! Boom and *scrape!*

The Starlight Wanderer slammed alongside the nearest coil. The violent jolt sent a shudder the whole length of the ship. Barin raged and wrestled the wheel, Fassof shrieked orders and obscenities from aloft, Cogga gaped at the monster, whilst Corin nearly lost his footing as the fleshy loop battered them again.

Ariane emerged from below, Cale gulping beside her. Together Queen and boy watched the sea monster bear down on them.

For the first time in his life Barin was unsure what to do. They stood no chance against this leviathan. Desperate, he yelled Cogga seek out Zallerak, who hadn't returned from below decks.

Corin followed the stocky sailor down the hatch. He grabbed

Clouter and returned above. Bleyne and Galed followed him, but there was no sign of the bard.

The kraken's monstrous head lowered toward the aft deck, allowing those snaggled teeth crunch timbers and snap boards. Meanwhile the tale lashed out, striking the furthest pirate ship and breaking it in two.

Barin seized Wyrmfang from Cogga, who had just surfaced with a bleary eyed Zallerak. The Northman commenced hacking into the scaly neck of the monster. At last the head withdrew. Barin paused to take a breath, but then the monster reared up again, all teeth and dripping maw.

Snap! K-plunk! The second fleeing pirate craft was broken by that tail. That left just one, beating a fast retreat north to where Rael's fleet showed black on the horizon.

Corin almost laughed at the irony of the situation. He leveled Clouter, poised to have a go at that neck. Beside him, Barin braced his legs, Wyrmfang square in front of him.

One, two...three—whack!

But then the monster changed tact. Its nearest loop slid under the hull, then came a flop as another coil wrapped around the mid deck. Following that, an atrocious racket came when planks, oars, and rails snapped like twigs as the kraken squeezed tight.

"Do something!" Corin yelled at Zallerak, who still stared, as startled as the rest.

"I can't. I wish I could, but I'm bloody knackered already, and quite frankly this is beyond me." Corin glanced at Barin. Both looked lost. Even Bleyne looked defeated, without his arrows. The hull splintered as the coils squeezed tight. Within minutes they would break apart.

Then the sea beast's head turned toward them again. The dinner-plate, wet eyes were almost mocking. Corin readied for the final blow. At least he'd take a few teeth.

Come on, you ugly...

***

Ariane had not been idle. She knew there was only one course of action left to them. She knelt on the foredeck, forgotten and forlorn. Elanion would aid them if she could, but even She had little sway over one of Her brother's creatures. Ariane uttered the words Dazaleon had taught her. That Summoning could only be used in direst need, and for help against a foe such as this.

Nothing happened. Ariane spoke the words again. Still nothing.

Goddess, save us! We've little time!

Ariane turned, saw Vervandi standing behind her.

"The Goddess cannot help you directly. This is not Her domain. But Elanion's brother might if the mood takes Him. But then, you never know with Sensuata." Vervandi wasn't smiling. She appeared edgy and annoyed.

"The Sea God?"

Vervandi nodded slowly. "Of course the Sea God, and my Uncle will demand a price."

"I will pay it!" Ariane yelled at the woman. "Just beg Him save us before it's too fucking late."

"He is coming," answered Vervandi, her beautiful face fading from view. Ariane staggered to her feet. Close by, the kraken's coils were biting hard into the hull. They had minutes, maybe only seconds. She heard Corin curse and the sound of steel on something hard. Then the vessel rocked and shuddered and she was thrown sprawling to the deck.

***

"Hoist me up!" Corin yelled at Barin, who after a blank look, seized his friend's legs and shoved him up onto his shoulders. Corin braced himself and readied Clouter as the monster's brutish mouth lowered toward him.

The mouth slammed shut but not before Corin had rammed Clouter up hard into the nearest eye—a huge lidless disc of jelly at least a foot in diameter. The monster's head jerked back, pitching man and longsword onto the deck and knocking Barin over.

The coils loosened their hold around the ship as the kraken shuddered in pain. Its tail lashed out in violent jerks and crashed down upon the last fleeing shark. That too sunk beneath the waves.

Corin would have laughed had there been time, but the kraken was rearing its head again with jaws wide enough to take them in one single gulp.

Corin knew they were on borrowed time. Weary, he scooped up Clouter for one last swing at the beastie. But then a Giant's head broke free of the waves and Corin dropped the longsword again.

***

Ariane chanted the words of protection as she watched the Sea God surface. Terrible Sensuata come to save them for a price, a price that only she could pay. Ariane stared wild eyed beside Galed and Cale. She hadn't even known they were close by.

The Sea God turned His gaze upon her and Ariane almost lost her footing. The face was a ravished mess of scaly scars, the hair tangled, long and unkempt, its color the blue-green-grey of churning waters.

Sensuata's arms and torso were a corded knot of muscle and scales. His skin was green and slimy beneath all that sinew. He reared before them, naked and terrible.

"Lord Sensuata, save us, You who rule the nine oceans!" Ariane yelled up at the god's face.

"WILL YOU PAY MY PRICE?" The Sea God's voice surged above them like an ocean gale. Sensuata's huge arms were folded across His barrel chest and that bewildering, mercurial green-grey gaze fell full upon the Queen, tiny and scared. Close by, Corin gripped the rail and tried to come to terms with what was happening.

"Price?" Corin yelled. "What price? What does He mean, Ariane? Don't do this! I love you!" She didn't hear him.

Instead she responded to the god, "I shall. I promise!" Ariane's little shout was almost lost by wave and echo.

"THEN SO BE IT."

Before he knew it, Corin's feet had brought him level with the Queen.

"What fucking price?" Ariane turned toward him then as one waking from a trance.

"Corin, I...we had no choice."

"There is always a choice."

"Not for such as us. And besides, it is already too late."

All watched then as the huge figure raised his left hand slowly and the kraken slunk submissive from the ship. *The Starlight Wanderer* pitched and tossed violently but somehow stayed upright as those great coils slid back across the deck. Timbers groaned and creaked, but miraculously the two masts held erect and the hull remained intact.

Then the Sea God uttered one long dreadful ululation bidding the kraken submerge beneath the waves. Within minutes the sea beast had gone, and only eddies and whirls showed where it had been.

Sensuata's gaze fell on Ariane once more.

"REMEMBER MY PRICE, LITTLE MORTAL. I SHALL CALL ON YOU TO PAY IT ONE DAY."

"I will remember." Ariane felt the tears glisten her cheek as the huge figure loomed over the ship.

"I LEAVE YOU SAFE. THE FOG WILL PROTECT YOU FOR A SHORT WHILE AND CONFUSE YOUR ENEMY."

As Sensuata boomed those last words, Ariane felt a damp chill brush her face. She turned and gazed behind to see misty columns rising like vapor out of the water. The fret was forming fast, congealing, blotting out the horizon. It gathered and swirled toward them, embracing the ship's timbers, sucking them into its damp, dewy mantle.

Nobody spoke. Corin chewed his lip and looked like he wanted to skewer someone. Beside him Barin sat hunched and aching. Bleyne stared at the giant figure of the Sea God. The devout archer was clearly terrified, as were Barin's crew. Even Fassof looked wan. Ariane stood alone. Cale, weeping at the Queen's words to Corin, and Galed had just vanished below again. And in a far corner by the wheel house, Zallerak fumbled at his harp, his long face troubled and forlorn.

The mist thickened to deep fog, swallowing the ship. Its chilling touch felt almost tangible, a massive spider web clinging to their faces like a dead lover's embrace.

Behind them the giant's bulk was slipping to stern, His face indiscernible and His body shrouded by the fog. The air hung silent and heavy. Zallerak plucked a chord, but the brave sound was swallowed by the murk. Ariane still watched. Within minutes the Sea God had vanished from view.

Ariane heard a soft tread behind her. She turned to see Corin standing there.

"I'll ask you one last time. What price? What did the giant mean?" His eyes were angry and confused.

Ariane smiled sadly up at him. She reached out with a hand, brushed dark locks away from his eyes.

"My soul belongs to the Sea God, Corin."

"That's bloody ridiculous."

"One day Sensuata will call on me to join Him. And when that happens I must depart."

"Why must you?" Behind him Corin half noticed the shadow of Cale reemerging to listen.

"Because we struck a bargain that not only saved us today but will keep Sensuata on our side in the future. He's a formidable ally, Corin."

"I don't give a toss about that. All I know is that I love you and I'm not letting you go. No man, monster, or even god can come between us, Ariane. Nor can those three meddling women change the way I feel."

"Ariane turned away. "I love you, too." Cale gulped. "But this isn't about you and me. We are part of something much bigger, Corin. And I am a Queen and have my people to protect."

"How can you protect them if that giant steals you away?"

"Because then I will be Sensuata's consort, with more influence to do good than any common mortal."

"More like His plaything."

"No. He is not as He appears, Corin. Sensuata is terrible, yes, but only because He suffers the eternal ache of loneliness."

"I don't understand, Ariane." Corin felt he was losing grip on reality. His body hurt and his mind raced. Everything was wrong.

The woman he loved was slipping away from him. And for what? A vain promise to a being without a soul. That giant might be god of the sea but He was no friend to mankind.

"Do you know the story of Miriel and the giant?" Corin didn't. "She was a mortal maiden who for a time loved the Sea God. But she was lost to Him, taken by one of His own storms."

"So?" Corin was barely listening.

"The Sea God suspected she had a lover and in His rage mustered a gigantic storm which destroyed her village. Unknown to Him, Miriel had returned there recently, and the storm took her, too. Sensuata was driven to despair, for in |His way He loved the maiden. They say Sensuata searched for Miriel for years, but no trace of the girl did He find. Since that time Sensuata has sought another bride, trawling the nine oceans with His nets."

"It's just a story."

Ariane smiled again, then on impulse turned, and reaching up, kissed Corin softly on the lips. Cale, watching, felt a tear trace his cheek. The boy felt a sadness he had never known. Even Roman's dying hadn't hit him this hard. Cale loved Ariane, but realized he loved Corin, too.

"And what of us?" Corin demanded.

"I will always love you, you fool," Ariane told Corin. "But our paths lie in different directions. Perhaps we can be lovers in the next life." Before Corin could respond Ariane had turned and faded into murk. Corin stared at the space where she had stood. He caught Cale's look and turned away.

"I am sorry," the boy said eventually.

Corin nodded. He gazed down at the murky water. No words could convey how he felt. Cale, on impulse, grasped Corin's shoulder and squeezed. If Corin noticed the boy's show of support he made no sign. Cale let go and, feeling awkward, departed gloomy below deck.

"She is not for you, smiling boy." Corin wasn't overly surprised to see Urdei perched on the broken rail behind him. The blonde girl's tresses were neatly combed and her pretty blue dress immaculate. She was winking at him, her expression sly.

"What do you want, you and your sisters?" Stuff the child. Corin wanted to go find Ariane, grab hold of her, and kiss her until their lips bled. Instead he stood stiff and angry, staring at the blonde girl.

"We want the best for you, beloved." Vervandi touched his left arm. Where had she come from?

"Or maybe the worst," cackled Skolde, the blood still trickling from her emaciated arms. The three were watching him: child, woman, and hag.

"Why me?"

"Because you are the chosen one," Vervandi said, her gold-green eyes hypnotic as ever. "That little Queen is not for you, even without her recent vow, which she will have to honor one day. Your destiny is higher, Corin, and we mean to help you reach it."

"Some of us might," scoffed Skolde while Urdei giggled.

"We all love you, actually." The girl-child pouted. "You're very popular, you know. Scolde's a miserable old hag, but she likes you really, smiling boy." The crone cackled.

"Well, you know what? I don't bloody well care. So why don't the three of you just piss off." Corin showed them his back. He groped through the fog, seeking the hatch. Bugger the lot of them: Sea God, Huntsman, Goddess, Assassin, Sorcerer, old Dog Face, the three jolly witches. He even doubted Vervandi now, suspecting she'd always had an agenda. And he wasn't giving up on Ariane. Not yet.

For a long moment he stared into the mist then, mind made up, Corin ventured below for one last try. He soon realized he'd lost his chance. The Queen was deep in discussion with Zallerak and Barin. All three looked tired and worried. Corin joined them and looked at Ariane, but she didn't return his gaze. It wasn't going to happen. The odds were stacked too high against them. The Queen and the mercenary—just a dream.

Up on deck the three sisters smiled knowingly at each other. A new game had commenced, one in which they all would partake.

∗∗∗

Barin had ordered Fassof get some lads to make repairs. Nothing vital was damaged, but they worked in somber silence.

They were drained, shattered. Even Barin was glum. Cale in particular was distraught. It was all too much for the boy. Galed comforted him in the master's cabin. The two were fast friends now.

Ariane retired without another word to Corin. Bleyne and those crew not on carpentry duty were sleeping, whilst Zallerak fiddled despondently with his instrument. Time passed deathly slow in the swirling fog. Several hours passed—or a day. It was impossible to tell. Nobody spoke save in whispers, above deck or below.

***

Ariane gazed through the porthole from her chair by the desk in her cabin. She had had no choice calling on the Sea God, but now Ariane wondered what would become of her. Would the giant summon her from His legendary palace? Legend said its fathomless halls lay deep beneath the farthest oceans. It was there he had kept Miriel as His Queen, His prisoner, His lover, and wife. Or would He rise up terrible from the surface of Lake Wynais one day and drown her as she rode, dragging her soul back to His domain. There was no point dwelling on it. If Sensuata came for her, so be it.

For now Ariane needed time to think, form a strategy against Caswallon. So far her lone gambit had been rescuing the Prince. But that had been achieved for her, and still she knew not where the shards were.

Truth was, she, like her friends, was still in shock: her capture and the fight, their flight from Kranek and Roman's death, then the kraken and the Sea God.

And Ariane mourned her champion. It would be hard in Wynais, making tough decisions without those gruff interruptions from her oldest friend.

Ariane felt alone and vulnerable. She wished Corin was with her. She really did love him. She couldn't deny it any longer. But he too had a part to play in this business. Corin was no ordinary mercenary. Ariane knew that. But who was he? And who would he eventually become?

Her feelings for Corin were irrelevant, she told herself, an indulgence she'd allowed herself to nurture, a flighty fancy more suited to a tavern wench than a Queen. Ariane's people needed her.

Enough. It was time she returned home, paid Corin his gold, and bid the fighter fond farewell. Doubtless he'd go back to Finnehalle. Perhaps if he stayed there he would be free from the shadows that stalked him. But Ariane knew that, like herself, Corin would never be free.

We are fate's children

With that last thought in mind Ariane turned and shut her eyes. When she woke, bright sunlight spilled through her porthole. The fog had gone and with it her last shadows of doubt.

***

They were seven sailors short. Four had been killed up on the square in Kranek and three lost to the leviathan's thrashings on the deck. Barin would be hard pressed to replace them. He now only had twenty-three men.

"Such hearty fellows are difficult to find," Barin grumbled in Corin's ear when his friend brought him up a horn of ale. "Good Valkador lads they were. Tough, resilient, been with me a long time."

Despite his words Barin owned to cheerfulness. The brig's master never stayed gloomy long. Close by, face swallowed by murk, sat Zallerak. Corin, looking at him, sensed a shadow lurking beneath those blue bewitching eyes.

"That kraken, what made it appear? Was it some fetch from Morak or Caswallon?" Corin's hard gaze pressed Zallerak until the bard shrugged and replied.

"Neither. Morak is too weak, especially now, and Caswallon lacks such power. That sea beast came from Yffarn, the underworld. The world fabric is wearing thin, Corin, allowing such horrors to enter Ansu."

"And the giant?"

"The gods, too, grow restless. With the Tekara shattered there's nothing to stop Their interfering. And They like interfering."

"And your part in all this?"

Zallerak smiled at him. "Get some sleep, Corin an Fol. I will see you in the morning." Zallerak stood up, folded his cloak, and faded into the gloom.

"He's an odd one," Barin mumbled, "but we owe him our lives."

"And Ariane, she saved us too."

Barin awarded him a sidelong stare. "I'm sorry about that. The boys and I had a feeling you two would end up together, ridiculous though that sounds."

"I know what you mean. She's a bloody Queen." Corin slurped a gulp. "How presumptuous of me. And now she's sold on this promise she made. What a waste, Barin."

"She's a strong woman." Barin struggled to find the right words. "But I didn't mean you weren't worthy of her, lad. Seems to me you pair are made for each other. Who knows, things might turn out alright. Don't lose heart, laddie. Love will find a way." Corin raised a brow at hearing such words from his friend.

"Not this time," Corin replied. "There is too much at stake. I argued against her, but I know she's right. Ariane has work to do and so do I. We have a Prince and crown to find."

Barin nodded. "I know, and part of me thinks the fun has just started."

"Me too, but for now let's forget about everything. I suggest you get the dice out. I'm going to beat you tonight."

Barin laughed. "I doubt that, but you never know." He winked at Corin then turned to the mate, who had just appeared with his arm in a fresh splint. "Ho, Fassof old chap. Go trouble Ruagon for some more ale."

"If I must."

"And Fassof."

"What?"

"Cheer up. We're still alive and afloat."

"Can't say I've noticed," responded the mate before adjusting his arm in the sling and grumbling off below deck.

"I don't know why he puts up with you," Corin said, tossing the dice. They were still playing and drinking when the sun burnt through the fog. Morning had come and with it new challenges. One thing remained the same. Corin was still crap at dice.

Later that day the Queen summoned them all below. Ariane smiled as they filed in to Barin's cabin and took seats. Corin marked how strong she looked, how resolved, her dark eyes bright and clear.

"Right then, you lot," Ariane announced, accepting a piping tea from Ruagon. "Listen in. This is what we're going to do."

***

The raven listens close by the storm hatch, then satisfied, hops across deck and takes urgent lofty wing. Up the bird soars through that clear bright sunny morning. Up and up to where its master awaits news beyond the fabric of this world.

Oroonin One Eye, gazing down from his roofless halls at the edge of time, sees the bird approach like a dark speck from below. The raven settles on His left shoulder and whispers runes in His ear. Moments later its twin returns from another place and time. This one also imparts its message.

The Huntsman nods as He feeds His ravens star flesh, their favorite. He has much to consider. War is coming, a third strife waged between the High Gods and their fallen brother, Old Night. He knows this will be the final conflict, will rage through the heavens until an outcome is decided, an end to all things.

But which side should He take this time? That would depend on many things. No need to be rash. He decides to watch and wait, let His intricate thoughts go wither they will. This time they take Him back to the beginning, to that distant moment when the Weaver weaved the world thread.

Back there again, Oroonin's canny mind contemplates the architecture of the heavens. All around Him worlds spin wildly on their axes. Suns burst forth into a billion miles of flame, scarlet dragons dancing their fiery dance across the universe.

Oroonin watches as life is weaved from the cosmic thread by the Maker. Time and space ebbs and flows in coruscating spirals. Everything is a beginning and an ending.

He sees stars explode and ancient worlds expire around Him. Past and future meld, becoming the now. All things die and are reborn. The cosmic circle turns and the universe throbs with the rhythm of the Maker's heart.

Oroonin is there at the beginning. His single, terrible eye witnesses the birth of the High Gods, He and His siblings, first children born of the universe, of the One ultimate creator. He sees himself as a young god striding among them, tall and terrible, with two eyes of silver fire, second in might only to His older brother, the Maker's first and most beautiful child.

Oroonin waits as others come dancing into the thread. These are the lesser gods and demigods, beings of light and darkness of every shape and form. He sees the lives of myriad races unfold around him, each one oblivious to the pattern of which they are a part.

Oroonin watches as the first nine planets are formed from raw matter. He sees His siblings take Their seats among the stars, at peace with each other, joyful in the embryonic fabric of the Weaver's tapestry. Great is Their wisdom, much power having been granted Them from Their father.

Ages pass and the High Gods prosper.

Serene in majesty, They rule Their domains well and are content. An age of golden peace thrives amongst the nine worlds. Much is accomplished during this period.

Time passes. The Weaver/Maker weaves new worlds, worlds of crystal oceans and copper fire; dark worlds and light worlds, ever making, ever weaving, and spinning through eternity in His twisting dance of light.

Time passes

Oroonin watches His Father weave the magic tapestry, blissfully unaware of the flaw in its thread. The Maker is far away and has forgotten His offspring in the endless, joyful dance.

But the Weaver's children feel neglected. Their clever minds reach inward, questioning Their purpose and wondering why Their Father has not returned to witness Their many achievements.

They begin to resent His neglect, believing He has kept secrets from Them, suspecting that He plans to spawn others that would usurp Their rightful stations.

Thus a wicked seed of discord is sown into Their hearts. The seed germinates, growing fast and strong, fed by Their jealousy and resentment.

Oroonin well remembers the shame of what follows, for He had been a party to it. And the stain of the seed's fruitless harvest still haunts Him.

He watches as his siblings quarrel, Himself among them, speaking out against Their Father in His absence. The High Gods have become proud in their towers, arrogant and aloof. They question the wisdom of the Weaver. Slowly, carefully, They plot His destruction and turn Their thoughts to bloody deeds. The seed takes root on the first planet, Ansu.

Time passes.

Oroonin witnesses the call to arms. He sees himself, a silver light of flame, joining that unholy rebellion, rising up against the Maker. Spurred on by the eldest and strongest among them, They rebel against the pattern in the tapestry.

So commences the first war in the heavens. Bright and terrible are Oroonin and His kin, riding Their star-wrought chariots across the Milky Way. But Their Father's wrath is greater still. He cleaves His children's pride asunder and They are cast down, defeated and chastised. Their high halls shatter to dust, and the ever-patient Maker reshapes the universe without Their participation.

Time passes and Oroonin watches.

Humbled and afraid, his kin set about redressing some of the wrong They have caused, seeking to placate the Maker until Their Father is appeased and loves them again.

Once more there is peace in the heavens.

But the eldest of his children is prouder than His kin. He cannot forget the glory of their challenge. Secretly and cunningly, this one plots against the Maker. The Firstborn is hungry for power and tainted by a new concept called vengeance.

A second wicked seed is born as He conspires, once again, to usurp the Maker's hold on the universe. The firstborn wants to create beauty out of nothing, but this is forbidden. Only the Maker can create life. Slowly, and with great patience, the eldest weaves His vengeful web.

The Maker is aware of this. He no longer trusts his children. He places a covenant on His rebellious son, naming him Cul-Saan, the overproud.

For a time Cul-Saan is afraid. He holds back, but his courage returns, urged on by His many new supporters.

He alone of the High Gods has surrounded Himself with acolytes and lesser beings. They placate His ego in return for favor. These lesser beings resent their low estates. They desire more power than they have been given.

Through millennia they woo their master, swelling His pride, filling His mind with dark thoughts until once again Cul-Saan rises up against his Creator, assaults the heavens, and wages a second war against the light.

Oroonin watches as Cul-Saan leads an army of fiends across the multiverse. Swarming like blowflies they descend on the bright hall of the Maker. And the Maker is afraid. He calls on His other children to join in war against this terrible son.

Joyfully they answer his call. They too have become wary of Cul-Saan's ambition, distrusting him and remembering the horror of their rebellion against their father, desiring only peace.

Oroonin recalls the greatness of that day. He sees the bright banners unfolding. He hears again the clarion call of trumpets as the host arrives. Foremost is His youngest brother, the Sky God, Telcanna, radiant and glorious, eclipsing the stars in His chariot of sapphire ice.

At His side strides another brother, Sensuata, Lord of all the Oceans, tall and terrible to behold. Their sister, Elanion of the Forests, is with Them. She, Oroonin's spouse, his sister, his mate, brandishes Her golden bow.

Behind Elanion ride the Faen, the faerie people, in a shim-

THE SHATTERED CROWN

mering host of green. Alongside His sister's chariot runs Borian of
the Winds, relentless in His wrath. Behind stormy Borian limps the
lame Smith, Croagon.

Then Oroonin sees the Lesser Gods: among them the twin sisters, Simiolanis the Dream Maiden and Undeyna of the shadows;
their cousin, beautiful Argonwui, and Crun Earth Shatterer before
he betrayed Them and became the Forsaken God. Many others
there are, all fearful to behold, an army of gods and immortals.

Last of all Oroonin sees himself, shrouded in His thought,
a black bird perched on either shoulder, the starlit spear Gloncal
gripped in His left hand.

Waiting for them at the edge of vision is the sable host of His
brother, Cul-Saan.

Once again war ravages the heavens. In that final battle Crun
and Undeyna switch sides. They trick Oroonin into facing Cul-Saan
alone, and His eye is torn out by His brother's hand. But Cul-Saan's
horde is swept aside, His rebellion crushed, and the Firstborn is
broken and cast down naked before the Maker.

Cul-Saan's punishment is grave, as are His followers'. The
Maker's anger is great this time. The war has been long and much
beauty is lost forever. He bids them break the proud one's body,
divide it into nine parts.

Each of these they place on one of the nine worlds and set a
fire demon to watch over it. The living head of Cul-Saan is buried
deep beneath a mountain in the steaming jungles of equatorial
Ansu. Great was the fall of Cul-Saan, once the most cherished and
powerful of the High Gods.

An age passes.

Beneath the mountain roots the fire demon sleeps, unaware
that its charge, Cul-Saan's severed head, a foul canker of corruption, seeps dark blood into the earth, staining all that it touches,
contaminating thought and bending wills.

Oroonin focuses His attention on this His favorite world. He
watches its peoples swell and ebb in war and peace, sees the dark
river of corruption seep throughout the lands until it taints all who
embrace it.

Many are held in thrall by the Dark One's sentient blood. They worship Him in secret groves. Old Night they name him, and bloody sacrifices are held to assay his wrath. Others flee his stain, calling on the protection of Elanion, the guardian of that world.

Time passes, the shadows lengthen. The cosmic pages unfold, revealing the rise of the golden Aralais and their dark brothers, the silent, shadowy, Urgolais. Years pass and these peoples wax in might. Like the High Gods before them, their powers grow alongside their pride.

The Aralais are a haughty race. Tall and beautiful, they ride upon chariots of glass, emulating the gods. They build high towers, seeking knowledge in the stars above. They come to despise their brethren the Urgolais, believing them a lesser race, as indeed they are in both stature and strength.

But the Urgolais are cunning. They too seek knowledge, but their gaze is downward, to the deep places of the world, where they are ensnared by the creeping taint of Cul-Saan's blood.

War comes to Ansu, the catastrophic war of the two races in which both are nearly destroyed. Oroonin witnesses the coming of the newcomers, the short-lived ones. Here at last was a race Oroonin could mold to his purpose.

These mortal creatures swell in strength and number. They are much like the Aralais in form, though they lack both the stateliness and beauty of the Golden Folk.

They scour the lands like locusts, breed and multiply, creating wide realms for themselves, and driving the Faen, Elanion's age-old custodians, deeper into the misty forests. These newcomers are easily tainted by Cul-Saan's blood, although many strive against it.

They fracture and quarrel, wage bloody wars amongst themselves throughout long bitter years. They too become overproud, and blasphemy is committed. They are punished by the Sea God, and the continent Gol is lost beneath the waves.

One warlord escapes the devastation with three ships. His name is Erun Cade, though history knows him as Kell, and he is wise though young in years, for he has seen much. Kell placates Sensuata's wrath with the aid of a Water Elemental, a creature similar to the Faen, and is allowed passage east across the endless ocean with his surviving people.

Oroonin sees Kell's folk disembark on the eastern shores, come to the aid of the Aralais in the final hour of that last apocalyptic battle with their ancient foe. It was said Elanion came to Kell, whom She loved in a dream, and bid him help the Golden Folk. Thus they turn the tide, and the Dog Lords power is broken.

The great days of the Aralais and Urgolais are finished. The ghosts of the shadowy ones flee into the deep places of the earth, and the few surviving Aralais offer Kell their lands in reward for his aid. Then they too retire.

The newcomers thrive in what are to become the Four Kingdoms. Kell's people flourish in knowledge and power, having been granted thirteen enchanted gifts from the Aralais. The greatest of these artifacts are the crystal crown, the Tekara, and the sword of light, Callanak.

***

A thousand years pass.

The Tekara keeps the stain of Cul-Saan at bay in the Four Kingdoms. But elsewhere it spreads, and Old Night's dominion widens throughout Ansu. His head stirs uneasy beneath the mountain, and His legions muster for a final war in the heavens. This time, He tells them, the dark will emerge victorious and a new dreadful age dawn.

Oroonin is restless. His Father is remote, lost in foreign worlds, a stranger. Perhaps it is time to switch allegiance—or maybe not just yet. Maybe He should have a crack at the top job. It could be argued that with Father away Oroonin had been running this cosmos for a while, no one else having shown any interest since Old Night's defeat. Promotion. Oroonin smiles. He likes the word.

Against the rules, of course, but rules change, especially when you are the one changing them. Cast the runes and see how they fall. Time will tell—but then He is outside time and has the edge.

This is why I need my army of dead souls. There is no Good there is no Evil. There is only I.

Oroonin laughs at His dilemma. He witnesses the shattering of the crown, knows the time is nigh for action. He summons his hounds and bids his ravens go hunt.

Time stops.

Oroonin rides out from that far high place. His guise is the One-Eyed Huntsman again, and the restless dead follow in his wake. He closes on his quarry, a lone ship beset by winter seas. At her prow stand a Northman and a scar-faced brooder. The Wild Hunt swoops low. Oroonin laughs. Let the new dance commence.

End of Part Two

Here Concludes Book Three
of *The Legends of Ansu.*

Get a sample preview of something special...
J.W. Webb's...

The Lost Prince

Chapter 1

Rascals

Silon hated Permio. It wasn't just the noise and smell of the place, or the constant threat of danger. This desert country had a different feel to it than anywhere within the Four Kingdoms. It was always so hot here. Not to mention the stink and noise. Gone were the cool breezes that blessed his beloved vineyards in Raleen. The merchant was less than a hundred miles from his home, but he found it impossible to relax.

He was in Cappel Cormac—the stinking, festering home of every villain and cutpurse imaginable. And in this city Silon was a wanted man.

News had reached the coffee rooms of Permio's second largest city concerning the events in Crenna last month. Silon knew he had little time here and must return home quickly. Nor did he wish to linger as every minute spent here was beyond dangerous.

The merchant waited restlessly for the contact he'd arranged to meet in this seedy place. A coffee house—dark, dirty and cluttered with unsavoury characters.

That man's choice not his. Silon would have preferred somewhere quieter—perhaps nearer the wealthy quarter of the city. But he had bowed to the other man's knowledge. Besides, this place was close to the quay and ships sailed frequently across to Raleen. It wouldn't prove difficult slipping aboard one should the sultan's soldiers spot him. They would be very keen to apprehend him, those soldiers. The sultan in his wisdom had placed a price on Silon's head of two thousand crannels.

A tidy sum. All because he was suspected of smuggling contraband across the bay. It was just as well they didn't know his real business.

The room was harsh with voices and swirling smoke stung Silon's eyes, both tobacco and subtler substances. The smell of coffee beans and body sweat clung to his nostrils. Silon looked down with practiced distain as a beggar held out a wooden bowl. The merchant signalled and the man was carried outside and pitched into the filthy street below. Cappel Cormac was a pitiless place. Any act of kindness would be noticed here.

Silon pulled the hood of his brown burnoose down over his forehead shrouding his features. Quietly he studied the occupants at the tables around him.

Over to his right, a couple of swarthy merchants were speaking in furtive whispers, glancing up occasionally from their piping bowls of coffee. Behind them leaned a tanned handsome warrior from Sedinadola by his look. He was flirting shamelessly with the dark eyed beauty in the corner.

The tavern was busy with folk coming and going. Silon noticed the odd northerner sweating in the dusty heat and looking uncomfortably conspicuous. At the back of the smoky room was seated a huge black warrior who appeared to be grinning at nothing in particular. He had a ferocious look and his teeth gleamed like perfect pearls. Silon locked eyes with the man briefly before dropping his gaze. It did not pay to stare too long in a place like this.

A soft sound. Silon glanced up carefully when the seat was taken beside him. He nodded slowly at the newcomer. His contact's face was deeply tanned beneath the scarlet shemagh. It was a hard face, lined with thin scars and dominated by a hooked nose.

The eyes were coaly black and crow-sharp as they apprised the merchant of Raleen.

"I trust that you are fit, my old friend?" the newcomer asked in a dry voice hinting the arid winds of the desert.

"Indeed I am, Barakani," replied Silon. "You look as vigorous as ever," he added. "I trust that your seven sons are all well."

"Yes," the desert chief grinned at Silon. "Their strength waxes alongside their impatience. Those boys have little time for our subtleties, my friend. They would prefer to act straight away, as indeed would I were the time right."

"That time draws close Barakani," Silon leaned forward to whisper in the other's ear. "However there is another issue that I hope you can assist me with."

Barakani raised a shrewd brow. "If I can."

"Something has occurred which I did not anticipate." Silon leaned closer. "Something of great import. I heard voices in the marketplace claiming a young nobleman from the north had recently passed through the city, seeking a guide into the deep desert. A strange request that don't you think?"

"Very strange," replied Barakani with a secret smile. "You wish to know his identity—this youth?" The merchant nodded slowly and Barakani continued in hushed tones.

"He is your missing prince. I am certain of it. I had one of my men follow him through the city seeing he came to no harm. The boy was dressed shabby and looked travel worn, but I would recognise Kelsalion's wayward son anywhere."

Silon smiled. "I sometimes forget how familiar you are with the northlands my old friend. Is it true you served in the Tigers for a time?"

"I wanted to learn how you northerners fight should you ever invade our lands again," grinned Barakani.

"Well, I am in your debt once again," responded Silon with a sigh of relief. "The fool boy was mad coming here alone, I doubt whether he would have made it out the docks without your help."

"Maybe not," replied Barakani. "But the boy didn't seem that helpless. Strangely everyone saw him and yet no one intervened—

something unheard of in Cappel Cormac. And why would he come here? There are far safer places to flee to even in Permio. It's very odd."

"Odder than you think."

"Ah..." Barakani took a slow sip from his piping coffee. He glanced about the crowded room before continuing with a sour expression. "The sultan's soldiers are crawling all over this city; his supreme ugliness suspects everyone, not just northern merchants, my friend. I saw no advantage in the prince being taken to Sedinadola for questioning. So I bid one of my men escort him into the desert, as was his wish."

"Where was Tarin's destination?" asked Silon.

"He wouldn't reveal it. Said only that he desired seeing the Crystal Mountains in the far south. A transparent lie or else a most peculiar desire—I couldn't tell which. "

"And risk the Ty-Tander's fiery breath!" Silon raised an eyebrow. "How bizarre. Stories concerning that beast have often been heard in the courtrooms at Kella City. Tarin will be well aware of the risk he's taking. And that prince is not known for his boldness."

"My own thoughts exactly," responded Barakani. "But just who has put him up to this, Silon? And why?"

"I don't know and it worries me, my friend," responded the merchant. Silon took a sip of his drink and sighed. "Another shadowy player in the game I suspect. At least we can assume he's not an ally of Caswallon."

"But what would the boy's mystery helper hope to achieve by such a venture?"

Silon winced as his coffee found a sensitive tooth. "Could it be what I think?" Barakani pressed him.

"It might be." the merchant smiled slightly and changed the subject, Barakani's hawk gaze was curious but patient. All in good time. These two needed each other—diplomacy was about give and take after all. And there were some subjects to dangerous even for whispers. Especially here.

"I am awaiting some friends from the north," Silon took another wary sip at his coffee. "The same lot that escaped Crenna a while ago on Captain Barin's ship. They can't be far from Raleen now. That's if they managed to evade the Assassin's pursuit."

Barakani grinned like an old wolf. "Rael Hakkenon won't be in a happy state of mind. He's not used to being thwarted so easily." The Assassin of Crenna was well known and feared in Permio too. There were rumours that Rael had accepted contracts from the sultan himself during the latter's early reign.

Silon nodded. "True enough. My spies sent me word from that island via pigeon to my villa the other week. A dangerous business for which I take some responsibility. Queen Ariane was involved and the mercenary Corin who I told you about. He in particular will be able to help us in this business as he knows Permio."

"The business being...?"

"Silon smiled slowly. Barakani always like playing these games. The wily desert chief was well aware of Silon's gambit. "We have to find the lost prince before our enemies do. That will involve individuals with specific skills. Corin being one. I need your assurance of their safe passage through the dunes."

Barakani laughed quietly, "You ask much, merchant. The sultan's spies are even more commonplace than his soldiers. And there are northern mercenaries in Permio already. I passed them several days ago. A rough lot I assume in the pay of Caswallon. Word must have got out to him of Tarin's intended destination. Though quite how I cannot guess."

"Gribble most likely."

"And who might he be?"

"A winged goblin—Caswallon's new spymaster. My people in Kella sent word about it."

"Interesting." Barakani let that one go. "Well, the mercenary captain I saw looked familiar. Tall. Lean. Hard grey eyes."

"That will be Hagan."

"The renegade Morwellan?"

"The same. You know him too?"

"I heard his reputation during the war," replied Barakani. "A cold proud bastard they say."

"Aye, that'll be him." Silon frowned. Hagan hadn't wasted

any time coming south, there were reports of his whereabouts in Kashorn village less than two months ago. Doubtless he'd been looking for Queen Ariane but fortunately had had no luck finding her. It was just as well Hagan hadn't come across Corin an Fol. Silon needed Corin focussing on the task ahead. Hagan and Silon's former employee for not the best of friends.

Silon studied the shrewd eyes of the man seated opposite him. Barakani was relaxed and at ease in the coffee room, despite a price on his head in this city that made Silon's two thousand crannels a paltry sum. Barakani wasn't called the Wolf of the Desert for nothing. He had earned his reputation as had his sons—all seven.

"I know I ask a lot, old friend," Silon whispered. "But no one knows the desert as well as you and your boys. I see a real chance here. We can thwart the sultan's plans placing you nearer to the throne of Permio—your rightful place."

"I will do what I can. When will your people arrive?"

"I don't know no and that worries me. Time is short and I expected them to arrive in Port Sarfe over a week ago. I've heard nothing since they escaped from Crenna."

"Perhaps they were delayed."

Silon nodded and took a long controlled sip from his now cooled coffee before continuing.

"One final question."

"Go on."

"Did Tarin carry a sack upon his person? A small bag perchance?"

Barakani shrugged shaking his head. "Of that I know nothing. But it would seem unlikely—even those unwilling to gut the boy would have taken his belongings. This *is* Cappel Cormac."

"Yes, that's what I feared."

"Leave these matters with me, Silon" Barakani's crafty eyes were scanning the tavern, "We have said enough," he added in a whisper. "We are being observed, my friend."

"Who?" answered Silon without looking round.

"A large fellow, black skinned—most likely a warrior from the distant south. They occasionally visit to trade. This one looks a confidant bastard. He is sitting in the far corner behind you. He's clever—I only just caught his eye. A spy for certain."

"Yes, I noticed him earlier," responded Silon. "Think you he's in the sultan's pay?" he asked in a whisper.

"I do not know," responded the desert chief. "But this is Cappel Cormac. Few strangers here are who they appear to be. You and I included, my friend."

They spoke for a while in hushed whispers before finishing their coffee in a leisurely manner. Silon stood up, made a show of fastidiously dusting his faded brown burnoose and then quietly left the tavern. He waited out of sight for some moments until he saw Barakani emerge. Silon nodded briefly in his direction and then faded subtle into the crowd.

Silon was worried. He'd better be getting back to his villa fast. If by some miracle Prince Tarin still had the remnants of the Tekara on his person they were in with a chance—be it a only fool's chance. But the idiot prince must be protected at all cost. And before they could protect him they needed to find him. And why would he make for the Crystal Mountains if he didn't have the remnants of the Tekara? Unless it was the only destination the prince had heard of. Those mountains were legendary after all. Who knew what mental state Tarin would be in after being holed up in Kranek Castle?

Silon would have to act fast. He needed Corin. Corin knew northern Permio better than he did. But where were they? The voyage south shouldn't have taken them this long. And just who has put Tarin up to this? Doubtless the same individual that freed the boy from the Assassin? And evidently some while before Queen Ariane's party arrived unwitting in Kranek harbour. It irked Silon that someone acted outside his circle of knowledge. A freelancer playing a subtle game. But just whose side was he on? And who was he?

The questions kept coming. Silon hurried down towards the dockyard, jostling his way through the bustling crowd. Angry faces glared at him as he shoved passed, and skinny dogs snarled and yapped. Down at the quayside he spotted a Morwellan trader—one of the few that recently escaped the sack of Vangaris harbour. She was making ready to leave port. Silon suspected that the vessel would stop off at Port Sarfe, before heading north for Calprissa now Vangaris had fallen to the barbarian fleet.

Silon stepped up his pace turning into a narrow alley.

Too late he realised his mistake.

Footsteps approaching fast from behind. The sound of steel slicing air. Silon ducked low as a robed figure with a purple sash swung a tulwar at him from behind.

He rammed his right shoulder back into his assailant's chest forcing the big man off balance. Then Silon twisted and rammed his knee up hard into his assailant's groin. The man buckled and Silon kicked him in the face sending him sprawling. Silon turned to run.

Again too late.

Two other men had arrived in the alley. These blocked his way ahead. Silon recognised them at once. They were the sultan's elite soldiery. They approached at speed barring his way. The first one swung his blade as he leapt at Silon. Again the whoosh of steel through air.

But Silon was ready. He grabbed the nearest soldier's out-thrust arm with his right hand. Then pulling him forward, Silon rammed his left palm hard up into the man's nose, snapping the bone. The soldier sunk to the floor the curved blade clattering beside him.

Clutching his secret dagger, Silon knelt swiftly despatching the sultan's soldier with a slice along his throat.

The remaining soldier hung back seeing his accomplice so easily bested. Then he grinned suddenly, seeing the first assailant regain his feet amid curses, and tulwar raised, approach Silon from behind. Now Silon was trapped in the dirty alley his back against the wall. They closed on him slowly each wishing to savour the moment. Their broad tulwars were held ready and hatred burned in their eyes.

Silon braced himself for the deathblow. He shut his eyes.

Moments passed—nothing.

Silon heard a loud grunt of pain followed by a meaty thud and the sound of a body hitting the dusty ground. A brief clang of steel followed then another groan and thud. Then a heavy voice laughed and Silon opened his eyes.

Standing before him, outlandishly dressed and grinning broadly, was the huge black warrior from the tavern. Slung across his back was the most extravagant array of weapons Silon had ever seen. In his sinewy left fist the huge stranger clutched a gold-capped cudgel. That gold was currently stained with the blood of the two soldiers he'd just brained. The stranger grinned as he reached down hoisting Silon to his feet. The merchant gasped for the man's grip was like iron.

"I am in your debt," he coughed. "May I ask your name?"

"I am Ulani, King of Yamondo," answered the stranger. His voice was rich, deep and musical. "I have been seeking a merchant from Port Sarfe by the name of Silon."

"Well I'm happy to report you have found him," responded Silon. Awhile later at the quayside, and after the merchant had booked his passage, the stranger told his tale. It was then that Silon realised their troubles had only just began.

Books available in print and digital formats:

Gol

The Shattered Crown

Made in the USA
San Bernardino, CA
18 August 2017